UNSUITABLE ENVIRONMENT

"McAndrew and Roker." Kleeman's voice came from the speakers, calm and superior. "There will be punishment unless you return at once."

I was at last at the airlock. McAndrew and Wicklund were there. Without speaking, McAndrew turned and pointed towards the wall of the lock. I looked, and felt a sudden sickness. The wall where the line of spacesuits should be hanging was empty.

"No suits?" I said stupidly.

He nodded. "Kleeman has been thinking a move ahead of you." There was a long and terrible pause. "I looked out," he said at last. "Through the viewport there. The ship's capsule is still where we left it."

"You're willing to chance it?" I looked at Wicklund, who stood there not following our conversation at all.

Mac nodded. "I am. But what about him?"

I walked forward and stood in front of Wicklund. "Do you still want to go with us? Leave the Ark forever?"

Wicklund licked his lips, then nodded.

"Into the lock." We moved forward together and I closed the inner door.

"Do not be foolish." It was Kleeman's voice, with a new expression of alarm. "There is nothing to be served by sacrificing yourselves to space. McAndrew, you are a rational man. Come back and we will discuss this together."

Mac swung open the outer airlock door. The air was gone in a puff of ice vapor. I saw the capsule at the top of the landing tower. To reach it we had to traverse sixth meters of the interstellar vacuum.

BAEN BOOKS by Charles Sheffield

The Compleat McAndrew
Convergent Series
Transvergence
The Mind Pool
Proteus in the Underworld
Borderlands of Science
My Brother's Keeper *(forthcoming)*

THE COMPLEAT McANDREW

CHARLES SHEFFIELD

THE COMPLEAT McANDREW

A Baen Books Original

Baen Publishing Enterprises
P.O. Box 1403
Riverdale, NY 10471

ISBN: 0-671-57857-X

Cover art by Dru Blair

First printing, April 2000

Distributed by Simon & Schuster
1230 Avenue of the Americas
New York, NY 10020

Typeset by Windhaven Press, Auburn, NH
Printed in the United States of America

Acknowledgements

Portions of this work have appeared previously in revised form, as follows:

"Killing Vector," © UPD Publications, 1978

"Moment of Inertia," © Davis Publications, 1980

"All the Colors of the Vacuum," © Davis Publications, 1981

"The Manna Hunt," © Davis Publications, 1982

"Rogue World," © Mercury Press, 1983

"Shadow World (The Hidden Matter of McAndrew)," © Davis Publications, 1992

"The Invariants of Nature," © Bantam Doubleday Dell, 1993

"Out of Focus," © Charles Sheffield, 1999 (first appeared in *SF Age*)

"The Fifth Commandment," © Charles Sheffield, 1999 (first appeared in *Analog*)

CONTENTS

Introduction 1

First Chronicle:
Killing Vector 5

Second Chronicle:
Moment of Inertia 25

Third Chronicle:
All the Colors of the Vacuum 65

Fourth Chronicle:
The Manna Hunt 103

Fifth Chronicle:
The Hidden Matter of McAndrew 147

Sixth Chronicle:
The Invariants of Nature 191

Seventh Chronicle:
Rogueworld 223

Eighth Chronicle:
With McAndrew, Out of Focus 277

Ninth Chronicle:
McAndrew and the Fifth Commandment 317

Appendix:
Science & Science Fiction 351

Introduction

A glance at the copyright dates on the stories in this book shows that McAndrew has been with me for almost as long as I have been writing fiction. My own manuscript notes make that point even more clearly: the first piece of fiction that I ever published appeared in the April, 1977 issue of *Galaxy* magazine. The handwritten date on the first page of the manuscript of "Killing Vector," my first McAndrew story, is just two months later: June 15, 1977. Since then, at apparently random intervals ranging from a few weeks to a few years, I have produced another tale of Arthur Morton McAndrew and his long-time and long-suffering companion, Jeanie Roker.

What's the fascination of these characters for me, and why do I return to them again and again? As a related question, is there any pattern to the stories?

First, let me point out that the order in which they appear in this volume is not the order in which the stories were written. Chronologically, the order would be "Killing Vector," "Moment of Inertia," "All the Colors of the Vacuum," "The Manna Hunt," "Rogueworld," "Shadow World," "The Invariants of Nature," "Out of Focus," and "The Fifth Commandment."

The most obvious point about these stories is that each revolves around some central issue of science. I go into that subject in detail in the Appendix at the end of the book. Whenever I become interested in something, especially when that something involves physics and astronomy, a McAndrew story is likely to emerge from my hindbrain.

That explains the chosen themes, but not McAndrew himself. I might suggest that he is some form of alter ego, the *me* that I wish I were, except that others have already assigned that role to Behrooz Wolf (of *Sight of Proteus*, *Proteus Unbound*, and *Proteus in the Underworld*).

Of course, I may have an alter ego suffering from multiple personality disorder. However, my better guess is that McAndrew is an *excuse*. I derive great pleasure from sitting around, reading and calculating on matters of no earthly value and importance. I do this happily for hours and days, limited only by the arguments of conscience that I ought to be doing something useful and productive. To give one example, I have for the past five years tried, sporadically and unsuccessfully, to analyze a particular mathematical game. I can state the game simply, and to avoid (or possibly create) reader frustration I may as well do so. Two players, A and B, take turns throwing a die. There is a probability p that the die will show a score of 2, and a probability of (1 - p) that the die will show a score of 1. Given a whole number N, what is the probability that player A will be the first to reach a score of at least N?

I cannot justify wasting so much time on such a trivial game, except to use the all-work-and-no-play defense. However, if an area of apparently useless interest can one day become the basis for a McAndrew story, I have a rationale for my actions. Surely, if I write and publish a story, no one can say that all my preliminary reading and calculating was pointless.

As for an overall pattern to the stories, I do see a general trend. However, I suspect that the trend mirrors changes not in science but in me. If I had to categorize myself at the time I wrote "Killing Vector," it would be as a practicing scientist whose knowledge of science fiction was mainly as a reader, a person who despite some first-hand experience of America and Americans was basically English, with an English wife and children. Today, twenty-one years and four or five million published words on, I would describe myself as a writer with a strong amateur interest in science; a person mostly American, with an American wife and children, albeit also a person with strong social and family ties to England and the English. And, a fact not to be dismissed, I am twenty-one years older. I am rather less interested in science, and more interested in people.

These changes affect the stories. When first we meet him, McAndrew the scientist is all there, but I don't think I could in the early tales ever have given him a child (as in "Rogueworld"), and still less a mother (as in "The Fifth Commandment"). That last story also points out an implicit element in most of the earlier stories: the relationship between Jeanie Roker and McAndrew is in some ways that of parent–child. He is the small boy whose rash actions lead him into trouble, she is the responsible and experienced adult who gets him out. I think *that's* who I would really like to be, the curious child who is not quite responsible for his own actions. That is the reason why I continue to write about Arthur Morton McAndrew.

Two other brief answers to questions: Will I ever write a McAndrew novel? An e-mail correspondent pointed out that although there are references to McAndrew in others of my novels, he has never had one of his own. My answer is, McAndrew will get a novel when I run across a neat scientific idea so large and complex that I can't get a handle on it in a story of ten to twenty thousand words.

And finally, is this really the *Complete* McAndrew, as the title suggests?

To this, I can only offer the Clintonian reply: it all depends on how you define the word, *is*. Certainly, at this time there exist no other McAndrew stories, so what you have is the complete McAndrew. Equally certainly, there will in the future be fascinating scientific ideas that just jump up and down, crying out, "Me, me, write about me."

I'm not sure I will be able to resist their pleas. But "The Incomplete McAndrew" makes a poor book title.

FIRST CHRONICLE:

Killing Vector

Everyone on the Control Stage found a reason to be working aft when Yifter came on board. There was maximum security, of course, so no one could get really close without a good reason. Even so, we all took the best look that we could manage—you don't often have a chance to see a man who has killed a billion people.

Bryson from the Planetary Coordinators' Office was at Yifter's elbow. The two men weren't shackled or anything melodramatic like that. Past a certain level of notoriety, criminals are treated with some deference and even respect. Bryson and Yifter were talking together in a friendly way, although they were in the middle of a group of top-rank security men, all heavily armed and watchful.

They were taking safety to extremes. When I stepped forward to greet Bryson and his prisoner, two guards carefully frisked me before I could get within hand-kill range, and they stood close beside me when the introductions were made. I haven't lived on Earth for a long time, and they must have known that I have no close

5

relatives there; but they were taking no chances. Yifter was a prime target for personal revenge. A billion people leave a lot of friends and relatives.

From a distance of one meter, Yifter's appearance did not match his reputation. He was of medium height, slightly built, with bushy, prematurely white hair and mild, sad eyes. He smiled at me in a tired, tolerant way as Bryson introduced us.

"I am sorry, Jeanie Roker," he said. "Your ship will be filled with strangers on this trip. I'll do my best to keep out of your way and let you do your job."

I hoped he could live up to his words. Since I took over the runs to Titan, I've carried most things in the connected set of cargo spheres that make up the Assembly. Apart from the kernels, and we carry a few of those on the outbound leg of every trip, we've had livestock, mega-crystals, the gravity simulator, and the circus. That's right, the circus. They must have had a terrible agent, that's all I can say. I took them both ways, to Titan and back to L-5. Even with all that, Yifter was still a novelty item. After he had been caught and the rest of the Lucies had gone underground, nobody had known quite what to do with him. He was Earth's hottest property, the natural target for a billion guns and knives. Until they decided how and when he would come to trial, they wanted him a long way from Earth. It was my job to deliver him to the Titan penal colony, and return him when they got themselves sorted out on Earth.

"I'll arrange for you and your guards to travel in a separate part of the Assembly," I said. "I assume that you will prefer privacy."

Yifter nodded agreeably, but Bryson wasn't having any.

"Captain Roker," he said. "Let me remind you that Mr. Yifter has not been found guilty on any charge. On this journey, and until his trial, he will be treated with proper courtesy. I expect you to house both of us here in the Control Stage, and I expect that you will invite us to take our meals here with you."

In principle, I could have told him to go and take a walk outside. As captain, I said who would travel in the Control Stage, and who would eat with me—and innocent people were not usually sent to the Titan penal colony, even before their trial. On the other hand, Bryson was from the Planetary Coordinators' office, and even off-Earth that carried weight. I suppressed my first reaction and said quietly, "What about the guards?"

"They can travel in the Second Section, right behind the Control Stage," replied Bryson.

I shrugged. If he wanted to make nonsense of Earth's security efforts, that was his choice. Nothing had ever happened on any of my two-month runs from Earth to Titan, and Bryson was probably quite right; nothing would happen this time. On the other hand, it seemed like a damned silly charade, to ship twenty-five guards to keep an eye on Yifter, then house them in a separate part of the Assembly.

Yifter, with an uncanny empathy, had read through my shrug. "Don't worry about security, Jeanie Roker," he said. He smiled again, that tired, soothing smile that began deep in his sad, brown eyes. "You have my assurance, I will be a model prisoner."

He and Bryson walked on past me, into the main quarters. Was that really Yifter, the bogey-man, the notorious head of the Hallucinogenic Freedom League? It seemed hard to believe. Three months earlier, the Lucies—under Yifter's messianic direction—had planted hallucinogenic drugs in the water supply lines of most of Earth's major cities. An eighth of the world had died in the resulting chaos. Starvation, epidemic, exposure, and mindless combat had revisited the Earth and exacted their age-old tribute. The monster who had conceived, planned, and directed that horror was difficult to match with Yifter, the seemingly mild and placid man.

My thoughts were quickly diverted to more immediate practical matters. We had the final masses of all the cargo, and it was time for the final balancing of the whole

Assembly. One might assume that just means balancing
the kernels correctly, since they out-mass everything else
by a factor of a million. But each Section containing a
kernel has an independent drive unit, powered by the
kernel itself. We leave those on Titan, and travel back
light, but on the trip out the dynamic balancing is quite
tricky.

I reviewed the final configuration, then looked around
for McAndrew. I wanted him to review the balance calculations. It's my responsibility, but he was the kernel
expert. I realized that he hadn't been present when Yifter
came aboard. Presumably he was over on one of the other
Sections, crooning over his beloved power sources.

I found him in Section Seven. The Assembly is made
up of a variable number of Sections, and there would be
twelve on this trip, plus the Control Stage. Until we
accelerate away from the Libration Colony station, all the
Sections are physically connected—with actual cables—to
each other and to the Control Stage. In flight, the coupling
is done electromagnetically, and the drives for the powered Sections are all controlled by a computer on the
Control Stage. The Assembly looks like a small bunch of
grapes, but the stalks are nonfunctional—there are no
cables in the System that could take the strains, even at
lowest acceleration. Moving among the spherical Sections
when we're in flight isn't easy. It means we have to cut the
drives, and turn off the coupling between the Sections.
That's why I thought the idea of having Yifter's guards in
a different Section was so dumb—from there, they couldn't
even reach the Control Stage when the drives were on.

I wanted McAndrew to check the configuration that
we would hold in flight, to see if he agreed that the
stresses were decently balanced among the different
Sections. We never run near the limit on any of them,
but there's a certain pride of workmanship in getting them
all approximately equal, and the stresses as low as possible.

He was standing on the ten-meter shield that surrounded the Section Seven kernel, peering through a long

boresight pointed in towards the center. He was aware of my presence but did not move or speak until the observation was complete. Finally he nodded in satisfaction, closed the boresight cap, and turned to me.

"Just checking the optical scalars," he said. "Spun up nicely, this one. So, what can I do for you, Jeanie?"

I led him outside the second shield before I handed him the trim calculations. I know a kernel shield has never failed, but I'm still not comfortable when I get too close to one. I once asked McAndrew how he felt about working within ten meters of Hell, where you could actually feel the gravity gradient and the inertial dragging. He looked at me with his little, introspective smile, and made a sort of throat-clearing noise—the only trace of his ancestry that I could ever find in him.

"Och," he said. "The shields are triply protected. They won't fail."

That would have reassured me, but then he had rubbed his high, balding forehead and added, "And if they do, it won't make any difference if you are ten meters away, or five hundred. That kernel would radiate at about two gigawatts, most of it high-energy gammas."

The trouble was, he always had the facts right. When I first met McAndrew, many years ago, we were taking the first shipment of kernels out to Titan. He had showed up with them, and I assumed that he was just another engineer—a good one, maybe, but I expected that. Five minutes of conversation with him told me that he had probably forgotten more about Kerr-Newman black holes—kernels—than I was ever likely to learn. I have degrees in Electrical Engineering and Gravitational Engineering, in my job I have to, but I'm really no gravity specialist. I felt like an idiot after our first talk. I made a few inquiries, and found that McAndrew was a full professor at the Penrose Institute, and probably the System's leading expert on space-time structure.

When we got to know each other better, I asked him why he would give up his job for four months of the year, to ride herd on a bunch of kernels being shipped around the Solar System. It was a milk-run, with lots of time and very little to do. Most people would be bored silly.

"I need it," he said simply. "It's very nice to work with colleagues, but in my line of business the real stuff is mostly worked out alone. And I can do experiments here that wouldn't be allowed back home."

After that, I accepted his way of working, and took vicarious pride in the stream of papers that appeared from McAndrew at the end of each Titan run. He was no trouble on the trips. He spent most of his time in the Sections carrying the kernels, only appearing in the Control Stage for his meals—and frequently missing them. He was a tinkerer as well as a theorist. Isaac Newton was his idol. His work had paid off in higher shielding efficiencies, better energy extraction methods, and more sensitive manipulation of the charged kernels. Each trip, we had something new.

I left the trim calculations with him, and he promised to check them over and give me his comments in an hour or two. I had to move along and check the rest of the cargo.

"By the way," I said, elaborately casual as I turned to go. "We'll be having company for dinner on this trip. Bryson insists that Yifter should eat with us."

He stood quietly for a moment, head slightly bowed. Then he nodded and ran his hand over his sandy, receding hair-line.

"That sounds like Bryson," he said. "Well, I doubt if Yifter will eat any of us for breakfast. I'm not sure he'll be any worse than the rest of you. I'll be there, Jeanie."

I breathed a small sigh of relief, and left him. McAndrew, as I knew from experience, was the Compleat Pacifist. I had wanted to be sure that he could stand the idea of meals with Yifter.

Four hours later, all our checks were complete. I switched on the fields. The dull grey exterior of each Section turned to silver, shattering the sunlight and turning

the Assembly to a cluster of brilliants. The cables linking the Sections were still in position, but now they were
hanging loose. All stresses had been picked up by the
balancing fields. In the Control Stage, I gradually turned
on the propulsion units of each powered Section. Plasma
was fed through the ergosphere of each kernel, picked
up energy, and streamed aft. The relative positions of the
Sections, Mossbauer-controlled to within fractions of a
micrometer, held steady. We accelerated slowly away from
L-5, and began the long spiral of a continuous-impulse
orbit to Titan.

My work was just about finished until crossover time.
The computers monitored the drive feeds, the accelerations, and all the balance of the Sections. On this trip,
we had three units without operating drive units: Section Two, where Yifter's guards were housed, just behind
the Control Stage; Section Seven, where McAndrew had
taken the kernel out of commission for his usual endless and mysterious experiments; and of course, the
Control Stage itself. I had made the mistake of asking
McAndrew what experiments he was planning for this
trip. He looked at me with his innocent blue eyes and
scribbled an answer full of twistor diagrams and spinor
notation—knowing damn well that I wouldn't be able to
follow it. He didn't like to talk about his work "half-
cooked," as he put it.

I had been more worried than I wanted to admit about
dinner on that first ship-evening. I knew we would all be
itching to ask Yifter about the Lucies, but there was no
easy way to introduce the subject into the conversation.
How could we do it? "By the way, I hear that you killed
a billion people a few months ago. I wonder if you would
like to say a few words on the subject? It would liven
up the table-talk at dinner." I could foresee that our
conversation might be a little strained.

As it turned out, my worries were unnecessary. The first
impression that I'd had of Yifter, of a mild and amiable

man, strengthened on longer exposure. It was Bryson, during dinner, who caused the first tricky moment.

"Most of Earth's problems are caused by the United Space Federation's influence," he said as the robo-server, always on best form at the beginning of the trip, rolled in the courses. "If it weren't for the USF, there wouldn't be as much discontent and rioting on Earth. It's all relative, living space and living standards, and the USF sets a bad example. We can't compete."

According to Bryson, three million people were causing all the problems for ten billion—eleven, before Yifter's handiwork. It was sheer nonsense, and as a USF citizen, I should have been the one to bridle; but it was McAndrew who made a growling noise of disapproval, down in his throat; and it was Yifter, of all people, who sensed the atmosphere quickest, and deftly steered the conversation to another subject.

"I think Earth's worst problems are caused by the power shortage," he said. "That affects everything else. Why doesn't Earth use the kernels for power, the way that the USF does?"

"Too afraid of an accident," replied McAndrew. His irritation evaporated immediately at the mention of his specialty. "If the shields ever failed, you would have a Kerr-Newman black hole sitting there, pumping out a thousand megawatts—mostly as high-energy radiation and fast particles. Worse than that, it would pull in free charge and become electrically neutral. As soon as that happened, there'd be no way to hold it electromagnetically. It would sink down and orbit inside the Earth. We couldn't afford to have that happen."

"But couldn't we use smaller kernels on Earth?" asked Yifter. "They would be less dangerous."

McAndrew shook his head. "It doesn't work that way. The smaller the black hole, the higher the effective temperature and the faster it radiates. You'd be better off with a much more massive black hole. But then you've got the problem of supporting it against Earth's gravity.

Even with the best electromagnetic control, anything that massive would sink down into the Earth."

"I suppose it wouldn't help to use a nonrotating, uncharged hole, either," said Yifter. "That might be easier to work with."

"A Schwarzschild hole?" McAndrew looked at him in disgust. "Now, Mr. Yifter, you know better than that." He grew eloquent. "A Schwarzschild hole gives you no control at all. You can't get a hold of it electromagnetically. It just sits there, spewing out energy all over the spectrum, and there's nothing you can do to change it—unless you want to charge it and spin it up, and make it into a kernel. With the kernels, now, you have control."

I tried to interrupt, but McAndrew was just getting warmed up. "A Schwarzschild hole is like a naked flame," he went on. "A caveman's device. A kernel is refined, it's controllable. You can spin it up and store energy, or you can use the ergosphere to pull energy out and spin it down. You can use the charge on it to move it about as you want. It's a real working instrument—not a bit of crudity from the Dark Ages."

I shook my head, and sighed in simulated despair. "McAndrew, you have an unconsummated love affair with those blasted kernels." I turned to Yifter and Bryson, who had watched McAndrew's outburst with some surprise. "He spends all his waking hours spinning those things up and down. All the last trip, he was working the kernels in gravitational focusing experiments. You know, using the fact that a gravity field bends light rays. He insists that one day we won't use lenses for optics—we'll focus light using arrays of kernels."

I made the old joke. "We hardly saw him on that trip. We were convinced that one day he'd get careless with the shields, fall into one of the kernels, and really make a spectacle of himself."

They didn't get it. Yifter and Bryson looked at me blankly, while McAndrew, who'd heard it all ten times before, chuckled. I knew his simple sense of humor—a bad joke is always funny, even if it's the hundredth time you've heard it told.

It's a strange thing, but after the first half-hour I had stopped thinking of Yifter as our prisoner. I could understand now why Bryson had objected to the idea of surrounding Yifter with armed guards. I'd have objected myself. He seemed the most civilized man in the group, with a warm personality and a very dry and subtle sense of humor.

When Bryson left the table, pleading a long day and a lack of familiarity with a space environment, Yifter, McAndrew and I stayed on, chatting about the previous trips I had made to Titan. I mentioned the time I had taken the circus.

"Do you know, I'd never seen most of those animals before," I said. "They were all on the list of endangered species. I don't think you could find them on Earth any more, except in a circus or a zoo."

There was a moment of silence, then Yifter spoke. His eyes were mild and smiling, and his voice sounded dreamy and distant.

"Endangered species," he said. "That's the heart of it. Earth has no room for failures. The weaker species, like weaker specimens of a species, must be eliminated. Only the strong—the mentally strong—may survive. The weak must be culled, for our own sake; whether that means one tenth, one half, or nine tenths of the total."

There was a chilling pause. I looked at Yifter, whose expression had not changed, then at McAndrew, whose face reflected the horror that I was feeling. Yet behind all that, I could feel the unique power of the man. My mind was rejecting Yifter, but I still had a sense of well-being, of warmth in the pit of my stomach, as he was speaking.

"We have made a beginning," went on Yifter quietly. "Just a beginning. Last time we were less successful than I had hoped. We had a breakdown in the distribution system for the drugs. I managed to eliminate the responsible individuals, but it was too late to correct the problem. Next time, God willing, it will be different."

He rose to his feet, white hair shining like silver, face beatific. "Good night, Captain. Good night, Professor McAndrew. Sleep well."

After he had left, McAndrew and I sat and looked at each other for a long time. Finally, he broke the spell.

"Now we know, Jeanie. We should have guessed it from the beginning. Mad as a hatter. The man's a raving lunatic. Completely psychotic."

That said most of it. McAndrew had used up all the good phrases. I nodded.

"But did you feel the strength in him?" went on McAndrew. "Like a big magnet."

I was glad that the penal colony was so far from Earth, and the avenues of communication so well-guarded. *Next time . . . it will be different.* Our two-month trip suddenly seemed to have doubled in length.

After that single, chilling moment, there were no more shocks for some time. Our regular meal-time conversations continued, and on several occasions McAndrew voiced views on pacifism and the protection of human life. Each time, I waited for Yifter's reply, expecting the worst. He never actually agreed with Mac—but he did not come out with any statement that resembled his comments of the first ship-evening.

We soon settled into the ship-board routine. McAndrew spent less and less time in the Control Stage, and more in Section Seven. On this trip, he had brought a new set of equipment for his experiments, and I was very curious to know what he was up to. He wouldn't tell. I had only one clue. Section Seven was drawing enormous energy from the other kernels in the rest of the Assembly. That energy could only be going to one place—into the kernel in Section Seven. I suspected that McAndrew must be spinning it up, making it closer to an "extreme"

kernel, a Kerr-Newman black hole where the rotation
energy matches the mass energy. I knew that couldn't be
the whole story. McAndrew had spun up the kernels
before, and he had told me that there was no direct way
of getting a really extreme kernel—that would take an
infinite amount of energy. This time, he was doing something different. He insisted that Section Seven had to be
off-limits to everybody.

I couldn't get him to talk about it. There would be a
couple of seconds of silence from him, then he would
stand there, cracking his finger joints as though he were
snapping out a coded message to me. He could be a real
sphinx when he chose.

Two weeks from Earth, we were drawing clear of the
main Asteroid Belt. I had just about concluded that my
worries for the trip were over when the radar reported
another ship, closing slowly with us from astern. Its
spectral signature identified it as the *Lesotho*, a cruise
liner that usually ran trajectories in the Inner System. It
was broadcasting a Mayday, and flying free under zero
drive power.

I thought about it for a moment, then posted Emergency Stations throughout the Assembly. The computed
trajectory showed that we would match velocities at a
separation of three kilometers. That was incredibly close,
far too close to be accidental. After closest approach,
we would pull away again—we were still under power,
accelerating outward, and would leave the *Lesotho*
behind.

I was still watching the displays, trying to decide whether
or not to take the next step—shutting off the drives—when
Bryson appeared, with Yifter just behind him.

"Captain Roker," he said, in his usual imperious manner. "That's an Earth ship there, giving you a distress
signal. Why aren't you doing anything about it?"

"If we wait just a few minutes," I said. "We'll be
within spitting distance of her. I see no point in rushing in, until we've had a good look at her. I can't think

what an Inner System ship would be doing, free-falling out here beyond the Belt."

That didn't cool him. "Can't you recognize an emergency when you see one?" he said. "If you won't do something productive with your people, I'll do something with mine."

I wondered what he wanted me to do, but he walked away without saying anything more, down the stairs that led to the rear communication area of the Control Stage. I turned back to the displays. The *Lesotho* was closing on us steadily, and now I could see that her locks were open. I cut our propulsion to zero and switched off all the drives. The other ship was tumbling slowly, drive lifeless and aft nacelles crumpled. Even from this distance, I could see that she would need extensive repairs before she could function again.

I was beginning to think that I had been over-cautious when two things happened. Yifter's guards, who had been housed behind the Control Stage in Section Two, began to float into view on the viewing screen that pointed towards the *Lesotho*. They were all in space armor and heavily weaponed. At the same time two suited figures appeared in the open forward lock of the other vessel. I cut in the suit frequencies on our main board.

"—shield failure," said the receiver. "Twenty-seven survivors, and bad injuries. We must have painkillers, medical help, water, food, oxygen and power-packs."

With that, one group of our guards outside began to move towards the two suited figures in the *Lesotho*'s lock, while the remainder stayed close to the Assembly, looking across at the other ship. Subconsciously, I noted the number of our guards in each party, then gave them my full attention and did a rapid re-count. Twenty-five. All our guards. I swore and cut in the transmitter.

"Sergeant, get half of those men back inside the Assembly shields. This is Captain Roker. I'm over-riding any other orders you may have received. Get the nearer party—"

I was interrupted. The display screen flashed blue-white, then over-loaded. The whole Control Stage rang like a great bell, as something slapped hard on the outer shield. I knew what it was: a huge pulse of hard radiation and highly energetic particles, smashing into us in a fraction of a microsecond.

Yifter had been floating within a couple of meters of me, watching the screens. He put his hand to the wall to orient himself as the Control Stage vibrated violently. "What was that?"

"Thermonuclear explosion," I said shortly. "Hundred megaton plus. On the *Lesotho*."

All the screens on that side were dead. I activated the standby system. The *Lesotho* had vanished. The guards had vanished with it, vaporized instantly. All the cables linking the parts of the Assembly, all the scanners and sensors that were not protected behind the shields, were gone. The Sections themselves were intact, but their coupling fields would have to be completely recalibrated. We wouldn't be arriving at Titan on schedule.

I looked again at Yifter. His face was now calm and thoughtful. He seemed to be waiting, listening expectantly. For what? If the *Lesotho* had been a suicide mission, manned by volunteers who sought revenge on Yifter, they hadn't had a chance. They couldn't destroy the Assembly, or get at Yifter. If revenge were not the purpose, what was the purpose?

I ran through in my mind the events of the past hour. With the drives switched off in the Assembly, we had an unprotected blind spot, dead astern. We had been putting all our attention on the *Lesotho*. Now, with the guards all dead, the Control Stage was undefended.

It was quicker to go aft and take a look than to call Bryson or McAndrew and ask them what they could see from the rear viewing screens of the Control Stage. Leaving Yifter, I dived head-first down the stairway—a risky maneuver if there were any chance that the drive might come back on, but I was sure it couldn't.

It took me about thirty seconds to travel the length of the Control Stage. By the time that I was halfway, I knew I had been thinking much too slowly. I heard the clang of a lock, a shout, and the sputtering crackle of a hand laser against solid metal. When I got to the rear compartment, it was all finished. Bryson, pale and open-mouthed, was floating against one wall. He seemed unhurt. McAndrew had fared less well. He was ten meters farther along, curled into a fetal ball. Floating near him I saw a family of four stubby pink worms with red-brown heads, still unclenching with muscle spasm. I could also see the deep burn on his side and chest, and his right hand, from which a laser had neatly clipped the fingers and cauterized the wound instantly as it did so. At the far end of the room, braced against the wall, were five suited figures, all well-armed.

Heroics would serve no purpose. I spread my arms wide to show that I was not carrying a weapon, and one of the newcomers pushed off from the wall and floated past me, heading towards the front of the Control Stage. I moved over to McAndrew and inspected his wounds. They looked bad, but not fatal. Fortunately, laser wounds are usually very clean. I could see that we would have problems with his lung unless we treated him quickly. A lobe had been penetrated, and his breathing was slowly breaking the seal of crisped tissue that the laser had made. Blood was beginning to well through and stain his clothing.

McAndrew's forehead was beaded with sweat. As the shock of his wound wore off, the pain was beginning. I pointed to the medical belt of one of the invaders, who nodded and tossed an ampoule across to me. I injected McAndrew at the big vein inside his right elbow.

The figure who had pushed past me was returning, followed by Yifter. The face plate of the suit was now open, revealing a dark-haired woman in her early thirties. She looked casually at the scene, nodded at last, and turned back to Yifter.

"Everything's under control here," she said. "But we'll

have to take a Section from the Assembly. The ship we were following in caught some of the blast from the *Lesotho*, and it's no good for powered flight now."

Yifter shook his head reprovingly. "Impatient as usual, Akhtar. I'll bet you were just too eager to get here. You must learn patience if you are to be of maximum value to us, my dear. Where did you leave the main group?"

"A few hours drive inward from here. We have waited for your rescue, before making any plans for the next phase."

Yifter, calm as ever, nodded approvingly. "The right decision. We can take a Section without difficulty. Most of them contain their own drives, but some are less effective than others."

He turned to me, smiling gently. "Jeanie Roker, which Section is the best equipped to carry us away from the Assembly? As you see, it is time for us to leave you and rejoin our colleagues."

His calm was worse than any number of threats. I floated next to McAndrew, trying to think of some way that we could delay or impede the Lucies' escape. It might take days for a rescue party to reach us. In that time, Yifter and his followers could be anywhere.

I hesitated. Yifter waited. "Come now," he said at last. "I'm sure you are as eager as I am to avoid any further annoyance"—he moved his hand, just a little, to indicate McAndrew and Bryson—"for your friends."

I shrugged. All the Sections contained emergency life-support systems, more than enough for a trip of a few hours. Section Two, where the guards had been housed, lacked a full, independent drive unit, but it was still capable of propulsion. I thought it might slow their escape enough for us somehow to track it.

"Section Two should be adequate," I said. "It housed your guards in comfort. Those poor devils certainly have no need for it now."

I paused. Beside me, McAndrew was painfully straightening from his contorted position. The drugs were beginning to work. He coughed, and red globules floated away across the room. That lung needed attention.

"No," he said faintly. "Not Two, Yifter. Seven. Section Seven."

He paused and coughed again, while I looked at him in surprise.

"Seven," he said at last. He looked at me. "No killing, Jeanie. No—Killing vector."

The woman was listening closely. She regarded both of us suspiciously. "What was all that about?"

My mouth was gaping open as wide as Bryson's. I had caught an idea of what McAndrew was trying to tell me, but I didn't want to say it. Fortunately, I was helped out by Yifter himself.

"No killing," he said. "My dear, you have to understand that Professor McAndrew is a devoted pacifist—and carrying his principles through admirably. He doesn't want to see any further killing. I think I can agree with that—for the present."

He looked at me and shook his head. "I won't inquire what dangers and drawbacks Section Two might contain, Captain—though I do seem to recall that it lacks a decent drive unit. I think we'll follow the Professor's advice and take Section Seven. Akhtar is a very competent engineer, and I'm sure she'll have no trouble coupling the drive to the kernel."

He looked at us with a strange expression. If it didn't sound so peculiar, I'd describe it as wistful. "I shall miss our conversations," he said. "But I must say goodbye now. I hope that Professor McAndrew will recover. He is one of the strong—unless he allows himself to be killed by his unfortunate pacifist fancies. We may not meet again, but I am sure that you will be hearing about us in the next few months."

They left. McAndrew, Bryson and I watched the screens in silence, as the Lucies made their way over to Section Seven and entered it. Once they were inside, I went over to McAndrew and took him by the left arm.

"Come on," I said. "We have to get a patch on that lung."

He shook his head weakly. "Not yet. It can wait a few minutes. After that, it might not be necessary."

His forehead was beading with sweat again—and this time it was not from pain. I felt my own tension mounting steadily. We stayed by the display screen, and as the seconds ticked away my own forehead began to film with perspiration. We did not speak. I had one question, but I was terribly afraid of the answer I might get. I think that Bryson spoke to both of us several times. I have no idea what he said.

Finally, a pale nimbus grew at the rear of the Section Seven drive unit.

"Now," said McAndrew. "He's going to tap the kernel."

I stopped breathing. There was a pause of a few seconds, stretching to infinity, then the image on the screen rippled slightly. Suddenly, we could see stars shining through that area. Section Seven was gone, vanished, with no sign that it had ever existed.

McAndrew took in a long, pained breath, wincing as his injured lung expanded. Somehow, he managed a little smile.

"Well now," he said. "That answers a theoretical question that I've had on my mind for some time."

I could breathe again, too. "I didn't know what was going to happen there," I said. "I was afraid all the energy might come out of that kernel in one go."

McAndrew nodded. "To be honest, that thought was in my head, too. At this range, the shields would have been useless. We'd have gone like last year's lovers."

Bryson had been watching the whole thing in confusion. We had been ignoring him completely. At last, pale and irritable, he spoke to us again.

"What are you two talking about? And what's happened to the Section with Yifter in it? I was watching on the screen, then it just seemed to disappear."

"McAndrew tried to tell us earlier," I said. "But he

didn't want the Lucies to know what he was getting at. He'd been fiddling with the kernel in that Section. You heard what he said—no Killing vector. I don't know what he did, but he fixed it so that the kernel in Section Seven had no Killing vector."

"I'm sure he did," said Bryson tartly. "Now perhaps you'll tell me what a Killing vector is."

"Well, Mac could tell you a lot better than I can. But a Killing vector is a standard sort of thing in relativity— I guess you never had any training in that. You get a Killing vector when a region of space-time has some sort of symmetry—say, about an axis of spin. And every sort of black hole, every sort of kernel we've ever encountered before, has at least one symmetry of that type. So if McAndrew changed the kernel and made it into something with no Killing vector, it's like no kernel we've ever seen. Right, Mac?"

He looked dreamy. The drugs had taken hold. "I took it past the extreme Kerr-Newman form," he said. "Put it into a different form, metastable equilibrium. Event horizon had disappeared, all the Killing vectors had disappeared."

"Christ!" I hadn't expected that. "No event horizon? Doesn't that mean you get—?"

McAndrew was still nodding, eye pupils dilated. "—a naked singularity. That's right, Jeanie, I had a naked singularity, sitting there in equilibrium in Section Seven. You don't get there by spinning-up—need different method." His speech was slurring, as though his tongue was swollen. "Didn't know what would happen if somebody tried to tap it, to use for a drive. Either the signature of space-time there would change, from three space dimensions and one time, to two space and two time. Or we might see the System's biggest explosion. All the mass coming out as radiation, in one flash."

It was slowly dawning on Bryson what we were saying. "But just where is Yifter now?" he asked.

"Gone a long way," I said. "Right out of this universe."

"And he can't be brought back?" asked Bryson.

"I hope not." I'd seen more than enough of Yifter.

"But I'm supposed to deliver him safely to Titan," said Bryson. "I'm responsible for his safe passage. What am I going to tell the Planetary Coordinators?"

I didn't have much sympathy. I was too busy looking at McAndrew's wounds. The fingers could be regenerated using the bio-feedback equipment on Titan, but the lung would need watching. It was still bleeding a little.

"Tell them you had a very singular experience," I said. McAndrew grunted as I probed the deep cut in his side. "Sorry, Mac. Have to do it. You know, you've ruined your reputation forever as far as I'm concerned. I thought you were a pacifist? All that preaching at us, then you send Yifter and his lot all the way to Hell—and good riddance to them."

McAndrew was drifting far away on his big dose of painkillers. He half-winked at me and made his curious throat-clearing noise.

"Och, I'm a pacifist all right. We pacifists have to look after each other. How could we ever hope for peace with people like Yifter around to stir up trouble? There's a bunch more of them, a few hours travel behind us. Fix me up quick, Jeanie. I should be tinkering with the other kernels a bit—just in case the other Lucies decide to pay us a visit later . . ."

SECOND CHRONICLE:

Moment of Inertia

"Now," said the interviewer, "tell us just what led you to the ideas for the inertia-less drive."

She was young and vulnerable-looking, and I think that was what saved her from a hot reply. As it was, McAndrew just shook his head and said quietly—but still with feeling—"Not the *inertia-less* drive. There's no such thing. It's a *balanced* drive."

She looked confused. "But it lets you accelerate at more than fifty gees, doesn't it? By making you so you don't feel any acceleration at all. Doesn't that mean you must have no inertia?"

McAndrew was shaking his head again. He looked pained and resigned. I suppose that he had to go through this explanation twice a day, every day of his life, with somebody.

I leaned forward and lowered the sound on the video unit. I had heard the story too often, and my sympathies were all with him. We had direct evidence that the McAndrew drive was anything but inertia-less. I doubt if he'll ever get that message across to the average person, even though he's most people's idea of the "great scientist," the ultimate professor.

I was there at the beginning of the whole thing. In fact, according to McAndrew I *was* the beginning. We had been winding our way back from the Titan Colony, travelling light as we usually did on the inbound leg. We had only four Sections in the Assembly, and only two of them carried power kernels and drive units, so I guess we massed about three billion tons for ship and cargo.

Halfway in, just after turnover point, we got an incoming request for medical help from the mining colony on Horus. I passed the word on to Luna Station, but we couldn't do much to help. Horus is in the Egyptian Cluster of asteroids, way out of the ecliptic, and it would take any aid mission a couple of weeks to get to them. By that time, I suspected their problem would be over—one way or another. So I was in a pretty gloomy mood when McAndrew and I sat down to dinner.

"I didn't know what to tell them, Mac. They know the score as well as I do, but they couldn't resist asking if we had a fast-passage ship that could help them. I had to tell them the truth, there's nothing that can get out there at better than two and a half gees, not with people on board. And they need doctors, not just drugs. Luna will have something on the way in a couple of days, but I don't think that will do it."

McAndrew nodded sympathetically. He knew that I needed to talk it out to somebody, and we've spent a lot of time together on those Titan runs. He's working on his own experiments most of the time, but I know when he needs company, too. It must be nice to be a famous scientist, but it can be lonely travelling all the time inside your own head.

"I wonder if we're meant for space, Mac," I went on—only half-joking. "We've got drives that will let us send unmanned probes out at better than a hundred gees of continuous acceleration, but we're the weak link. I could take the Assembly here up to five gee—we'd be home in a couple of days instead of another month—but you and I couldn't take it. Can't you and some of your staff at the Institute come up with a system so that we don't get crushed flat by high accelerations? A thing like that, an inertia-less drive, it would change space exploration completely."

I was wandering on, just to keep my mind off the problems they had out on Horus, but what I was saying was sound enough. We had the power on the ships, only the humans were the obstacle. McAndrew was listening to me seriously, but he was shaking his head.

"So far as I know, Jeanie, an inertia-less drive is a theoretical impossibility. Unless somebody a lot brighter than I am can come up with an entirely new theory of physics, we'll not see your inertia-less drive."

That was a pretty definitive answer. There *were* no people brighter than McAndrew, at least in the area of physics. If Mac didn't think it could be done, you'd not find many people arguing with him. Some people were fooled by the fact that he took time off to make trips with me out to Titan, but that was all part of his way of working.

If you deduce from this that I'm not up at that rarefied level of thought, you're quite right. I can follow McAndrew's explanations—sometimes. But when he really gets going he loses me in the first two sentences.

This time, his words seemed clear enough for anyone to follow them. I poured myself another glass of ouzo and wondered how many centuries it would be before the man or woman with the completely new theory came along. Sitting across from me, Mac had begun to rub at his sandy, receding hairline. His expression had become vacant. I've learned not to interrupt when he's got that look on his face. It means he's thinking in a way that I can't follow. One of the other professors at the Penrose Institute says that Mac has a mind that can see round corners, and I have a little inkling what he means by that.

"Why inertia-less, Jeanie?" said McAndrew after a few minutes.

Maybe he hadn't been listening after all. "So we can use high accelerations. So we can get people to go at the same speeds as the unmanned probes. They'd be flattened at fifty gee, you know that. We need an inertia-less drive so that we can stand that acceleration without being squashed to a mush."

"But that's not the same thing at all. I told you that a drive with no inertia isn't possible—and it isn't. What you're asking for, now, it seems to me that we should be able . . ."

His voice drifted off to nothing, he stood up, and without another word he left the cabin. I wondered what I'd started.

If that was the beginning of the McAndrew drive— as I think it was—then, yes, I was there at the very beginning.

So far as I could tell, it wasn't only the beginning. It was also the end. Mac didn't talk about the subject again on our way in to Luna rendezvous, even though I tried to nudge him a couple of times. He was always the same, he didn't like to talk about his ideas when they were "half-cooked," as he called it.

When we got to Luna, McAndrew went off back to the Institute, and I took a cargo out to Cybele. End of story, and it gradually faded from my thoughts, until the time came, seven months later, for the next run to Titan.

For the first time in five years, McAndrew didn't make the trip. He didn't call me, but I got a brief message that he was busy with an off-Earth project, and wouldn't be free for several months. I wondered, not too seriously, if Mac's absence could be connected with inertia-less spaceships, and then went on with the cargo to Titan.

That was the trip where some lunatic in the United Space Federation's upper bureaucracy decided that Titan was overdue for some favorable publicity, as a thriving colony where culture would be welcomed. Fine. They decided to combine culture and nostalgia, and hold on Titan a full-scale, old-fashioned Miss & Mister Universe competition. It apparently never occurred to the organizers—who must have had minds that could not see in straight lines, let alone around corners—that the participants were bound to take the thing seriously once it was started. Beauty is not something that good-looking people are willing to take lightly. I had the whole Assembly filled with gorgeous, jealous contestants, screaming managers, horny and ever-hopeful newshounds from every media outlet in the System, and any number of vengeful and vigilant wives, lovers and mistresses of both sexes. On one of my earlier runs I took a circus and zoo out to Titan, but that was nothing compared with this trip. Thank Heaven that the ship is computer-controlled. All my time was spent in keeping some of the passengers together and the rest apart.

It also hadn't occurred to the organizers, back on Earth, that a good part of the Titan colony is the prison. When I saw the first interaction of the prisoners and the contestants I realized that the trip out to Titan had been a picnic compared with what was about to follow. I chickened out and went back to the ship until it was all over.

I couldn't really escape, though. When it was all over, when the winners had finally been chosen, when the protests and the counter-protests had all been lodged, when the battered remnants of the more persistent prisoners had been carried back to custody, when mayhem was stilled, and when the colonists of Titan must have felt that they had enjoyed as much of Inner System culture as they could stand for another twenty or thirty years, after all that it was my job to get the group back on board again, and home to Earth without further violence. The contestants hated their managers, the managers hated the judges, the judges hated the news media, and everyone hated the winners. It seemed to me that McAndrew may have had advance information about the trip, and drawn a correct conclusion.

I would like to have skipped it myself. Since I was stuck with it, I separated the Sections of the Assembly as much as I could, put everything onto automatic, and devoted myself to consoling one of the losers, a smooth-skinned armful from one of the larger asteroids.

We finally got there. On that day of rejoicing, the whole ghastly gaggle connected with the contest left the Assembly, I said a lingering farewell to my friend from Vesta—a most inappropriate origin for that particular contestant—and settled back for a needed rest.

It lasted for about eight hours. As soon as I called into the Com Center for news and messages, I got a terse summons on the com display: GO TO PENROSE INSTITUTE, L-4 STATION. MACAVITY.

Not an alarming message, on the face of it, but it worried me. It was from McAndrew, and I doubt if three people knew that I had given him that nickname when I found he was a specialist on theories of gravity ("Old Possum's Book Of Practical Cats" didn't seem to be widely read among Mac's colleagues).

Why hadn't he called me directly, instead of sending a com-link message? The fact that we were back from Titan would have been widely reported. I sat down at the terminal and placed a link to the Institute, person-to-person to McAndrew.

I didn't feel any better when the call went through. Instead of Mac's familiar face, I was looking at the coal-black complexion of Professor Limperis, the head of the Institute. He nodded at me seriously.

"Captain Roker, your timing is impressive. If we had received no response to Professor McAndrew's coded message in the next eight hours, we would have proceeded without you. Can you help?"

He hesitated, seeing my confused expression. "Did your message tell you the background of the problem?"

"Dr. Limperis, all I've had so far is half a dozen words—to go to the L-4 branch of the Institute. I can do that easily enough, but I have no idea what the problem is, or what use I could possibly be on it. Where's Mac?"

"I wish to God I could answer that." He sat silent for a moment, chewing on his lower lip, then shrugged. "Professor McAndrew insisted that we send for you—left a message specifically for you. He told us that you were the stimulus for beginning the whole thing."

"*What* whole thing?"

He looked at me in even greater surprise. "Why, the high acceleration drive—the balanced drive that McAndrew has been developing for the past year. McAndrew has disappeared testing the prototype. Can you come at once to the Institute?"

The trip out to the Institute, creeping along in the Space Tug from Luna Station, was one of the low points of my life. There was no particular logic to it—after all, I'd done nothing wrong. But I couldn't get rid of the feeling that I'd wasted a critical eight hours after the passengers had left the Assembly. If I hadn't been obsessed with sex on the trip back, maybe I would have gone straight to the com-link instead of taking a sleep break. And maybe then I would have been on my way that much earlier, and that would have been the difference between saving Mac and failing to save him . . .

You can see how my mind was running. Without any real facts, you can make bears out of bushes just as well in space as you can on Earth. All I had been told by Limperis was that McAndrew had left a week earlier on a test of the prototype of a new ship. If he was not back within a hundred and fifty hours, he had left that terse coded message for me, and instructions—orders might be a better word—to take me along on any attempted search for him.

Dr. Limperis had been very apologetic about it. "I'm only quoting Professor McAndrew, you understand. He said that he didn't want any rescue party setting out in the *Dotterel* if you weren't part of it. He said"—Limperis coughed uncomfortably—"we had a real need for your common sense and natural cowardice. We'll be waiting for you here as soon as you can arrange passage. The least

we can do for Professor McAndrew in the circumstances
is to honor his wishes on this."

I couldn't decide if I was being complimented or not.
As L-4 Station crept into view on the forward screen, I
peered at it on highest magnification, trying to see what
the rescue ship looked like. I could see the bulk of the
Institute structure but no sign of anything that ought to
be a ship. I had visions of a sort of super-Assembly, a huge
cluster of electromagnetically linked spheres. All I could
see were living quarters and docking facilities, and, as we
came in to dock, a peculiar construction like a flat, shiny
plate with a long thin spike protruding from the center.
It looked nothing like any USF ship, passenger or cargo.

Limperis may have spent his whole life in pure research,
but he knew how to organize for emergency action. There
were just five people in our meeting inside the Institute.
I had never met them in person, but they were all familiar to me through McAndrew's descriptions, and from
media coverage. Limperis himself had made a life study
of high-density matter. He knew every kernel below lunar
mass out to a couple of hundred astronomical units—many
of them he had visited, and a few of the small ones he had
shunted back with him to the Inner System, to use as power
supplies.

Siclaro was the specialist in kernel energy extraction.
The Kerr-Newman black holes were well-understood
theoretically, but efficient use of them was still a matter for experts. When the USF wanted to know the best
way to draw off power, for drives or for general use,
Siclaro was usually called in. His name on a recommendation was like a stamp of approval that few would think
to question.

With Gowers there as an expert in multiple kernel
arrays, Macedo as the System authority in electromagnetic
coupling, and Wenig the master of compressed matter
stability, the combined intellect in that one room in the
Institute was overpowering. I looked at the three men
and two women who had just been introduced to me, and

felt like a gorilla in a ballet. I might make the right movements, but I wouldn't know what was going on.

"Look, Dr. Limperis," I said, "I know what Professor McAndrew wants, but I'm not sure he's right." Might as well hit them with my worries at the beginning, and not waste everybody's time. "I can run a ship, sure—it's not hard. But I've no idea how to run something with a McAndrew drive on it. Any one of you could probably do a better job."

Limperis was looking apologetic again. "Yes and no, Captain Roker. We could all handle the ship, any one of us. The concepts behind it are simple—a hundred and fifty years old. And the engineering has been kept simple, too, since we are dealing with a prototype."

"Then what do you want me for?" I won't say I was angry, but I was uneasy and unhappy, and there's a fine line between irritation and discomfort.

"Dr. Wenig will drive the *Dotterel*, he has handled it before in an earlier test. Actually, he handled the *Merganser*, the ship that Dr. McAndrew has disappeared in, but the *Dotterel* has identical design and equipment. Controlling the ship is easy—if everything behaves as we expected. If something goes wrong—and something must have gone wrong, or McAndrew would be back before this—then neither Dr. Wenig, nor any of the rest of us, has the experience that will be needed. We want you to tell Dr. Wenig what *not* to do. You've been through dangerous times before." He looked pleading. "Will you observe our actions, and use your experience to advise us?"

Uninvited, I flopped down into a seat and stared at the five of them. "You want me to be a bloody canary!"

"A canary?" Wenig was small and slight, with a luxuriant black mustache. He had a strong accent, and I think he was suspecting himself of a translation error.

"Right. Back when people used to go down deep in the earth to mine coal, they used to take a canary along with them. It was more sensitive to poisonous gases than they were. When it fell off the perch, they knew it was time to leave. The rest of you will fly the ship, and watch for me to fall off my seat."

They looked at each other, and finally Limperis nodded. "We need a canary, Captain Roker. None of us here knows how to sing at the right time. Will you do it?"

I had no choice. Not after Mac's personal cry for help. I could see one problem—I'd be telling them everything they did was dangerous. When you have a new piece of technology, it *is* risky, *whatever* you do with it.

"You mean you'll let me overrule all the rest of you, if I don't feel comfortable?"

"We would." Limperis was quite firm about it. "But the question will not arise. The *Merganser* and the *Dotterel* are both two-person ships. We saw no point in making them larger. Dr. Wenig will fly the *Dotterel*, and you will be the only other person aboard. It just takes one person to handle the controls. You will be there to advise of hidden problems."

I stood up. "Let's go. I don't think I can see danger any better than you can, but I may be wrong. If Mac's on his own out there, wherever he is, we'd better get moving. I'm ready when you are, Dr. Wenig."

Nobody moved. Maybe McAndrew and Limperis were right about my antennae, because at that moment I had a premonition of new problems. I looked around at the uncomfortable faces.

"Professor McAndrew isn't actually *alone* on the *Merganser*." It was Emma Gowers who spoke first. "He has a passenger with him on the ship."

"Someone from the Institute?"

She shook her head. "Nina Velez is with him."

"Nina Velez? You don't mean President Velez's daughter—the one with AG News?"

She nodded. "The same."

I sat down again in my chair. Hard. Maybe the Body-beautiful run to Titan had been an easier trip than I had realized.

✧ ✧ ✧

Wenig may have come to piloting second-hand, but he certainly knew his ship. He wanted me to know it, too. Before we left the Institute, we'd done the lot—schematics, models, components, power, life support, mechanicals, electricals, electronics, controls, and backups.

When the ship was explained to me, I decided that McAndrew didn't really see round corners when he thought. It was just that things were obvious to him before they were explained, and obvious to other people afterwards. I had been saying "inertia-less" to Mac, and he had been just as often saying "impossible." But we hadn't been communicating very well. All I wanted was a drive that would let us accelerate at multiple gees without flattening the passengers. To McAndrew, that was a simple requirement, one that he could easily satisfy—but there was no question of doing away with inertia, of passengers or ship.

"Take it back to basics," said Wenig, when he was showing me how the *Dotterel* worked. "Remember the equivalence principle? That's at the heart of it. There is no way of distinguishing an accelerated motion from a gravitational field force, right?"

I had no trouble with that. It was freshman physics. "Sure. You'd be flattened just as well in a really high gravity field as you would in a ship accelerating at fifty gee. But where does it get you?"

"Imagine that you were standing on something with a hefty gravity field—Jupiter, say. You'd experience a downward force of about two and a half gee. Now suppose that somebody could accelerate Jupiter *away* from you, downwards, at two and a half gee. You'd fall towards it, but you'd never reach it—it would be accelerating at the same rate as you are. And you'd feel as though you were in free fall, but so far as the rest of the Universe is concerned you'd be accelerating at two and a half gee, same as Jupiter. That's what the equivalence principle is telling us, that acceleration and gravity can cancel out, if they're set up to be equal and opposite."

As soon as you got used to Wenig's accent, he was easy to follow—I doubt if anybody could get into the Institute unless he was more than bright enough to explain concepts in easy terms.

I nodded. "I can understand that easily enough. But you've just replaced one problem with a worse one. You can't find any drive in the Universe that could accelerate Jupiter at two and a half gee."

"We cannot—not yet, at any rate. Luckily, we don't need to use Jupiter. We can do it with something a lot smaller, and a lot closer. Let's look at the *Dotterel* and the *Merganser*. At McAndrew's request I designed the mass element for both of them."

He went across to the window that looked out from the inside of the Institute to raw space. The *Dotterel* was floating about ten kilometers away, close enough to see the main components.

"See the plate on the bottom? It's a hundred meter diameter disk of compressed matter, electromagnetically stabilized and one meter thick. Density's about eleven hundred and seventy tons per cubic centimeter—pretty high, but nothing near as high as we've worked with here at the Institute. Less than you get in anything but the top couple of centimeters of a neutron star, and nowhere near approaching kernel densities. Now, if you were sitting right at the center of that disk, you'd experience a *gravitational* acceleration of fifty gee pulling you down to the disk. Tidal forces on you would be one gee per meter—not enough to trouble you. If you stayed on the axis of the disk, and moved away from it, you'd feel an attractive force of *one* gee when you were two hundred and forty-six meters from the center of the disk. See the column growing out from the disk? It's four meters across and two hundred and fifty meters long."

I looked at it through the scope. The long central spike seemed to be completely featureless, a slim column of grey metal.

"What's inside it?"

"Mostly nothing." Wenig picked up a model of the *Dotterel* and cracked it open lengthwise, so that I could see the interior structure. "When the drives are off, the living-capsule is out here at the far end, two hundred and fifty meters from the dense disk. Gravity feels like one gee, toward the center of the disk. See the drives here, on the disk itself? They accelerate the whole thing *away* from the center column, so the disk stays flat and perpendicular to the motion. The bigger the acceleration that the drives produce, the closer to the disk we move the living-capsule up the central column here. We keep it so the total force in the capsule, gravity less acceleration, is always one gee, *toward* the disk."

He slid the capsule along an electromechanical ladder closer to the disk. "It's easy to compute the right distance for any acceleration—the computer has it built-in, but you could do it by hand in a few minutes. When the drives are accelerating the whole thing at fourteen gee, the capsule is held a little less than fifty meters from the disk. I've been on a test run in the *Merganser* where we got up to almost twenty gee. Professor McAndrew intended to take it up to higher accelerations on this test. To accelerate at thirty-two gee, the capsule must be about twenty meters from the disk to keep effective gravity inside to one gee. The plan was to take the system all the way up to design maximum—fifty gee thrust acceleration, so that the passengers in the capsule would be right up against the disk, and feel as though they were in free fall. Gravity and thrust accelerations will exactly balance."

I was getting goose bumps along the back of my neck. I knew the performance of the unmanned med ships. They would zip you from inside the orbit of Mercury out to Pluto in a couple of days, standing start to standing finish. Once in a while you'd get a passenger on them—accident or suicide. The flattened thing that they unpacked at the other end showed what the human body thought of a hundred gee.

"What would happen if the drives went off suddenly?" I said.

"You mean when the capsule is up against the disk—at maximum thrust?" Wenig shook his head. "We designed a safeguard system to prevent that, even on the prototypes. If there were a sign of the drive cutting off, the capsule would be moved back up the column, away from the disk. The system for that is built-in."

"Yeah. But McAndrew hasn't come back." I had the urge to get on our way. "I've seen built-in-safe systems before. The more foolproof you think something is, the worse the failure when it happens. Can't we get moving?"

"Come on." Wenig stood up. "Any teacher will tell you, you can't get much into an impatient learner. I'll give you the rest of the story as we go. We'll head out along the same path as McAndrew did—that's plotted out in the records back here."

"You think McAndrew went along with the nominal flight plan?"

"We know he didn't." Wenig looked a lot less sure of himself. "You see, when the drives are on maximum the plasma round the living-capsule column interferes with radio signals. Fifty hours after they left the Institute, the *Merganser* was tracked from Triton Station. McAndrew came back into the Solar System, decelerating at fifty gee. He didn't cut the drive at all—just went right through the System and accelerated out again in a slightly different direction. We got the log, but we have no idea what he was doing. There was no way to get a signal to him or from him with the drive on."

"So they got all the way up to the maximum drive! And they came back here. God, why didn't Limperis tell me that when we were in the first meeting?" I went to the locker and pulled out a suit. "He took it up all the way, fifty gee or better. Let's get after him. If he kept that up, he'll be halfway to Alpha Centauri by now."

The living-capsule was about three meters across and

simply furnished. I was surprised at the amount of room, until Wenig pointed out to me how equipment and supplies that could take higher accelerations were situated on the outside of the capsule, on the side away from the gravity disk.

We had started with McAndrew's flight plan for only a few minutes when I took Limperis at his word that I'd be boss and changed the procedure. If we were to reach McAndrew, the less time we spent shooting off in the wrong direction, the better. He had come right through the System, and we ought to head in the direction that he was last seen to be heading.

"I'll take us up to fifty gee," said Wenig. "That way, we'll experience the same perturbing forces as the *Merganser* did. All right?"

"Christ, no." My stomach turned over. "Not all right. Look, we don't know what happened to Mac, but chances are it was some problem with the ship. If we do just what he did, we may finish up with the same trouble."

Wenig took his hands off the controls and turned to me, palms spread. "But then what can we do? We don't know where they were going, all we can do is try and follow the same track."

"I'm not sure. All I know is what we're *not* going to do—and we're not trying for top acceleration. Didn't you say you'd flown *Merganser* at twenty gee?"

"Several times."

"Then take us out along Mac's trajectory at twenty gee until we're outside the System. Then cut the drive. I want to use our sensors, and we won't be able to do that from the middle of a ball of plasma."

Wenig looked at me. I know he was mentally accusing me of cowardice. "Captain Roker," he said quietly. "I thought we were in a hurry. We may be weeks following *Merganser* the way you are proposing."

"Yeah. But we'll get there. Can Mac's support system last that long?"

"Easily."

"Then don't let's kick it around any more. Let's do it. Twenty gee, as soon as you can give it to us."

The *Dotterel* worked like a dream. At twenty gee acceleration relative to the Solar System, we didn't feel anything unusual at all. The disk pulled us towards it at twenty-one gee, the acceleration of the ship pulled us away from it at twenty gee, and we sat there in the middle at a snug and comfortable standard gravity. I couldn't even feel the tidal forces, though I knew they were there. We had poor communications with the Penrose Institute, but we'd known that and expected to make up for it when we cut the drive.

Oddly enough, the first phase of the trip wasn't scary—it was boring. I wanted to get up to a good cruise speed before we coasted free. It gave me the chance to probe another mystery—one that seemed at least as strange as the disappearance of the *Merganser*.

"What were you doing at the Institute, allowing Nina Velez aboard the ship?"

"She heard that we were developing a new drive—don't ask me how. Maybe she saw the Institute's budget." Wenig sniffed. "I don't trust the security at the USF Headquarters."

"And you let her talk her way in, and you forced McAndrew to take her with him on a *test flight*?"

If I sounded mad, I felt madder. Mac's life meant more than the dignity of some smooth-assed bureaucrat in the Institute's front office.

Dr. Wenig looked at me coldly. "I think you misunderstand the situation. Nina Velez was not forced onto Professor McAndrew by the "front office"—for one thing, we have no such thing. The Institute is run by its members. You want to know why Miss Velez is on board the *Merganser*? I'll tell you. McAndrew insisted that she go with him."

"Bullshit!" There were some things I couldn't believe. "Why the hell would Mac let himself go along with that? I know him, even if you don't. Over his dead body."

Wenig sighed. He was leaning on a couch across from me, sipping a glass of white wine—no hardship tours for him.

"Four weeks ago I'd have echoed your comments exactly," he said. "Professor McAndrew would never agree to such a thing, right? But he did. Putting this simply, Captain Roker, it is a case of infatuation. A bad one. I think that—"

He stopped, outraged. I had started to laugh, in spite of the seriousness of our situation.

"What's so funny, Captain?"

"Well." I shrugged. "The whole thing's funny. Not funny, it's preposterous. McAndrew is a great physicist, and Nina Velez may be the President's daughter, but she's just a young newswoman. Anyway, he and I—he wouldn't—"

Now I stopped. I wondered if Wenig was going to get up and hit me, he looked so mad.

"Captain Roker, I don't like your insinuation," he said. "McAndrew is a physicist—so am I. You may not be smart enough to realize it, but physics is a *field of study*, not a surgical operation. Castration isn't part of the Ph.D. exams, you know." His tone dripped sarcasm. I wouldn't have liked a two-month trip to Titan with young Dr. Wenig.

"Anyway," he went on. "You have managed to jump to a wrong conclusion. It was not Professor McAndrew who suffered the initial infatuation. It was Nina Velez. She thinks he is wonderful. She came to do an interview, and before any of us knew what was going on she was in his office all day. All night, too, after the first week."

I was wrong. I know that now, and I think I knew it then, but I was too peeved to make an immediate apology to Wenig. Instead, I said, "But if she was the one that wanted him, couldn't he just throw her out?"

"Nina Velez?" Wenig gave a bark of laughter. "You've never met her, I assume? She's a President's daughter, and whatever Nina wants, Nina gets. She started it, but inside a couple of days she had Professor McAndrew behaving like a true fool. It was disgusting, the way he went on."

(*You're jealous, Wenig*, I said, *jealous of Mac's good luck*—but I said it to myself.)

"And she persuaded McAndrew to let her go out on the *Merganser*? What were the rest of you doing?"

He reddened. "Professor McAndrew was not the only one behaving like a fool. Why do you think Limperis, Siclaro and I feel like murderers? The two women on the team, Gowers and Macedo, insisted that Nina Velez should not go near the ships. We overruled them. Now, Captain Roker, maybe you see why each of us wanted to come after McAndrew. We drew lots, and I was the winner.

"And maybe you should think of one other thing. While you are looking at our motives, and laughing at them, maybe you ought to look at your own. You look angry. I think you are jealous—jealous of Nina Velez."

It's a good thing that we had to follow our flight plan at that point, and prepare to cut the drive, or I don't know what I would have done to Dr. Wenig. I'm a shade taller than he is, and I outweigh him by maybe ten pounds, but he looked fit and wiry. It wouldn't have been a foregone conclusion, not at all.

Our descent into savagery was saved by the insistent buzzer of the computer, telling us to be ready for the drive reduction. We sat there, furious and not looking at each other, as the acceleration was slowly throttled back and the capsule moved away from the disk to resume its free-flight position two hundred and fifty meters behind it. The move took ten minutes. By the time it was over we had cooled off. I managed a graceless apology for my implied insults, and Wenig just as uncomfortably accepted it and said that he was sorry for what he had been saying and thinking.

I didn't ask him what he had been thinking—there was a hint that it was much worse than anything that he had said.

We had cut the drive at a little more than one hundred astronomical units from the Sun and were coasting along at a quarter of the speed of light. The computer gave us automatic Doppler compensation, so that we could hold an accurate communication link back to the Institute, through Triton Station. Conversation wasn't easy, because the round-trip delay for signals was almost twenty-eight hours—all we expected to be able to do was send "doing fine" messages to Limperis and the others.

Our forward motion was completely imperceptible, though I fancied that I could see a reddening of stars astern and a bluer burn to stars ahead of us. We were well beyond the edge of the planetary part of the System, out where only the comets and the kernels lived. I put all our sensors onto maximum gain and Wenig and I settled in to a quiet spell of close watching. He had asked me what we were looking for. I had told him the truth: I had no idea, of what or when.

We crept on, farther and farther out. I don't know if you can actually creep at a quarter of light speed, but that's the way it felt; blackness, the unchanging stars, and a dwarfed Solar System far behind us.

Our eyes were all wide open: radio receivers, infrared scanners, telescopes, flux meters, radar and mass detectors. For two days we found nothing, no signal above the hiss and shimmer of the perennial interstellar background. Wenig was growing more impatient, and his tone was barely civil. He wanted us to get the drive back on high, and dash off after McAndrew—wherever that might be.

He was fidgeting on his bunk and ignoring the scopes when I caught the first trace.

"Dr. Wenig. What am I seeing? Can you tune that IR receiver?"

He came alert and was over to the console in a single movement. After a few seconds of adjustment he shook his head and swore. "It's natural, not man-made. Look at that trace. We're seeing a hot collapsed body. About seven hundred degrees, that's why there's peak power in the five micrometer band. We can call back to Limperis if you like, but he's sure to have it in his catalog already. There must be lots of these within a few days flight of us."

He left the display and slumped back on his bunk. I went over and stared at it for a couple of minutes. "Would McAndrew know that this is here?"

That made him think instead of just brooding. "There's a good chance that he would. Collapsed and high-density matter is Doctor Limperis's special study, but McAndrew probably put a library of them into *Merganser*'s computer before he left. He wouldn't want to run into something unexpected out here."

"We have McAndrew's probable trajectory stored there too?"

"We know how he left the System, where he was heading. If he cut the drive, or turned after he was outside tracking range, we don't have any information on it."

"Never mind that. Give me the library access codes, and let me get at the input console. I want to see if Mac's path shows intersection with any of the high-density objects out here."

Wenig looked skeptical. "The chances of such a close encounter are very small. One in millions or billions."

I was already calling up the access sequence. "By accident? I'd agree with you. But McAndrew must have had some reason to fly back through the System, and make the slight course change that you recorded. I think he was telling us where he was going. And the only place he could have been going between here and Sirius would be one of the collapsed bodies out in the Halo."

"But why?" Wenig was standing at my shoulder, fingers twitching.

"Don't know that." I stood up. "Here, you do it, you must have had plenty of experience with *Dotterel*'s computer. Set it for anything that would put *Merganser* within five million kilometers of a high-density body. That's as close as I think we can rely on trajectory intersection."

Wenig's fingers were flying over the keys—he should have been a concert pianist. I've never seen anybody handle a programming sequence at that rate. While he was doing it the com-link whistled for attention. I turned to it, leaving Wenig calling out displays and index files.

"It's Limperis," I said. "Problems. President Velez is starting to breathe down his neck. Wants to know what has happened to Nina. When will she be back? Why did Limperis and the rest of you let her go on a test trip? How can the Institute be so irresponsible?"

"We expected that." Wenig didn't look up. "Velez is just blowing off steam. There's no way that any other ship could get out here to us in less than three months. Does he have anything useful to suggest?"

"No. He's threatening Limperis with punitive measures against the Institute. Says he'll want a review of the whole organization."

"Limperis is asking for our reply?"

"Yes."

Wenig keyed in a final sequence of commands and sat back in his seat. "Tell him Velez should go fuck himself. We've got enough to do without interference."

I was still reading the incoming signals from Triton Station. "I think Dr. Limperis has already sent that message to the President's Office, in not quite those words. We'd better get Nina back safely."

"I know that." Wenig hit a couple of keys and an output stream began to fill the scope. "Here it comes. Closest approach distances for every body within five hundred AU, assuming McAndrew held the same course and acceleration all the way out. I've set it to stop if we get anything better than a million kilometers, and display everything that's five million or closer."

Before I could learn how to read the display, Wenig banged both hands down on the desk and leaned forward,

"Look at that!" His voice showed his surprise and excitement. "See it? That's HC-183. It's 322 AU from the Sun, and almost dead ahead of us. The computer shows a fly-by distance for *Merganser* too small to compute—that's an underflow where we ought to see a distance."

"Suppose that McAndrew decelerated as he got nearer to it?"

"Wouldn't make much difference, he'd still be close to rendezvous—speeds in orbit are small that far out. But why would he want to rendezvous with HC-183?"

I couldn't answer that, but maybe we were at least going to find *Merganser*. Even if it was only a vaporized trace on the surface of HC-183, where the ship hit it.

"Let's get back with our drive," I said. "What's the mass of HC-183?"

"Pretty high." Wenig frowned at the display. "We show a five thousand kilometer diameter and a mass that's half of Jupiter's. Must be a good lump of collapsed matter at the center of it. How close do you want to take us? And what acceleration for the drive?"

"Give us a trajectory that lets us take a close look from bound orbit. A million kilometers ought to be enough. And keep us down to twenty gee or better. I'll send a message back to the Institute. If they have any more information on HC-183, we want it."

Wenig had been impatient before, when we weren't going anywhere in particular. Now that we had a target he couldn't sit still. He was all over our three-meter living-capsule, fiddling with the scopes, the computer, and the control console. He kept looking wistfully at the drive setting, then at me.

I wasn't having any. I felt as impatient as he did, but when we had come this far I didn't want to find we'd duplicated *all* McAndrew's actions, including the one that might have been fatal. We smoothly turned after twenty-two hours, so our drive began to decelerate us, and waited out the interminable delay as we crept closer to the dark mass of HC-183. We couldn't see a sign of it on any of the sensors, but we knew it had to be there, hidden behind the plasma ball of the drive.

When our drive went off and we were in orbit around the black mass of the hidden proto-planet, Wenig was at the display console for visible wavelengths.

"I can see it," he shouted.

My first feeling of relief and excitement lasted only a split second. There was no way we would be able to spot the *Merganser* from a million kilometers out.

"What are you seeing? Infrared emission from HC-183?"

"No, you noodle. I can see the ship—McAndrew's ship."

"You can't be. We'd have to be right next to it to be able to pick it up with our magnifications." I spun my seat around and looked at the screen.

Wenig was laughing, hysterical with relief. "Don't you understand? I'm seeing the *drive*, not *Merganser* itself. Look at it, isn't it beautiful?"

He was right. I felt as though I was losing my reason. McAndrew might have gone into orbit about the body, or if he were unlucky he might have run into it—but it made no sense that he'd be sitting here with the drive on. And from the look of the long tail of glowing plasma that stretched across twenty degrees of the screen, that drive was on a high setting.

"Give me a Doppler read-out," I said. "Let's find out what sort of orbit he's in. Damn it, what's he doing there, sight-seeing?"

Now that it looked as though we had found them, I was irrationally angry with McAndrew. He had brought us haring out beyond the limits of the System, and he was sitting there waiting when we arrived. Waiting, and that was all.

Wenig had called up a display and was sitting there staring at it in perplexity. "No motion relative to HC-183," he said. "He's not in an orbit around it, he's got the ship just hanging there, with the drive balancing the gravitational attraction. Want me to take us alongside, so we can use a radar signal? That's the only way he'll hear us through the drive interference."

"I guess we'll have to. Take us up close to them." I stared at the screen, random thoughts spinning around my head. "No, wait a minute. Damn it, once we set up the computer to take us in there, it will do automatic drive control. Before we go in, let's find out what we're in for. Can you estimate the strength of HC-183's gravitational attraction at the distance that *Merganser* is at? Got enough data for it?"

"Give me a second." Wenig's fingers flew over the console again. If he ever decided that he didn't want to work at the Penrose Institute, he'd make the best space-racer in the System.

He looked at the output for a second, frowned, and said, "I think I must have made an error."

"Why?"

"I'm coming up with a distance from the surface of about nine thousand kilometers. That means the *Merganser* would be feeling a pull of fifty gee—their drive would be full on, as high as it's designed to go. It wouldn't make sense for them to hang there like that, on full drive. Want to go on down to them?"

"No. Hold it where we are." I leaned back and closed my eyes. "There has to be a pattern to what Mac's been doing. He went right through the System back there with the drive full on, now he's hanging close in to a high-density object with the drive still full on. What the hell's he up to?"

"You won't find out unless we can get in touch with him." Wenig was sounding impatient again. "I say we should go on down there. Now we know where he is it's easiest to just go and ask him."

It was hard to argue with him, but I couldn't get an uneasy feeling out of the back of my head. Mac was holding a constant position, fifty gees of thrust balancing the fifty gee pull of HC-183. We couldn't get alongside him unless we were willing to increase *Dotterel's* drive to a matching fifty gee.

"Give me five more minutes. Remember why I'm here. It's to keep you from doing anything too brave. Look, if we were to hang on our drive with a twenty gee thrust, how close could we get to the *Dotterel*?"

"We'd have to make sure we didn't fry them with our drive," said Wenig. He was busy for a couple of minutes at the computer, while I tried again to make sense of the pieces.

"We can get so we're about sixty thousand kilometers from them," said Wenig at last. "If we want to talk to them through the microwave radar link, the best geometry would be one where we're seeing them side-on. We'd have decent clearance from both drives there. Ready to do it?"

"One minute more." I was getting a feeling, a sense that everything that McAndrew had done had been guided by a single logic. "Look, I asked you what would happen if the drive failed when the life-capsule was up close to the mass disk, and you said the system would move the capsule back out again. But look at it the other way round now. Suppose the drive works fine—and suppose it was the system that's supposed to move the life-capsule up and down the column that wouldn't work? What would that do?"

Wenig stroked at his luxuriant mustache. "I don't think it could happen, the design looked good. If it did, everything would depend where the capsule stuck."

"Suppose it stuck up near the disk, when the ship was on a high-thrust drive."

"Well, that would mean there was a big gravitational acceleration. You'd have to cancel it out with the drive, or the passengers would be flattened." He paused. "It would be a bugger. You wouldn't dare to turn the drive *off*—you'd need it on all the time, so that your acceleration compensated for the gravity of the disk."

"Damn right. If you couldn't get yourself farther from the disk, you'd be forced to keep on accelerating. That's what happened to the *Merganser*, I'll bet my pension on it. Get the designs of the capsule movement-train up on the screen, and let's see if we can spot anything wrong with it."

"You're an optimist, Captain Roker." He shrugged. "We

can do it, but those designs have been looked at twenty times. Look, I see what you're saying, but I find it hard to swallow. What was McAndrew doing when he came back through the system and then out again?"

"The only thing he *could* do. He couldn't switch the drive off, even though he could turn the ship around. He could fly off to God knows where in a straight line—that way we'd never have found him. Or he could fly in bloody great circles, and we'd have been able to see him but never get near to him for more than a couple of minutes at a time—there's no other manned ship that could match that fifty gee thrust. Or he could do what he did do. He flew back through the System to tell us the direction he was heading, out to HC-183. And he balanced here on his drive tail, and sat and waited for us to get smart enough to figure out what he was doing."

I paused for breath, highly pleased with myself. Out of a sphere of trillions of cubic miles, we had tracked the *Merganser* to its destination. Wenig was shaking his head and looking very unhappy.

"What's wrong," I said cockily. "Find the logic hard to follow?"

"Not at all. A rather trivial exercise." He looked down his nose at me. "But you don't seem able to follow your own ideas to a conclusion. McAndrew knows all about *this* ship. He knows it can accelerate at the same rate as *Merganser*. So your idea that he couldn't fly around in big circles and wait for us to match his position can't be right—the *Dotterel* could do that."

He was right.

"So why didn't Mac do that? Why did he come out all this way?"

"I can only think of one answer. He's had the chance to look at the reason the life capsule can't be moved back along the axis, so the drive mustn't be switched off. And he thinks that this ship has the same problem."

I nodded. "See now why I wouldn't let you take the *Dotterel* all the way up to fifty gee?"

"I do. You were right, and I would have taken us into trouble if you hadn't been along. Now then"—Wenig looked gloomier than ever at some new thought—"let's take the logic a step farther. McAndrew is hanging down there near HC-183 in a fifty gee gravity field. We can't get there to help him unless we do the same, and we're agreed that we dare not do that, or we'll end up with the same difficulty that he has, and we won't be able to turn off the drive."

I looked out of the port, toward the dark bulk of HC-183 and the *Merganser*, hovering on its plume of high-temperature plasma. Wenig was right. We daren't go down there.

"So how are we going to get them out?"

Wenig shrugged, "I wish I could tell you. Maybe McAndrew has an answer. If not, they're as inaccessible as if they were halfway to Alpha Centauri and still accelerating. We've got to get into communication with them."

When I was about eleven years old, just before puberty, I had a disturbing series of dreams. Night after night, for maybe three months, I seemed to wake on the steep face of a cliff. It was dark, and I could barely see handholds and toeholds in the rock.

I had to get to the top—something was hidden below, invisible behind the curve of the black cliff face. I didn't know what it was, but it was awful.

Every night I would climb, as carefully as I could; and every night there would come a time when I missed a handhold, and began to slide downwards, down into the pit and the waiting monster.

I woke just as I reached the bottom, just as I was waiting for the first sight of my pit beast.

I never saw it. Puberty arrived, sex dreams replaced my fantasy. I forgot all about the cliff face, the terror, the feeling of force that could not be resisted. Forgot it totally—except that dream memories never disappear completely, they lie at some deep submerged level of the mind, until something pulls them out again.

And here I was again, back on the same cliff face, sliding steadily to my fate, powerless to prevent it. I woke up with my heart rate higher by thirty beats a minute, with cold perspiration on my forehead and neck. It took me a long time to return to the present, to banish the bygone fall into the pit.

I finally forced myself up to full consciousness and looked at the screen above me. The purple blaze of a plasma drive danced against the black backdrop of HC-183 and its surrounding star field. It hung there, falling forever but suspended on the feathery stalk of the drive exhaust. I lay there for about ten minutes, just watching, then looked across at Wenig. He was staring at me, his eyes unblinking.

"Awake at last," He made a sort of coughing noise, something that I think was intended to be a laugh. "You're a cool one, Captain Roker. I couldn't sleep with that hanging there"—he jerked his thumb at the screen—"even if you doped me up with everything in the robodoc."

"How long did I sleep?"

"About three hours. Ready to give up now?"

I was. It had been my idea, an insistence that we ought to try and get some sleep before we did the next phase of our maneuver around HC-183. Wenig had opposed it, had wanted to go on at once, but I thought we'd benefit from the rest. So I was wrong.

"I'm ready." My eyes felt as though they'd been filled with grit, and my throat was dry and sore, but talking about that to Wenig wouldn't do much for McAndrew or Nina Velez. "Let's get into position and try the radar."

While Wenig juggled us over to the best position, sixty thousand kilometers from HC-183 and about the same distance from the *Merganser,* I wondered again about my companion. They had drawn lots to come with me, and he had won. The other four scientists back at the Institute seemed a little naive and unworldly, but not Wenig. He was tough and shrewd, and I had seen the speed of those hands, dancing over the keyboard. Had

he done a bit of juggling when they drew lots, a touch
of hand-faster-than-the-eye?

I thought of his look when he spoke about Nina. If
McAndrew was infatuated, perhaps Wenig shared the spell.
Something strong was driving him along, some force that
could keep him awake and alert for days on end. I
wouldn't know if I was right or not unless we could find
a way to haul *Merganser* back out of the field. The ship
still hovered over its pendant of blue ionized gases,
motionless as ever.

"How about this?" Wenig interrupted my thoughts. "I
don't think I can get the geometry any better than it is now."

We were hanging there too, farther out from the
proto-planet than the *Merganser* but close enough to see
the black disk occulting the star field. We could beam short
bursts of microwaves at our sister ship and hope there was
enough signal strength to bore through the sheaths of
plasma emitted by the drives. It would be touch and go—
I had never tried to send a signal to an unmanned ship on
high-drive, but our signal-to-noise ratio stood right on the
borderline of system acceptance. As it was, we'd have to
settle for voice-links only.

I nodded, and Wenig sent out our first pulses, the
simple ship ID codes. We sent it for a couple of minutes, then waited with our attention fixed on the screen.

After a while Wenig shook his head. "We're not getting through. It wouldn't take that long to respond to our
signal."

"Send it with reduced information rate and more
redundancy. We have to give McAndrew enough to filter out the noise."

He was still in send mode when the display screen
began to crawl with green patterns of light. Something
was coming in. The computer was performing a frequency
analysis to pick out the signal content from the background, smoothing it, and speeding it up to standard
communication rate. We were looking at the Fourier
analysis that preceded signal presentation.

"Voice mode," said Wenig quietly.

"*Merganser*." The computer reconstruction of McAndrew's voice was slow and hollow. "This is McAndrew from the *Merganser*. We're certainly glad to hear from you, *Dotterel*. Well, Jeanie, what kept you?"

"Roker speaking." I leaned forward and spoke into the vocal input system—too fast, but the computer would take care of that at the other end. "Mac, we're hanging about sixty kay out from you. Is everything all right in *Merganser*?"

"Yes."

"No," broke in another voice. "Get us out of here. We've been stuck in this damned metal box for sixteen days now."

"Nina," said Wenig. "We'd love to get you out—but we don't know how. Didn't Dr. McAndrew tell you the problem?"

"He said we couldn't leave here until the ship you are on came for us."

Wenig grimaced at me and turned away from the input link. "I ought to have realized that. McAndrew hasn't told her the problem with the drives—not all of it."

"Maybe he knows an answer." I faced back to the microphone. "Mac, as we see it we shouldn't put the *Dotterel* up as high as fifty gee thrust. Correct?"

"Of course." McAndrew sounded faintly surprised at my question. "Why do you think I went to such lengths to get to this holding position out here? When you go to maximum setting for the drive, the electromechanical coupling for moving the life-capsule gets distorted, too."

"How did we miss it on the design?" Wenig sounded unconvinced.

"Remember the last-minute increase in stabilizing fields for the mass plate?"

"It was my recommendation—I'm not likely to forget it."

"We recalculated the effects on the drive and on the exhaust region, but not the magnetostrictive effects on the life-support column. We thought they were second-order changes."

"And they're not? I ought to be drawn and quartered—that was my job!" Wenig was sitting there, fists clenched and face red.

"Was it now? Och, your job, eh? And I've been sitting here thinking all this time it was *my* job." For someone in a hopeless position thirty billion miles from home, McAndrew sounded amazingly cool. "Come on now, we can sort out whose doing it was when we're all back at the Institute."

Wenig looked startled, then turned to me again. "Go along with him on this—I'm sure he's doing it for Nina's sake. He doesn't want her worried."

I nodded—but this time I was unconvinced. Mac must have something hidden away inside his head, or not even Nina Velez would justify his optimistic tone.

"What should we do, Mac?" I said. "We'd get the same effects if we were to accelerate too hard. We can't get down to you, and you can't get up to us without accelerating out past us. How are we going to get you out of there?"

"Right." The laugh that came over the com-link sounded forced and hollow, but that may have been just the tone that the computer filters gave it. "You might guess that's been on my mind too. The problem's in the mechanical coupling that moves the life-capsule along the column. It's easy enough to see, once you imagine that you've had a two millimeter decrease in column diameter—that's the effects of the added field on the mass plate."

Wenig was already calling the schematics out onto a second display. "I'll check that. Keep talking."

"You'll see that when the drive's up to maximum, the capsule catches on the side of the column. It's a simple ratchet effect. I've tried varying the drive thrust up and down a couple of gee, but that won't free it."

"I see where you mean." Wenig had a lightpen out and

was circling parts of the column for larger scale displays. "I don't see how we can do anything about it. It would take a lateral impact to free it—you'll not do it by varying your drive."

"Agreed. We need some lateral force on us. That's what I'm hoping you'll provide."

"What is all this?" It was Nina's voice again, and she sounded angry. "Why do you just keep on talking like that? Anybody who knew what he was doing would have us out by now—would never have got us into it in the first place if he had any sense."

I raised an eyebrow at Wenig. "The voice of infatuation? I think the bloom's off the rose down there."

He looked startled, then pleased, then excited—and then tried to appear nonchalant. "I don't know what McAndrew is getting at. How could we provide any help?" He turned to the input system. "Dr. McAndrew, how's that possible? We can't provide a lateral force on *Merganser* from here, and we can't come down safely."

"Of course you can." McAndrew's voice sounded pleased, and I was sure he was enjoying making the rest of us try and work out his idea. "It's very easy for you to come down here."

"How, Mac?"

"In a free-fall trajectory. We're in a fifty gee gravity field because we're in a stationary position relative to HC-183. But if you were to let yourself fall in a free orbit, you'd be able to swing in right past us, and away again, and never feel anything but free fall. Agreed?"

"Right. We'd feel tidal effects, but they'd be small." Wenig was calling out displays as he talked, fingers a blur over the computer console. "We can fly right past you, but we'd be there and away in a split second. What could we do in so short a time?"

"Why, what we need." McAndrew sounded surprised by the question. "Just give us a good bang on the side as you go by."

❖   ❖   ❖

It sounded easy, as McAndrew so glibly and casually suggested it. When we went into details, there were three problem areas. If we went too close, we'd be fried in the *Merganser*'s drive. Too far off, and we'd never get a strong enough interaction. If all that was worked out correctly, we still had one big obstacle. For the capsule to be freed as *Dotterel* applied sideways pressure, the drive on the other ship would have to cut off completely. Only for a split second, but during that time McAndrew and Nina would feel a full fifty gee on them.

That's not quite as bad as it sounds—people have survived instantaneous accelerations of more than a hundred gee in short pulses. But it's not a picnic, either. Mac continued to sound cheerful and casual, mainly for Nina Velez's benefit. But when he listed the preparations that he was taking inside *Merganser*, I knew he was dealing with a touch-and-go situation.

After all the calculations (performed independently on the two ships, cross-checked and double-checked) we had started our free-fall orbit. It was designed to take us skimming past the *Merganser*, with a closest separation of less than two hundred meters. We daren't go nearer without risking crippling effects from their drive. We would be flying right through its region of turbulence.

Four hours of discussion between McAndrew and Wenig—with interruptions from Nina and me—had fixed the sequence for the vital half-second when we would be passing the *Merganser*. The ships would exert gravitational forces on each other, but that was useless for providing the lateral thrust on the life capsule system that McAndrew thought was needed. We had to give a more direct and harder push some other way.

Timing was crucial, and very tricky.

Whatever we threw at the other ship would have to pass through the drive exhaust region before it could impact the life-capsule column. If the drive were on, nothing could get through it—at those temperatures any material we had would be vaporized on the way, even if

it were there for only a fraction of a second. The sequence
had to be: launch mass from *Dotterel*; just before it got
there, kill drive on *Merganser*; hold drive off just long
enough for the *Dotterel* to clear the area and for the mass
to impact the *Merganser* support column; and back on
with their drive, at once, because when the drive was off
the *Merganser's* passengers would be feeling the full fifty
gees of the mass plate's gravity.

McAndrew and Wenig cut the time of approach of the
two ships into millisecond pieces. They decided exactly how
long each phase should last. Then they let the two on-board
computers of the ships talk to each other, to make sure that
everything was synchronized between them—at the rate
things would be happening, there was no way that humans
could control them. Not even Wenig, with his super-fast
reflexes. We'd all be spectators, while the two computers
did the real work and I nursed the abort switch.

There was one argument. McAndrew wanted to use
a storage tank as the missile that we would eject from
our ship to impact theirs. It would provide high momentum transfer for a very brief period. Wenig argued that
we should trade off time against intensity, and use a liquid
mass instead of a solid one. Endless discussion and calculations, until Mac was convinced too. We would use all
our spare water supply, about a ton and a half of it. That
left enough for drinking water on a twenty gee return to
the Inner System, but nothing spare for other uses. It
would be a scratchy and smelly trip home for *Dotterel's*
passengers.

Drive off, we felt only the one-gee pull of our mass
plate as we dropped in to close approach. On *Merganser*, McAndrew and Nina Velez were lying in water bunks,
cushioned with everything soft on the ship. We were on
an impact course with them, one that would change to
a near-miss after we ejected the water ballast. It looked
like a suicide mission, running straight into the blue
furnace of their drive.

The sequence took place so fast it was anti-climactic.

I saw the drive cut off ahead of us and felt the vibration along the support column as our mass driver threw the ballast hard towards *Merganser*. The brief pulse from our drive that took us clear of them was too quick for me to feel.

We cleared the drive region. Then there seemed to be a wait that lasted for hours. McAndrew and Nina were now in a ship with drive off, dropping towards HC-183. They were exposed to the full fifty gees of their mass plate. Under that force, I knew what happened to the human body. It had not been designed to operate when it suddenly weighed more than four tons. Membranes ruptured, valves burst, veins collapsed. The heart had never evolved to pump blood weighing hundreds of pounds up a gravity hill of fifty gees. The only thing that Mac and Nina had going for them was the natural inertia of matter. If the period of high gee were short enough, the huge accelerations would not have time to produce those shattering physical effects.

Wenig and I watched on our screens for a long, long moment, until the computer on *Merganser* counted off the last microsecond and switched on the drive again. If the life-capsule was free to move along its column, the computer would now begin the slow climb out of HC-183's gravity well. No action was needed from the passengers. When we completed our own orbit we hoped we would see the other ship out at a safe distance, ready for the long trip home.

And on board the ship? I wasn't sure. If the encounter had lasted too long, we might find no more than two limp and broken sacks of blood, tissue and bone.

It was another long day, waiting until we had been carried around in our orbit and could try to rendezvous the two ships. As soon as we were within radar range, Nina Velez appeared on the com screen. The drive was cut back, so we could get good visual signals. My heart sank when I saw the expression on her face.

"Can you get over to this ship—quickly?" she said.

I could see why all the professors at the Institute had lost their senses. She was small and slight, with a child-like look of trust and sad blue eyes. All a sham, according to everything I'd been told, but there was no way of seeing the strong personality behind the soft looks. I took a deep breath.

"What's happening there?" I said.

"We're back under low gee drive, and that's fine. But I haven't been able to wake him. He's breathing, but there's blood on his lips. He needs a doctor."

"I'm the nearest thing to that in thirty billion miles." I was pulling a suit towards me, sick with a sudden fear. "I've had some medical training as part of the Master's License. And I think I know what's wrong with McAndrew. He lost part of a lung lobe a couple of years ago. If anything's likely to be hemorrhaging, that's it. Dr. Wenig, can you arrange a rendezvous with the mass plates at maximum separation and the drives off?"

"I'll need control of their computer." He was pulling his suit on, too. I didn't want him along, but I might need somebody to return to the *Dotterel* for medical supplies.

"What should I be doing?" Thank heaven Nina showed no signs of panic. She sounded impatient, with the touch of President Velez in her voice. "I've sat around in this ship for weeks with nothing to do. Now we need action but I daren't take it."

"What field are you in now? What net field?"

"One gee. The drive's off now, and we've got the life-capsule right out at the end of the column."

"Right. I want to you stay in that position, but set the drive at one gee acceleration. I want McAndrew in a zero-gee environment to slow the bleeding. Dr. Wenig, can you dictate instructions for that while we are rendezvousing?"

"No problem." He was an irritating devil, but I'd choose him in a crisis. He was doing three things at once, putting on his suit, watching the computer action for the rendezvous, and giving exact and concise instructions to Nina.

Getting ourselves from one ship to the other through open space wasn't as easy as it might sound. We had both ships under one gee acceleration drives, complicated by the combined attraction of the two mass plates. The total field acting on us was small, but we had to be careful not to forget it. If we lost contact with the ships, the nearest landing point was back on Triton Station, thirty billion miles away.

Nina in the flesh was even more impressive than she was over the video link, but I gave her little more than a cursory once-over. McAndrew's color was bad and even while I was cracking my suit open and hustling out of it I could hear a frightening bubbling sound in his breathing. Thank God I had learned how to work in zero gee— required part of any space medicine course. I leaned over him, vaguely aware of the two others intently watching. The robodoc beside me was clucking and flashing busily, muttering a faint complaint at McAndrew's condition and the zero-gee working environment. Standard diagnosis conditions called for at least a partial gravity field.

I took the preliminary diagnosis and prepared to act on it while the doc was still making up its mind. Five cc's of cerebral stimulant, five cc's of metabolic depressant, and a reduction in cabin pressure. It should bring Mac up to consciousness if his brain was still in working order. I worried about a cerebral hemorrhage, the quiet and deadly by-product of super-high gees. Ten minutes and I would know one way or the other.

I turned to Wenig and Nina who were still watching the robodoc's silent body trace. "I don't know how he is yet. We may need emergency treatment facilities ready for us as soon as we get back to the System. Can you go over to *Dotterel*, cut the drive and try to make contact with Triton Station? By the time you have the connection we should have the full diagnosis here."

I watched them leave the ship, saw how carefully

Wenig helped Nina to the transfer, and then I heard the first faint noise behind me. It was a sigh, with a little mutter of protest behind it. The most wonderful sound I ever heard in my life. I glanced over at the doc. Concussion—not too bad—and a little more bleeding than I wanted to see from the left lung. Hell, that was nothing. I could patch the lung myself, maybe even start the feedback regeneration for it. I felt a big grin of delight spreading like a heat wave over my face.

"Take it easy, Mac. You're doing all right, just don't try and rush yourself. We've got lots of time." I secured his left arm so that he couldn't disturb the rib cage on that side.

He groaned. "Doing fine, am I?" He suddenly opened his eyes and stared up at me, "Holy water, Jeanie, that's just like a medic. I'm in agony, and you say it's a little discomfort. How's Nina doing?"

"Not a mark on her. She's not like you, Mac, an old bag of bones. You're getting too old for this sort of crap."

"Where is she?"

"Over on *Dotterel*, with Wenig. What's the matter, still infatuated?"

He managed a faint smile. "Ah, none of that now. We were stuck on *Merganser* for more than two weeks, locked up in a three meter living sphere. Show me an infatuation, and I'll show you a cure for it."

The com-link behind me was buzzing. I cut it in, so that we could see Wenig's worried face.

"All right here," I said, before he had time to worry any more. "We'll be able to take our time going back. How are you? Got enough water?"

He nodded. "I took some of your reserve supply to make up for what we threw at you. What should we do now?"

"Head on back. Tell Nina that Mac's all right, and say we'll see you both back at the Institute."

He nodded again, then leaned closer to the screen and spoke with a curious intensity. "We don't want to run the risk of having a stuck life capsule again. I'd better keep us down to less than ten gee acceleration."

He cut off communication, without another word. I turned to McAndrew. "How high an acceleration before you'd run into trouble with these ships?"

He was staring at the blank screen, a confused look on his thin face. "At least forty gee. What the devil's got into Wenig? And what are you laughing at, you silly bitch?"

I came over to him and took his right hand in mine. "To each his own, Mac. I wondered why Wenig was so keen to get here. He wants *his* shot at Nina—out here, where nobody else can compete. What did *you* tell her— some sweet talk about her lovely eyes?"

He closed his eyes again and smiled a secret smile. "Ah, come on Jeanie. Are you telling me you've been on your best behavior since I last saw you? Gi' me a bit of peace. I'm not soft on Nina now."

"I'll see." I went across to the drive and moved us up to forty gee. "Wait until the crew on Titan hear about all this. You'll lose your reputation."

He sighed. "All right, I'll play the game. What's the price of silence?"

"How long would it take a ship like this to get out to Alpha Centauri?"

"You'd not want this one. We'll have the next one up to a hundred gee. Forty-four ship days would get you there, standing start to standing finish."

I nodded, came back to his side and held his hand again. "All right, Mac, that's my price. I want one of the tickets."

He groaned again, just a bit. But I knew from the dose the doc had put into him that it wasn't a headache this time.

THIRD CHRONICLE:

All the Colors of the Vacuum

As soon as the ship got back from the midyear run to Titan, I went down to Earth and asked Woolford for a leave of absence. I had been working hard enough for six people, and he knew it. He nodded agreeably as soon as I made the formal request.

"I think you've earned it, Captain Roker, no doubt about that. But don't you have quite a bit of leave time saved up? Wouldn't that be enough?" He stopped staring out of the window at the orange-brown sky and called my records onto the screen in front of him.

"That won't do it," I said, while he was still looking.

Woolford frowned and became less formal. "It won't? Well, according to this, Jeanie, you've got at least . . ." He looked up. "Just how long do you want to take off?"

"I'm not exactly sure. Somewhere between nine and sixteen years, I think."

I would have liked to break the news more gently, but maybe there was no graceful way.

✧   ✧   ✧

It had taken McAndrew a while to deliver on his promise. The design of the more advanced ship contained no new theory, but this time he intended that the initial tests would be conducted more systematically. I kept pushing him along, while he tried to wriggle out of the commitment. He had been full of drugs and painkillers at the time, he said—surely I didn't consider it fair, to hold him to what he'd been silly enough to promise then?

Fair or not, I wouldn't listen. I had called him as soon as we were on the final leg of the Titan run.

"Yes, she's ready enough to go." He had a strange expression on his face, somewhere between excitement and perplexity. "You've still got your mind set on going, then, Jeanie?"

I didn't dignify that question with a reply. Instead I said, "How soon can I come out to the Institute?"

He cleared his throat, making that odd sound that spoke to me of his Scots ancestry. "Och, if you're set on it, come as soon as you please. I'll have things to tell you when you get here, but that can wait."

That was when I went down and made my request to Woolford for a long leave of absence. McAndrew had been strangely reluctant to discuss our destination, but I couldn't imagine that we'd be going out past Sirius. Alpha Centauri was my guess, and that would mean we would only be away about nine Earth years. Shipboard time would be three months, allowing a few days at the other end for exploration. If I knew McAndrew, he would have beaten the hundred gee acceleration that he projected for the interstellar prototype. He was never a man to talk big about what he was going to do.

The Penrose Institute had been moved out to Mars orbit since the last time I was there, so it took me a couple of weeks of impatient ship-hopping to get to it. When we finally closed to visible range I could see the old test ships, *Merganser* and *Dotterel*, floating a few kilometers from the main body of the Institute. They were easy to recognize from the flat mass disc with its protruding central spike. And floating near them, quite a bit bigger, was a new ship of gleaming silver. That had to be the *Hoatzin*, McAndrew's newest plaything. The disc was twice the size, and the spike three times as long, but *Hoatzin* was clearly *Merganser*'s big brother.

It was Professor Limperis, the head of the Institute, who greeted me when I entered. He had put on weight since I last saw him, but that pudgy black face still hid a razor-sharp mind and a bottomless memory.

"Good to see you again, Captain Roker. I haven't told McAndrew this, but I'm very glad you'll be going along to keep an eye on him." He gave what he once described as his "hand-clapping minstrel-show laugh"—a sure sign he was nervous about something.

"Well, I don't know that I'll be much use. I'm expecting to be just a sort of passenger. Don't worry. If my instincts are anything to go by there won't be much danger in a simple stellar rendezvous and return."

"Er, yes." He wouldn't meet my eye. "That was my own reaction. I gather that Professor McAndrew has not mentioned to you his change of target?"

"Change of target? He didn't mention any target at all." Now my own worry bead was beginning to throb. "Are you suggesting that the trip will *not* be to a stellar rendezvous?"

He shrugged and waved his hands, pointing along the corridor. "Not if McAndrew gets his way. Come along, he's inside at the computer. I think it's best if he is present when we talk about this further."

Pure evasion. Whatever the bad news was, Limperis wanted me to hear it from McAndrew himself.

We found him staring vacantly at a completely blank display screen. Normally I would never interrupt him when he looks as imbecilic as that—it means that he is thinking with a breadth and depth that I'll never comprehend. I often wonder what it would be like to have a mind like that. Humans, with rare exceptions, must seem like trained apes, with muddied thoughts and no ability for abstract analysis.

Tough luck. It was time one of the trained apes had some of her worries put to rest. I walked up behind McAndrew and put my hands on his shoulders.

"Here I am. I'm ready to go—if you'll tell me where we're going."

He turned in his chair. After a moment his slack jaw firmed up and the eyes brought me into focus.

"Hello, Jeanie." No doubt about it, as soon as he recognized me he had that same shifty look I had noticed in Limperis. "I didn't expect you here so soon. We're still making up a flight profile."

"That's all right. I'll help you." I sat down opposite him, studying his face closely. As usual he looked tired, but that was normal. Geniuses work harder than anyone else, not less hard. His face was thinner, and he had lost a little more hair from that sandy, receding mop. My argument with him over that was long in the past.

"Why don't you grow it back?" I'd said. "It's such a minor job, a couple of hours with the machines every few months and you'd have a full head of hair again."

He had sniffed. "Why don't you try and get me to grow a tail, or hair all over my body? Or maybe make my arms a bit longer, so they'll let me run along with them touching the ground. Jeanie, I'll not abuse a bio-feedback machine to run evolution in the wrong direction. We're getting less hairy all the time. I know your fondness for monkeys"—a nasty crack about an engineering friend of mine on Ceres, who was a bit hairy for even my accommodating tastes—"but I'll be just as happy when I have no hair at all. It gets in the way, it grows all the time, and it serves no purpose whatsoever."

McAndrew resented the time it took him to clip his fingernails, and I'm sure that he regarded his fondness for food as a shameful weakness. Meanwhile, I wondered who in the Penrose Institute cut his hair. Maybe they had a staff assistant, whose job it was to shear the absent-minded once a month.

"What destination are you planning for the first trip out?" If he was thinking of chasing a comet, I wanted that out in the open.

McAndrew looked at Limperis. Limperis looked at McAndrew, handing it back to him. Mac cleared his throat.

"We've discussed it here and we're all agreed. The first trip of the *Hoatzin* won't be to a star system." He cleared his throat again. "It will be to pursue and rendezvous with the Ark of Massingham. It's a shorter trip than any of the star systems," he added hopefully. He could read my expression. "They are less than two light-years out. With the *Hoatzin* we can be there and docked with the Ark in less than thirty-five ship days."

If he was trying to make me feel better, McAndrew was going about it in quite the wrong way.

Back in the twenties, the resources of the Solar System must have seemed inexhaustible. No one had been able to *catalog* the planetoids, still less analyze their composition and probable value. Now we know everything out to Neptune that's bigger than a hundred meters across, and the navigation groups want that down to fifty meters in the next twenty years. The idea of grabbing an asteroid a couple of kilometers across and using it how you choose sounds like major theft. But it hadn't merely been permitted—it had been encouraged.

The first space colonies had been conceived as utopias, planned by Earth idealists who wouldn't learn from history. New frontiers may attract visionaries, but more than that they attract oddities. Anyone who is more than three sigma away from the norm, in any direction, seems to finish out there on the frontier. No surprise in that. If a person can't fit, for whatever reason, he'll move away from the main group of humanity. They'll push him, and he'll want to go. How do I know? Look, you don't pilot to Titan without learning a lot about your own personality. Before we found the right way to use people like me, I would probably have been on one of the Arks.

The United Space Federation had assisted in the launch of seventeen of them, between ninety and forty years ago. Each of them was self-supporting, a converted asteroid that would hold between three and ten thousand people at departure time. The idea was that there would be enough raw materials and space to let the Ark grow as the population grew. A two-kilometer asteroid holds five to twenty billion tons of material, total life-support system for one human needs less than ten tons of that.

The Arks had left long before the discovery of the McAndrew balanced drive, before the discovery of even the Mattin Drive. They were multi-generation ships, bumbling along into the interstellar void with speeds that were only a few percent of light speed.

And who was on-board them when they left? Any fairly homogeneous group of strange people, who shared enough of a common philosophy or delusion to prefer the uncertainties of star travel to the known problems within the Solar System. It took courage to set out like that, to sever all your ties with home except occasional laser and radio communication. Courage, or an overpowering conviction that you were part of a unique and chosen group.

To put that another way, McAndrew was proposing to take us out to meet a community about which we knew little, except that by the usual standards they were descended from madmen.

"Mac, I don't remember which one was the Ark of Massingham. How long ago did it leave?"

Even mad people can have sane children. Four of the Arks, as I recalled, had turned around and were on their way back to the System.

"About seventy-five years ago. It's one of the earlier ones, with a final speed a bit less than three percent of light speed."

"Is it one of the Arks that has turned back?"

He shook his head. "No. They're still on their way. Target star is Tau Ceti. They won't get there for another three hundred years."

"Well, why pick them out? What's so special about the Ark of Massingham?" I had a sudden thought. "Are they having some problem that we could help with?"

We had saved two of the Arks in the past twenty years. For one of them we had been able to diagnose a recessive genetic element that was appearing in the children, and pass the test information and sperm filter technique over the communications link. The other had needed the use of an unmanned high-acceleration probe, to carry a couple of tons of cadmium out to them. They had been unlucky enough to choose a freak asteroid, one that apparently lacked the element even in the tiniest traces.

"They don't report any problem," said Mac. "We've never had a response to any messages we've sent to them, so far as the records on Triton Station are concerned. But we know that they are doing all right, because every three or four years a message has come in from them. Never anything about the Ark itself, it has always been . . . scientific information."

McAndrew had hesitated as he said that last phrase. That was the lure, no doubt about it.

"What kind of information?" I said. "Surely we know everything that they know. We have hundreds of thousands of scientists in the System, they can't have more than a few hundred of them."

"I'm sure you're right on the numbers." Professor Limperis spoke when McAndrew showed no inclination to do so. "I'm not sure it's relevant. How many scientists does it require to produce the work of one Einstein, or one McAndrew? You can't just sit down and count numbers, as though you were dealing with—with bars of soap, or poker chips. You have to deal with individuals."

"There's a genius on the Ark of Massingham," said McAndrew suddenly. His eyes were gleaming. "A man or woman who has been cut off from most of physics for a whole lifetime, working alone. It's worse than Ramanujan."

"How do you know that?" I had seldom seen McAndrew so filled with feeling. "Maybe they've been getting messages from somebody in the System here."

McAndrew laughed, a humorless bark. "I'll tell you why, Jeanie. You flew the *Merganser*. Tell me how the drive worked."

"Well, the mass plate at the front balanced the acceleration, so we didn't get any sensation of fifty gee." I shrugged. "I didn't work out the math for myself, but I'm sure I could have if I felt like it."

I could have, too. I was a bit rusty, but you never lose the basics once you have them planted deep enough in your head.

"I don't mean the balancing mechanism, that was just common sense." He shook his head. "I mean the *drive*. Didn't it occur to you that we were accelerating a mass of trillions of tons at fifty gee? If you work out the mass conversion rate you will need, you find that even with an ideal photon drive you'll consume the whole mass in a few days. The *Merganser* got its drive by accelerating charged particles up to within millimeters a second of light speed. That was the reaction mass. But how did it get the energy to do it?"

I felt like telling him that when I had been on *Merganser* there had been other details—such as survival—on my mind. I thought for a few moments, then shook my head.

"You can't get more energy out of matter than the rest mass energy, I know that. But you're telling me that the drives on *Merganser* and *Hoatzin* do it. That Einstein was wrong."

"No!" McAndrew looked horrified at the thought that he might have been criticizing one of his senior idols. "All I've done is build on what Einstein did. Look, you've done a fair amount of quantum mechanics. You know that when you calculate the energy for the vacuum state of a system you don't get zero. You get a positive value."

I had a hazy recollection of a formula swimming back across the years. What was it? h/4πw, said a distant voice.

"But you can set that to zero!" I was proud at remembering so much. "The zero point of energy is arbitrary."

"In quantum theory it is. But not in general relativity." McAndrew was beating back my mental defenses. As usual when I spoke with him on theoretical subjects, I began to feel I would know less at the end of the conversation than I did at the beginning.

"In general relativity," he went on, "energy implies space-time curvature. If the zero-point energy is not zero, the vacuum self-energy is real. It can be tapped, if you know what you are doing. That's where *Hoatzin* draws its energy. The reaction mass it needs is very small. You can get that by scooping up matter as you go along, or if you prefer it you can use a fraction—a very small fraction—of the mass plate."

"All right." I knew McAndrew. If I let him get going he would talk all day about physical principles. "But I don't see how that has anything to do with the Ark of Massingham. It has an old-fashioned drive, surely. You said it was launched seventy-five years ago."

"It was." This was Limperis again, gently insistent. "But you see, Captain Roker, nobody outside the Penrose Institute knows how Professor McAndrew has been able to tap the vacuum self-energy. We have been very careful not to broadcast that information until we were ready. The potential for destructive use is enormous. It destroys the old idea that you cannot create more energy at a point than the rest mass of the matter residing there. There was nothing known in the rest of the System about this use until two weeks ago."

"And then you released the information?" I was beginning to feel dizzy.

"No. The basic equations for accessing the vacuum self-energy were received by laser communication. They were sent, with no other message, from the Ark of Massingham."

Suddenly it made sense. It wasn't just McAndrew who

was itching to get in and find out what there was on the Ark—it was everyone at the Penrose Institute. I could sense the excitement in Limperis, and he was the most guarded and politically astute of all the Members. If some physicist, working out there alone two light-years from Sol, had managed to parallel McAndrew's development, that was a momentous event. It implied a level of genius that was difficult to imagine.

I knew *Hoatzin* would be on the way in a few days, whether I wanted to go or stay. But there was one more key question.

"I can't believe that the Ark of Massingham was started by a bunch of physicists. What was the original composition of the group that colonized it?"

"Not physicists." Limperis had suddenly sobered. "By no means physicists. That is why I am glad you will be accompanying Professor McAndrew. The leader of the original group was Jules Massingham. In the past few days I have taken the time to obtain all the System records on him. He was a man of great personal drive and convictions. His ambition was to apply the old principles of eugenics to a whole society. Two themes run through all his writings: the creation of the superior human, and the idea of that superior being as an integrated part of a whole society. He was ruthless in his pursuit of those ends."

He looked at me, black face impassive. "From the evidence available, Captain, one might suggest that he succeeded in his aims."

Hoatzin was a step up from *Merganser* and *Dotterel*. Maximum acceleration was a hundred and ten gees, and the living-capsule was a four-meter sphere. I had cursed the staff of the Institute, publicly and privately, but I had got nowhere. They were obsessed with the idea of the lonely genius out there in the void, and no one would consider any other first trip for *Hoatzin*. So at least I would check out every aspect of the system before we went, while

McAndrew was looking at the rendezvous problem and making a final flight plan. We sent a message to the Ark, telling them of our trip and estimated arrival time. It would take two years to get there, Earth-time, but we would take even longer. They would be able to prepare for our arrival however they chose, with garlands or gallows.

On the trip out, McAndrew tried again to explain to me his methods for tapping the vacuum self-energy. The available energies made up a quasi-continuous "spectrum," corresponding to a large number of very high frequencies of vibration and associated wavelengths. Tuned resonators in the *Hoatzin* drive units selected certain wavelengths which were excited by the corresponding components in the vacuum self energy. These "colors," as McAndrew thought of them, could feed vacuum energy to the drive system. The results that had come from the Ark of Massingham suggested that McAndrew's system for energy extraction could be generalized, so that all the "colors" of the vacuum self-energy should become available.

If that were true, the potential acceleration produced by the drive could go up by a couple of orders of magnitude. He was still working out what the consequences of that would be. At speeds that approached within a nanometer per second of light speed, a single proton would mass enough to weigh its impact on a sensitive balance.

I let him babble on to his heart's content. My own attention was mostly on the history of the Ark of Massingham. It was an oddity among oddities. Six of the Arks had disappeared without trace. They didn't respond to signals from Earth, and they didn't send signals of their own. Most people assumed that they had wiped themselves out, with accidents, wars, strange sexual practices, or all three. Four of the Arks had swung back towards normalcy and were heading in again for the System. Six were still heading out, but two of them were in deep trouble if the messages that came back to Triton

Station were any guide. One was full of messianic rant-
ing, a crusade of human folly propagating itself out to
the stars (let's hope they never met anyone out there
whose good opinion we would later desire). Another was
quietly and peacefully insane, sending messages that
spoke only of new rules for the interpretation of dreams.
They were convinced that they would find the world of
the Norse legends when they finally arrived at Eta
Cassiopeia, complete with Jotunheim, Niflheim, and all
the assembly of gods and heroes. It would be six hundred years before they arrived there, time enough for
moves to rationality or to extinction.

Among this set, the Ark of Massingham provided a
bright mixture of sanity and strangeness. They had sent
messages back since first they left, messages that assumed
the Ark was the carrier of human hopes and a superior
civilization. Nothing that we sent—questions, comments,
information, or acknowledgements—ever stimulated a
reply. And nothing that they sent ever discussed life
aboard the Ark. We had no idea if they lived in poverty
or plenty, if they were increasing or decreasing in numbers, if they were receiving our transmissions, if they had
material problems of any kind. Everything that came back
to the solar system was science, delivered in a smug and
self-satisfied tone. From all that science, the recent transmission on physics was the only one to excite more than
a mild curiosity from our own scientists. Usually the Ark
sent "discoveries" that had been made here long ago.

Once the drive of the *Hoatzin* was up to full thrust
there was no way that we could see anything or communicate with anyone. The drive was fixed to the mass plate
on the front of the ship, and the particles that streamed
past us and out to the rear were visible only when they
were in collision with the rare atoms of hydrogen drifting in free space. We had actually settled for less than
a maximum drive and were using a slightly dispersed
exhaust. A tightly focused and collimated beam wouldn't
harm us any, but we didn't want to generate a death ray

behind us that would disintegrate anything in its path for a few light-years.

Six days into the trip, our journey out shared the most common feature of all long distance travel. It was boring. When McAndrew wasn't busy inside his head, staring at the wall in front of him and performing the mental acrobatics that he called theoretical physics, we talked, played and exercised. I was astonished again that a man who knew so much about so much could know nothing about some things.

"You mean to tell me," he said once, as we lay in companionable darkness, with the side port showing the eldritch and unpredictable blue sparks of atomic collision. "You mean that *Lungfish* wasn't the first space station. All the books and records show it that way."

"No, they don't. If they do, they're wrong. It's a common mistake. Like the idea back at the beginning of flight itself, that Lindbergh was the first man to fly across the Atlantic Ocean. He was more like the hundredth." I saw McAndrew turn his head towards me. "Yes, you heard me. A couple of airships had been over before him, and a couple of other people in aircraft. He was just the first person to fly *alone*. *Lungfish* was the first truly *permanent* space station, that's all. And I'll tell you something else. Did you know that in the earliest flights, even ones that lasted for months, the crews were usually all men? Think of that for a while."

He was silent for a moment. "I don't see anything wrong with it. It would simplify some of the plumbing, maybe some other things, too."

"You don't understand, Mac. That was at a time when it was regarded as morally wrong for men to form sexual relationships with men, or women with women."

There was what I might describe as a startled silence.

"Oh," said McAndrew at last. Then, after a few moments more, "My God. How much did they have to pay them? Or was coercion used?"

"It was considered an honor to be chosen."

He didn't say any more about it; but I don't think he believed me, either. Politeness is one of the first things you learn on long trips.

We cut off the drive briefly at crossover, but there was nothing to be seen and there was still no way we could receive messages. We were crowding light speed so closely that anything from Triton Station would scarcely be catching up with us. The Institute's message was still on its way to the Ark of Massingham, and we would be there ourselves not long after it. The *Hoatzin* was behaving perfectly, with none of the problems that had almost done us in on the earlier test ships. The massive disc of dense matter at the front of the ship protected us from most of our collisions with stray dust and free hydrogen. If we didn't come back, the next ship out could follow our path exactly, tracking our swath of ionization.

During deceleration I began to search the sky beyond the *Hoatzin* every day, with an all-frequency sweep that ought to pick up signals as soon as our drive went to reduced thrust. We didn't pick up the Ark until the final day and it was no more than a point on the microwave screen for most of that. The image we finally built up on the monitor showed a lumpy, uneven ball, pierced by black shafts. Spiky antennas and angled gantries stood up like spines on its dull grey surface. I had seen the images of the Ark before it left the Solar System, and all the surface structures were new. The colonists had been busy in the seventy-seven years since they accelerated away from Ganymede orbit.

We moved in to five thousand kilometers, cut the drive, and sent a calling sequence. I don't remember a longer five seconds, waiting for their response. When it came it was an anti-climax. A pleasant-looking middle-aged woman appeared on our screen.

"Hello," she said cheerfully. "We received a message that you were on your way here. My name is Kleeman. Link in your computer and we'll dock you. There will be a few formalities before you can come inside."

I put the central computer into distributed mode and linked a navigation module through the com-net. She sounded friendly and normal but I didn't want her to have override control of all the *Hoatzin's* movements. We moved to a position about fifty kilometers away from the Ark, then Kleeman appeared again on the screen.

"I didn't realize your ship had so much mass. We'll hold there, and you can come in on a pod. All right?"

We usually called it a capsule these days, but I knew what she meant. I made McAndrew put on a suit, to his disgust, and we entered the small transfer vessel. It was just big enough for four people, with no air lock and a simple electric drive. We drifted in to the Ark, with the capsule's computer slaved through the *Hoatzin*. As we got nearer I had a better feel for size. Two kilometers is small for an asteroid, but it's awfully big compared with a human. We nosed into contact with a landing tower, like a fly landing on the side of a wasp's nest. I hoped that would prove to be a poor analogy.

We left the capsule open and went hand-over-hand down the landing tower rather than wait for an electric lift. It was impossible to believe that we were moving at almost nine thousand kilometers a second away from Earth. The stars were in the same familiar constellations, and it took a while to pick out the Sun. It was a bright star, but a good deal less bright than Sirius. I stood at the bottom of the tower for a few seconds, peering about me before entering the air lock that led to the interior of the Ark. It was a strange, alien landscape, with the few surface lights throwing black angular shadows across the uneven rock. My trips to Titan suddenly felt like local hops around the comfortable backyard of the Solar System.

"Come on, Jeanie." That was McAndrew, all brisk efficiency and already standing in the air lock. He was much keener than I to penetrate that unfamiliar world of the interior.

I took a last look at the stars, and fixed in my mind the position of the transfer capsule—an old habit that pays off once in a thousand times. Then I followed McAndrew down into the lock.

A few formalities before you can come inside. Kleeman had a gift for understatement. We found out what she meant when we stepped in through the inner lock, to an office-cum-schoolroom equipped with a couple of impressive consoles and displays. Kleeman met us there, as pleasant and rosy-faced in the flesh as she had seemed over the com-link.

She waved us to the terminals. "This is an improved version of the equipment that was on the original ship, before it left your system. Please sit down. Before anyone can enter our main Home, they must take tests. It has been that way since Massingham first showed us how our society could be built."

We sat at the terminals, back-to-back. McAndrew was frowning at the delay. "What's the test, then?" he grumbled.

"Just watch the screen. I don't think that either of you will have any trouble."

She smiled and left us to it. I wondered what the penalty was if you failed. We were a long way from home. It seemed clear that if they had been improving this equipment after they left Ganymede, they must apply it to their own people. We were certainly the first visitors they had seen for seventy-five years. How had they been able to accept our arrival so calmly?

Before I could pursue that thought the screen was alive. I read the instructions as they appeared there, and followed them as carefully as possible. After a few minutes I got the knack of it. We had tests rather like it when I first applied to go into space. To say that we were taking an intelligence test would be an oversimplification—many other aptitudes were tested, as well as knowledge and mechanical skills. That was the only consolation I had. McAndrew must be wiping the floor with me on all the parts that called for straight brain-power, but I knew that his coordination was terrible. He could unwrap a set of interlocking, multiply-connected figures mentally and tell you how they came apart, but ask him to do the same thing with real objects and he wouldn't be able to start.

After three hours we were finished. Both screens suddenly went blank. We swung to face each other.

"What's next?" I said. He shrugged and began to look at the terminal itself. The design hadn't been used in the System for fifty years. I took a quick float around the walls—we had entered the Ark near a pole, where the effective gravity caused by its rotation was negligible. Even on the Ark's equator I estimated that we wouldn't feel more than a tenth of a gee at the most.

No signs of what I was looking for, but that didn't mean much. Microphones could be disguised in a hundred ways.

"Mac, who do you think she is?"

He looked up from the terminal. "Why, she's the woman assigned to . . ." He stopped. He had caught my point. When you are two light-years from Sol and you have your first visitors for seventy-five years, who leads the reception party? Not the man and woman who recycle the garbage. Kleeman ought to be somebody important on the Ark.

"I can assist your speculation," said a voice from the wall. So much for our privacy. As I expected, we had been observed throughout—no honor system on this test. "I am Kal Massingham Kleeman, the daughter of Jules Massingham, and I am senior member of Home outside the Council of Intellects. Wait there for one more moment. I will join you with good news."

She was beaming when she reappeared. Whatever they were going to do with us, it didn't seem likely they would be flinging us out into the void.

"You are both prime stock, genetically and individually," she said. "I thought that would be the case when first I saw you."

She looked down at a green card in her hand. "I notice that you both failed to answer one small part of the inquiry on your background. Captain Roker, your medical record indicates that you bore one child. But what is its sex, condition, and present status?"

I heard McAndrew suck in his breath past his teeth, while I suppressed my own shock as best I could. It was clear that the standards of privacy in the System and on the Ark had diverged widely in the past seventy-seven years.

"It is a female." I hope I kept my voice steady. "Healthy, and with no neuroses. She is in first level education on Luna."

"The father?"

"Unknown."

I shouldn't have been pleased to see that now Kleeman was shocked, but I was. She looked as distressed as I felt. After a few seconds she grabbed control of her emotions, swallowed, and nodded.

"We are not ignorant of the unplanned matings that your System permits. But hearing of such things and encountering them directly are not the same." She looked again at her green card. "McAndrew, you show no children. Is that true?"

He had taken his lead from me and managed a calm and literal reply. "No recorded children."

"Incredible." Kleeman was shaking her head. "That a man of your talents should be permitted to go so long without suitable mating . . ."

She looked at him hungrily, the way that I have seen McAndrew eye an untapped set of experimental data from out in the Halo. I could imagine how he had performed on the intellectual sections of the test.

"Come along," she said at last, still eyeing McAndrew in a curiously intense and possessive way. "I would like to show you some of Home, and arrange for you to have living quarters for your use."

"Don't you want more details of why we are here?" burst out Mac. "We've come nearly two light-years to get to the Ark."

"You have been receiving our messages of the advances

that we have made?" Kleeman's manner had a vast self-confidence. "Then why should we be surprised when superior men and women from your system wish to come here? We are only surprised that it took you so long to develop a suitably efficient ship. Your vessel is new?"

"Very new." I spoke before McAndrew could get a word in. Kleeman's assumption that we were on the Ark to stay had ominous overtones. We needed to know more about the way the place functioned before we told her that we were planning only a brief visit.

"We have been developing the drive for our ship using results that parallel some of those found by your scientists," I went on. I gave Mac a look that kept him quiet for a little while longer. "When we have finished with the entry preliminaries, Professor McAndrew would very much like to meet your physicists."

She smiled serenely at him. "Of course. McAndrew, you should be part of our Council of Intellects. I do not know how high your position was back in your system, but I feel sure you have nothing as exalted—and as respected—as our Council. Well,"—she placed the two green cards she was holding in the pocket of her yellow smock—"there will be plenty of time to discuss induction to the Council when you have settled in here. The entry formalities are complete. Let me show you Home. There has never been anything like it in the whole of human history."

Over the next four hours we followed Kleeman obediently through the interior of the Ark. McAndrew was itching to locate his fellow-physicists, but he knew he was at the mercy of Kleeman's decisions. From our first meeting with others on the Ark, there was no doubt who was the boss there.

How can I describe the interior of the Ark? Imagine a free-space beehive, full of hard-working bees that had retained an element of independence of action. Everyone on the Ark of Massingham seemed industrious, cooperative, and intelligent. But they were missing a dimension, the touch of orneriness and unpredictability that you would find on Luna or on Titan. Nobody was cursing, nobody was irrational. Kleeman guided us through a clean, slightly dull Utopia.

The technology of the Ark was simpler to evaluate. Despite the immense pride with which Kleeman showed off every item of development, they were half a century behind us. The sprawling, overcrowded chaos of Earth was hard to live with, but it provided a constant pressure towards innovation. New inventions come fast when ten billion people are there to push you to new ideas. In those terms, life on the Ark was spacious and leisurely. The colony had constructed its network of interlocking tunnels to a point where it would take months to explore all the passages and corridors, but they were nowhere near exhausting their available space and resources.

"How many people would the Ark hold?" I asked McAndrew as we trailed along behind Kleeman. It would have taken only a minute or two to work it out for myself, but you get lazy when you live for a while with a born calculator.

"If they don't use the interior material to extend the surface of the Ark?" he said. "Give them the same room as we'd allow on Earth, six meters by six meters by two meters. They could hold nearly sixty million. Halve that, maybe, to allow for recycling and maintenance equipment."

"But that is not our aim," said Kleeman. She had overheard my question. "We are stabilized at ten thousand. We are not like the fools back on Earth. Quality is our aim, not mindless numbers."

She had that tone in her voice again, the one that had made me instinctively avoid the question of how long we would be staying on the Ark. Heredity is a potent influence. I couldn't speak about Jules Massingham, the founder of this Ark, but his daughter was a fanatic. I have seen others like her over the years. Nothing would be allowed to interfere with the prime objective: build the

Ark's population on sound eugenic principles. Kleeman was polite to me—I was "prime stock"—but she had her eye mainly on McAndrew. He would be a wonderful addition to her available gene pool.

Well, the lady had taste. I shared some of that attitude myself. "Father unknown" was literally true and Mac and I had not chosen to elaborate. Our daughter had rights, too, and Jan's parentage would not be officially known unless she chose after puberty to take the chromosome matching tests.

Over the next six days, McAndrew and I worked our way into the life pattern aboard the Ark. The place ran like a clock, everything according to a schedule and everything in the right position. I had a good deal of leisure time, which I used to explore the less-popular corridors, up near the Hub. McAndrew was still obsessed with his search for physicists.

"No sense here," he growled to me, after a meal in the central dining area out on the Ark's equator. As I had guessed, effective gravity there was about a tenth of a gee. "I've spoken to a couple of dozen of their scientists. There's not one of them would last a week at the Institute. Muddled minds and bad experiments."

He was angry. Usually McAndrew was polite to all scientists, even ones who couldn't understand what he was doing, still less add to it.

"Have you seen them all? Maybe Kleeman is keeping some of them from us."

"I've had that thought. She's talked to me every day about the Council of Intellects, and I've seen some of the things they've produced. But I've yet to meet one of them, in person." He shrugged, and rubbed at his sandy, receding hairline. "After we've slept I'm going to try another tack. There's a schoolroom over on the other side of the Ark, where I gather Kleeman keeps people who don't seem quite to fit into her ideas. Want to take a look there with me, tomorrow?"

"Maybe. I'm wondering what Kleeman has in mind for

me. I think I know her plans for you, she sees you as another of her senior brains." I saw the woman herself approaching us across the wide room, with its gently curving floor. "You'd like it, I suspect. It seems to be like the Institute, but members of the Council have a lot more prestige."

I had immediate proof that I was right. Kleeman seemed to have made up her mind. "We need a commitment from you now, McAndrew," she said. "There is a coming vacancy on the Council. You are the best person to fill it."

McAndrew looked flattered but uncomfortable. The trouble was, it really *did* interest him, I could tell that. The idea of a top-level brains trust had appeal.

"All right," he said after a few moments. He looked at me, and I could tell what he was thinking. If we were going to be on our way back home soon, it would do no harm to help the Ark while he was here. They could use all the help available.

Kleeman clapped her hands together softly; plump white hands that pointed out her high position—most people on the Ark had manual duties to keep the place running, with strict duty rosters.

"Wonderful! I will plan for your induction tomorrow. Let me make the announcement tonight, and we can speed up the proceedings for the outgoing member."

"You always have a fixed number of members?" asked McAndrew.

She seemed slightly puzzled by his question. "Of course. Exactly twelve. The system was designed for that number."

She nodded at me and hurried away across the dining area, a determined little woman who always got her way. Since we first arrived she had never ceased to tell McAndrew that he must become the father of many children; scores of children; hundreds of children. He looked more and more worried as she increased the number of his future progeny.

The next morning I went on with my own exploration of the Ark, while McAndrew made a visit to the Ark's oddities, the people who didn't seem to fit Kleeman's expectations. We met to eat together, as usual, and I had a lot on my mind. I had come across an area in the center of the Ark where power supply lines and general purpose tube inputs increased enormously, but it did not seem to be a living area. Everything led to one central area, but one accessible only with a suitable code. I puzzled over it while I waited for McAndrew to appear.

The whole Ark was bustling with excitement. Kleeman had made the announcement of McAndrew's coming incorporation to the Council of Intellects. People who had scarcely spoken to him before stopped us and shook his hand solemnly, wishing him well and thanking him for his devotion to the welfare of the Ark. While I drank an aperitif of glucose and dilute ascorbic acid, preparations for a big ceremony were going on around me. A new Council member was a big event.

When I saw McAndrew threading his way towards me past a network of new scaffolding, I knew his morning had been more successful than mine. His thin face was flushed with excitement and pleasure. He slid into the seat opposite me.

"You found your physicist?" I hardly needed to ask the question.

He nodded. "Up on the other side, in a maximum gravity segment right across from here. He's—you have no idea—he's—" McAndrew was practically gibbering in his excitement.

"Start from the beginning." I leaned across and took his hands in mine.

"Yes. I went out on the other side of the Ark, where there's a sort of tower built out from the surface. We must have passed it on the way over from the *Hoatzin* but I didn't notice it then. Kleeman never took us there—never mentioned it to me."

He reached out with one hand across the table,

grabbed my drink and took a great gulp of it. "Och, Jeanie, I needed that. I've not stopped since I first opened my eyes. Where was I? I went on up to that tower, and there was nobody to stop me or to say a word. And I went on inside, farther out, to the very end of it. The last segment has a window all the way round, so when you're there you can see the stars and the nebulae wheeling round past your head." McAndrew was unusually stirred and his last sentence proved it. The stars were normally considered fit subjects only for theory and computation.

"He was out in that last room," he went on. "After I'd given up hope of finding anybody in this whole place who could have derived those results we got back through Triton Station. Jeanie, he looks no more than a boy. So blond, and so young. I couldn't believe that he was the one who worked out that theory. But he is. We sat right down at the terminal there, and I started to run over the background for the way that I renormalize the vacuum self-energy. It's nothing like his way. He has a completely different approach, different invariants, different quantization conditions. I think his method is a good deal more easy to generalize. That's why he can get multiple vacuum colors out when we look for resonance conditions.

"Jeanie, you should have seen his face when I told him that we probably had fifty people at the Institute who would be able to follow his proofs. He's been completely alone here. There's not another one who can even get close to following him, he says. When he sent back those equations, he didn't tell people how important he thought they might be. He says they worry more about controlling what comes in from the System, rather than what goes out from here. I'm awful glad we came. He's an accident, a sport that shows up only once in a couple of centuries—and he was born out here in the void! Did you know, he's taken all the old path integral methods, and he has a form of quantum theory that looks so simple, you'd never believe it if you didn't see it . . ."

He was off again. I had to break in, or he would have

talked without stopping, right through our meal. McAndrew doesn't babble often, but when he does he's hard to stop.

"Mac, hold on. Something here doesn't make sense. What about the Council of Intellects?"

"What about it?" He looked as though he had no possible interest in the Council of Intellects—even though the bustle that was going on all around us, with new structures being erected, was all to mark McAndrew's elevation to the Council.

"Look, just yesterday we agreed that the work you're interested in here must have originated with the Council. You told me you hadn't met one person who knew anything worth discussing. Are you telling me now that this work on the vacuum energy *doesn't* come from the people on the Council?"

"I'm sure it doesn't. I doubted that even before I met Wicklund, up there in the tower." McAndrew was looking at me impatiently, "Jeanie, if that's the impression I gave, it's not what I meant. A thing like this is almost always the work of a single person. It's not initiated by a group, even though a group may help to apply it to practice. This work, the vacuum color work, that's all Wicklund—the Council knows nothing of it."

"So what *does* the Council do? I hope you haven't forgotten that you're going to join it later today. I don't think Kleeman would take it well if you said you wanted to change your mind."

He waved an impatient arm at me. "Now, Jeanie, you know I've no time for that. The Council of Intellects is some sort of guiding and advising group, and I'm willing to serve on it and do what I can for the Ark. But not now. I have to get back over to Wicklund and sort out some of the real details. Did I mention that I've explained all about the drive to him? He mops up new material like a sponge. If we can get him back to the Institute he'll catch up on fifty years of system science development in a few months. You know, I'd better go and talk to Kleeman about this council of hers. What's the use of calling it a Council of Intellects, when people like Wicklund are not on it? And I'll have to tell her we want to take him back with us. I've already mentioned it to him. He's interested, but he's a bit scared of the idea. This is home to him, the only place he knows. Here, is that Kleeman over there by the scaffolding? I'd better catch her now."

He was up and out of his seat before I could stop him. He hurried over to her, took her to one side and began to speak to her urgently. He was gesturing and cracking his finger joints, in the way that he always did when he was wound up on something. As I moved to join them I could see Kleeman's expression changing from a friendly interest to a solid determination.

"We can't change things now, McAndrew," she was saying. "The departing member has already been removed from the Council. It is imperative that the replacement be installed as soon as possible. That ceremony must take place tonight."

"But I want to continue my meetings with—"

"The ceremony will take place tonight. Don't you understand? The Council cannot function without all twelve members. I cannot discuss this further. There is nothing to discuss."

She turned and walked away. Just as well, McAndrew was all set to tell her that he was not about to join her precious council, and he was planning to leave the Ark without fathering hundreds, scores, or even ones of children. And he was taking one of her colonists—her subjects—with him. I took his arm firmly and dragged him back to our table.

"Calm down, Mac." I spoke as urgently as I could. "Don't fly off wild now. Let's get this stupid council initiation rite out of the way today, and then let's wait a while and approach Kleeman on all this when she's in a more reasonable mood. All right?"

"That damned, obstinate, overbearing woman. Who the hell does she think she is?"

"She thinks she's the boss of the Ark of Massingham, and she *is* the boss of the Ark of Massingham. Face facts. Slow down now, and go back to Wicklund. See if he's interested in leaving when we leave, but don't push it too hard. Let's wait a few days, there's nothing to be lost from that."

How naive can you get? Kleeman had told us exactly what was going on, but we hadn't listened. People hear what they expect to hear.

I found out the truth the idiot's way. After McAndrew had gone off again, calm enough to talk to his new protege, I had about four hours to kill. The great ceremony in which McAndrew would become part of the Council of Intellects would not take place until after the next meal. I decided I would have another look at the closed room that I had seen on my earlier roaming.

The room was still locked, but this time there was a servicewoman working on the pipes that led into it. She recognized me as one of the two recent arrivals on the Ark—the less important one, according to Ark standards.

"Tonight's the big event," she said to me, her manner friendly. "You've come to take a look at the place your friend will be, have you? You know, we really need him. The Council has been almost useless for the past two years, with one member almost gone. Kleeman knew that, but she didn't seem happy to provide a new member until she met McAndrew."

She obviously assumed I knew all about the Council and its workings. I stepped closer, keeping my voice casual and companionable. "I'll see all this for myself tonight. McAndrew will be in here, right? I wonder if I could take a peek now, I've never been inside before."

"Sure." She went to the door and keyed in a combination. "There's been talk for a while of moving the Council to another part of Home, where there's less vibration from construction work. No sign of it happening yet, though. Here we go. You won't be able to go inside the inner room, of course, but you'll find you can see most things from the service area."

As the door slid open I stepped through into a long, brightly-lit room. It was empty.

My heart began to pound urgently and my mouth was as dry as Ceres. Strange, how the absence of something can produce such a powerful effect on the body.

"Where are they?" I said at last. "The Council. You said they are in this room."

She looked at me in comical disbelief. "Well, you didn't expect to find them sitting out in the open, did you? Take a look through the hatch at the end there."

We walked forward together and peered through a transparent panel at the far end of the room. It led through to another, smaller chamber, this one dimly lit by a soft green glow.

My eyes took a few seconds to adapt. The big, translucent tank in the center of the room slowly came into definition. All around it, equally spaced, were twelve smaller sections, all inter-connected through a massive set of branching cables and optic bundles.

"Well, there they are," said the servicewoman. "Doesn't look right, does it, with one of them missing like this? It doesn't work, either. The information linkages are all built for a set of exactly twelve units, with a twelve-by-twelve transfer matrix."

Now I could see that one of the small tanks was empty. In each of the eleven others, coupled to a set of thin plastic tubes and contact wires, was a complex shape, a dark-grey ovoid swimming in a bath of green fluid. The surfaces were folded and convoluted, glistening with the sticky sheen of animal tissues. At the lower end, each human brain thinned away past the brain stem to the spinal cord.

I remember asking her just one question: "What would happen if the twelfth member of the Council of Intellects were not connected in today?"

"It would be bad." She looked shocked. "Very bad. I don't know the details, but I think all the potentials would run wild in a day or two, and destroy the other eleven.

It has never happened. There have always been twelve members of the Council, since Massingham created it. He is the one over there, on the far right."

We must have spoken further, but already my mind was winging its way back to the dining area. I was to meet McAndrew one hour before the big ceremony. *Incorporation*, that was what Kleeman had called it, incorporation into the Council. De-corporation would be a better name for the process. But the Council of Intellects was well-named. After someone has been pared down, flesh, bone and organs, to a brain and a spinal column, intellect is all that can remain. Perhaps the thing that upset me more than anything in that inner room was their decision to leave the eyes intact. They were there, attached to each brain by the protruding stalks of their optic nerves. They looked like the horns of a snail, blue, grey or brown balls projecting from the frontal lobes. Since there were no muscles left to change the focal length of the eye lenses, they were directed to display screens set at fixed distances from the tanks.

The wait in the dining area was a terrible period. I had been all right on the way back from the Council Chamber, there had been movement to make the tension tolerable, but when McAndrew finally appeared my nerves had become awfully ragged. He was all set to burble on about his physics discussions. I cut him off before he could get out one word.

"Mac, don't speak and don't make any quick move. We have to leave the Ark. Now."

"Jeanie!" Then he saw my face. "What about Sven Wicklund? We've talked again and he wants to go with us—but he's not ready."

I shook my head and looked down at the table top. It was the worst possible complication. We had to move through the Ark and transfer across to the *Hoatzin*, without being noticed. If Kleeman sensed our intentions, Mac might still make it to the Council. My fate was less certain but probably even worse—if a worse fate is imaginable.

It would be hard enough doing what we had to do without the addition of a nervous and inexperienced young physicist. But I knew McAndrew.

"Go get him," I said at last. "Remember the lock we came in by?"

He nodded. "I can get us there. When?"

"Half an hour. Don't let him bring anything with him—we'll be working with a narrow margin."

He stood up and walked away without another word. He probably wouldn't have agreed to go without Wicklund; but he hadn't asked me for any explanation, hadn't insisted on a reason why we had to leave. That sort of trust isn't built up overnight. I was scared shitless as I stood up and left the dining area, but in an obscure way I was feeling that warm glow you only feel when two people touch deeply. McAndrew had sensed a life-or-death issue, and trusted me without question.

Back at our sleeping quarters I picked up the com-link that gave me coded access to the computer on the *Hoatzin*. We had to make sure the ship was still in the same position. I followed my own directive and took nothing else. Kal Massingham Kleeman was a lady whose anger was best experienced from a distance. I had in mind a light-year or two, but at the moment I was concerned only with the first couple of kilometers. I wanted to move out of the Ark in a hurry.

The interior of the Ark was a great warren of connecting tunnels, so there were a hundred ways between any two points. That was just as well. I changed my path whenever I saw anyone else approaching, but I was still able to move steadily in the direction of our entry lock.

Twenty minutes since McAndrew had left. Now the speaker system crackled and came to life.

"Everyone will assemble in Main Hall Five."

The ceremony was ready to begin. Kleeman was going to produce Hamlet without the Prince. I stepped up my pace. The trip through the interior of the Ark was taking longer than I had expected, and I was going to be late.

Thirty minutes, and I was still one corridor away. The monitors in the passage ceiling suddenly came to life, their red lenses glowing. All I could do was keep moving. There was no way of avoiding those monitors, they extended through the whole interior of the Ark.

"McAndrew and Roker." It was Kleeman's voice, calm and superior. "We are waiting for you. There will be punishment unless you come at once to Main Hall Five. Your presence in the outer section has been noted. A collection detail will arrive there at any moment. McAndrew, do not forget that the Council awaits you. You are abusing a great honor by your actions."

I was at last at the lock. McAndrew stood there listening to Kleeman's voice. The young man by his side—as Mac had said, so blond, so young—had to be Sven Wicklund. Behind those soft blue eyes lay a brain that even McAndrew found impressive. Wicklund was frowning now, his expression indecisive. All his ideas on life had been turned upside down in the past days, and Kleeman's latest words must be giving him second thoughts about our escape.

Without speaking, McAndrew turned and pointed towards the wall of the lock. I looked, and felt a sudden sickness. The wall where the line of suits should be hanging was empty.

"No suits?" I said stupidly.

He nodded. "Kleeman has been thinking a move ahead of you."

"You know what joining the Council would imply?"

He nodded again. His face was grey. "Sven told me as we came over here. I couldn't believe it at first. I asked him, what about the children Kleeman wanted me to sire? They would drain me for the sperm bank before they . . ." He swallowed.

There was a long and terrible pause. "I looked out," he said at last. "Through the viewport there. The capsule is still where we left it."

"You're willing to chance it?" I looked at Wicklund, who stood there not following our conversation at all.

Mac nodded. "I am. But what about him? There's no Sturm Invocation for people here on the Ark."

As I had feared, Wicklund was a major complication.

I walked forward and stood in front of him. "Do you still want to go with us?"

He licked his lips, then nodded.

"Into the lock." We moved forward together and I closed the inner door.

"Do not be foolish." It was Kleeman's voice again, this time with a new expression of alarm. "There is nothing to be served by sacrificing yourselves to space. McAndrew, you are a rational man. Come back, and we will discuss this together. Do not waste your potential by a pointless death."

I took a quick look through the port of the outer lock. The capsule was there all right, it looked just the same as when we left it. Wicklund was staring out in horror. Until Kleeman had spoken, it did not seem to have occurred to him that we were facing death in the void.

"Mac!" I said urgently.

He nodded, and gently took Wicklund by the shoulders, swinging him around. I stepped up behind Wicklund and dug hard into the nerve centers at the base of his neck. He was unconscious in two seconds.

"Ready, Mac?"

Another quick nod. I checked that Wicklund's eyelids were closed, and that his breathing was shallow. He would be unconscious for another couple of minutes, pulse rate low and oxygen need reduced.

McAndrew stood at the outer lock, ready to open it. I pulled the whistle from the lapel of my jacket and blew hard. The varying triple tone sounded through the lock. Penalty for improper use of any Sturm Invocation was severe, whether you used spoken, whistled, or electronic methods. I had never invoked it before, but anyone who goes into space, even if it is just a short trip from Earth to Moon, must receive Sturm vacuum

survival programming. One person in a million uses it.
I stood in the lock, waiting to see what would happen
to me.

The sensation was strange. I still had full command of
my movements, but a new set of involuntary activities came
into play. Without any conscious decision to do so I found
that I was breathing hard, hyper-ventilating in great gulps.
My eye-blinking pattern had reversed. Instead of open eyes
with rapid blinks to moisten and clean the eyeball, my lids
were closed except for brief instants. I saw the lock and
the space outside as quick snapshots.

The Sturm Invocation had the same effect an McAndrew,
as his own deep programming took over for vacuum exposure. When I nodded, he swung open the outer lock door.
The air was gone in a puff of ice vapor. As my eyes flicked
open I saw the capsule at the top of the landing tower. To
reach it we had to traverse sixty meters of the interstellar
vacuum. And we had to carry Sven Wicklund's unconscious
body between us.

For some reason I had imagined that the Sturm
vacuum programming would make me insensitive to all
pain. Quite illogical, since you could permanently damage your body all too easily in that situation. I felt the
agony of expansion through my intestines, as the air
rushed out of all my body cavities. My mouth was performing an automatic yawning and gasping, emptying the
Eustachian tube to protect my ear drums and delicate
inner ear. My eyes were closed to protect the eyeballs
from freezing, and open just often enough to guide my
body movements.

Holding Wicklund between us, McAndrew and I
pushed off into the open depths of space. Ten seconds
later, we intersected the landing tower about twenty
meters up. Sturm couldn't make a human comfortable in
space, but he had provided a set of natural movements
that corresponded to a zero-gee environment. They were
needed. If we missed the tower there was no other landing point within light-years.

The metal of the landing tower was at a temperature several hundred degrees below freezing. Our hands were unprotected, and I could feel the ripping of skin at each contact. That was perhaps the worst pain. The feeling that I was a ball, over-inflated and ready to burst, was not a pain. What was it? That calls for the same sort of skills as describing sight to a blind man. All I can say is that once in a lifetime is more than enough.

Thirty seconds in the vacuum, and we were still fifteen meters from the capsule. I was getting the first feeling of anoxia, the first moment of panic. As we dropped into the capsule and tagged shut the hatch I could feel the black clouds moving around me, dark nebulae that blanked out the bright star field.

The transfer capsule had no real air lock. When I hit the air supply, the whole interior began to fill with warm oxygen. As the concentration grew to a perceptible fraction of an atmosphere, I felt something turn off abruptly within me. My eye blinking went back to the usual pattern, my mouth closed instead of gaping and gasping, and the black patches started to dwindle and fragment.

I turned on the drive of the transfer vessel to take us on our fifty kilometer trip to the *Hoatzin* and glanced quickly at the other two. Wicklund was still unconscious, eyes closed but breathing normally. He had come through well. McAndrew was something else. There was blood flowing from the corner of his mouth and he was barely conscious. He must have been much closer to collapse than I when we dropped into the capsule, but he had not loosened his grip on Wicklund.

I felt a moment of irritation. Damn that man. He had assured me that he would replace that damaged lung lobe after our last trip but I was pretty sure he had done nothing about it. This time I would see he had the operation, if I had to take him there myself.

He began to cough weakly and his eyes opened. When he saw that we were in the capsule and Wicklund was between us, he smiled a little and let his eyes close again. I put the drive on maximum and noticed for the first time the blood that was running from my left hand. The palm and fingers were raw flesh, skin ripped off by the hellish cold of the landing tower. I reached behind me and pulled out the capsule's small medical kit. Major fix-ups would have to wait until we were on the *Hoatzin*. The surrogate flesh was bright yellow, like a thick mustard, but it took away the pain. I smeared it over my own hand, then reached across and did the same for McAndrew. His face was beginning to blaze with the bright red of broken capillaries, and I was sure that I looked just the same. That was nothing. It was the bright blood dribbling down his blue tunic that I didn't like.

Wicklund was awake. He winced and held his hands up to his ears. There might be a burst eardrum there, something else we would have to take care of when we got to the *Hoatzin*.

"How did I get here?" he said wonderingly.

"Across the vacuum. Sorry we had to put you out like that, but I didn't think you could have faced a vacuum passage when you were conscious."

His gaze turned slowly to McAndrew. "Is he all right?"

"I hope so. There may be some lung damage that we'll have to take care of. Want to do something to help?"

He nodded, then turned back to look at the ball of the Ark, dwindling behind us. "They can't catch us now, can they?"

"They might try, but I don't think so. Kleeman probably considers anybody who wants to leave the Ark is not worth having. Here, take the blue tube out of the kit behind you and smear it on your face and hands. Do the same for McAndrew. It will speed up the repair of the ruptured blood vessels in your skin."

Wicklund took the blue salve and began to apply it tenderly to McAndrew's face.

After a couple of seconds Mac opened his eyes and smiled. "Thank you, lad," he said softly. "I'd talk more physics with you, but somehow I don't quite feel that I'm up to it."

"Just lie there quiet." There was hero worship in Wicklund's voice. I had a sudden premonition of what the return trip was going to be like. McAndrew and Sven Wicklund in a mutual admiration society, and all the talk of physics.

After we had the capsule back on board the *Hoatzin* I felt secure for the first time. We installed McAndrew comfortably on one of the bunks while I went to the drive unit and set a maximum-acceleration course back to the Solar System. Wicklund's attention was torn between his need to talk to McAndrew and his fascination with the drive and the ship. How would Einstein have felt in 1905, if someone could have shown him a working nuclear reactor just a few months after he had developed the mass-energy relation? It must have been like that for Wicklund.

"Want to take a last look?" I said, my hand on the drive keyboard.

He came across and gazed at the Ark, still set on its long journey to Tau Ceti. He looked sad, and I felt guilty.

"I'm sorry," I said. "But I'm afraid there's no going back now."

"I know." He hesitated. "You found Home a bad place, I could tell from what McAndrew said. But it's not so bad. To me, it was home for my whole life."

"We'll talk to the Ark again. There may be a chance to come here later, when we've had more time to study the life that you lived. I hope you'll find a new life in the System."

I meant it, but I was having a sudden vision of the Earth we were heading back to. Crowded, noisy, short of all resources. Wicklund might find it as hellish as we had found life on the Ark of Massingham. It was too late to do anything about it now. Fortunately, this sort of problem probably meant less to Wicklund than it would to most people. Like McAndrew, his real life was lived inside his own head, and all else was secondary to that private vision.

I pressed the key sequence and the drive went on. Within seconds, the Ark had vanished from sight.

I turned back and was surprised to see that McAndrew was sitting up in his bunk. He looked terrible, but he must be feeling better. His hands were yellow paws of surrogate flesh, his face and neck a bright blue coating of the ointment that Wicklund had applied to them. The dribble of blood that had come from his mouth had spread its bright stain down his chin and over the front of his tunic, mixing in with the blue fabric to produce a horrible purple splash.

"How are you, Mac?" I said.

"Not bad. Not bad at all." He forced a smile.

"You know, it's not good enough. You promised me ages ago that you'd schedule a repair for that lung—and you didn't do it. If you think I'm prepared to keep dragging you around bleeding and bubbling, you're wrong. When we get back, you have that lung fixed properly—if I have to drag you to the medics myself."

"Och, Jeanie." He gave a feeble shrug. "We'll see. It takes so much time away from work. Let's get on home, though, and we'll see. I've learned a lot on this trip, more than I ever expected. It's all been well worth it."

He caught my skeptical look. "Honest, now, this is more important than you realize. We'll make the next trip out together, the way I promised you. Maybe next time we'll get to the stars. I'm sorry that you got nothing out of this one."

I stared at him. He looked like a circus clown, all smears and streaks of different clashing colors. I shook my head. "You're wrong. I got something out of it."

He looked puzzled. "How's that?"

"I listen to you and the other physicists all the time, and usually I don't understand a word of it. This time I know just what you mean. Lie still, and you can see for yourself. I'll be back in a second."

All the colors of the vacuum? That was McAndrew. If a picture is worth a thousand words, there are times when a mirror is worth more than that. I wanted to watch Mac's face when he saw his own reflection.

FOURTH CHRONICLE:

The Manna Hunt

We had been working hard for two months, preparing for the first long trip. Neither McAndrew nor I would admit to feeling excited, but every day I could see the pleasure and anticipation just bubbling up in him. I doubt that I was any harder to read.

It meant sixteen-hour work spells, day after day, checking every detail of the ship and mission. On an exploration that would take us away for four months of shipboard time and almost nine years of Earth-time, all the thinking had to be finished before we left the Institute.

Finally the launch date was only four days away.

That made the news of cancellation—when they plucked up the courage to tell us about it—hard to take.

I had been over on the *Hoatzin*, checking the condition of the big massplate at the front of the ship. It took longer than I expected. By the time I flew my inspection pinnace on its ten thousand kilometer hop back to the Penrose Institute we were well into the sleep period. I hadn't expected anyone in the dining hall when I slipped in to dial a late meal—and certainly I didn't expect to find Professor Limperis in close conversation with McAndrew.

"Working late—" I said. Then I saw their faces. Even Limperis, black as he was, looked drawn and a shade paler. I sat down opposite them. "What's happened?"

McAndrew shrugged without speaking and jerked his head towards Limperis.

"We've had a directive from USF Headquarters," said the older man. He seemed to be picking his words carefully. "Signed by Korata—right from the top. There was a meeting last week between the Food and Energy Council of Earth and the United Space Federation. They called me two hours ago. The Penrose Institute is instructed to support certain high priority Council activities. This requires that we—"

"They've cancelled us, Jeanie," cut in McAndrew harshly. "The bastards. Without one word of discussion with anybody here. Our Alpha Centauri mission is dead—*finito.*"

I gawped at Limperis. He nodded in an embarrassed way. "Postponed, at least. With no new date set."

"They can't do that." I was beginning to feel my own anger rising. "The Institute doesn't answer to the Food and Energy Council, how the hell can they claim to order you around? This is an independent organization. Tell them to go away and play with themselves. You have the authority to do that, don't you?"

"Well . . ." Limperis looked even more embarrassed. "In principle, Captain Roker, it is as you say. I have the authority. But you know that's an oversimplification of the real world. We need political support as much as any other group—we rely partly on public funding. I like to pretend that we're pure research, answering to no one. In practice, we have our own political constituency in the Councils. I tried to explain this just now"—McAndrew grunted and glowered down at the table—"to point out why I can't really fight it without losing an awful lot. Three of our big supporters, Councilors who've done us big favors in the past, called me ten minutes after we got the first word. They want to use their credit on this one. The Alpha Centauri mission is off. The Council needs the use of the *Hoatzin* for other purposes."

"*No way.*" I leaned forward until our faces were only six inches apart. "That's our ship—we've slaved over it. If they think they can call in and take it away from me and Mac without even asking, and leave us—"

"They want you, too, Jeanie." Limperis leaned back a bit. In my excitement I was spitting all over him. "Both of you. The orders are very clear. They want you and McAndrew and the ship."

"And what the hell for?"

"For a mission of their own." He looked more baffled than irritated now. "For a mission so secret they wouldn't tell me anything about it."

That was the first shock. The others dribbled in one by one as McAndrew and I made our way from the Penrose Institute to the headquarters of the Food and Energy Council.

The Institute had been parked out near Mars orbit. With the *Hoatzin*, and its hundred gee drive, or even with one of the prototypes like *Merganser* at fifty gee, we could have been to Earth in half a day. But Professor Limperis still insisted that the McAndrew Drive should never be employed in the Inner System, and McAndrew himself backed that decision completely. We were stuck with a slow boat and a ten day journey.

Surprise Number One came soon after we powered away from the Institute. I had assumed that we would be running a confidential mission for the *Energy* Department of the full Food and Energy Council. We had worked together on high-energy projects in the past, and I knew McAndrew was a real expert on the subject. But our travel documents instructed us to report to the *Food* Department. What did food programs need with a theoretical physicist, a spacecraft captain, and a high-acceleration ship?

Three days from Earth we were hit with another surprise. The information came in as a brief, impersonal directive that could be neither amplified nor questioned. I would not be the captain of the new mission. Despite the fact that I had more experience with the McAndrew Drive than anyone else in the System, a Food Department official would give me my orders. I became even angrier when, two days from Earth, we learned the rest of it. McAndrew and I would serve as "special advisors" reporting to a crew from the Food and Energy Council. We would have about as much decision-making authority on the mission as the robochef. I had descended from captain to cabin boy.

For me, maybe they could persuade themselves that it was a reasonable decision; some people have more deep space experience than I do (but not much more) and you could say that my talent is nothing more than tricks for staying alive and out of trouble. But McAndrew was another matter. To assign him a role as a simple information source suggested an ignorance or an arrogance beyond my belief.

All right, so I'm a McAndrew fan; I won't deny it. When I got to Earth I would have words with the bureaucrats of the Food Department.

I needed to talk it out with somebody, but Mac was no use. He wasn't interested in arguments on nontechnical subjects. Instead, he retreated as usual into his private world of tensors and twistors, and despite my own respectable scientific background I couldn't follow him there. For most of the journey he sat slack-jawed on his bunk, perfectly content, gazing at the blank wall and performing the invisible mental gymnastics that had earned him his reputation.

That sort of thinking is beyond me. I spent the long hours brooding, and by the time we were led into the Council's offices I was loaded for bear.

The Food Department enjoys a bigger staff and budget than anything else in System Government, and the opulence of its fittings was quite a contrast to the spartan furnishings of the Institute. We were conducted through four luxurious outer offices, each with its own secretaries and screening procedure. Ample working space spoke of prestige and power. The room we finally came to held a conference table big enough for forty people.

A woman was seated alone at the massive desk. I looked at her elegant dress, beautifully made-up eyes and carefully coiffured hair, and I suddenly felt scruffy and out of place. Mac and I were dressed for space work, in one-piece beige coveralls and loafers. My hair had been cropped to a few centimeters long. His thin, straggly mop as usual dipped untidily over his high forehead. Neither of us was wearing a touch of make-up.

"Professor McAndrew?" She stood up and smiled at us. I glowered back at her. "And Captain Roker, I assume. I must apologize for treating you in such cavalier fashion. You have had a long trip here, and no adequate explanation."

Good disarming waffle, the sort you get from an experienced politician or the highest level of bureaucrat, but her smile was broad and friendly. She came forward and held out a pudgy hand. As I took it I made a closer inspection of her appearance: thirty-five years old, maybe, and a bit overweight. Perhaps this messy situation wasn't her fault. I restrained my scowl and muttered conventional words of greeting.

She gestured us to sit down.

"I am Anna Lisa Griss," she went on. "Head of Programs for the Food Department. Welcome to Headquarters. Other staff members will join us in a few minutes, but first I want to point out the need for secrecy. What you will learn here cannot be mentioned to anyone outside this room without my permission. I will come to the point at once. Look at this."

She exuded an air of complete control. As she was speaking the lights dimmed and an image became visible on the screen at the far end of the room. It showed a column of calendar years, and alongside it two other columns of figures.

"Total System food reserves, present and projected," said Griss. "Look at the trend—it's a log scale—then look particularly at the behavior thirty years from now."

I was still trying to assimilate the first few numbers when McAndrew grunted and put his hand up to his face.

"That's ridiculous," he said. "You're showing a factor of two drop in less than three decades. What's the basis for that projection?"

If she felt surprise at his speed of response, she didn't show it. "We included population patterns, available acreages, plant yields, and capacity to manufacture synthetics. Would you like to see the details on any one of them?"

McAndrew shook his head. "Never mind the details. That's disaster and starvation flashing on your screen."

"It is. It's the reason that you are here." She brought the lights back up to what I regarded as a dim, conspiratorial level and dropped her voice to match. "You can imagine the effect when that projection becomes public knowledge, especially if no one can see any way out. Even though we're talking about many years in the future, we'd see stockpiling—probably food wars."

I was feeling a growing anger. There had been rumors of a major future food shortage flying around the System for a long time. The Administration had denied every one, dismissing all gloomy forecasts as alarmist.

"If you're correct in your projections, you can't keep this a secret," I said. "People have a right to know so they can work on solutions."

McAndrew frowned at me, while Anna Lisa Griss gave me a quick probing glance (no smile now) and raised her dark eyebrows. The man's easy, her look said, but this one needs persuading.

"The problem is clear enough," she agreed. "It has been known to my group for almost a decade. Fairly soon it may be obvious to everybody. But it's the possible solution I want to talk about now. And involving the general public wouldn't help a bit—there's no chance that they could provide new insights."

I didn't like her superior manner, but in spite of my irritation I was becoming interested. "It has to be a supply-side answer," I said. "The population growth won't budge."

"Obviously." She smiled again, a bit too broadly, and sneaked a look at her watch. "But think about that supply side. We'd like to increase the planted acreage, of course. But how? We're using every spare inch, unless we can move the lunar agricultural experiments to massive production—and nobody feels optimistic about that. Plant yields are as high as they will go—we're seeing bad effects of plant overbreeding already. No hope there. So what's left?"

Before we could chance an answer or she could provide one, the door behind us opened. A skinny man with plastered-down grey hair entered and stood deferentially at the threshold.

"Come in, Bayes." Anna Lisa Griss looked again at her watch. "You're late."

"Sorry." He remained at the door, hesitating.

"I began without you. Come in and sit down." She turned to face us without offering introductions. "There was one area still to be examined: alternative supplies of organic materials that might easily be converted to food. Six years ago, everyone thought that was a hopeless avenue. Now, with the Griss-Lanhoff Theory"—I could hear the capital letters in her voice as she proclaimed the name—"we have new hope."

I was watching Bayes' face as she spoke. His lips tightened when Anna Lisa Griss pronounced the name of the theory, but he remained silent.

McAndrew cleared his throat.

"I'm afraid that I'm not as well up on the literature of food production as I ought to be," he said. "Lanhoff's a familiar name. If it's the same person, I knew him fairly well ten years ago, when he was working on porphyrin syntheses. What's he doing now?"

"We don't know. Maybe you can help us to find out."
She leaned forward and looked at us intently. "Lanhoff
has disappeared—out in the Halo, testing our theory.
Two weeks ago I learned that you have available a
high-acceleration ship with an inertia-less drive." (I saw
McAndrew wince and mutter "not inertia-less" to himself.) "We need the use of that, for a mission of the
highest priority. We have to find out what happened to
Lanhoff's project. Three days from now we must be on
our way to the Halo."

It said something for the lack of efficiency of the
Food Department that they would drag McAndrew and
me all the way to Earth for a meeting, then shuttle us
back to the Penrose Institute and the *Hoatzin* on a
Government-owned ship less than four hours after we
arrived. Anna Lisa Griss would follow to the Institute
in another and even fancier vessel, but Bayes went with
us to continue the briefing on the way. Without his boss
around he lost his intimidated look and became a much
cheerier person.

"Let's start with Lanhoff's ideas," he said. "Though after
listening to Anna back in her office it's apparently going
to be called the Griss-Lanhoff Theory, at least while
Lanhoff's not on the scene. I'll keep it short, but I'm not
sure where to begin. In the Halo, I guess. Professor
McAndrew, do you know anything about the Halo?" He
cackled with laughter at his joke.

Griss had asked McAndrew that same question when
she was giving us our first briefing. I had watched Bayes'
eyes bulge with astonishment. I felt the same way myself.
McAndrew probably knew more about the Halo and the
outer parts of the extended Solar System than anyone,
living or dead—he had developed the entire theory that
predicted the existence of the kernel ring, the broad belt
of Kerr-Newman black holes that girdles the ecliptic at
four hundred AU, ten times the distance of Pluto. And
of course he had travelled out there himself, in the first

test of the McAndrew balanced drive. I assumed that any scientist worth the name would know all about McAndrew and his work, but apparently Anna Lisa Griss proved me wrong.

McAndrew laughed. He and Will Bayes had needed only ten minutes alone together to discover a mutual fascination with bad jokes, and they were getting along famously. I thought ahead to a long trip with the two of them and shuddered at the prospect.

"Lanhoff wandered into our offices six or seven years back," went on Bayes after he had had a good giggle at his own wit. "He'd been analyzing the results of Halo remote chemistry probes. Didn't you do some of that yourself, a few years ago?"

McAndrew rubbed at his sandy, receding hairline. "Och, just a little bit. I wanted to find power kernels, not low-density fragments, but as part of the survey we sneaked in a look at some other stuff as well. Most of the Oort cloud's so poorly surveyed, you know, it's a crime not to explore it whenever you have the chance. But I never looked out more than a few hundred AU—it was before we had the drive, and probes were too expensive. I'm sure Lanhoff had all my results to work with when he started."

"He certainly knew your work," said Bayes. "And he remembered you well. You made quite an impression on him. He's an organic chemist, and he had been looking at all the data on the Halo, and plotting body chemical composition as a function of distance from the Sun. He has a special algorithm that allows him to look at the fractional composition of each object—I think it came from Minga's team. You probably don't remember Minga, he never published much himself. I met him once or twice, way back . . . no, maybe I'm thinking of Rooney. You know, he was the one who did the high-energy work, I think it was for the Emerald Project, wasn't it? Yes, I think so . . ."

It's probably a kindness if I edit Will Bayes' briefing

of McAndrew and me. He tried hard enough, but everything he said reminded him of something else, and that something else had to be explained, too, and all the people involved in it reminded him or other people, and what they had done. Regression, *ad infinitum*.

We didn't mind too much, with a two-day journey before we were back at the Institute, but I must say I thought a bit more kindly of Anna Griss before the trip was over. Staff meetings with Bayes must be hell.

Boiling Will's verbiage down to a minimum, it was a simple story: Lanhoff had done a systematic chemical analysis of the cometary Halo, from its beginnings beyond the Edgeworth-Kuiper Belt, all the way to the fading outer edge nearly half a light-year away, where the Sun's gravitational hold is so weak that the frozen bodies drift around in orbits with periods of millions of years.

That's the Oort cloud, a great ball of loosely-held matter centered on the Sun. There are several hundred billion comets out there, ranging from near-planet-sized monsters a few hundred kilometers across to snowballs no bigger than your fist. Chapman's Rule applies as well to the cometary Halo as it does to the asteroid belt: for every object of given diameter, there are ten objects with one-third of that diameter.

The Halo has been described and studied since the middle of the twentieth century, but Lanhoff's interests were different. He divided the solar vicinity into regions of different distances and inclinations to the plane of the ecliptic, and he looked at the percentage of different organic materials within each orbital regime. Naturally, with a trillion objects to work with he could only look at a tiny sample of the total, but even so the analysis took him eight years. And he found something new and surprising. In a part of the Halo about 3200 AU from the Sun, running out to maybe 4,000 AU, the complexity of chemical compounds increases enormously. Instead of simple organic molecules like cyanogen, formaldehyde, and methane, his program told him he was finding higher compounds and complex polymers—macromolecules like polysaccharide chains.

"Like what?" At that point in the discussion I had interrupted Will Bayes' rambling. Organic chemistry is low on the list of educational priorities for controlling a spacecraft.

"Organic polymers," said McAndrew thoughtfully. He had been frowning hard as Bayes talked of the chemical composition. "Chains of glucose molecules, to make starches and cellulose." He turned back to Bayes. "Did Lanhoff find any evidence of porphyrins, or nitrogen compounds like purines and pyrimidines?"

Bayes blinked. "You seem to know all about this already. Did Anna already brief you? Lanhoff's work is all supposed to be a big secret."

I had some sympathy with him. Briefing McAndrew is an unrewarding experience. At the end he seems to know everything you know and be able to explain it and apply it better. Now Mac was shaking his head and looking puzzled.

"She didn't mention any of this to us. But I knew most of it years ago. Not the particular place in the Halo where we might find complex organic materials, but at least the fact that they might be there. It's not a new theory at all. Hoyle suggested it more than a hundred years ago. I just don't understand why there's anything secret about it. A finding like this one ought to be available to anyone."

"There's a reason. Wait until you know Anna Griss a bit better and you'll understand." Bayes was looking outside for his first glimpse of the *Hoatzin*, which was now only a couple of hundred kilometers away. "She's the hardest worker I know, but she's super-ambitious. She wants to run the whole Council someday—tomorrow, if she had her way. When Lanhoff came to her with his proposal, the first thing she did was hit it with a classified label."

"Didn't anyone argue with her?" I said.

"No. Try it. It's not something you'll do more than once. There were a few mutterings, that was all. Anna offered some positive incentives, too. She thinks this will make her famous, and push everybody in the Department ten rungs up the management ladder."

"Just because we've got a bit more information about the composition of the Halo? Not much chance of that." McAndrew snorted his disbelief.

"No." Bayes was still peering out of the port. "Lanhoff persuaded her that he had the only answer to the System food problem. All he needed was money and a ship, and USF permission to make some orbit changes to a few bodies out in the Halo. Good God!" He turned back from the scope. "There's the oddest-looking ship out there. Surely we're not proposing to chase after Lanhoff in that thing?"

Lanhoff's suggestion sounded reasonable until you sat down to think about it. Out in the Halo, off where the Sun was nothing more than an extra-bright star, mountains of matter drift through space, moving to the tug of a faint gravitational current. Most of them are frozen or rocky fragments, water ice and ammonia ice bonding metals and silicates. But swarms of them, in a toroidal region three hundred billion miles from Earth, are made of more complex organic molecules. If Lanhoff were correct, we would find an endless supply of useful compounds there—all the prebiotic materials from which foodstuffs are easily made. They needed only warmth and a supply of the right enzymes to serve as catalytic agents. Cellulose, polypeptides, carotenoids, and porphyrins could be transformed to sugars, starches, proteins, and edible fats. The food supply of the whole solar system would be assured for a million years.

Now sit down and think about it again. How do you seed a hundred million worlds and turn them to giant candymountains, when the nearest of them is so far away. How do you heat them; how do you get them back where they will be useable?

If you are Arne Lanhoff, none of those questions will deter you. The enzymes you need are available in small amounts in the inner system; once a body has been seeded and heat is available from a fusion reactor, enzyme production can proceed at an explosive pace. It will suffice to begin with just a few hundred thousand tons of the right enzymes, and make the rest where the supply of raw materials is assured. The types of enzymes needed to split polymer chains are well known, but the only sort of ship that can carry this much load is a boost-and-coast vessel with a maximum short-duration acceleration of only two-tenths of a gee. So be it. Plan on a trip out to the Halo that will take a couple of years, and allow another year or two to trundle around from one cometary body to the next, seeding and performing necessary orbital adjustments. The continuous-thrust engines that will be attached to each body add another two million tons to the ship's initial payload. So be it. Fusion heaters to warm the frozen interiors will add a million more. Don't worry about it. For a project of this size and importance, the Food and Energy Council will find the money and equipment.

McAndrew had shaken his head when Will Bayes described the plan to place the seeded bodies into radial orbits, thrusting in toward the Sun. "Man, do you realize what it will take to stop one of them? We'll be trying to catch a billion tons travelling at two thousand kilometers a second."

"Arne Lanhoff knew that before he left. He was planning just enough drive to bring them to the Inner System in twenty years. By that time they'll be warmed and transformed in content." Bayes smiled contentedly. "He felt sure that you'd find ways to catch them and slow them. It's the sort of thing your group finds challenging."

"Challenging! He's insane." But two minutes later McAndrew was miles away, working on his new puzzle. Arne Lanhoff knew his man rather well.

The ship that had left the Inner System four years ago

did so with no fanfares or publicity. The *Star Harvester* was a massive set of linked cargo spheres with electromagnetic coupling. Each Section had an independent drive unit powered by its own kernel. It was quite similar to the Assembly that I pilot on the Earth-Titan run, and I was glad to know that I'd have no trouble handling it if the need arose.

That need might well arise. The Food Department had received regular communications from the *Star Harvester* crew during the long trip out—two years Earth-time, and the ship was too slow to make it noticeably shorter in shipboard time. Lanhoff had finally reached his first suitable target, a fifteen-kilometer chunk of ice and organics. He had officially named the body *Cornucopia*, planted the enzyme package, the fusion furnace, and the drive, and then started it on the long drop in towards the Sun. Without the drive it would fall for millennia. With a little continuous-thrust assistance *Cornucopia* would be crossing the orbit of Jupiter sixteen years from now. By that time it would be a fertile mass of the raw materials of nutrition, enough to feed the entire solar system for five years.

"No problems. Complete success in all phases," read Arne Lanhoff's message as they moved on to the next selected target, a mere five hundred million miles away.

The mission had operated perfectly for another five targets—each one named, processed, and directed toward the Inner System. *Ambrosia; Harvest Festival; Persephone; Food of the Gods;* and *Demeter.*

Then the pattern was broken. The seventh target had been reached ninety days ago. After an initial message announcing contact with the body *Manna*, a huge organic fragment sixty kilometers in length and incredibly rich in complex compounds, *Star Harvester* became inexplicably silent. A query beamed to it from Triton Station fled off on its nineteen-day journey, and an automatic signal of message receipt finally returned. But no message originated in the ship's transmission equipment. Arne Lanhoff and his crew of four had vanished into the void, three hundred billion miles from home.

Our troubles didn't wait until we were out in the Halo. As soon as Anna Lisa Griss arrived on board the *Hoatzin*, only six hours before our scheduled departure time, we had a problem. She looked around the living quarters disbelievingly.

"You mean we're supposed to stay in this little space— all of us? It can't be more than three meters across."

"Nearer to four." I paused in my run-through of firing sequence checks. "We left information about that with you before we came here didn't you look at it?"

"I looked at the size of the ship, and the column for the living quarters was hundreds of meters long. Why can't we use all of it?"

I sighed. She had the authority to commandeer the *Hoatzin* but had never bothered to learn the first thing about how it operated.

"The living-capsule moves up and down that column," I said. "Farther from or closer to the mass disk, depending on the ship's acceleration. We can put the supplies outside the capsule area, but if we want to live in a one-gee environment we're stuck with this part—it's not bad, plenty of space for four people."

"But what about my staff?" She gestured at the five people who had followed her into the *Hoatzin*. I realized for the first time that they might be more than merely carriers of luggage.

"Sorry." I tried to sound it. "This ship is rated for a four-person crew, maximum."

"Change it." She gave me the full force of her imperial manner. I suddenly understood why Will Bayes chose not to argue with her.

I stared back at her without blinking.

"I can't. I didn't make that rule—check with the USF back at Lunar Base if you like, but they'll confirm what I'm telling you."

She took her lower lip between her teeth, turned her head to survey the cabin, and finally nodded. "I believe you. Damnation. But if there is a four-man limit we still have a problem. I need Bayes and I want my own pilot. And I need McAndrew. You'll have to stay behind."

She didn't look at me this time. I took a deep breath. I didn't want to do it, but if we were going to bang heads we might as well get it over with. Now was as good a time as any.

"I suggest that you discuss this with McAndrew," I said. "Better talk to your pilot, too, while you're at it. I think you'll find that Mac will refuse to go along without me— just as I wouldn't go without him. This is not a conventional vessel. Ask your own pilot how many hours of experience he has with the McAndrew Drive. Mac and I have essential experience and skills for the successful performance of this mission. Take your pick. Both, or neither."

My voice sounded trembly. Instead of replying she turned to head for the steps to the lower level of the living-capsule.

"Prepare us for departure," she said over her shoulder as she went. Her voice was so calm that I was shocked by my own tension. "I will talk to Bayes. He must assume additional duties on this project." She turned again when just her head and shoulders were visible. "Did you ever consider taking a job down on Earth? You have abilities that are wasted out here in the middle of nowhere."

I swivelled my chair to face the console screen and wondered what sort of victory I had won—if any. Anna Lisa Griss was wise in the ways of political infighting, while I was a raw novice. But I was damned if I'd give up my place on this trip without a struggle. The ship was easy to handle, but I'd never admit that to Anna Griss.

Will Bayes came in to stand beside me while I was still having trouble getting my attention back to the status reports.

"Now you've done it," he said. "What did you say to her? I've never seen her in such a weird mood. I can't read her at all. She just told Mauchly and the rest of her staff to get back to Headquarters—no explanation. And I've been given double duty for the duration."

I ran the trajectory parameters out onto the screen, jabbing viciously at the buttons. Then I gave him a quick sideways glance. "I had to make a choice. Which would you rather have: Anna Lisa Griss in a peculiar mood, or a ship run by people who don't know the McAndrew Drive from a laser-sail?"

He grunted and stared gloomily at the screen. "That's not an easy decision. You've never seen Anna when she's really annoyed. I have. Let me tell you, it's not something I want to go through again." He leaned forward. "Hey, Jeanie. Surely that's not the plot of our flight out you've got on the display there."

"It certainly is." I rotated axes so that all coordinates were in ecliptic spherical polars and stored the result. "Don't you like it?"

"But it looks so simple." He moved his finger along the screen. "I mean, it's just a straight line. Not a real trajectory at all. What about the Sun's gravitational field? And you're not making any allowance for the movement of *Manna* while we're flying out there."

"I know." I loaded the flight profile to main memory and as I did so the knot in my stomach seemed to loosen. "That's why I'll be piloting this ship, Will, rather than one of your buddies. We'll be accelerating away from the Sun at a hundred gee, agreed? Did you know that the Sun's acceleration on us here near Mars orbit is only one three hundred thousandth of that? It has tiny effects on our motion."

"But what about *Manna*'s movement in its orbit while we're on the way there? You've ignored that as well."

"For two reasons. First, *Manna* is so far out that it's not moving very fast in its orbit—only half a kilometer a second. More important, we don't know how far Lanhoff's team went in processing *Manna*. Is the body in its original orbit, or did they start it moving in toward the Sun?"

"I've no idea."

"Nor have I. The only thing we can do is fly out there and find out."

I looked at the clock. Time to get moving. "Better say your goodbyes," I went on. "There'll be plenty of chances for us to talk to each other in the next couple of weeks. Probably too many. Two hours from now we'll be on our way. Then we'll be deaf to outside signals until we're out in the Halo and turn off the drive."

"Is that so?" He looked intrigued. "But what about orders that come—"

"Bayes." Anna Griss was calling softly from below.

Will was gone before I could swivel my chair.

I don't envy the life of the Downsiders, ten billion of them crawling over each other looking for a little breathing space. But there are certain experiences available on Earth and nowhere else in the Solar System.

For instance, I'm told that, during the great circular storms that sweep from the Earth tropics to the northern latitudes, there is an area at the very center—the "eye of the hurricane" as the Downsiders call it—where the wind drops to perfect stillness and the sky overhead turns to deep blue. That's something I'd like to see, just once.

The eye of the hurricane. That was the area of the living-capsule surrounding McAndrew during the *Hoatzin's* flight out to rendezvous with *Manna*.

With me, Anna Griss was in constant battle.

"What are you talking about, no messages?" she said. "I have to be in daily contact with Headquarters."

"Then I'll have to switch off the drive," I explained. "We can't get signals through the plasma shell."

"But that will slow us down! I told Headquarters that we'd only be away for one month—and it's a two-week trip each way even if we keep the drive on all the time."

We were standing by the robochef and I was programming the next meal. It took a few seconds for her last statement to penetrate.

"You told Headquarters *what*? That we'll only be away for a month?"

"That's right. Three days should be long enough to find out what's happening to *Star Harvester*. You said that yourself, and McAndrew agreed."

I turned to face her, noticing again the care she took to make her appearance as well-groomed and attractive as possible.

"Three days should be long enough, sure it should. But you'll be away for a lot more than a month. The trip is two weeks each way *in shipboard time*. It's twenty-five days each way in Earth-time. There's no possible way you can get back home in a month."

Her face flushed red and her eyes glowed—she looked more attractive than ever. "How can that happen?"

"I don't know, but it's standard physics. Ask McAndrew." (I knew well enough, but I'd had more than I wanted of this conversation.)

It was like that all the time. We found it hard to agree on anything, and it became clear as soon as we were on the way that Anna Griss was used to delegating and not to doing. Poor old Will Bayes did triple duty. Luckily there was not too much that *could* be done without a communications link to Earth—except shout at Will and keep him on the run.

Yet McAndrew—I thought at first I was imagining it—McAndrew was the eye of the hurricane. When she was within two yards of him, Anna Griss became all sweetness and light. She humbly asked him questions about the drive and about time dilation; she deferred to his opinions on everything from diet to Dostoevski; and she hung first on his word and then on his arm, blinking her eyelashes at him.

It was sickening.

And McAndrew—the great lout—he lapped it up.

"What's she doing?" I said to Bayes when the other two were out of earshot. "She's making a fool of herself."

He winked at me. "You think so, and I think so—but

does *he* think so? Before we left she told me to get a full dossier about him and bring it on this trip. She's been reading it, too. You have to know Anna. What she wants, she gets. Wouldn't look bad for her personal records, would it, to have a five-year cohab contract with the most famous scientist in the System?"

"Don't be silly. She doesn't even like him."

"She does, you know." He stepped closer and lowered his voice. "I know Anna. She has appetites. She wants him, and I think she'd like a cohab contract."

I snorted. "With Mac? That's ridiculous! He belongs to—to science." And I fully believed it, until one morning I found myself applying a pheromonal amplifier behind my ears, and dressing in a new lime-green uniform that fitted a lot closer than my standard garb.

And McAndrew—the great lout—he never noticed or said one word.

While this was going on, we were hurtling outward away from the Sun. With our acceleration at a hundred gee, the living-capsule was snuggled in close to the massplate. The plate's gravitational attraction just about balanced the body force on us produced by the ship's acceleration, leaving us in a comfortable and relaxing half-gee environment. The tidal forces caused by the gravity gradient were noticeable only if you looked for them. McAndrew's vacuum drive worked flawlessly, as usual, tapping the zero point energy—"sucking the marrow out of spacetime," as one of Mac's colleagues put it.

"I don't understand," I'd once said to him. "It gets energy out of nothing."

McAndrew looked at me reproachfully. "That's what they used to say in 1910, when mad scientists thought you might get energy from the nucleus of an atom. Jeanie, I thought better of you."

All right, I was squelched—but I didn't understand the drive one bit better.

❖   ❖   ❖

At the halfway mark we rotated the ship to begin deceleration and I cut the drive while we did it. Anna Griss had an opportunity to send her backlog of messages, and finally gave Will Bayes a few hours of peace. I was amused to see that her communications gave the impression that she was running everything on the *Hoatzin*. Her increased absence from Headquarters she attributed to delays on the trip. If the level of scientific expertise in the Food Department matched her own, she would probably get away with it.

For me, this should have been the best part of the mission, the reason I remain in space and never look for a Downside job. With the drive off we flew starward in perfect silence. I stayed by the port, watching the wheel of heaven as the ship turned.

The *Hoatzin* was within five percent of light-speed. As we performed our end-over-end maneuver, the colors of the starscape Doppler-shifted slowly from red to blue. I caught a last glimpse of Sol and its attendants before the massplate shielded them from view. Jupiter was visible through the optical telescope, a tiny point of light a fifth of a degree away from the Sun's dazzling disk. Earth was gone. Its reflected photons had been lost on their hundred-and-fifty-billion mile outward journey.

I turned the telescope ahead, in a hopeless search for *Manna*. It was a speck in the star-sea, as far ahead of us as the Sun was behind. We would not detect its presence for another two weeks. I looked for it anyway. Then the shield came on to protect us from the sleet of hard radiation and particles caused by our light-chasing velocity. The stars blinked out. I could pay attention again to events inside the *Hoatzin*.

With little else to occupy her attention, Anna delegated her chores to Will Bayes and concentrated everything on charming McAndrew. Will and I received the disdain and the dog work. I sat on my anger and bided my time.

As for Mac, he had disappeared again inside his head. We had loaded a library of references on Lanhoff and the organic materials of the Halo into the computer before we left the Institute. He spent many hours absorbing that information and processing it in the curiously structured personal computer he carries inside his skull. I knew better than to interrupt him. After just a couple of futile attempts to divert him, Anna learned the same lesson. No doubt about it: she was quick. No scientist, but when it came to handling people she did instinctively what I had taken years to learn. Instead of social chit-chat, she studied the same data that McAndrew had been analyzing and asked him questions about it.

"I can see why there ought to be a lot of prebiotic organic stuff out in the Halo," she said during one of our planned exercise sessions. She was dressed in a tight blue leotard and pedaling hard at the stationary cycle. "But I never did follow Lanhoff's argument that there may be primitive life there, too. Surely the temperature's far too cold."

It was still the "Griss-Lanhoff" Theory for official records, but with us Anna had dropped her pretence of detailed knowledge of Lanhoff's ideas. She had been the driving force to carry his ideas to practical evaluation. We all knew it; for the moment that was enough for her. I had no doubt that we would see another change when we arrived back in the Inner System.

McAndrew was idly lifting and lowering a weighted bar. He hated exercise, but he grudgingly went along with general USF orders for spaceborne personnel.

"It is cold in the Halo," he said. "Just a few degrees above absolute zero, in most of the bodies. But it may not be *too* cold."

"It's much too cold for us."

"Certainly. That's Lanhoff's point. We know only about the enzymes found on Earth. They allow chemical reactions to proceed in a certain temperature regime. Why shouldn't there be other life-supporting enzymes that can operate at far lower temperatures?"

Anna stopped pedaling, and I paused in my toe-touching. "Even at the temperatures here in the Halo?" she said.

"I think so." McAndrew paused in his leisurely bar-lifting. "Lanhoff argues that with plenty of complex organic molecules and with a hundred billion separate bodies available, a lot of things might develop in four billion years. He expected to find life somewhere out here—primitive life, probably, but recognizable to us. He was prepared to find it, and the *Star Harvester* was equipped to bring back samples."

We dropped the subject there, but it went running on in my mind while Anna took McAndrew off to program an elaborate meal. I could hear her giggling from the next room, while visions of a Halo civilization ran wild through my brain. Life had appeared there, evolved to intelligence. The Halo society had been disturbed by the arrival of our exploring ship. Lanhoff was a prisoner. His ship had been destroyed. The Inner System and the Halo would go to war . . .

All complete rubbish. I knew that even as I fantasized, and McAndrew pointed out why when we discussed it later.

"We got the way we are, Jeanie, because life on Earth is one long fight for limited resources. Our bloody-mindedness all started out as food battles, three billion years ago. The Halo isn't like that—*everything* will be part of the food supply. How much evolving would we have done if it rained soup every day and the mountains of Earth had been made of cheese? We'd still be single-celled organisms, happy as clams."

It sounded plausible. McAndrew was so bright that you tended not to question him after a while. But an hour or two later I was worrying again. It occurred to me that Mac was a physicist—when it came to biology he was way outside his field. And *something* had happened to Lanhoff and his ship. What could it have been?

I didn't mention it again, but I worried and fretted, while McAndrew and Anna Griss talked and laughed in the sleeping area and Will Bayes sat next to me in the control area, miserable with his own thoughts. He was so dominated by Anna that I often lost sight of him as an independent person when she was around. Now I found out what made him tick—security.

Poor Will. Looking for security he had joined the safest, most stable organization in Earth's government: the Food Department. That was the place for a solid, Earthbound, risk-free job. He had no desire for adventure, no wish to travel more than a mile from his little apartment. He had been in space only once before, as part of a meeting between the Council and the United Space Federation. Now he was embarked on a mission so far from home that he might survive even if the Sun went nova.

How had it happened? He didn't know. It didn't occur to him to blame Anna. He sat about, uncertain and unhappy. I kept him company, my own worry bump throbbing randomly until at last it was time to throttle the drive and begin final search and rendezvous. *Manna* should be less than ten million kilometers ahead of us.

"QUERY DISTANCE FOR *STAR HARVESTER* APPROACH? DEFAULT VALUE: ZERO."

Our computer began talking to us while we were still scanning ahead for first visual contact. No matter what had happened to the vessel's crew, *Star Harvester*'s guidance and control system was still working. Automatic communication for identification and position-matching had begun between the two ships as soon as drive interference was low enough to permit signal transfer.

"Fifty thousand kilometers." I didn't want an immediate rendezvous. "Manual control."

"FIFTY THOUSAND KILOMETERS. CONTROL TRANSFERRED."

"We'll see nothing from that distance." Anna was impatiently watching the hi-mag viewing screen. "We're wasting time. Take us in closer."

We could now see the rough-cut oblong of *Manna* on the imaging radar. A bright cluster of point reflections at one end had to be the *Star Harvester*'s assembly of sections. I suddenly had a new feel for the size of the body we were approaching. Lanhoff's ship was of the largest class in the USF fleet. Next to *Manna* it looked like specks of dust.

"Didn't you hear me?" Anna spoke more loudly. "I don't want a view from a million miles away—take us in closer. That's an order."

I turned to face her. "I think we should be cautious until we know what's going on. We can do a lot of over-all checking from this distance. It's safer."

"And it wastes time." Her voice was impatient. "I'm the senior officer on this ship. Now, do as I say, and let's get in closer."

"Sorry." I couldn't delay this moment any longer. "You're the senior officer while we're in free flight, I agree. But when we're in a rendezvous mode with another ship, the pilot automatically has senior decision authority. Check the manuals. I have final say on our movements until we're on the way back to Earth."

There was a long pause while we sat eyeball to eyeball. Anna's face took on a touch of higher color on the cheeks. McAndrew and Will Bayes held an uncomfortable silence.

"You've had this in mind all along, haven't you?" Anna said softly. Her voice was as cold as Charon. "Damn you, you counted on this. You're going to waste everybody's time while you play at being the boss."

She went through to the other communications department, and I heard the rapid tapping of keys. I didn't know if she was making an entry into the log, or merely calling out the section of the Manual that defines the transfer of authority to the pilot during approach and rendezvous. I didn't care. Super-caution has always paid off for me in the past. Why change a winning hand, even for Anna Griss? I concentrated my attention on the incoming data streams.

Half an hour later Anna came back and sat down without speaking. I was uncomfortably aware of her critical attention over my shoulder. I gestured to the central display screen, where the second series of remotely sensed observations from *Manna* were now appearing. The computer automatically checked everything for anomalies. One new set was displayed in flashing red for our attention.

"That's why I didn't want to rush. I don't think we've been wasting time at all. Mac, look at those radioactivity readings. What do you think of them?"

The computer had done its preliminary analysis, taking the ratio of radioactivity measurements from *Manna* to typical Halo bodies and to the general local background. McAndrew frowned at the smoothed values for a few seconds, then nodded.

"Uh-uh. They're high. About six hundred times as big as I would expect."

I took a deep breath. "So I think we know what happened to Lanhoff. One of the fusion units must have run wild when they were installing it. See now why I'm cautious, folks?"

Anna Griss looked stunned. "Then the crew all got a fatal overdose of radiation?"

"Looks like it." I had proved my point, but not in a way that gave me any satisfaction. I felt sick inside. When a fusion plant blows, there's no hope for the crew.

"No, Jeanie." McAndrew was frowning and rubbing at his sandy hairline. "You're jumping to conclusions. I said the radioactivity was six hundred times as big as it should be, and it is. But it's still low—you could live in it for years, and it wouldn't do you much harm. If a fusion plant had gone, the reading from *Manna* would be a hundred thousand times what we're measuring."

"But what else could give us abnormally high values?"

"I've no idea." He looked at me apologetically. "And we'll never know from this distance. Seems to me that Anna's right. We may have to get in a lot closer for a good look if we really want to find out."

Perhaps the idea that Lanhoff and his crew were almost certainly dead was hitting Anna hard for the first time. At any rate, there was no triumph in her expression as she watched me ease us gingerly forward until we were only ten thousand kilometers from the planetoid. We went slowly, all our sensor input channels wide open. I set the control system to hold us at a constant distance from the surface of *Manna*.

"That's as far as I'm willing to take us," I said. "We're a long way from home, and I won't risk our only way of getting back. Any closer look will have to be done with the transfer pod. Mac, I've not had time to watch the inputs. Is there anything about the ship or about *Manna* that's looking out of line?"

He had been muttering to himself over by a display screen. Now he frowned and pressed a sequence of control keys.

"Maybe. While you were busy I did a complete data transfer from *Star Harvester*'s computer to ours. Lanhoff and his crew stopped feeding in new inputs a hundred and fifteen days ago—that's when the signals to Oberon Station cut off—but the automatic sensors kept right on recording. See, here's the very first radioactivity reading from *Manna* when they arrived, and there's one taken just a few minutes ago. Look at 'em. Identical. And now look at this. This is the thermal profile of a cross-section through *Manna*'s center."

A multi-colored blob filled the screen. It was a set of concentric ellipses, color coded to run from a dark red in its center portion to a violet on the outer boundary.

"Different colors represent different temperatures." McAndrew touched a button, and a dark ellipse appeared around the red and orange portions at the center of the image. "I've just put in the contour for zero degrees Celsius. See? Significant, eh?"

"See what?" said Anna. She was sitting close to McAndrew, their shoulders touching.

"The inside—inside the curve. It's warmer than the melting-point of ice. If *Manna* has a water-ice core, it must be liquid. There's a couple of kilometers of frozen surface, then that liquid interior."

"But we're out in the Halo," I protested. "We're billions of miles from a source of heat. Unless—did Lanhoff already put one of his fusion plants in there?"

"No." McAndrew shook his head. His eyes were sparkling. "The temperature distribution inside was like this before Lanhoff arrived. You're right, Jeanie, it looks impossible—but there it is. *Manna* is three hundred degrees warmer than it has any right to be."

There was a long silence. Finally Will Bayes cleared his throat. "All right, I'll be the dummy. How can that happen?"

McAndrew gave a little bark of excitement. "Man, if I had a definite answer to that I wouldn't hold out on you. But I can make a good guess. There has to be a natural internal source of heat, something like uranium or thorium deep inside. That's consistent with the high radioactivity value, too." He turned to me. "Jeanie, you have to get us over there, so we can take a good look at the inside."

I hesitated. "Will it be safe?" I said at last. "If it's uranium and water—you can make a nuclear reactor from them."

"Yes—if you try really hard. But it wouldn't happen in nature. Be reasonable, Jeanie."

He was looking at me expectantly, while Anna sat silent. She liked to see him putting the pressure on me for a change.

I shook my head. "If you want to go over there and explore, I won't try to stop you. But my job is the safety of this ship. I'm staying right here." Logic was all on my side. But even as I spoke I felt that I was giving the coward's answer.

From a distance of fifty kilometers, *Manna* already filled the sky ahead, a black bulk against the star field. *Star Harvester* hung as a cluster of glittering spheres near one end of the planetoid. It steadily grew in size on the screen as the pod moved in, one of its television cameras sending a crisp image back to my observing post on the *Hoatzin*. I could see the dozen Sections and the narrow connectors between them, hollow tubes that were flexible now but electromagnetically stiffened when the drive went on.

"Approaching outermost cargo sphere," said McAndrew. I could see him on the screen that showed the inside of the pod, and a third image showed and recorded for me the pod control settings exactly as he saw them himself.

"Everything still appears perfectly normal," he went on. "We'll make our entry of *Star Harvester* through the Control Section. What is it, Anna?"

He turned to where she was monitoring another sensor, one for which I was not receiving coverage.

"Cut in Unit Four." I said quickly.

At my command the computers sent the image Anna and Will were watching to fill the center screen. I saw a long shaft that extended from a cargo hold of *Star Harvester* and drove down to penetrate the rough surface of *Manna*. The camera tracked its length, switching to deep radar frequencies to generate an image where the shaft plunged below the planetoid's surface.

"Is that a drilling shaft?" I asked. "It looks as though they were getting ready to put a fusion plant in the middle of *Manna*."

"Wouldn't make sense." McAndrew spoke in an abstracted grunt, and I saw him rubbing at the balding spot on the back of his head. "Lanhoff knew quite well that *Manna* has a liquid core—he had the same computer base to look at as we do. With that core he didn't need a fusion plant at all. The interior would be warm enough already for his enzymes to thrive."

"Was he looking for radioactive material?" I asked; but I could answer that question myself. "It wouldn't make sense. He could locate them the same way we did, from remote measurement. So why would he drill into the core?"

"I'll tell you why," said Anna suddenly. "That's the way Arne always was. Anytime he saw something that he didn't understand he wanted to investigate—he couldn't resist it. I'll bet he drilled to the core to take a closer look at something he'd detected in there—something he couldn't examine closely enough from outside."

The pod had been creeping in nearer and nearer to the hatches on the Control Section. I suddenly realized that once the three of them went inside I would be blind.

"Mac, as soon as you get in there, turn on all the monitors and tell the computer to send the signals back to me here on the *Hoatzin*." I raised my voice. "And one of you has to stay in the Control Section if you go down to the surface. D'you hear me?"

He nodded vaguely, but he was already moving toward the hatch. Anna followed him. The last thing I saw before the camera could no longer keep them in view was Will Bayes' face as he turned to take a last worried look around the pod.

Deserted, but in perfect working order; that was the conclusion after a thorough examination of the Control Section of *Star Harvester*.

I had followed on the remote monitors as the other three made their inspection, step by step, and I could not fault them for lack of caution.

"We'll not find Lanhoff and his crew here," said McAndrew finally, when they were back in the main control room. "They must have gone down into the interior of *Manna*. Look at this."

A computer-generated profile of the shaft leading down from the ship to the surface appeared on the screen in front of me. It penetrated the frozen outer crust and terminated in an airlock leading to the liquid core. In the graphics display the broad shaft looked like a hair-thin needle piercing an egg. I was astonished again by the size of the planetoid. Its liquid core held half a million cubic kilometers of liquid. Maybe we would never find Lanhoff and the other crew members.

"We know they went down there," went on McAndrew, as though he was reading my thoughts. He held up a big clear container full of a cloudy yellow fluid. "See? They brought back samples. I'll send you the analysis, but I can tell you now that the results are just what Lanhoff predicted."

"It's high-level organic materials," added Anna. She was looking at me in triumph. "I told you we had to come here to find anything useful. This is just as we expected, but even more concentrated than I hoped. We've found a mother lode. The whole inside of *Manna* is like a rich soup—one of us could probably drink it for dinner and feel well-fed."

Will Bayes was staring at it dubiously, as though he expected Anna to tell him to go ahead and take a swig. "There's things *living* in it," he said.

My old fears came running back. "Mac, be careful how you handle that. If there are organisms there . . ."

"Just single-celled ones." McAndrew was excited. "Lanhoff thought he might find primitive life here, and he was quite right."

"And it's DNA-based," added Anna. "The same as we are."

I looked more closely at the yellow broth. "So the old theories must be right? Life came to Earth from outside."

"That's the real significance of what they found on *Manna*," said McAndrew. "Life didn't originate on Earth. It began out here in the Halo, or somewhere even farther out, and drifted in to Earth—maybe in the head of a comet, or as smaller meteorites. But see the difference; down on Earth we've had pressures to make us evolve away from a single cell form. Here, there's heat from the radioactive materials in the middle of the planetoid, and there's food galore. There's no reason for evolution as we know it. That's why I don't share your worries, Jeanie, about going down to the interior. There's no evolutionary reason for predators on *Manna*. We won't find sharks and tigers here. It's the Garden of Eden."

Anna nodded her agreement and squeezed his arm. They were both so excited, I wondered if I were the irrational one. The more enthusiastic they became, the more uneasy I felt. No sharks and tigers, maybe—but wouldn't there still be natural selection, even if it went on very slowly?

Shades of Malthusian Doctrine: the number of organisms would follow an increasing geometric progression, and the food resources were finite. Eventually there would have to be a balance, a steady state where dying organisms were just replaced by new ones; and then natural selection ought to take over, with competition between different forms. I didn't have that logic explicitly in mind, all I knew was that something seemed wrong. And I knew that Mac was no biologist. I stared at the screen and shook my head.

"So what happened to Lanhoff and his crew?" I said.

There was a long, uneasy silence.

"Quite right, Jeanie," said McAndrew at last. "We still have no answer to that. But we're going to find one. Will can stay here, and Anna and I will go down there now."

"No." My pulse began to race. "I won't allow it. It's too dangerous."

"We don't agree," said Anna softly. "You heard McAndrew, he says we should look down there—and we'll go in our suits, so we'll be well protected."

Fools rush in where angels fear to tread. Anna Griss knew how to survive in an Earthbound bureaucratic free-for-all, but she was a long way from her home ground. And if she was relying on Mac's instincts to save their skins . . .

"*No.*" My voice cracked. "Didn't you hear me? I absolutely forbid it. That's an order."

"Is it?" Anna didn't raise her voice. "But you see, we're not in the spacecraft rendezvous mode now, Captain Roker. The *Star Harvester* is tethered to the planetoid. That means I command here, not you." She turned to McAndrew. "Come on, let's make sure we're fully prepared. We don't want to take any risks."

Before I could speak again she reached forward to the

monitor. I suddenly found that I was looking into a blank screen.

It took me a long five minutes to patch in a substitute communications link between the computers of the *Hoatzin* and the *Star Harvester*.

When the auxiliary screen came alive I saw Will Bayes fiddling with the control bank.

"Where are they, Will?"

He turned quickly. "They're on the way down to the surface. Jeanie, I couldn't stop them. I said they shouldn't go, but Anna wouldn't take any notice of me. And she has Mac convinced, too."

I knew McAndrew—he hadn't taken any convincing at all. Show him an interesting intellectual problem, and preservation of life and limb came a poor second to curiosity.

"Don't worry about that, Will. Link me to the computer on board the transfer pod."

"What are you going to do?"

"Go after them. Maybe Mac is right, and they'll be fine, and in no danger. But I want to be the rearguard and trail along behind them, just in case."

Will could have probably flown the pod to pick me up in an emergency, and I knew that the computer could have done it with a single rendezvous command from me. But Will and the computer would have followed the book on permissible rates of acceleration and docking distances. I took remote control of the pod myself, overrode the computer, broke every rule in the manual, and had the pod docked at the *Hoatzin* in less than fifteen minutes. Going back to the *Star Harvester* we beat that time by a hundred seconds.

Will was waiting at the main lock with his suit on. "Something has gone wrong," he said. "They told me they would send a signal every ten minutes, but it's been over twenty since the last one. I was going to go down and see what's happening."

"Did you see any weapons on board when you were looking over the ship earlier?"

"Weapons?" Will frowned. "No. Lanhoff had no reason to carry anything like that. Wait a minute, though, what about a construction laser? That can be pretty dangerous, and there are plenty of those in Section Six."

"Get one." I was preparing the transfer pod for a rapid departure from *Star Harvester* if we needed it. One time in a thousand, a precaution like that pays off.

"I'll get two."

Will was off along the tube between the Sections before I could argue with him. I didn't want him with me in the middle of *Manna*—I wanted him available to help me out if I ran into trouble myself.

What was I expecting? I had no idea, but I felt a lot better when I had my suit firmly closed and a portable construction laser tucked under one arm. Will and I went together to the entrance of the long tunnel that led down to the interior of *Manna*.

"Right. No farther for you." I looked at the peculiar way he was holding the laser, and wondered what would happen if he had to use it. "You stay here, at the head of the shaft. I'll send you a signal every ten minutes."

"That's what Anna said." His words echoed after me as I dropped away down the broad shaft.

The illumination came only from the light on my suit. Seen from the inside, the shaft out of the cargo hold dropped away in front of me like a dark, endless tunnel. *Manna's* gravity was negligible, so there were none of the Earth dangers of an accelerated fall. But I had to take care to remain clear of the side of the tunnel—it narrowed as we went deeper into the planetoid's crust. I drifted out to the center of the shaft, turned on the coupling between the suit's conducting circuits and the pulsed field in the tunnel wall, and made a swift, noiseless descent.

The three kilometer downward swoop took less than a minute. All the way to the airlock at the bottom I watched carefully for any sign that McAndrew and Anna had met trouble there. Everything was normal.

The drilling mechanism at the end of the shaft was still in position. Normally the shaft could extend itself through hard, frozen ice at a hundred feet an hour. When they came to the liquid interior, however, Lanhoff had arrested the progress of the drill and installed the airlock. It was a cylindrical double chamber about six meters across, with a movable metal wall separating the two halves.

I cycled through the first part of the lock, closed the wall, and went forward to the second barrier. I hesitated in front of it. The wall was damp with a viscous fluid The airlock had been used recently. Anna and McAndrew had passed through here to the liquid core of the planetoid. If I wished to find them I must do the same.

Was there a port? I wanted to take a good look at the interior of *Manna* before I was willing even to consider going through into it.

The only transparent area was a tiny section a few inches across, where a small panel had been removed and replaced by a thin sheet of clear plastic. Lanhoff must have arranged it this way, to make an observation point before he would risk a venture beyond the lock. Despite his curiosity referred to by Anna, it suggested that he was a cautious man—and it seemed to increase the odds against me. I was diving blind, and in a hurry.

I drifted across and put the faceplate of my suit flat against the transparent plate. The only illumination in the interior was coming from my suit, and because it had to shine through the port I was confused by back-scattered light. I held my hand to shield my eyes, and peered in.

My first impression was of a snowstorm. Great drifting white flakes swam lazily across the field of view. As I adjusted to the odd lighting, the objects resolved themselves to white, feathery snowballs, ranging in size from a grape to a closed fist. The outer parts were in constant vibration, providing a soft-edged, uncertain shimmer as they moved through the pale yellow fluid of *Manna's* interior.

Even as I watched, the number and density of the white objects was increasing. The snowfall became a blizzard. And floating far away from me, almost at the limit of vision, I saw two great white shapes. They were travesties of the human form, bloated and blurred outlines like giant snowmen. Every second they grew bigger, as more and more snowballs approached and adhered to their surfaces. They were swelling steadily, rounding to become perfect spheres.

I shivered in my suit. Alien. The figures looked totally alien, but I knew what I had found. At their centers, unable to see, move, or send messages, were McAndrew and Anna. As I watched I thought of the guardian white corpuscles in my own blood-stream. The feathery balls were like them, busy leukocytes crowding around to engulf and destroy the foreign organisms that dared to invade the body of *Manna*.

How could I rescue them? They were in no danger for the first few minutes, but the snowballs would muffle the escape of heat from the suits. Unless the clinging balls were cleared away, Anna and McAndrew would soon die a blind and stifling death.

My first instinct was to open the lock and plunge through to the interior. Another look at the feathery snowballs changed my mind about that. They were thicker than ever, drifting up from the deep interior of the planetoid. If I went out there they would have me covered in less than a minute. The laser that I had brought with me was useless. If I used it in water, it would waste its energy turning a small volume close to me to steam.

And I had no other weapon with me.

Return to the *Star Harvester*, and look for inspiration there? It might be too late for McAndrew and Anna.

I went across to the side of the lock. There was a dual set of controls for the drilling shaft there, installed so that drilling progress could be monitored and modified on the spot. If I started the drill, the fluid ahead would offer little resistance. The tunnel would extend further into the liquid, far enough to enclose the area where the two misshapen spheres were floating. So if I opened the lock first, then activated the drill . . .

The timing would be crucial. Once the lock was open, liquid would be drawn into the evacuated area around me. Then I would have to operate the drill unit so that the open lock moved to enclose the two swollen masses of snowballs, close the lock again, and pump the liquid out. But if I was too slow, the blizzard of snow would close in on me, too, and I would be as helpless as McAndrew and Anna.

Delay wouldn't help. I pressed the lever that opened the lock, moved to the side of the chamber, and started the drill extender.

Liquid rushed in through the opening aperture. I struggled to move forward against its pressure, fighting my way back to the lock control.

There was a swirling tide of white all around me. Feathered balls hit my suit and stuck to it, coating the faceplate in an opaque layer. Within thirty seconds I could not see anything, and my arms and legs were sluggish in their movements as I clung to the lock lever.

I had not anticipated that I would become blind so quickly. Were McAndrew and Anna already swept into the chamber by the advancing drill and the opened lock? I had no way of knowing. I waited as long as I dared, then heaved at the lever. My arm moved slowly, hampered by the mass of snow-spheres clinging to it. I felt the control close, and sensed the muffled roar of the pump. I tried to thrash my arms, to shake off the layers that clogged their movement. It was useless. Soon I was unable to move at all. I was in darkness. If the snowballs could tolerate vacuum, McAndrew and Anna and I would go the same way as Lanhoff; we'd be trapped inside our suits, our communication units useless, until the heat built up to kill us.

It was a long, long wait (only ten minutes, according to the communications link on board the ship—it felt like days). Suddenly there was a lightening of the darkness in front of my faceplate. I could move my arms again. The feather balls were falling off me and being pumped out through the airlock.

I turned around, peering through the one clear spot on my faceplate. There were two spherical blobs with me in the chamber, and they were gradually taking on human shapes. After another five minutes I could see parts of their suits.

"Anna! Mac! Turn around."

They clumsily rotated to face me. I saw them staring out of the faceplates, white-faced but undeniably alive.

"Come on. Let's get out of here."

"Wait." McAndrew was taking a bag from the side of his suit, opening it, and scooping up samples of liquid and snowballs. I decided that he was terminally crazy.

"Don't fool with that, Mac—let's get out of here."

What was the danger now? I didn't know, and I wasn't going to wait to find out. I reached out, grabbed his arm, and began to haul him back through to the other chamber. We were still sloshing in a chaos of fluid and floating feather balls.

Anna grabbed at my arm, so I was towing both of them. I could hear her teeth chattering.

"God," she said. "I thought we were dead. I knew it, it was just like being dead, no sound, nothing to see, not able to move."

"I know the feeling," I grunted—they were a weighty pair. "How did you get caught? I mean, why didn't you get back into the airlock as soon as the snowballs arrived?"

We were scooting back up the tunnel as fast as we could, McAndrew still clinging to his bucket of specimens.

"We didn't see any danger." Anna was gradually getting control of herself, and her grip on my arm had loosened. "When we first came through the lock there were maybe half a dozen of those fuzzballs in sight. McAndrew said we ought to get a specimen before we left, because they were a more complex life-form than any that Lanhoff had reported. And then they started to arrive in millions, from all directions. Our suits were covered before we could get away—we didn't have a chance."

"But what are they—and what were they doing?" I said.

We had reached the top of the tunnel and entered the cargo sphere. There was no sign of Will Bayes—it occurred to me that I hadn't sent him a single signal of any kind since I left. He must be frantic. I hit the switch that would fill the chamber with air. For some reason I was keener to get out of that suit than I had ever been.

McAndrew placed his container on the floor and we all began to work our way free, starting with the helmets.

"What were they doing? Now that's a good question," he said. "While we were stuck in the middle of them down there, I had time to give it some thought."

Well, that sounded right. When McAndrew stops thinking, he'll be dead.

"Lanhoff and I made a big goof," he went on, "and for him it was a fatal one. We both argued that the food supply here was so plentiful that there'd be no pressure to evolve. But we forgot a basic fact. An organism needs more than food to survive."

"What else? You mean moisture?" I had my suit off, and air had never tasted so good.

"Moisture, sure. But as well as that it needs warmth. Here on *Manna*, the evolutionary pressure is to get near a heat source. If you're out too far from the center, you become part of the frozen outer layer. Those snowballs normally live down near the middle, getting as close as they can to the radioactive fragments that provide the warmth."

Anna was out of her suit. Now that we were safe, she was making a tremendous effort to gain her self-possession. Her shivering had stopped and she was even patting at her damp and tangled hair. She peered curiously down at the container of feathered snowballs. They were still moving slowly around in the yellow liquid.

"The radioactivity must speed up their rate of evolution, too," she said. "And I was thinking they wanted to eat us."

"I doubt that we're very appetizing, compared with their free soup," said McAndrew. "No, if there hadn't been so many of them they'd have been harmless enough. But when we came along, they sensed the heat given off by our suits, and they tried to cuddle up to us. They didn't want to eat us, all they were after was a place by the fireside."

Anna nodded. "This is going to create a sensation when we get back to Earth. We'll have to take a lot of specimens back with us."

She was reaching down towards the open container. One of the snowballs had fully opened and was a delicate white mass of feathery cilia. She put out her forefinger as though she intended to touch it.

"*Don't do that!*" I shouted.

Maybe she was not even considering any such thing, but my loud command made her stiffen. She looked up at me angrily.

"You saved us, Captain Roker, and I appreciate that. But don't forget who is in charge of this expedition. And don't try to order me around—ever."

"Don't be a fool," I said. "I wasn't ordering you around—I was speaking for your own good. Don't you have any idea what might be dangerous?"

My own tone must have betrayed my impatience and anger. Anna stiffened, and her color went from white to red.

"McAndrew has pointed out that these lifeforms would have been quite harmless if there had not been so many of them," she said. And then she reached forward into the container and deliberately touched the expanded snowball with her forefinger. She looked up at me. "Satisfied? They're perfectly harmless."

Then she screamed. The ball was clinging to her finger as she withdrew it, and the cilia had enveloped it as far as the second joint.

"It won't come off!" She began shaking her hand desperately. "It hurts."

I swung my helmet hard at her finger, and the edge caught the ball near its middle. It was jarred loose and flew across the chamber. Anna stood and looked ruefully at her hand. The finger was reddened and swollen.

"Damnation. It stings like hell." She turned accusingly to McAndrew and held forward her injured hand. "You fool. You told me they're harmless, and now look at my finger. This is your fault."

We all stared at her hand. The swelling on her forefinger seemed to be getting bigger and redder.

McAndrew had been standing there with a startled and perplexed expression on his face. Before I could stop him he picked up the laser that I had laid on the floor, aimed it at Anna, and pressed the switch. There was a crackle from the wall behind Anna, and the smoke of burned tissue. Her arm had been neatly severed above the elbow, and the wound cauterized with a single sweep of the instrument.

Anna looked at the stump with bulging eyes, groaned, and started to fall sideways to the floor.

"Mac!" I grabbed for the laser. "What the hell are you doing?"

His face was pale. "Come on," he said. "Let's get her to the robodoc. This isn't too serious—she'll have to wait to regenerate it until we get home and find a biofeedback machine, but we can't help that."

"But why did you do it?"

"I made one bad mistake, back there outside the air lock." We were hurrying back through the ship, supporting Anna between us.

"I don't want to make another one," he went on. "Lanhoff's notes on the single-celled organisms inside *Manna* pointed out that they didn't have a sexual method of reproduction, but they have something that resembles the plasmids down on Earth—they swap sections of DNA with each other, to get the mixing of offspring characteristics. I wondered about that when I read it, because it suggests a mechanism for speeding up an evolutionary process. But I skipped on past it, because I was so sure there would be no evolutionary pressures at work inside *Manna*."

We were almost at the Control Section of *Star Harvester*. Unless Will had gone mad and flown off in the transfer pod, we were only twenty minutes away from the *Hoatzin*'s robodoc. Anna was coming out of her faint, and groaning a little.

"Mac, I still don't see it. Why does the evolution method of the creatures inside *Manna* mean you had to burn off Anna's arm?"

"If they do swap tissue regularly, their immune reaction systems have to recognize and tolerate the exchange. But we're not made like that—Anna's immune reaction system might mop up the materials that the snowball transferred to her bloodstream, but more likely the stuff would have killed her. I daren't take the chance."

We had come to the hatch that led to the transfer pod. Will Bayes stood there. For a fraction of a second he looked relieved, then he took in the whole scene. We were all pale and panting. I was dragging Anna along while she lay in a near-faint with only a stump of a right arm; and McAndrew, wild-eyed and lunatic, was bounding along behind us, still brandishing the laser.

Will backed away in horror, his hands held in front of him. "Come on, man, don't just stand there," said McAndrew. "Get out of the way. We've got to get Anna over to our ship and let the doc have a go at her. The sooner the better."

Will took a hesitant step to one side. "She's not dead, then?"

"Of course she's not dead—she'll be good as new once she's been through a regeneration treatment. We'll have to keep her sedated for the trip back, but she'll be all right."

I went to the controls of the pod, ready to take us back to the *Hoatzin*. It hadn't occurred to me that Anna would be quieted down now for the return trip, but I wouldn't be the one to complain.

"You mean we're actually going home?" asked Will. His tone suggested that he had never expected to see Earth again.

"Just for a while." McAndrew had settled Anna as comfortably as he could, and now he was looking disconsolately around him for the bucket of lifeform samples that we had left behind in the Control Section of *Star Harvester*.

"We'll be back, Will, don't you worry," he said. "Anna was quite right: when Lanhoff found *Manna* he stumbled across a real treasure trove. We've hardly scratched the surface. As soon as we can get organized, there'll be another party from the Food Department. And I'm sure we'll all be here with it."

My attention was mainly on the controls, so I'm not sure that I heard Will's low mumble correctly. But I think he was saying something about a transfer to the Energy Department.

FIFTH CHRONICLE:

The Hidden Matter of McAndrew

The message was concise and clear:

Dear Captain Roker,

The Institute is sending a party to explore a region approximately half a light-year from Sol, for the purpose of verifying dark matter conjectures in current cosmological theories. Our projected departure date is six days hence. Knowing of your experience with *Hoatzin*-class ships employing the balanced drive, we wonder if you might be available to serve as a crew member for Project Missing Matter. If you are interested in so serving, I invite you to contact me or Dr. Dorian Jarver, at the above address.

Sincerely,
Arthur Morton McAndrew,
Research Scientist,
Penrose Institute.

Clear, but also totally baffling. It was no surprise that McAndrew wanted to test obscure scientific theories. That was his stock-in-trade. People who knew physics as I would never know it told me that McAndrew was better than anyone else alive, a name to be mentioned in the same breath as Newton and Einstein.

It was also predictable that he might be heading far out of the Solar System. He had done that whenever he thought there was something interesting to look at, or just when he needed a little time and space for serious solitary thinking. "I have to have it, Jeanie," he'd said to me, a score of times. "It's very nice to work with colleagues, but in my line of business the real stuff is mostly worked out alone."

Nor was it odd that I was learning about the trip so late—a couple of times he had hared off on wild sorties far outside the Solar System, and I had been forced to chase after him and drag him out of trouble.

But now for the mysteries: He had never, in all the many years since first we met, sent a letter to "Captain Roker," or signed himself with his full name. I was always "Jeanie" when he wrote to me, while he signed as "Mac" or "Macavity"—my private Old Possum-ish name for him, because like Macavity the Mystery Cat, McAndrew did things that seemed to break the law of gravity.

Second, he didn't *write* when he was planning an expedition. There would be a random call, at any hour of the day or night. He was thinking of making a trip, he'd say vaguely. Would I perhaps like to go along?

Third—a detail, but one that chafed my ego—I was invited to go on the Project Missing Matter expedition as a *crew member*. Mac knew that I'd served as ship's captain, and only as captain, for fifteen years.

Fourth, the whole tone of the letter was too stilted and officious to be genuine McAndrew. He couldn't sound that formal if he tried.

And one more mystery, to round out the set. Who the

devil was Dorian Jarver? I thought I knew all the key scientists at the Penrose Institute.

That question was fifth on the list, and the least important until I tried to call McAndrew for an explanation. Then instead of the old direct-access lines into individual offices at the Penrose Institute, I found myself dumped to a Message Center where my call was at once rerouted from McAndrew to Dorian Jarver. Director Jarver is unavailable, said a polite voice. Please leave your name, and he will return the call as soon as possible.

I hung up without waiting to learn if the voice at the other end was live or recorded. *Director* Jarver? What had happened to my old friend Professor Limperis, the blackest man alive, who had run the Institute since long before my first visit?

Finding the answer to that was not difficult. I tapped one of the general data bases and queried for the staff file of the Penrose Institute. Professor Limperis was listed, sure enough—but as professor *emeritus* and *ex*-Director. The new director was Dr. Dorian Jarver, former head of the Terran science applications group, and—bad sign—nephew of Councilor Griss, head of Terran Food and Energy.

Anna Lisa Griss, that was, a lady whose arm McAndrew had once, with the best of possible intentions, cut off with a power laser out in the Oort cloud. It would have been regrown, long since; but I doubted that the memory had faded with the scar.

I followed an old McAndrew principle, and went to a publications data base. Dorian Jarver was there, with eight or nine decent-sounding physics papers credited to him; but they were not recent. The newest one was eleven years old. The new director of the Penrose Institute appeared to be an ex-physicist.

McAndrew was anything but an ex-physicist. Why would he cite his own name and *Jarver's* as someone I might contact?

When I received the message from McAndrew I was

on the tail end of a routine run home from Titan. As soon as the Assembly I had been piloting was tucked away and all its Sections placed in a stable parking orbit, I signed off and headed straight for the Penrose Institute aboard one of the 5-gee mini-versions of the McAndrew balanced drive.

"I invite you to contact me or Dr. Dorian Jarver," the letter had said. *Contact* can surely include a visit.

The outline of the Institute at last appeared as a lumpy and spiky double-egg during my final approach. I examined it closely. It would wander around the Inner Solar System depending on research needs, anywhere between Mercury and the Belt, but its facilities shouldn't change. They hadn't. As we docked I could see the *Dotterel* and the *Merganser* moored in the external hoists. They were the first prototypes using the McAndrew balanced drive (which everyone else, to Mac's intense annoyance, insists on calling the McAndrew inertia-less drive). Those early ships were no longer in use. They had been replaced by a more advanced design, embodied in the *Hoatzin*. I could see its bulky massplate and longer central spike off in the distance. It appeared slightly grubby and battered-looking, as befitted the first and only ship to visit both the Ark of Massingham and the Oort cloud.

The changes began inside, as soon as I passed through the lock. In the old Institute the visitor found herself wading at once through a junkyard of obsolete equipment waiting for disposal. It would have been quite an obstacle course in an emergency, but nobody had ever seemed worried about that.

Now I found myself in a clean and uncluttered chamber. The walls were painted white, the floor was polished grey, and in the middle of the room sat something that the Institute had surely never seen before: a long desk, two receptionists, and in front of them, a sign-in terminal and a tray of badges.

The woman behind the desk went on fiddling with a great bank of controls in front of her, all flickering lights and low humming, but the man glanced up at me inquiringly.

"I'm here to see McAndrew," I said, and started towards the corridor on the left. I'd been here scores of times, and I knew where Mac hung out, in a cluttered room that made even the old entry to the Institute look elegant. Mac didn't throw away junk equipment. He kept it in his office.

"Not that way, ma'am," said the man politely. "Professor McAndrew is the other way now. You will need an escort. And if you'd first please check in . . ."

McAndrew's voice was starting to whisper in my ear. By the time that I had signed in, stated my identity, had my ID independently checked with a DNA mapper, been assigned a badge, and refused refreshments (how long did they expect me to be in the reception area?) Mac's voice was shouting at me. "Help, Jeanie," it screamed. "Help, help, help!"

This wasn't the Penrose Institute that I had known, the place of casual procedure and superb science where Mac had worked for half his life. It had become a clone of a thousand Earthside technology offices.

And it got worse. When I, checked and signed and badged, was led away towards the new working offices, I still did not reach McAndrew. "In a few minutes," said my guide, in answer to my question. "But first, the Director."

I was ushered into a new chamber, starkly clean and sparsely furnished. My guide left at once and I looked around. There was no desk, no terminal. Over in one corner on an angular white chair sat an equally angular and thoughtful man, fingertips touching in front of his face.

"Captain Roker," he said, and stood up. He smiled, very white teeth in a thin-lipped, worried countenance. "I'm Dorian Jarver, the Director of the Penrose Institute. I must say I didn't expect a visit until you'd heard more about the project. But it's a blessing that you're here, because now we can all do our best to persuade you."

"I'm persuaded already." I realized that was true, and had been since I saw that ritzy new entrance foyer. "I'm reporting for duty right now."

"For the expedition described in Professor McAndrew's letter to you? But the mission and your role in it are not yet fully defined."

"You can define that later. I'm here, and I'm ready to start."

Dorian Jarver must have been surprised at both my arrival and my instant acceptance. "I'm delighted to hear that," he said, though he didn't sound it. "You come to us with the highest recommendations. And I have to admit that I've been a little worried about this proposed expedition. It could be dangerous, and Professor McAndrew is too valuable to risk. He's one of our most priceless assets."

No matter what else he didn't know, he obviously understood McAndrew. It *could* be dangerous, because Mac would charge into Hell itself if he saw some intriguing scientific fact sitting in the innermost circle. He *was* too valuable to risk. But Jarver's final word was disturbing to me. Not a scientist, not a human being. An *asset*.

"You have been to the Institute before?" added Jarver.

I nodded. I didn't know what Mac had told him about me, but I suspected that the new director had no idea how close we were.

"Then you'll have noticed the changes here. The Council had been worrying about the Institute for quite a while. When Director Limperis retired and I came in, the Council insisted that from now on operations would have to be organized rather differently."

He talked about those changes for the next few minutes. Better equipment and facilities for the scientists. Bigger and cleaner offices. More attention by support staff to routine maintenance functions. Removal of the need for top scientists to waste their time on calls and letters and incoming requests for information, trivia that could be handled just as well by junior staff.

It all sounded terrific. But McAndrew's strangely awkward letter stuck in my head. I wanted to see him, and make sure that he was all right.

With my mind on McAndrew as Jarver went on talking, I didn't think that I was saying much in reply. But it must have been enough for the director, because after another few minutes he seemed to lose interest in the conversation, nodded, and said, "Now, Captain Roker, I'm sure you'll be wanting to hear more about the expedition itself. Project Missing Matter will be testing some of the most fundamental ideas in cosmology; of course, you'll get that better from McAndrew than you'll ever get it from me."

As we stood up I thought that I had Dorian Jarver pegged. I had seen him before, many times. Not the man himself, but the type. The upper levels of Terran government were full of them: competent, hard-working men and women, who started out as scientists, found that they were never going to be better than average, and at an early age substituted management and administration for research. Jarver had changed over the years from scientist to calculating bureaucrat.

Well, I've been wrong before. Let's call that my first mistake on Project Missing Matter.

The director led me to an office down at the far end of the corridor and opened the door. It was big, far bigger than McAndrew's old, cluttered den. It had the same antiseptic look as the rest of the new Institute. But even Jarver couldn't do much about the appearance of the occupant.

McAndrew was lolling in an easy chair, staring vacantly at the wall. His shoes were off, his feet were bare and grubby. His thinning, sandy hair was standing up in little wispy spikes as though he had been running his hands through it, which he tended to do when he was thinking, and I could see from the redness of his finger and toe joints that he had been pulling them and cracking them, in the way that I hated.

He glanced up as we came in, swinging his chair casually in our direction.

"Jeanie Roker," he said. He didn't stand up, and he didn't seem in the least surprised at my unexpected arrival. I glanced at Jarver out of the corner of my eye. If Mac wanted to convince the director that he hardly knew me, he should have acted quite differently.

"Professor McAndrew," said Jarver to me. It could have been an introduction, or possibly an apology. "If you'll excuse me, Captain Roker, I'll leave the two of you to discuss the expedition. I'll meet with you again later."

As soon as he was gone I bent over and gave McAndrew a six-month separation hug. The hell with formal handshakes. He hugged me right back, then I flopped into the seat opposite and said, "Mac. What the hell is going on here?"

"You saw it already." His face took on a gloomy, give-up expression that I didn't like at all. "New offices, new procedures, all the other folderol. Now tell me, did I *need* a new office?"

"Does it matter that much? You can work as well in here as you could in your old place, and it's nice to visit and sit on something softer than an optical scalar calibrator. And Jarver's right, the Institute was getting a bit run-down. It looks good now. You're becoming crabby in your old age."

He glared at me. "If that were the whole of it, I might agree with you . . . but it's not. You had that letter. Didn't it make you wonder a bit?"

"Why d'you think I'm here?"

I don't believe he heard me. *"Due procedure,"* he said, "that's what they call it. But it's beyond that. No messages or memos or papers or letters go out from here without stamps of official approval on them. You saw how my letter to you sounded after they'd done messing with it. All the incoming mail is opened, too—personal as well as professional—before we get to see it. Spoken messages are just as bad. Incoming and outgoing calls are all logged and recorded. Did you see that blasted bank of equipment in the front area, with administrative staff snooping on everything? I'm telling you, it's like being in a bloody prison."

"Mac, you're overreacting. Jarver is used to running things Earth-style. They're hot on procedure. It'll take him a while to learn Institute ways. You and your buddies will sort him out."

"Will we now?" McAndrew snorted. "Me and my buddies will sort him out, will we—when Emma Gowers and Wenig and Lucky Macedo have already resigned and left."

That was a shocker. I knew all three, and there wasn't one who didn't make me feel, without their ever intending it, about as bright as a chimps' tea-party drop-out.

"Mac, that proves my point. If Jarver's losing high-caliber people like that, he must know that he won't last another three months. Unless he's too dumb even to realize what he's driving away?"

I saw a change in McAndrew's expression. He's the system's most honest man, even when it undermines his own arguments. Now he looked guilty.

"That's maybe the worst of it," he said. "Jarver's not stupid at all. He got the job here, likely, because he's a relative of Anna Griss. She's no lover of the Institute after what I did to her. But Jarver didn't come here wanting to destroy the place. He's a good physicist, see, with a real sense for what's important."

"That's not what I thought when I looked at his publication record. Not many papers to his credit, and all written a long time ago."

"Jeanie." McAndrew stared at me with the disappointed expression of a man whose dog has slipped back into non-housebroken ways. "How many times have I told you, a publication record tells you *nothing*. Any clod can spew out words and equations, year in and year out, and push them into print. Papers don't count for *anything*, unless other people use 'em. You should have looked at the

Citation Index, to see how often Jarver's work is given as a reference by other people. If you'd done that, you'd have seen hundreds of them. He's not publishing now, true enough, but when he did, he was *good*."

Poor old McAndrew. I was beginning to see the real problem. Here was a new director who did everything that Mac disliked, a man whom he would love to hate and disparage. But he couldn't do that. Jarver was a good physicist, and therefore almost beyond censure.

"But if he's that bright, you ought to be able to work with him. *Persuade* him."

"Damn it, I *have* persuaded him. That's what the new expedition is all about. I've got Jarver convinced that we have to go out a long way from Sol. Then we stop, and sit still, and do our measurements, and learn more than anyone has ever known about the distribution of missing matter."

I had to find out more about that, but this wasn't the time for it. Half a light-year from Sol was a long trip, even with a hundred gees of continuous acceleration and the relativity squeeze that our high speed would provide us. We'd have weeks to talk about missing matter, Mac's experiments, and everything else in the Universe. But it would be nice to know why we had to go out there at all.

"Why not do your experiments here at the Institute?"

"Because it's too damned *noisy* near in." McAndrew became more like his old self as the conversation turned closer to physics. I decided there was hope—maybe he wasn't a broken man after all. "It's the Sun's fault," he went on. "Sol generates such an infernal din, gravitationally and in almost every electromagnetic wavelength you can think of, that you can't do a decently sensitive experiment closer than half a light-year. It's like listening for a pin drop, when somebody's banging a bass drum right next to your ear. We have to go out, out where the interstellar medium is nice and quiet."

"But that's exactly what you will be doing. You'll be

flying out on the *Hoatzin*, and as far from the Institute as you want to be. So why aren't you pleased?" I had a horrible thought. "Unless you're telling me that Jarver proposes to go along with us."

"No, no, no." McAndrew went right back to being gloomy. "He says he'd like to, but he's far too busy running the Institute. He's not going. But he's sending his aunt's pet bully-boys, Lyle and Parmikan, along to keep an eye on things and report back. Now *that's* what really has me going, Jeanie. That's the reason I sent you the letter."

I got very annoyed with McAndrew. He was taking a perfectly natural decision, from Jarver's point of view, and blowing it up out of all proportion.

Of course, this was before I met Van Lyle and Stefan Parmikan.

The doubtful pleasure of that meeting was not long delayed. It came the same afternoon, when McAndrew dragged me along to the weekly seminar, a tradition of the Penrose Institute for as long as I had been visiting it.

The old meeting room, with its poor air circulation and white plastic hard-backed chairs, had vanished. In its place was a hall with tiers of plushy seats running in banks up towards the rear. It could hold maybe three hundred. The seminars that I remembered might draw fifty if they were on a really hot subject.

Today there were no more than thirty people in the room. McAndrew and I took seats at the end of the last occupied row. I tried to recognize the people I knew from the look of the backs of their heads. I did pretty well, over half the audience. Wenig and Gowers and Macedo might be gone, but most of the other old-timers at the Institute hadn't given up yet.

The lecturer, Siclaro—another Institute perennial—was already in position and raring to go.

"The first ten-thousandth of a second after the Big Bang is far more interesting than the entire rest of the history of the Universe." That was his first sentence. I couldn't tell you what his second sentence was. I didn't *expect* to understand the seminar, you see, because I never had in the past. But I might still enjoy it. Like the psychologist at the burlesque show I concentrated on the audience, examining the newcomers to try to guess their specialties and how good they were at them.

A futile exercise, of course. Emma Gowers, the System's top expert on multiple kernel arrays, looks and dresses like a high-class whore. Wenig could be her pimp, and McAndrew himself resembles an accountant in need of a haircut and a good meal.

You just can't *tell*. Brains won't correlate with appearance.

Over to the far left of our row sat a group of three. I saw Dorian Jarver. He was leaning forward, intent on the presentation. To his immediate right were two men of particular interest to me—because they too were taking no notice of the lecture and showing a lot of interest in the audience. I nudged McAndrew, just as someone hurried in from the back of the room and leaned over to whisper in Jarver's ear. He sighed, shook his head, and followed the woman quickly out of the hall.

"What?" said McAndrew at last. He had missed the whole episode with Jarver.

"Those two men. Who are they?"

He snorted. "Them two? Van Lyle. Stefan Parmikan."

I stared with redoubled curiosity. Van Lyle (I found out later which was which) was a big, broad-shouldered fellow with curly blond hair and a handsome, craggy profile. He made no pretence of listening to the lecture, but he observed the audience with open interest. At his side the little, round-shouldered figure of Stefan Parmikan was far more discreet. To a casual observer he was following everything that Siclaro said—but every few seconds his head would turn for a moment and his eyes would flicker over everyone. When they met mine he at once turned away.

"Mac," I said. And paused.

He had slipped away from my side. I saw him down by the lecturer's podium next to Siclaro, one hand pointed at the screen.

"You know the problem," he was saying. "We all believe that the amount of matter in the universe is *just* enough to keep it expanding forever. That gives asymptotically flat spacetime, an idea we have half a dozen good theoretical reasons for wanting to believe. But the bright matter—the stuff we can see—only accounts for maybe a hundredth of what's needed to close spacetime. So, where's the rest of it? Where's the missing matter?

"I agree with Siclaro, it's the devil to answer that question from any experiments we've been able to do so far. I wouldn't propose to try. But we've designed a whole new set of crucial experiments that we can do if we are far out from Sol, where there's not so much interference."

He was getting into a discussion of the hidden matter, the reason for taking the *Hoatzin* on its light-year round-trip. But I couldn't listen to him, because I was no longer alone. The two men next to Jarver had slid quietly across from the other side of the room and were now by my side.

"Captain Roker?" said the blond-haired man. "I wanted to say hello. I hear we're going to be shipmates."

He gazed sincerely into my eyes, took my hand in his big, meaty paw, and held on a few seconds longer than necessary.

"Pleased to meet you," added his companion, leaning across and taking my hand in turn. "I'm Stefan Parmikan. I've heard a lot about you." His smile was a wet, shapeless version of Van Lyle's intimate grin. And instead of riveting me like Lyle, his brown eyes would look anywhere but into mine.

"You heard about me?" I was surprised. McAndrew is closer than a clam. "From whom?"

"The boss. Councilor Griss."

His limp grip was like a lump of wet gristle, much

worse than Van Lyle's intimate clutch; but that wasn't what
bothered me.

Suddenly, I could put it all together. So far my thinking
had managed to get everything wrong. Anna Lisa Griss
could push her relatives into high places, and no one
would be surprised by that. Nepotism never changes. She
had arranged for Dorian Jarver to take over the Penrose
Institute.

But it was her bad luck that Jarver happened to be
genuine, a conscientious scientist with a real feel for
physics and science. She couldn't change his nature. What
she *could* do, though, and had done, was to install as his
assistants her chosen few: people with no feeling for
science, who would follow the Councilor's style of operation and do exactly what she said. She had told them to
mold the Institute to her own taste, to change it to a copy
of the standard Terran bureaucracy that she understood
and controlled so well.

And they were doing it. I was now convinced that
the real author of the message to me had not been
McAndrew. Lyle or Parmikan had structured it, with
Anna Griss behind them. Mac had asked for my help,
but *she* had been the manipulator. She wanted me on
board the *Hoatzin*, for a trip that she would control,
through Van Lyle and Stefan Parmikan, from beginning
to end.

What made me so sure? There's one point that I
neglected to mention about the run-in that we had with
Anna Griss out in the Oort cloud. McAndrew had cut
off her arm, which was bad enough but maybe forgiv-
able since he thought he was doing it to save her life.
But before that I had stared her down, overridden her
authority, and asserted my own position as ship's captain. She had been forced to accept it. But knowing
Anna, I knew that would never be forgiven, or forgotten. Not even when she had taken an eye for an eye—
or an arm for an arm.

I heard the door at the back of the room open. Jarver

was coming back in, and Lyle and Parmikan dutifully hurried back to his side. I shivered, and sat up straight in my seat. Something creepy had brushed by me in the past few minutes, and I didn't yet know what it was.

"So that's it," McAndrew was saying from the podium. "The two best candidates for the missing material needed to flatten the universe are *hot* dark matter—probably energetic neutrinos with a small rest mass, generated soon after the Big Bang; or maybe *cold* dark matter, particles like the axions needed for charge-parity conservation, or the photinos and other more massive objects required by supersymmetry theories.

"So which should we believe in, the hot or the cold? We don't know. They both have problems describing the way that the galaxies formed.

"Worse than that, we aren't measuring nearly enough of *either* kind of matter. Add everything together, and we still have less than half the mass density needed to make a flat universe. We must be badly underestimating either the cold dark matter or the hot.

"Which? Theory still can't provide the answer. Most of the events that decide all this began happening in the first 10^{-35} seconds after the origin of the universe, when we weren't around to do experiments; when even the laws of physics may not have been the same.

"We may never know the composition of the missing matter, until we can put our instruments in the right place for observation—deep in interstellar space."

He halted. Siclaro nodded his appreciation, and Mac came ambling back to his seat.

Naturally, he had missed the whole interaction with Lyle and Parmikan. He'd have missed it even if it had happened under his nose, because he never saw anything when he was talking about physics. He had temporarily forgotten his annoyance at the changes to the Institute, and he seemed quite pleased with life.

I wasn't. I had been brought to the Institute so that McAndrew and I could fly half a light-year from home with Lyle and Parmikan. Anna Griss had engineered my arrival. It was inconceivable that the surprises were all over.

What little goodies were in store when Anna's bully-boys and I were flying far off in the *Hoatzin*?

I lost track of that question in the busy days before departure. The *Hoatzin* was primed and ready, but I hadn't performed my engine inspection or any of the other preparations that I like to do. I went over the ship, checking everything, and found nothing worse than a slight imbalance in the drive that would have meant a mid-course correction at ship turn-around, a quarter of a light-year from Sol.

Neither Lyle nor Parmikan gave me any trouble. In fact, I hardly saw them until the four of us assembled for final check-in and departure. Then Stefan Parmikan rolled up with about ten times as much baggage as he was allowed.

He objected strongly when I told him to take it away. "All that space." He pointed outside, to the *Hoatzin* with its hundred meter mass disk and the four hundred meter axle sticking out like a great grey spike from its center. "There's oceans of room for my stuff."

How could a man reach adulthood today, and know so little about the McAndrew balanced drive?

"The disk you're pointing at is solid compressed matter," I said. "Density is twelve hundred tons per cubic centimeter, and surface gravity is a hundred and ten gees. If you want to strap your luggage on the outside of that, good luck to you."

"What about the axle? I can see that it's hollow."

"It is. And it has to stay that way, so the living-capsule can move up and down it. Otherwise we couldn't balance the gravitational and inertial accelerations. Either we move the capsule in closer to the disk as we increase the acceleration, or you tell me how we're going to survive a hundred gees." When he still didn't show much sign of understanding me, I waved my hand. "The total living accommodation of the *Hoatzin* is that four-meter sphere. I'm not going to spend the next month falling over your stuff. And I'm not going to waste time arguing. That luggage isn't going with us. That's final. Get it out of here, so we can prepare to board."

Parmikan glowered and grumbled, and finally dragged it away. When he reappeared an hour later with a much smaller package I hustled everyone onto the *Hoatzin* as quickly as possible to avoid any more hold-ups. Maybe I wasn't as thorough as I should have been inspecting luggage. But I suspect it would have done no good if I had been. There must be a definite threat before you start opening people's personal effects. I was anticipating rudeness and arguments and possible discipline problems, but not danger.

Let's call that my second mistake in Project Missing Matter.

Once we were under way I felt a lot better. With the drive on the perimeter of the mass disk turned on, the *Hoatzin* is surrounded by a sheath of highly relativistic plasma. Signals won't penetrate it. Communications with Anna Griss, or anyone else back in the Solar System, were blocked. That suited me fine.

By the end of the first twenty-four hours at full drive we were doing well. We were up to a quarter of light-speed, heading out from Sol at right angles to the plane of the ecliptic and already at the distance of Neptune. We had settled into a typical shipboard routine, each person giving the others as much space as possible. You do that when you know you have to spend a long time packed together into a space no bigger than a fair-sized kitchen.

And then, unexpectedly, our communications silence caused trouble.

The *Hoatzin* had been pleasantly quiet for hours. McAndrew had donned a suit, one of the new transparent models so light that you could sit in high vacuum and hardly realize you had a suit on at all.

He was going outside. Most people would be terrified at the prospect of leaving the capsule when the drive is on—if for any reason it turned off, the capsule would automatically spring out to the far end of the axle, to hold the interior field at one gee. But anyone not firmly secured to the capsule would fall at a hundred gee acceleration towards the mass disk. A quick end, and a messy one.

It never occurred to McAndrew that his inventions might fail. He had happily gone outside, for a status check of one of the new mass detectors that he would be using when we reached our destination in the middle of nowhere. We were heading for the region of lowest matter density known, out beyond the limits of the Oort cloud where we would find less than one atom per hundred cubic meters.

I was looking at the outside display screens, partly to scan the plume of plasma behind the *Hoatzin* for any sign of drive variability, and partly, to tell the truth, because I wanted to keep my eye on McAndrew. He doesn't believe the balanced drive can give trouble, despite the fact that its very first use nearly killed him.

While I had my attention on the screens, Stefan Parmikan crept up behind me. I didn't know he was there until I heard a soft, sibilant voice in my ear. "I am required to send a report to the Council every day, and be able to receive messages from them."

I jerked around. Parmikan's face was only a foot from mine. It was probably not his fault, but why was his mouth always so wet-looking?

"But Professor McAndrew tells me that we cannot send messages to Terra when the drive is turned on," he continued.

"Quite right. To Terra, or anywhere else. The signals can't get through."

"In that case, the drive must be turned off once every shipboard day."

"Forget it." I was a bit brusque, but Lyle and Parmikan seemed to have come along on the expedition without learning a thing about the ship, the drive, or anything else.

And Parmikan didn't sound like he was asking—he was telling. "We lose a couple of hours every time we turn power on and off," I went on. "And you'd have the living-capsule going up and down the axle like a yo-yo, to balance the change in acceleration from a hundred gee to zero. And anyway, once we're a long way out the signal travel time is so long the messages would be useless."

"But it is technologically feasible to turn off the drive, and to send and receive messages?"

"It is. And practically ridiculous. We won't do it."

Parmikan smiled his wet smile, and for once he appeared to be genuinely pleased about something.

"We will, Ms. Roker. Or rather, you will. You will turn the drive off once a day, for communication with Earth."

He drew a yellow document from his pocket, stamped prominently with the Council seal, and handed it to me.

Not *Captain* Roker. Ms. Roker. It took only a few seconds to scan the paper and understand what it was. I was holding Parmikan's appointment as captain of the *Hoatzin* for this mission. In all the excitement of preparing for our departure I had completely forgotten the original letter to me. An invitation to serve as *crew member* on the expedition, not captain. For the days before our departure I had instinctively and naturally assumed the senior position. And Lyle and Parmikan had been sly enough to go along with me, even addressing me as "Captain Roker" until we were on our way and it was too late to do anything about it.

"Well, Ms. Roker? Do you question the authority assigned by this document?"

"I question its wisdom. But I accept its validity." I scanned down the rest of the page. Parmikan's command extended from the time we left the Penrose Institute until the moment when we docked on our return. No loopholes. "I agree, you're the captain. I don't see anything here defining my duties, though, or saying that I'll agree to them. So if you want to turn the drive off yourself, without my help . . ."

Stefan Parmikan said nothing, but his sliding brown eyes met mine for one triumphant split-second. He reached into his pocket, pulled out a tiny playback unit, and turned it on.

"I'm reporting for duty right now," said a voice. It was my own.

"For the expedition described in Professor McAndrew's letter to you? But the mission and your role in it are not yet fully defined." That was Dorian Jarver.

"You can define that later. I'm here, and I'm ready to start."

There was a pause, as that section of the recording ended. Then Jarver's voice came again: "In accordance with Captain Jean Pelham Roker's earlier statement, this serves to define her duties on the *Hoatzin* mission identified as *Project Missing Matter*. Ms. Roker will serve as a general crew member, taking her orders and assignments from Captain Stefan Parmikan and from Senior Officer Van Lyle."

Set-up. But my own fault completely. I had felt bad vibrations the moment I met Parmikan and Lyle. Then I had gone right ahead and ignored my own instincts. Let's call that my third mistake.

McAndrew was climbing back in through the tiny airlock. I turned to him. "Mac, suppose we turned the drive off every day for a minute or two, long enough to send a burst mode message back to Earth. Allowing for the time we need to power the drive down and back up, how much would that add to our total trip?"

He stared at me for a moment, then his jaw dropped and his face took on a strange half-witted vacancy. That was fine. It just meant that he was off in his own world, thinking and calculating. I had given up trying to understand what went on inside McAndrew's head when he was solving a problem. Even though what I had asked him was straightforward and I could have done the calculation myself given a little time, I would bet money that he was not using any technique I'd have chosen. As one of the Institute members told me years ago, McAndrew has a mind that sees round corners.

"Five days," he said after a few seconds. "Of course, that's *shipboard* days. Two months Terran, allowing for time squeeze."

"Quite acceptable," said Parmikan. "Ms. Roker, please work out the necessary arrangements and bring them to me."

He turned and headed off for the private area of his own bunk, leaving me to fume and curse. And then, after a few minutes, to sit down and work out the best times for a regular interruption to the drive. I had to work it into other activities, so that Parmikan would make his daily call with minimum disruption to ship routine.

McAndrew came to me when I was almost finished. "Jeanie, I didn't catch on to what he wanted when you asked me that, or I'd have said it was hard to do. You don't have to take this sort of guff from him."

"I do." I picked up the results of my efforts, aware that Van Lyle had been watching me all the time I was working. "You know the first rule of space travel as well as I do: Like it or not, you can only have one captain. Parmikan is the captain of the *Hoatzin*."

I carried the schedule I had generated across to Parmikan's curtained rest area. The little private spaces allotted to each of us were intentionally set as far apart from each other as possible, around the perimeter of the living capsule. I rapped on the curtain rail. "This is my recommended schedule," I said, when Parmikan's head poked through. I held it out to him, but he did not take it.

"Is it a simple procedure?" he asked.

"I believe so. I've done my best to make it as simple as possible."

"Good. Then you should have no trouble carrying it out. Notify me when the drive is off, and we are ready for our first communication opportunity with Terra. By then I'll have another assignment for you."

His head vanished back through the curtain. I had an insight into Parmikan's style of command. He would give all the orders. I would do all the work. This was Anna Lisa Griss's revenge for my asserting my authority over her. I would have to obey Parmikan's every random whim for two months.

I was still naive enough to think that would be enough to satisfy her. My fourth mistake, was that? I'm beginning to lose count.

I stayed angry at being ordered around, until I remembered Lyle and Parmikan's general ignorance of shipboard matters. Then I thought, Hey, it's better like this. How would you feel if Parmikan took over the controls *himself*? And I went away to set up the program to power down the drive at regular intervals.

Except that McAndrew had heard my exchange with Parmikan, and he was feeling sorry for me. He insisted that he would do the tedious job of changing the drive program schedule. I let him. It was quite safe to do so, because Mac's such a perfectionist on this sort of thing that he sometimes makes me feel sloppy.

But Mac is only devious in scientific matters. He didn't catch something in the *Hoatzin*'s overall mission profile that I would have noticed at once.

I discovered it much later, and almost too late. Call that my fifth mistake, and let's stop counting.

To me, the interruptions to our outward progress were a useless nuisance. I have no idea what was sent or received by Parmikan and Lyle in their daily communications. I was specifically excluded from them, and in any case Parmikan had me far too busy with a hundred other things to worry much about messages—he had an absolute genius for thinking up demeaning and pointless tasks. I do know, though, that the person sending or receiving at the other end was not Dorian Jarver. The link was set up to a location on Terra, not to the Penrose Institute.

And McAndrew, being McAndrew, contrived to turn the periods when the drive was off into an opportunity.

He decided that he could use those few dead minutes every day to perform his first experiments. One morning right after breakfast I went to the rear of the living capsule to escape from Van Lyle—he, and his probing eyes, followed me everywhere. I found McAndrew sitting beside his instrument panel, frowning at the wall.

"Problems?"

He shrugged, and scratched at the back of his balding head. "I'd have said no. Everything passes the internal checks. But look at this." He pulled up a display. "I've got the most sensitive mass detectors ever, lined up on our final destination. All the other instruments confirm that there's absolutely nothing out there. But see these."

He pointed to small blips in the output level of the instruments.

"Noise?" I suggested. "Or the result of our high velocity? Or maybe a local effect, something on the *Hoatzin*?" He had told me that his new instruments were supernaturally sensitive to disturbance.

"No, they're definitely external, and far-off. And *regular*. That's just the signals I'd be getting if massive objects were flying, evenly spaced, across my field of view. Except there's nothing there. It's a total mystery."

"Then you'll just have to be patient. We're already past turn-around. In twelve days we'll be there, and you'll be able to see for your—"

"Crewman Roker!" It was Parmikan's voice, ringing through the living capsule. "Come here immediately. I have a task that must be performed at once."

I took a deep breath, and held it. Another fun-filled day was beginning. Twelve more to go, before we came to rest in the most perfect nothingness known to humans, half a light-year from the Sun.

With the whole habitable space of the *Hoatzin* only four meters across, I knew before we left the Institute that we'd be living close. But given the lack of privacy, there was one form of closeness I had never expected.

The surprise came late in the evening on the twenty-third day out, when Mac was in the shielded rear of the living capsule muttering over his still-anomalous instrument readings. The blips were growing. With Parmikan's consent Mac had gradually changed our course, angling the ship's direction of travel towards the strongest source of signal. We would arrive a tenth of a light-year away from our original destination, but as McAndrew pointed out, the choice of that had been more or less arbitrary. Any place where the matter density was unusually low would serve his purpose equally well.

By eleven o'clock Stefan Parmikan was asleep. I was sitting cross-legged on my bunk, listening to an Institute lecture from my talking library. It was "Modern Physics for Engineers," by Gowers, Siclaro, and McAndrew, a course designed to be less high-powered than the straight two-hundred-proof Institute seminar presentations. There were three other series available, of rapidly descending levels of difficulty. They each had official names, but inside the Institute they were known as "Physics for Animals," "Physics for Vegetables," and "Physics for Football Players."

I had brought all four, just in case, but I was holding my own with "Physics for Engineers." I was finally gaining a clearer idea of just why we had to charge off half a light-year from Sol.

Something was absent from the Universe, something that the best brains around thought had to be there: Missing matter.

The "bright stuff"—visible matter—isn't nearly enough to make the Universe hover on the fine line between expanding forever, and collapsing back one day to the Big Crunch. That's what the theorists want, but there's only about one percent of the mass needed in the bright stuff. You can pick up a factor of ten or so from matter that's pretty much the same as visible matter, but happens to be too cold to see, and that's all.

This leaves you about a factor of ten short on mass.

And there you stick. You have to start laying bets on other, less familiar materials.

Neutrinos moving up close to the speed of light—hot dark matter—are one candidate. There are scads of neutrinos around, generated soon after the Big Bang but damnably difficult to find by experiment. Neutrinos don't interact much with ordinary matter. They'd slip through light-years of solid lead, if you happened to *have* light-years of lead available. They're a candidate for the missing matter, but they're not the front runner. They don't give a Universe with the right lumpy structure, and anyway they come up short on total mass.

The other candidates are much slower and heavier than neutrinos. They're the cold dark matter school, axions and photinos and gravitinos, and *they* don't give the right lumpiness to the Universe, either. Even adding them to the neutrino mass, the whole thing still came up too small. McAndrew was saying, in effect, we've gone as far as theories can go. Let's get out there, where the experiments have a chance to succeed, and *measure* how much hot dark matter and cold dark matter is around. Then we'll know where we stand.

It was all fairly new to me. I was concentrating deeply, struggling with the theories of WIMPs—Weakly Interacting Massive Particles—when I was interrupted.

For the past three days I had been aware of Van Lyle hanging around me. I became a lot more aware of him when two arms suddenly went around me from behind, and two hands clasped my breasts.

"Hey, Jeanie," Lyle's voice whispered in my ear. "You've got lovely tits. It's going to be nice and quiet for a while. Want to get friendly?"

I jerked forward along the bunk, untangling my legs and trying to pull myself free. He was hanging on tight. That *hurt*.

"Get your damned hands off me." I wanted to say something a lot worse, but I knew we were going to be cooped up in the same space for another few weeks, no matter what. I had been trained to avoid onboard confrontations, and I wanted to stay cool and end this politely.

I swung around to face him and pushed myself away.

"Oh, don't be like that." He was grinning, a big, smarmy God's-gift-to-women grin. "Come on. Lighten up. We could have some real fun."

He reached out towards my breast again, and I pushed his hand away. "Quit that, Lyle! I tell you, I'm not having any."

"You haven't tried it. Lots of women could tell you, you won't be disappointed. Want to have a look at my testimonials?" And then, as I pushed his groping hand away again, this time when it reached towards my crotch, "Hey, Jeanie, you're *strong*. I just love strong women."

"You do, do you?" I'd had it. "*This* strong enough for you?"

I swung with all my body behind it as his face came forward, and got him with my fist right on the bridge of his nose.

It hurt like hell—hurt *me*, I mean. I didn't care how much it hurt him. But I don't think he enjoyed it, because as the blood spurted out of his flattened nose and splashed all over my bunk, he let out a terrible howl that brought McAndrew running.

Just as well, because by that time I was upright, off my bunk, and all set to kick Lyle in the balls at least ten times as hard as I'd punched his nose. McAndrew got in the way before I could do it. He leaned close to Van Lyle, a rag in his hand to mop up blood.

"What happened?"

Lyle produced only a horrible snorting noise.

"Tripped as he was coming in here," I said, "and banged his face on the edge of the bunk. Get the medical kit."

McAndrew glanced at the bunk as Stefan Parmikan finally appeared. I knew that Mac was doing an instant height and angle match, and rejecting it. But he never said a thing. Nor did Lyle, unless you count the groans when Parmikan was moving his broken nose around in an attempt to achieve a reasonably straight result.

We fixed the nose, more or less, and sedated Lyle. Parmikan went back to bed. During the sleep period, McAndrew leaned over the edge of my bunk and whispered to me. "Jeanie? I know you're awake. Are you all right?"

"I'm just fine." I didn't want him as furious as I was.

"He didn't bang himself on the bunk, did he? He made advances to you, and you hit him."

"What makes you think that?" Mac's insights were supposed to be into Nature, but not human nature.

"He was talking about you two days ago, when you weren't present. He said he wanted to take you to bed. Get a piece, he said."

"And you were *there*? Why for God's sake didn't you stop him? Tell him that you and I are lovers, have been for years."

There was a long, worried pause. "It wouldn't have been right, talking about you like that. And Jeanie, I don't *own* you, you know."

McAndrew, McAndrew. If I weren't so fond of you, I'd wring your scrupulous Puritan neck.

"But you know what?" he went on, "I'm afraid that it's going to make for a more difficult working atmosphere during the experiments."

It's a good thing it was dark, so I couldn't take a shot at *his* nose, too.

The first twenty-three days of the trip out had seemed pretty bad. I learned the next morning that the remaining five were going to be a lot worse—and then after that we had the period of McAndrew's experiments to look forward to, followed by a four-week return journey to the Institute.

The pattern was established on the twenty-fourth day. Van Lyle was back on his feet early. The bruise from his broken nose had mysteriously spread, to give him two purple-black eyes. With a white, rigid plaster across the middle of his face, he resembled a vengeful owl as he staggered out of his bunk. He glared around him.

"The inside of this capsule is dirty. It must be cleaned."

"It's not bad," I said. "It's just the way you'd expect the ship to look after three weeks."

"I'll be the judge of that." Lyle picked up a dish of soggy cereal, inverted it, and deliberately dropped it to the floor. "Get to work. This cabin first, then my quarters. I'll be back to inspect your progress this afternoon."

I held myself in—just. When Stefan Parmikan appeared ten minutes later, I had all the cleaning equipment out of the ceiling racks and ready for use.

He looked, not at me but past me. "What do you think you are doing?"

"Getting ready to clean the cabin. Following Officer Lyle's instruction."

"Very well. You can do that later. I need you to explain the procedure for ship automatic course tracking to me."

Unbelievable. Could it be that Stefan Parmikan was at last taking an interest in the way that the *Hoatzin* worked? I rose to follow him, but he turned and pointed to the cleaning equipment.

"Put those away first, back in the ceiling racks. I'm not going to spend the whole day falling over your stuff. And I'm not going to waste time arguing. You can get everything out again later."

It didn't help to recognize that Parmikan was quoting my own words, about the luggage of his that I had refused to allow aboard.

I began to put away the cleaning equipment, and thought favorably of Fletcher Christian.

No one on the *Hoatzin* seemed happy for the next five days. Parmikan and Lyle constantly tried to push me over the edge, and were constantly disappointed. They came close, but I certainly wasn't going to give them the pleasure of knowing *how* close.

And McAndrew, who should have been as happy as a pig because the time of his experiments had arrived, had become intense and introverted. The *Hoatzin* had homed in close to his strongest anomalous signal, but it did not seem to have resolved his problem.

"Look at this, Jeanie," he said, during one of my rare breaks from slavery. I had just checked that the ship had achieved its final location and velocity, and confirmed that we were at rest again relative to Sol. "These are *real-time* signals, happening right this minute. I've got instruments focused on a region only two light-seconds from here. You can see the visual display of it on the left half of the screen."

I looked. Other than a triangle of three bright reference stars, the visible wavelength display was blank.

"Nothing there," I said.

"Quite right. And now, the input from the mass detectors. They're set up to scan the same field, and I've got them in imaging mode focused for two light-seconds away." McAndrew popped the mass detector result on the right, as a split-screen display.

I stared. I expected to see nothing on the right side of the screen, either, and that's exactly what I saw. The region two light-seconds from us, where McAndrew's mass detection instruments were focused, was empty of matter—more empty, in fact, than any other known region.

"Well," I began to say. And then something impossible happened. The left-hand screen at visible wavelengths continued to show nothing but distant reference stars; but the screen displaying the mass imaging system inputs showed an object floating steadily across it, from top to bottom. The blob was clean-edged and irregular in shape, its outline like a fat, curved and pimpled cigar. It took maybe ten seconds from the first appearance on the top of the screen to its leisurely disappearance from the lower boundary. It must be moving at just a few miles a second relative to the *Hoatzin*.

"Mac, you've got the displays set up wrong. Those have to be showing different fields of view."

"They're not, Jeanie. I've checked a dozen times. They're showing the same part of the sky."

"Rerun it. Let me see it again."

"I don't need to. Wait twenty seconds, and you'll see another one. About one a minute."

We waited. At last a second shape, apparently identical to the first, came floating across the mass detector screen. And again the visible wavelength screen remained blank.

"Ultra-violet," I said. "Or infrared, or microwave . . ."

"I've checked them all. Nothing, from radiation or particle sensors. Only the signal from the mass detectors."

"So they're *black holes*. Kernels. They have to be."

"That's exactly what I thought, when we were a ways off and the signal was just a fuzzy blob with no structure. But just you look at the shape of that"—a third shape like a thick, warty banana was crossing the screen—"when you know as well as I do that any black hole has to have at least rotational symmetry. Those things have no axis of symmetry at all. And another thing. I did an *active* test. I sent a particle stream off to intercept one of those objects. If it were a black hole, you'd get a return radiation signal as the particles were gravitationally caught. But I got *nothing*. The particles went right on through as though there wasn't anything there at all."

I had a strange, prickly feeling up the back of my neck. We were observing nothing, a vacuum specter, a lost memory of matter. *By a knight of ghosts and shadows, I summoned am to tourney, ten leagues beyond the wide world's end* . . . Except that in our case, ten leagues had grown to half a light-year.

"Mac, they're *impossible*. They can't exist."

"They do, though." McAndrew's eyes were gleaming. I realized that I had mistaken his emotion. It wasn't frustration. It was immense, pent-up excitement and secret delight. "And now I've seen them in more detail, I know what they are."

"What, then?"

"I'll tell you—but not until we get a chance for a real close-up look. Come on, Jeanie."

He headed straight for Parmikan's private quarters, banged on the wall, and pulled the curtain to one side without waiting for an invitation. Parmikan and Lyle were both inside, heads close together. They had kept to themselves completely since the previous day, after an unusually long message to or from Earth. They jerked apart as McAndrew barged through.

"We want to move the *Hoatzin* a bit," he said without preamble. "And I have to go outside. I'd like Captain Roker to go with me."

If he was asking permission, calling me "Captain Roker" to Stefan Parmikan was the worst way to go about getting it. I expected an instant refusal. Instead a rapid glance passed between the two men, then Parmikan turned to McAndrew.

"What do you mean, move the ship?"

"Just a smidgeon, a couple of light-seconds. There's something I need to look at as part of my experiments. As soon as we're in the right position I need to take a couple of mass detectors outside with me and examine a structure. It will take a few hours, that's all. But it's a two-person job, and I'll need help."

I certainly didn't expect that Lyle or Parmikan would volunteer for the job of helper, but equally I didn't expect that they'd agree to my doing it—if I were outside, how could they give me disgusting chores? But Parmikan nodded his head at once.

"Right," said McAndrew. His diffident manner had vanished. "Jeanie, while I get the equipment ready I want you to take the *Hoatzin* to encounter one of the anomalies. Put us smack in the middle, and set us to hold at zero relative velocity."

I didn't argue. But as he went off to the rear of the living-capsule, I did exactly half of what he had requested. A small, watchful region of my brain was awakening, from

a slumber it must have been in ever since I decided to reply
to McAndrew's letter by flying straight to the Institute. Now
I closed in on one of the objects and set us to zero relative velocity—but I kept our ship a couple of kilometers
clear rather than providing McAndrew's requested encounter. He might know exactly what he was dealing with, and
be sure that it was safe. Until I had that knowledge, too,
I was going to regard any region of empty space occupied
by a mystery as possibly dangerous.

As I was completing my task I noticed a minor oddity in the operations of the *Hoatzin's* computer. The
program was functioning flawlessly, but as I directed each
change in position or speed, a status light indicated that
an extra data storage was being performed. The response
time was a fraction of a second longer than usual.

I'd probably have caught it when at Parmikan's insis-
tence we switched the drive on and off every day, but
Mac had programmed all those changes as a favor to me.
And if McAndrew had been ready to go outside at once,
I might have ignored it now. Instead, I took a look to
see where the generated data were being stored.

I found a Dummy's Delight.

The data I was creating were being placed in a trajectory control program of a type much despised by
professionals. It was the sort of thing that anyone could
use and no one ever did, because it was guaranteed to
be inefficient. In a Dummy's Delight, for every move
made by the ship the inverse move was generated and
stored. If the program were then executed, the ship would
return to its point of origin along whatever convoluted
trajectory it may have taken to fly out.

The program's only advantage was simplicity. One push
of a button, and all need for piloting went away.

But there was no way that *we* would fly back along
our original trajectory—there were much more efficient
thrust patterns. And I certainly hadn't given the command
to place the required data into the Dummy's Delight
before the *Hoatzin* left the Penrose Institute.

Had Mac done it? And if so, why?

My wariness node had started to work overtime. On impulse I wiped from memory the whole Dummy's Delight sequence, and left a message on the control screen: AUTOMATIC RETURN PROGRAM TO TERRA HAS BEEN ERASED BY CAPTAIN ROKER. It seemed reasonable when I did it, but I started to have second thoughts as I hurried to join McAndrew. He had his mass detector survey instruments working as free-standing units and was already in his suit.

"Mac." I waited until I had my own suit on, and was absolutely sure that we could not be overheard by Van Lyle or Stefan Parmikan. "Did you set up a Dummy's Delight in the *Hoatzin's* computer?"

He was busy, guiding the bulky detectors into the lock. "Now why would I do a daft thing like that?" he said, and vanished into the lock himself.

Why *would* he do a thing like that? I asked myself. Why would *anyone* do it?—unless they suspected that no competent pilot, like me or McAndrew, would be around to fly the *Hoatzin* on its return journey to Sol.

Paranoid? You bet. It's the only way to fly.

I emerged from the lock into that great forever silence that fills all the space between the stars. Sol was dwindled, indistinguishable from dozens of others. I picked it out from its position, not its superior brightness. The region I floated in appeared totally empty and featureless, despite the suit's vision enhancement systems. Particles were fewer here, the vacuum a little harder. But the human observer would never know the difference.

I glanced back at Sol. Look at the situation any way you liked; if I blew it and something went wrong, it was a long walk home.

I propelled myself gently away from the ship and towards McAndrew. He was staring at his mass detector readings in great irritation.

"Jeanie, you've made a mistake. We're kilometers away from the source."

"We certainly are. Two kilometers, to be exact. I know you can see right through it and it looks like nothing's there, but I want to approach this particular nothing very carefully."

He gave the patient sigh of a long-suffering martyr. "Ah, Jeanie. There's no *danger* here, the way you're thinking. I know just what this is."

"Maybe. But you haven't told me."

"I will, though, right now. It's *shadow matter*." And then, seeing my stare, "I'm surprised you've not heard of it."

"I know, Mac. I'm a constant disappointment to you. But I haven't. So tell me."

"It's wonderful. Right out of supersymmetry theory. Soon after the Big Bang—about 10^{-43} seconds after it, actually, before anything else we know about happened—*gravity* decoupled from everything else. Sort of like the way that radiation decoupled from matter, but the gravity decoupling happened much earlier. So then you had a symmetry breaking, a sort of splitting, and two types of matter were created: ordinary matter and shadow matter. Just like matter and anti-matter—except that matter and shadow matter can't interact by strong nuclear forces, or radiation, or the weak nuclear force. They can *only* interact by gravitational influence. You'd never detect shadow matter by firing particles at it. We proved that for ourselves. The particles feel the gravitational force, but that's tens of orders of magnitude too weak to do anything noticeable."

I stared at nothing, in the direction that the mass detectors were pointing. "You're saying that whatever is out there is as real as we are—but we can't see it?"

"Can't see it, never will be able to see it. Seeing depends on interaction with radiation. The only way to learn what we've found is through these." He pointed at the mass detectors. "We're safe enough, as I said. But we have to do some detailed mapping. Who knows what that is out there? It could be a shadow matter star—we don't have any idea how big a star might be in that universe, or what the laws of force are. Or maybe we're detecting a set of interstellar shadow matter spaceships, or a column of shadow matter ants marching in a shadow matter superworld.

"You think I'm joking, but I'm not. It could be anything. The only way we'll get any idea what we've found is by plotting structure. That's why I need you—it's a two-person job, to make transects."

We're safe enough, he had said. But maybe only while we were outside the *Hoatzln*.

"Mac, before we start your work we've got to talk. I think we have a bad problem." I told him about the Dummy's Delight on the ship's computer.

He frowned through his suit visor. "But why would they waste data storage on a thing like that?"

"So they could get home, even if something happened to both of us." I took the last mental step, the one I had been resisting. "Mac, we're not intended to return from this trip. The plan is for us to vanish while we're out here. If the drive of the ship were turned on now, who'd ever know what had happened to us?"

He turned to stare at the *Hoatzin*. "They wouldn't *dare*."

"Not now they wouldn't. I wiped the program they were relying on to fly them back. So they need us." *Or one of us*. But I didn't say that. "We're safe enough for the moment."

"But what about when we go back inside? We can't stay out here forever."

"I don't have an answer for you. We've got enough air for six or seven hours. We have to think of something— soon."

We *had* to think of something. But we didn't succeed. My mind stayed blank. McAndrew is a superbrain, but not when it comes to this sort of problem. After half an hour floating free not far from the ship, he shook his head.

"It's got me beat. But this is silly. There's no point in sitting here doing nothing. We might as well get on with the measurements."

He placed one mass detector in my care, with its inertial position sensor tuned to the *Hoatzin* as reference, and started to steer me under his direction from one fixed place to another, while he moved himself in constant relative motion. He apparently knew exactly what he wanted. That was just as well. My own thoughts were all on the situation aboard the ship. What would we do when our air ran low?

I worried that problem with no result while McAndrew made four straight-line passages, right through the middle of the kilometer-wide region that he described as shadow matter. The mass detectors confirmed that something was there. I saw absolutely nothing.

On the fifth passage through, McAndrew paused halfway. He called to me to move closer, while he carried his own detector through a complicated spiral in space. At the end of it he left his mass detector where it was, flew across to me, and examined the recording on my instrument.

"Well, I'm damned," he said. "Jeanie, I think you were right. Stay there." And leaving me mystified and feeling about as intelligent as a marker post, he flew away. This time he moved his mass detector through an even more complex path in space, pausing often and proceeding very cautiously.

"I've still no idea what this is, overall," he said when he came back. "But I'll tell you one thing for sure. There are structures in shadow space that I've never met in our spacetime."

"Right about *what*?" I asked. "You just said I was right. But what was I right about?"

"That we ought not to set the ship in the middle of that, without knowing more about it. I'm seeing evidence of gravitational line singularities, or something very like them, running across the shadow matter region. You don't find those in our universe. If we had flown in too close to one of them, we might have found ourselves in trouble."

"You mean we're not in trouble *now*? With Lyle and Parmikan waiting for us."

"I've been thinking about that, too." He came close, and his face was earnest and unshaven within his visor. "I think you're overreacting. There's no evidence at all that Lyle and Parmikan even knew there was a Dummy's Delight set up in the *Hoatzin's* computer. And certainly there's no evidence they mean us any harm. But *anyway*," he went on, before I could interrupt, "one thing's for sure: When we go back in the lock, I should enter first while you stay outside. I know both of them, they respect me, and they'll not do anything to hurt me."

McAndrew is a pathetically bad liar. I didn't argue with him. But when we were a few meters from the lock I said, "You've got it backwards. *I'm* the one they won't hurt, because they need a pilot to get home. And you don't know how to work our only weapon. Don't stand too near the hatch of the lock."

I dived for the airlock, pulled myself inside, and swung it closed in one movement, leaving Mac to bang on the outside. While the lock was filling with air I did a little work of my own. It required that three separate safety procedures be overridden, so it took a few minutes. At last I moved forward to open the inner lock door, then jumped back at once to stand by the outer one.

I didn't know what I was expecting. Lyle and Parmikan, going about the normal business of the ship, with a stack of messy chores ready for me? Or waiting to complain that I had for no reason at all wiped out a program that one of them had set up in the computer, for a wholly innocent purpose?

What I hadn't expected was a projectile weapon, held in Van Lyle's hand and pointed right at my belly-button. I rammed my left fist down on the lock control, as the thought flashed through my head that there should have been a more thorough luggage inspection when we boarded the *Hoatzin*.

I moved as fast as I could, but they had been ready and waiting. I was too slow. Lyle pressed the trigger.

As he did so two things happened. Parmikan smacked at Lyle's hand and screamed, "Don't kill her! We need her to get us back." That saved me, spoiling Lyle's aim. In the same moment the outer lock door, its final safety trigger broken by the force of my fist, blew outward in a rush of air.

I flew out with it, knowing that my last-ditch plan to fight back had failed. I was hit. And my secret weapon was useless, because Lyle and Parmikan were already wearing suits.

I felt the fainting weakness that comes with a sudden drop of blood pressure. Then my suit resealed, and a few seconds later McAndrew was grabbing at me to halt my spin. He had followed me as I emerged in that crystal cloud of cooling air.

I felt pain for the first time, and looked down. Half the calf of my left leg was missing. The automatic tourniquet had cut in and tightened below the knee. The flow of blood from the wound had already stopped. I would live—if we somehow survived the next few minutes.

Which didn't seem likely. Lyle and Parmikan had emerged from the lock, and Lyle still had his gun. He raised it. And shot me again.

Or he would have done, had he been the least bit familiar with freefall kinematics and momentum conservation. Instead the recoil of his gun sent him rolling into a backward somersault, while the bolt itself flew who knows where.

Before Lyle could sort himself out and fire again, McAndrew was dragging me away, using his suit propulsion system at maximum setting to carry both of us along. One nice thing about Mac, he didn't need much data to form a conclusion.

"Don't try a long shot." That was Parmikan to Lyle, over the suit radio. "She's injured. Get in close. Then we finish him and grab her. But *don't kill her*—she's taking us home."

"I won't kill her." That was Lyle, the white plaster on his nose vivid through the suit's visor. "Not 'til I'm done with the bitch. She'll wish she was dead before that."

They were coming after us, knowing that we had no place to hide. It was our misfortune to find ourselves, weaponless and pursued, in the emptiest quarter of known space. Nowhere to run to, and soon we would be out of air.

McAndrew was retreating anyway, dragging me along with him, but not in a simple, straight-line run. We were zigzagging up and across and sideways, rolling all over the sky; which made good sense if you were trying to evade being shot, and no sense at all when your enemy had just declared that he would not shoot until he got close.

Then we stopped dead. Mac glanced all around him, sighting for Parmikan and Lyle, the two mass detectors just where we had left them, and the shape of the *Hoatzin*, further off. He lifted us a few meters upward, and halted again.

"Here we are, then," he muttered. "And here we stay."

Lyle and Parmikan hadn't moved while Mac and I had been corkscrewing our way around in space. Now they started towards us. Soon I could see their faces, white in the reflected glow of the visors' built-in instruments.

Still McAndrew didn't move. The feeling of distance and unreality that had swamped me the moment I was shot started to fade. At last I was scared. But when I started my propulsion system, ready to take off again away from the advancing men, Mac held out his hand to stop me.

"No, Jeanie. Hold by, and don't move."

They were closing on us. Parmikan was two or three meters in the lead. Lyle still held the gun, but he had learned his lesson. He would not fire again until he was at point-blank range, too close to be thrown off in his aim by the effects of free-fall rotation.

"Mac!" We couldn't stand still and be slaughtered like sheep. I swung to argue with him, and saw the expression on his face. He was agonized and biting his lower lip. "Mac, come on. We can't just give in."

But he was shaking his head at me. "I'm sorry, Jeanie," he said. "This isn't me. I can't go through with it. No matter what happens next, I have to give them a chance." And he lifted his arm towards Lyle and Parmikan. "Don't come any closer. Stay right there. You are in terrible danger."

That stopped them—for a second or two. They stared all around, and saw nothing. Lyle snorted through his broken nose, while Parmikan laughed aloud for the first time since I had met him.

"Don't try that on us, McAndrew," he said. "We weren't born yesterday. If you stand still, I promise you'll get yours clean and quick."

He was moving forward again. My suit's vision enhancement showed the grin on his shapeless mouth. He looked as happy as I had ever seen him. And then the clean white of his suit was broken by a thin black line that ran across Stefan Parmikan from hip to hip, about two inches below his navel.

He stared down at himself as the line widened. He started to scream, and tried to back up.

It was too late. His motion carried him forward. As it did so he *shrank*, shortening and squeezing in towards his hips. The thin black line became a rolling tunnel of red and purple across his whole body. Twisted internal organs were moving into it from above and below. Then Parmikan had passed all the way through.

The scream ended. A pair of legs, still held together at the top, came floating on towards us. Separate from it moved a torso, cleanly severed. Blood gouted out and froze as a fine icy spray.

Lyle, a few meters behind, had enough time to stop. He paused, still holding the gun.

"Hand that over." I summoned what little energy I had and spoke over the suit radio before McAndrew had time to react. And then, when Lyle hesitated, I said, "Hand it over *right now*. Or get just the same as he did."

He hardly seemed to be listening. His eyes were following the horror of Parmikan's severed body. But he nodded and released the gun, which floated gently away from him.

It's a measure of how far gone I was that I actually started out towards it, until McAndrew grabbed me.

"You stay where you are, too," he said. "And Lyle, don't move a millimeter until we come around and get you. There's other gravitational line singularities through this whole volume."

We began to move again, McAndrew hauling me along like ballast in a strange helical path that wound its way towards Van Lyle. Finally McAndrew was able to reach out and snag the gun.

"All right." He waved it at Lyle, then towards the *Hoatzin*. "We've got a clear run from here to the ship. You start that way. And remember that I understand freefall ballistics a lot better than you do. I won't miss."

The three of us drifted slowly back to the lock, but McAndrew would not let Van Lyle enter. He handed me the gun. "You first, Jeanie. Can you fix the lock so it works?"

"I think so." I moved inside. "I just have to reset the safety interlocks."

I made it sound trivial, and it should have been. But I kept half blacking-out before I was done and able at last to refill the interior of the *Hoatzin* with air.

It seemed forever before the lock cycled again. I wondered and stayed tense. I had the gun. Suppose Lyle had taken advantage of that and overpowered McAndrew?

I dropped those worries when Lyle emerged from the inner lock. His manner and bearing were of a crushed man with no fight left in him. I made him take his suit off, but I kept my own on until McAndrew finally came through the lock.

He didn't give Lyle a look. He came straight across to me and examined my injured leg.

"I'm sorry, Jeanie," he said, as he helped me ease out of my suit. "I know I put us in danger, warning them the way I did. If Parmikan had stopped in time we might have been killed. But I couldn't let them go on moving into that line singularity, without giving them at least a chance to stop. I just couldn't do that. You'd have done the same thing, wouldn't you?"

"Of course I would."

Like hell. If it had been up to me, Lyle would be floating around in two halves, the same as Stefan Parmikan. But then, compared with McAndrew I'm a barbaric, vengeful throwback. "Don't worry about it, Mac. What you did was the right thing."

I winced, as the suit came free from my calf and caught on crusted blood. "So whose idea was it, Van Lyle?" I said. "Who decided that on this expedition, McAndrew and I wouldn't be going back?"

He had been sitting slumped over, staring at the floor. He looked up, opened his mouth to speak, then changed his mind. He shook his head.

I didn't blame him. When we arrived home he would be charged and surely convicted; but nothing the system authorities could do to him was half as bad as Anna Lisa Griss's vengeance if he betrayed her.

McAndrew had gone across to the capsule's medical center and was returning with two spray syringes. "I'm going to put you under, Jeanie, while I dress your leg," he said. "You'll have to wait until we're home for a full repair. But first, to be safe . . ."

He went to Van Lyle and pressed the loaded syringe against the back of the stooped man's neck. Lyle tried to stand up, with a startled expression on his face. It was already too late.

"Better if we keep him under all the way back," Mac said,

as after a few struggling seconds Lyle slid forward and fell face-down on the floor. "That way we don't have to worry."

I wasn't worrying. I was going to be next, and physically I was ready for it. My calf was beginning to throb mercilessly. Still I held up my hand in protest. "Mac, wait a minute. We shouldn't head back until you've finished your experiments. And you've hardly started."

He moved behind me. "Don't be daft, Jeanie. I can come here anytime. And I surely will. There's big questions to be answered. I need to map the structure of those shadow matter objects in more detail. And now we've got another candidate for the hidden matter. How much is cold dark matter, how much hot dark matter, how much *shadow* matter?"

The cool nozzle of the syringe touched the back of my neck, and the spray diffused through my skin. I felt the effect at once as a pleasant, relaxing warmth that spread through my whole body.

"Mac," I said, as the capsule of the *Hoatzin* began to blur around me. "You saved us, but I don't know how you did it. How did you know where to go, to put that gravity singularity right between us and those two?"

"Easy enough," he said. "I had the measurements from the mass detectors. That made it a standard problem of inverse potential theory: Given the field, where are the masses needed to generate it? I already felt sure that there were line singularities of shadow matter, ones that would work—gravitationally—on anything in our universe that encountered them. But just where were they? I worked that out while you were inside the lock, playing your fun and games with Lyle and Parmikan. Of course, I had to make simplifying assumptions and hope they wouldn't affect the answer. And it would have been really nice to have a computer. But there was no time for that. I did what I could."

I did what I could. What he had done, in the few minutes before I was blown out of the lock in a gust of freezing air, was to solve, mentally, a problem that would have taken me half a day to set up, and a computer to solve. And he had done it while knowing that the next half hour might end his own life.

Cold Dark Matter, Hot Dark Matter, Shadow Matter. The words spun through my mind as the world darkened, and McAndrew's earnest face faded before my eyes. *Cold Dark Matter, Hot Dark Matter, Shadow Matter.*

Which one had dominated our past, to create the present structure of the Universe?

I had no idea. All I knew for sure as I slid into unconsciousness was that the *future* of our Universe was going to be dominated by *cool grey matter*; the sort that McAndrew and a few rare others like him have between their ears.

SIXTH CHRONICLE:

The Invariants of Nature

"I must say it was a surprise to me that you came here at all," Van Lyle said pleasantly. "You really have to hand it to the Director. Anna Griss predicted all of this, you know—the effect of the announcement, McAndrew's arrival, and then yours. Very perceptive of her. But, then, isn't that exactly why she has the job of Administrator, and we do not?"

He was standing in front of a huge pair of metal doors, checking a set of dials built into the frame. On the other side of them lay the processing vats, where all organic tissues—muscles, bones, nails, skin and hair—were dissolved to basic biotic molecules. Warning signals were splashed all over the chamber, and on both the doors: CONTROLLED ACCESS—DANGER, CORROSIVE GASES AND LIQUIDS—DO NOT PROCEED WITHOUT PROTECTIVE SUITS—OFFICIAL DEPARTMENT REPRESENTATIVES ONLY PERMITTED BEYOND THIS POINT.

Van Lyle turned to me questioningly. "Impressive, wouldn't you say? Don't be coy, Captain. I'd really like to hear your opinions on all this."

I rolled my eyes at him. I was sitting upright in a metal wheelchair. My wrists and elbows were bound to the chair arms with broad fiber tape, the sort that is hard to unstick and just about impossible to break. My lower legs were lashed to the chair's metal struts with the same material. A broad sticky strip of it covered my face, from just below my nose to the point of my chin.

"Ah, I see the problem," Lyle went on. "But are you ready to talk nicely now, and not make a fuss?"

I nodded—one of the few degrees of freedom available to me.

Van Lyle nodded back. "Very good! And just in case you feel tempted to change your mind, let me point out that it would be quite pointless. This part of the installation is all automated. No one is here but the two of us."

He came across to me and touched one end of the tape that covered my mouth. But instead of pulling it loose, he paused to run his fingers along one side of my nose, and back down the other.

"What a nice, shapely adornment," he said. "Not at all like mine, eh? Before we finish, we'll have to do something about that."

I hadn't realized until that moment just how much he hated me. His nose was bent and slightly flattened, detracting from his rugged blond good looks. The mouth beneath the crooked nose twisted with anger as he ripped the tape away from my mouth.

I worked my lips against each other, wincing. A layer of skin had been torn away by the super-adhesive tape, along with every fine hair on my face. I felt a trickle of blood down my chin.

The less discussion of noses, though, the better. I had broken Van Lyle's, half a light-year away from Sol, when he wouldn't take his lecherous hands off me. That had been long ago, but unfortunately he didn't seem willing to forget it.

"You know McAndrew," I said. "All it took was the right

word, and he was ready to head for Earth. Nothing that I said could stop him from coming."

"So I understand." Lyle nodded. "But you, Jeanie—surely you're much more sophisticated than that? I would have bet money against you following him down here."

Van Lyle's calling me Jeanie made my flesh crawl, but he was right. I didn't have the excuse that Mac had, the siren song, the magic words that had left him helpless: *a new invariant of nature.*

"You don't understand," I said. "I've spent half my life chasing after Mac when he got into trouble. By now it's second nature. But usually it's to some place halfway to the stars—not a trip down to Earth."

I had no real interest in telling any of this to Van Lyle, true as it might be. I was merely stalling, postponing the moment when he would tape my mouth again and carry out the next stage of the proceedings. I had little doubt what that was going to be. Lyle hadn't hauled me down to this processing plant, far offshore and a hundred meters beneath the surface of the sea, just to show off the advanced technology of Earth's Food Department.

It was also a very bad sign that he had mentioned the name of Anna Griss. In the past he had always refused to admit that he worked for her.

I wondered what he was waiting for now. It shows how desperate I was feeling, but I actually hoped he might be planning another shot at raping me. Let him do anything—anything that might provide enough time for help to arrive, or give me a thin chance of resistance. That was better than being strapped in the wheelchair, able only to move my head and trunk from side to side.

I didn't have much hope. This wasn't my environment, it was theirs. I might have an edge in deep space, but down on Earth, Van Lyle and Anna Griss held home field advantage.

And suddenly I had no hope at all. Because I heard the steel doors at the back of the chamber open, the ones through which I had been wheeled in. There was the squeak of unoiled bearings, and a few seconds later another wheelchair was rolled alongside mine.

McAndrew sat in it, his legs and arms tied to the chair's metal struts, not by sticky tape but by thick, knotted cords. His mouth was not covered.

He stared across at me miserably. "I'm sorry, Jeanie," he said. "I really am. This is all my fault, every bit of it."

I tried to smile at him, and winced at raw, stripped skin. My lips began to bleed again. "Don't feel bad, Mac," I mumbled. "If it's your fault, it's my responsibility."

It had started at the Penrose Institute, over a month ago. I had been on the way home after a routine Europan delivery run. Orbital geometries happened to be favorable, so it was the most natural thing in the world for me to drop in on McAndrew. The Institute, after a disastrous couple of years of bureaucratic rule, was once more under the steady but informal guiding hand of old Dr. Limperis, dragged out of retirement to put things right. I wanted to see how everything was going, and renew old acquaintances.

I headed straight for Mac's working quarters. He was not there. Instead, Emma Gowers was loafing in his favorite chair and staring at a display.

"Off in the communications center," she said. "He'll be back in a few minutes. You might as well wait here." She was as blond, beautiful and blowzy as ever. And presumably as brilliant. She was the Institute's resident expert on multiple kernel arrays.

"Is he all right?" I asked. Mac usually had to be dragged out of his own office, unless he was off somewhere running an experiment.

"Oh, he's fine." Emma pushed her mass of blond hair higher on her head. "But you know McAndrew. He's got another pet project going. You can hardly talk to him any more."

I nodded. It was the most natural thing in the world

to find McAndrew in the grip of a new scientific obsession. He would be delighted to see me, I knew that. But he might also be only vaguely aware of my presence.

I sat down next to Emma. "What is it this time?"

"There's talk of a new fundamental invariant. I'm skeptical, frankly, but he's a believer—at least enough to want to check it out for himself."

"Educate me, Emma. What do you mean, a fundamental invariant?"

Simple explanations were not Dr. Gowers' forte. She frowned at me. "Oh, you know. Things that don't change under transformation. Like the determinant of a linear system under orthogonal rotation, or the Newtonian equations of motion with a Galilean transformation, or Maxwell's equations with a Lorentz transformation."

It's an odd thing about Emma Gowers. Her own taste in men is for primitive specimens, dim and hairy objects who apparently decided to stop evolving somewhere in the early Pleistocene. Yet she insisted on assuming that McAndrew and I were on the same intellectual plane, just because we were long-time intimates.

"Uh?" I wanted to say; but I was saved from new admissions of stupidity and ignorance by McAndrew's own bustling arrival.

"Using my chair *and* my data banks again, Emma," he said. "Out, out, out." And then to me, as though we had not been separated for months, "Jeanie, this is perfect timing."

Most people think that I tolerate behavior in McAndrew that I would never stand in any other human being, just because he's a genius. He is that, the best combination of theorist and experimenter to arise in physics since Isaac Newton—at least, that's what those few equipped to make the evaluation all tell me. But genius has nothing to do with my own tolerance of Mac, or his of me.

I can't do better than to say that we click. We are very different, but we touch at just enough points to make us stick.

McAndrew puts it differently. "A hydrogen bond," he has said to me, often enough to make it irritating. "Not an *ionic* bond, that's all set and rigid, or even a *covalent* bond, where things are actually shared. No. We're a *hydrogen* bond, loose and fluid and easy-going."

I'll just say that we like each other. And if he thinks I'm so dim that everything he says to me about science has to be deliberately "dumbed down," and if I think he is so wrapped up in abstractions that he ought not to be allowed outside in the real world without a keeper—well, that's acceptable to both of us.

This time he responded to my hug, but in an automatic and absent-minded way. "If you're heading inward," he went on, "as I suspect you are, then I'll hitch a ride with you."

The space structure that houses the Penrose Institute is mobile, and at the time of my visit it was again drifting free, well outside the orbit of Mars. But *inward*? Mac's interests usually lay well beyond the edge of the Solar System.

"To Earth," he explained. And, as my eyebrows rose, "Och, don't worry, I'm not asking you to come with me. Drop me off at a libration point, Jeanie. That will do fine."

He knew my aversion to Earth, overcrowded and noisy and smelly. But I had always thought that he shared it, and he and I had other good reasons to avoid going there. One of Earth's most powerful people was Anna Griss, former head of Earth's Food Department, and now Administrator of the full Food and Energy Council. Mac had cut off her arm with a power laser, out in the Oort cloud. It had been done with the best of intentions, and it had saved her life; but I knew Anna. She would not have forgotten, or forgiven.

As for me, I had been a target for her hatred since the same trip, perhaps even more so, because I had challenged her authority—and proved her wrong.

It's no surprise that there are people like Anna Griss in the world. There always have been. Go back fifty thousand years, to a time when most of us were just grubbing along, looking for a decent bush of ripe berries or a fresher lump of meat. A few, like McAndrew, were busy inventing language or numbers, or painting the walls of the cave. And some, just a handful but too many in every generation, were seeking an edge over the rest of us: Water access, or mating rules, or restricted entry to heaven. No matter how few they were, Anna Griss would have been one of them.

So McAndrew knew very well what I was driving at when I stared at him and said, "Earth? Do you think that's a good idea?"

"It's a must," he said. "I'm going to visit the Energy Council. To be specific, I'm going to the laboratory of Ernesto Kugel, where there is evidence that something wonderful has been discovered: a new Invariant of Nature."

You could hear the capital letters.

"Told you so," said Emma Gowers. And she stood up, tugged her short dress down as close to her dimpled knees as it would go, and swept out.

If McAndrew's words were designed to impress me, they failed.

"Mac," I said. "With me, three invariants and a dollar will get you a cup of coffee."

"You're a barbarian, Jeanie," he said amiably. "I'm just using the term that Kugel used: *a new invariant of nature*. Would it help if I rephrased that, and said that he claims to have found an important new conservation law?"

It did help, because I have been around McAndrew for a long time. But it didn't help much.

"New, how?" I asked. "I mean, I know that energy is conserved, and momentum is conserved—"

"In a closed system."

"In a closed system, fine. But how can there be a *new* conservation law?"

"Well, that's where things get interesting. Now and again, physicists realize that certain things that they used to think of as independent are actually different aspects of the same thing. For example, a few hundred years ago, heat and motion and light used to be thought of as quite separate entities. But then, after lots of work by people like Rumford and Joule and Kelvin, scientists realized that those separate things were all forms of *energy*. And though different types of energy can be converted, one to another, they decided that the total could never be changed. That was the principle of conservation of energy.

"Starting with the work of chemists like Lavoisier, people also observed that mass is conserved, too, in every form of physical and chemical reaction. So you had conservation of energy, and you had conservation of mass. But the big breakthrough came in 1905, when Einstein showed that mass and energy are equivalent, and that their *total* is the thing that is conserved, rather than either one. And he also showed that it didn't matter which reference frame you use for the measurements. The energy-momentum four-vector is invariant. That single principle helped to unify the whole field of physics.

"The same thing happened with angular momentum. For a while it looked as though it wasn't conserved in nuclear reactions. But then workers in quantum theory found that an *internal* angular momentum had to be added to the picture for many particles—spin—and after that angular momentum became a fully conserved quantity. That, too, was a terrific generalizing idea. Did you know that in 1931 Pauli deduced the existence of a new particle, the neutrino, just because the principles of conservation of energy and of angular momentum required that it exist?"

"I did know that, Mac"—once—"and you haven't answered my question. I realize very well that there are conservation principles. But how can there possibly be a *new* one?"

"I can give you two possible answers to that. The first is that the physical laws of the universe, as we already know them, admit some conserved quantity that we simply haven't recognized yet."

"Isn't that unlikely?"

"You might think so, after all the time and effort we've put into searching for that sort of invariance principle, for the past hundred and fifty years, with nothing to show for it. But there's another possible answer, one that at first doesn't sound much more likely. It could be that Ernesto Kugel's lab has discovered a new fundamental form of physical law."

McAndrew was starting to make sense to me, which should have been a tipoff right there that something was about to go wrong. Usually, the longer that we talk, the more confused I become.

"You mean, a new force? Something like discovering gravity for the first time?"

"That will do nicely. We happen to have been aware of gravity for as long as humans existed, and we've had theories of it for over five hundred years. We've known the electromagnetic force for three centuries, and the strong and weak forces that govern nuclear interactions for just a couple. But gravity is actually a very weak force, something we only feel because very large bodies are involved. Suppose that we had evolved as tiny creatures, no bigger than fleas, in the middle of an energetic plasma? Then gravity wouldn't have much immediate effect on our lives. We'd have learned about electromagnetism early, but we might still not know about gravity."

I was finally getting the head-swirling buzz that usually accompanied a McAndrew explanation. "But we *didn't* evolve smaller than fleas, in the middle of a plasma."

"No. But different environments make it easy to detect different forces."

"But less than a year ago you were telling me that the place to look for new laws of nature is out in deep space where we've never been, out where the sun and planets don't interfere with observations."

"I did say that. But suppose I'm *wrong*. Wouldn't that be exciting, Jeanie? A new law of nature, sitting there under our noses all this time, and detectable down on the surface of Earth."

And there you had it. Most people hate to learn that they are wrong. Not McAndrew. When he's proved wrong, he's ecstatic. It means he's learned something new, and that's his main reason for existence.

But I still hated the idea that he'd be going to Earth. "This Ernesto Kugel. If he's in the Energy Department, that means he works for Anna Griss."

"So?"

"Do you know him?"

"Not personally. But I know his work, very well. Ernesto Kugel built the *Geotron*."

Capital letters again. I resisted the urge to be distracted by that. "Is he the sort of person you believe might make a fundamental new discovery?"

"Oh, no."

"Well . . ."

"Not *him*. He's an engineer—and a first-rate one—but he's no physicist. Someone in his lab would have done the work. Someone I don't know. Kugel would probably put his own name on the report just to make people pay attention."

"But surely you don't think that some total *unknown* would have come up with a big scientific breakthrough?"

"Jeanie, the big breakthroughs *always* come from some total unknown. And genius can pop up anywhere. Kugel got lucky."

"Maybe. But Kugel works for Anna Griss, and she hates your guts. Don't you remember what you did to her?"

"Ah, away with you." He ran his fingers through his thinning hair. "Jeanie, I'm sure that's all long forgotten. The invitation to visit Kugel's lab was *approved* by Anna. She signed off on it."

"Did she?" I said. "Well, of course that makes everything fine, doesn't it?"

I should have known better. Irony is totally wasted on McAndrew.

He beamed at me. "I knew you'd see it my way when you had the facts, Jeanie. How soon can we leave?"

✧   ✧   ✧

I think my inner voices are pretty good when it comes to warning of trouble. The problem is, I don't always listen to them.

This time I allowed another event to occupy my mind when I ought to have been worrying about McAndrew's visit to Earth. In my own defense, I must say that the intrusion came from outside. When the linked spheres of the Assembly were halfway to Earth, with Mac and me cozy in the Control Section, I received a message from Hermann Jaynsie at the United Space Federation Headquarters.

It was long and wordy, because Hermann is long and wordy, but I can boil it down. It said, in essence, "What the devil did you do, Captain Roker, on your last cargo haul from the Jovian system to Earth? We thought we had a deal with them for four billion tons of vegetable foodstuffs, grown in our Europan ocean farms. Now Earth is telling us they don't want to take delivery of any more shipments."

The lightspeed round-trip travel time to USF Headquarters was seven minutes, so I couldn't exactly chitchat back and forth. But I did send him a pretty long reply, which again can be boiled down to, "Damned if I know, Hermann. They seemed happy enough with what I dropped off last time."

My livelihood wasn't hurt by the cancellation of a food supply contract with Earth; but my ego was, and I spent a good deal of time fuming. Was it Anna Griss, getting at me in a remarkably indirect way? I knew she was capable of subtle malice. But I still looked for a more logical explanation. I couldn't see even Anna risking Earth's food supply just to get at me.

I had no intention of going to Earth, or wasting another minute thinking of Ernesto Kugel and his mysterious invariant. So when we arrived at the Colony drop-off point, where the Assembly would be moored until its next trip out, McAndrew and I went our own ways. He headed down on a shuttle, as excited as a child on his way to a birthday party. I mothballed the ship, and handed it over to the local USF maintenance crew.

That took me three days. And then on the fourth morning, without thinking about what I was doing, I found myself aboard a shuttle vessel.

Heading for Earth.

I had been given a number to reach McAndrew, and I forwarded a message to tell him that I was on the way, and when and where I would arrive. I didn't ask, but I rather hoped he might be waiting for me.

He wasn't. And it was one of life's less pleasant experiences to pass through entry formalities, search for Mac's face, and see Van Lyle waiting for me on the other side of the barrier.

"Captain Jeanie Roker." He reached out and took my hand. "It's been a while."

I shook his hand, but my feelings must have showed on my face, because he laughed and said, "Don't say anything. You did what you did, and I thoroughly deserved it. Let bygones be bygones."

But he touched his fingertips to his bent nose.

I said, "McAndrew—"

"Is having too much fun, Captain, to tear himself away from the Geotron facility. He asked me to come to the port, and take you there to join him."

It sounded awfully plausible. But I couldn't put the past behind me as easily as he claimed to have done. "Professor McAndrew *asked* you to come and meet me?"

Instead of answering, Lyle took a palm-sized phone from his pocket and tapped in a string of numbers. "Four one seven," he said into the unit. After a few seconds' pause he handed me the phone.

I found myself staring into the tiny screen at a familiar high-cheekboned face. His wispy hair was sticking up in little random spikes, and his color was a fraction ruddier than usual. I couldn't see his fingers, but I could bet that he was cracking the joints.

"Jeanie," he said, as soon as he saw me. "I didn't expect to hear from you until you arrived at the Geotron. What's wrong? Are you having problems getting underwater?"

Underwater? But it was McAndrew, without a doubt. McAndrew live, healthy, unrestrained, and by the look of it having the time of his life. He actually did not sound too thrilled by the news of my arrival.

"No problems," I said. "I touched down just a few minutes ago."

"Right then. I'll have to go. We're very busy here." And his picture promptly vanished. The phone link disconnected.

That was the genuine McAndrew, without a doubt, and he was clearly all right. The smart thing to have done at that point would have been to apologize to Van Lyle for my rudeness, plead prior job commitments off Earth, and turn right around and head back to space. Instead I handed the little phone back, sighed, and said, "Before I make a complete fool of myself, tell me one thing. What *is* a Geotron, and *where* is a Geotron?"

Van Lyle stared at me. I think I had actually managed to surprise him.

"You're asking *me* what a Geotron is?"

"I am."

"But didn't Professor McAndrew explain to you?"

"He would have done—if I had given him half a chance."

"Well . . . I'm not a scientist, as you know very well."

"Nor am I. That ought to make things easier for both of us." We started walking toward a sleek high-speed aircar, as Van Lyle said, "Well, you know what neutrinos are, don't you?"

"Yes. They're elementary particles, with no charge, and a tiny rest mass. Their discovery was predicted by Pauli in 1931, because they were needed to preserve the laws of conservation of energy and angular momentum."

That was gross intellectual dishonesty, and I knew it. But Lyle didn't. He looked quite impressed.

"Right," he said. "All they have are spin and energy. And they don't interact much with ordinary matter, uness they have very *high* energy. That makes them the devil to detect. A free neutrino can easily pass right through the Earth. But sometimes that can be an advantage. Like if you want to do down-deep exploration. And you decide to build a Geotron."

He explained the rest of it as we took off and he flew us west at Mach Ten. The staff of Earth's Food and Energy Council had done all the easy exploration of Earth's interior that they could do—which meant prospecting to about twenty kilometers down. Now they were forced to search deeper, or else be dependent on off-planet resources. The Geotron was nothing more than a huge kind of X-ray machine, for examining the inner structure of the Earth. But instead of X-ray radiation, which would penetrate no more than a few feet, the machine generated tight beams of high-energy neutrinos. They could be sent in any direction. They passed right through the middle of the Earth, scattering off structures in the interior, and emerged at points around the world where their numbers were measured. Then a very fancy set of computer programs took the information on the detected neutrinos and used that to deduce the interior structures that they had encountered in their path from the Geotron to the detection chambers.

"Looking for primordial methane, as the primary target," Lyle explained. "Pockets of compressed methane left over from the time of the Earth's formation, and still trapped deep inside."

"To use as fuel?"

"Lord, no. Methane's far too valuable an organic material to burn—even if the laws permitted it. We use it for complex hydrocarbon synthesis."

"Have you been finding any?"

"More than you would believe."

It occurred to me that I had an explanation to offer Hermann Jaynsie for Earth's lack of interest in the food supply contracts. There would never be a shortage of nitrogen on Earth, with an atmosphere that was nearly eighty percent that gas. If they now had enough hydrocarbons, and enough energy, elemental food synthesis would be a snap.

The most surprising thing was Van Lyle's willingness to tell all this to me, an outsider. Didn't Earth's Food and Energy Council *care* any more who knew what? Or were there missing pieces that were not being mentioned?

"I understand the Geotron," I said. "But what was that about being underwater?"

"Well, you don't think we'd put it on land, do you? Solid surface is too precious. We put it on the seabed." And then, when I looked puzzled. "Captain Roker, just how big do you think the Geotron is?"

"I've no idea."

"Then I'll tell you. The main ring is forty kilometers across."

Forty kilometers. A long day's walk. Or in this case, a long day's swim.

"So it was built on the Malvinas' continental shelf," he went on. "Where there's a lot of available seabed, and the water is only fifty to a hundred meters deep."

"Malvinas?"

"Off the east coast of Patagonia. We'll be there in half an hour. Then you can see it for yourself."

In the next few minutes I learned that the Malvinas' coastal zone was now Earth's hottest development area, site not only of the Geotron but also of the world's most modern food facilities and genetic laboratories; all, naturally, off-shore, in the shallow seas that ran for hundreds of kilometers east of the mainland.

And while Lyle talked, I struggled to remember where Patagonia was. Southern hemisphere? Definitely. South America? Probably. It occurred to me that although I could quote the size and approximate orbital parameters for every major body from Mercury to the edge of the Oort cloud, I did not know the geography of Earth.

We were flying near the edge of the atmosphere. I

stared up at the familiar black sky, with the brightest stars showing, then turned my eyes down to wisps of white cloud, with far below them the alien sea.

I felt, as usual when I was on Earth, a long way from home.

Our descent to the Geotron did nothing to ease my feeling of alienation. I had not realized that our aircar was amphibious, until we were skimming a few feet above long, rolling waves. We touched down, planing across the surface in a cloud of spray. Lyle took his hands off the controls.

And instead of bobbing on the rollers, we kept descending. After a few moments of panic, while the water level rose past the windows and plunged us into a green gloom, I realized that the aircraft was not only an amphibian, it was also a submersible. I could hear the thrum of engines aft, and see the yellow beams of light that lit the way ahead and behind us for many meters.

"Lights for passenger viewing only," explained Lyle. "Just so you can enjoy the sights. I haven't been controlling the craft since we touched down on the waves. We'll be homed in to the Geotron facility automatically—sonic control, of course, not radio. Radio signals won't travel through water."

"How far is it?"

"Just a couple of kilometers. There was no point in landing too far away, but the final approach is interesting."

We had been angling steadily downward. The natural sunlight was vanishing, breaking to cloudy patches of darkening green. Shoals of silver-green fish and what looked like endless thousands of purple squids darted through the beams of our headlights. Then they too were gone, and I had my first sight of Earth's sea-floor, a smooth grey-brown carpet of fine sediments that swirled up like an ominous mist behind us in the wake of our propulsion jets.

That alien fog made me uneasy. I was much comforted when the huge silver wall of the outer Geotron ring appeared ahead, and we moved to an underwater docking. That felt quite familiar to me. An inward pressure of seawater replaced the space environment's outward pressure against vacuum, but the same sort of locks were needed. And once we were inside, we could have been in any controlled one-gravity environment between the Vulcan Nexus and the Hyperion Deep Vault.

Van Lyle led the way through the set of connected chambers that formed the control nexus for the Geotron. Other maintenance areas were spaced all around the rim of the main rings, a couple of kilometers apart. After a final up-and-down ride over the top of the inner ring, we were finally spilled by a moving stairway into a big square room, partitioned off into dozens of small work cubicles.

McAndrew sat in one of them with a man and a woman in their early twenties. His shoes and socks were off and he was staring at a listing that filled the whole of the cubicle wall. He looked well, was obviously unrestrained, and gave every impression of a man totally at home and thoroughly enjoying himself.

"There he is," said Lyle. "I was wondering, why does he take his shoes and socks off when he's working?"

"In case he needs to count to more than ten." But I didn't know the real answer, any more than Lyle did, and I had known Mac for a long time. At least he wasn't cracking his toe joints at the moment.

We walked forward. Mac saw me first, and stood up. "Jeanie! This is Merle Thursoe and Tom O'Dell. We're setting up a really great experiment."

He nodded to me, almost dismissively, and turned back to the display. Then something—maybe my snort of anger—must have told him that this wouldn't quite do for someone who had come so far to see him.

"Tom, Merle," he said, "would you carry on without me for a few minutes?" And then, turning back to me and standing up, "Jeanie, I don't think you know Ernesto Kugel. Come on. You have to meet him."

He walked me right through the complicated center of the room, to a cubicle no bigger or better furnished than any of the others. Sitting at a desk there, facing outward, was a serious little man wearing a formal black suit, white shirt, and dark blue neckerchief. A matching blue rose adorned his lapel.

"Director Ernesto Kugel." McAndrew was at his most formal. "May I present Captain Jeanie Roker."

Kugel stood, came around his desk, and bowed, giving me a splendid view of the top of a hairless scalp as smooth and white and round as an ostrich egg. His whole head was free of hair, except for the neatly trimmed black moustache on his upper lip. I decided that nature could never have created the effect. Ernesto Kugel had worked on it.

I was all set to dislike the man, when he straightened up and took my hand.

"I am delighted to meet you, Captain Roker," he said, in a deep, smooth voice. "Professor McAndrew told me that you are most competent. What he did not mention is that you are also elegant and beautiful."

I stared at him. "Does that line work often?"

He gazed back, unblinking and unashamed, his brown eyes as bright and lively as a bird's. "Not so often." He suddenly smiled, and it transformed his face. "But let us say, it works often enough."

"And I suppose that joking about it works, too?"

"Sometimes. Most times. And if it does not"—he shrugged—"what harm has been done? God made two sexes, Captain Jeanie—and luckily that was exactly the right number."

I suddenly found it impossible to dislike him at all. We stood grinning at each other, until McAndrew said, "I want a word in private. Just the three of us."

"Of course." Kugel nodded his head toward the cubicle. "But this is as private as we get. I believe it is bad if I hide myself away from where the real work is done. Bad for my staff—and worst of all for me." Kugel waved to us to sit down. His desk was as neat and organized as Mac's was usually messy.

McAndrew didn't waste any time. "Ernesto, I could explain our discussions to Captain Roker—to Jeanie. But I would feel much more comfortable if you were to do that."

"Of course." Kugel leaned toward me, and spoke in his low, confidential voice. "You should sleep with him, you know. You two should have children."

I turned on McAndrew. "You brought me in here, just to hear a proposition on your behalf? You ought to be old enough to handle your own public relations."

"That's not what I meant!" Mac waved at the other man. "Keep going, Ernesto."

"Of course." Kugel was chuckling to himself. "What I mean, Captain Jeanie, is that the man standing before you, Arthur Morton McAndrew, is a great genius. His genes, and your genes, should be preserved and cherished. I knew his reputation long before he came here, but now I realize that he is one of the immortals."

"But I'm not fit to carry Dr. Kugel's coat, when it comes to large-scale engineering," McAndrew added. Praise of his abilities makes him terribly uncomfortable.

I sighed. It was obviously a mutual admiration society. Apparently I had travelled the distance from Moon to Earth, just to hear the two of them compliment each other.

"But to be specific," Kugel said, after a long pause in which they sat nodding and smiling. "Before Professor McAndrew's arrival, I and my staff had operated the Geotron for three months. In all that time, we had observed an inexplicable loss of neutrinos. We know how many the machine produces. And we know how many we are finding, in each of our mobile detectors. From that it is a simple calculation to estimate the total number escaping over the whole of the Earth's surface. There were too few of them, less than we were creating—and not by a number within the reasonable bounds of statistical error. There were *far* too few. For a long time we thought that it must be a matter of phase changes, or instrument calibration. Finally we decided that could not be the case.

"We had no explanation. Until two of my brightest young staff, Thursoe and O'Dell, became involved."

"Jeanie met them both," McAndrew said.

"Then you must know, Captain, that both of them are far brighter than I. They proposed a specific physical reason for the absence of neutrinos, arguing by analogy to the conserved vector current theory of Feynman and Gell-Mann. That would imply the existence of a new kind of weak force, and a new physical invariant. It was speculative, but I thought it looked very interesting. I mentioned the work and the theory in my weekly report of activities to the Food and Energy Council. I did not expect that it would receive external circulation—until the sudden arrival of Professor McAndrew's request to visit the Geotron facility, and review the evidence."

He turned to Mac. "Now I think that you should continue."

"Well . . ." McAndrew became uneasy. "I don't like to criticize other people's work, you know, and the O'Dell and Thursoe theory is highly ingenious; but it did occur to me that there could be a simpler explanation."

"You knew it," Kugel said flatly. "Knew it before you ever left the Penrose Institute."

"No. Everything depended on the experimental results." McAndrew turned back to me. "You see, Jeanie, the Geotron had been operating at a very precise and very high neutrino energy, a domain that to my knowledge had not been explored before in any detail. It seemed to me that the explanation for the loss of neutrinos could be something as simple as resonance capture. Certain materials, common in Earth's interior, may have a very high capture cross-section for neutrinos of the Geotron energy. And that could account for the observed difference between production and detection. It would also be a most important scientific discovery, because such a resonance is not predicted by current theories."

"Mph," I said. It meant, Mac, I have now heard more than I wish to know about lost neutrinos.

But McAndrew, as it turned out, was close to the end. "And there's a very simple way to tell if I'm right," he said. "In less than twelve hours we can do an experiment with a modulated Geotron energy, far from possible resonance, and get an instant neutrino count. That's what O'Dell, Thursoe, and I have been working on. And we are just about ready for final set up."

As I said, I've known McAndrew for a long time; long enough to interpret what he had just told me: he was all ready to do a neat physics experiment, and for the next half day nothing in heaven or earth would budge him from the Geotron facility.

That conviction was at once reinforced by Ernesto Kugel.

"You are of course welcome to remain here during the experiment," he said to me placatingly. "On the other hand, one of the Administrator's own staff members suggests that you might find a visit to our new food production plant, a few kilometers away, much more intriguing. He would be happy to serve as your escort."

"More than happy." And dead on cue, Van Lyle was standing at the entrance to the cubicle. "Ready when you are, Captain Roker."

It was all fine—and all just a little bit too pat.

"I need to go to the bathroom," I said, "before we leave."

"Sure."

Inside the stall I sat down on the toilet seat, put my head in my hands, and thought.

I was uncomfortable. What was the source of my discomfort? Nothing that I could put a name on, except that maybe the leopard had changed his spots a little too completely. This Van Lyle was not the Van Lyle I had known.

But what then were the dangers? Nothing that I could think of.

I was being paranoid. I went back out. I gave McAndrew a farewell hug, while Ernesto Kugel looked on approvingly. But as I was doing it I whispered in Mac's ear, "I'm going to look at the food production center with Van Lyle. If I'm not back in twelve hours, you come after me."

McAndrew is not good at this sort of thing. "What?" he said loudly.

"You heard." I did not raise my voice. "See you soon— I hope."

Earth is an amazing place. It's a spent force, a used-up relic, a crusted dinosaur that the rest of the System looks back on and shakes its head.

But it doesn't know that—or at least it won't admit it.

The Malvinas' food production facility was astonishing. On the seabed, powered by abundant fusion energy and with nothing but the raw elements as working material, the production center was making foodstuffs as good as any I'd tasted through the whole system. No wonder that Earth, with a ten thousand year supply of primordial methane promised by Ernesto Kugel, wanted to renege on supply contracts. It had little interest in what it saw as extortion from the Outer System.

Earth looked like—dare I say it?—the planet of the future.

Maybe it was that, the total unreality of the experience, that made me lower my guard. Lyle and I were walking through a chamber where vat after vat of synthesized milk and beef extract stood in ferment.

"We'll visit the organic recycling center next," he said. "But first, smell this." We paused in front of an open container, much smaller than the others. "It is Roquefort cheese. Synthesized, but you'd never know it. Lean over, stick your head in, and take a good sniff. Then I'll give you a taste."

I leaned over the tub. And I passed out cold, without ever knowing that I had gone.

When I came to I was in a wheelchair, bound but not yet gagged. Lyle was standing at my side.

"Ah, there you are, Jeanie," he said in a cheerful voice. "Back with us at last. Are you ready for action?"

My head reeled, and a cloying smell was still in my nostrils. How long had I been out? I didn't know, but it felt like an age. McAndrew might arrive at any moment. I had to think, and I had to survive until that happened.

"I don't know what you're up to," I said, "but I know it won't work. They'll come after me."

"Will they now?" Lyle cocked his head politely. "Don't take this wrong, Jeanie, but I think you are mistaken. Though I have to say that I am looking forward to the appearance of Professor McAndrew. The show wouldn't be the same without him. I also think it would be better for the time being if your mouth were taped, just in case." And a minute later, "I must say it was a surprise to me that you came here at all."

That, I think, is just where we came in. And a couple of minutes later it was Mac's arrival in a second wheelchair, pushed by Anna Griss herself, that sent me to a final misery.

"Mac," I whispered, after he had been rolled up alongside me. I was already full of an awful suspicion. "Where are the others?"

"Others?" He frowned at me, high forehead wrinkling. "Others? I came by myself."

McAndrew had done what I asked him to do—literally. He had come after me. Alone.

Well, at least there were few illusions left. And when Anna Griss came forward to stand in front of us, there were none. She was, as ever, elegantly dressed, carefully made up, and totally self-confident. She stared at us for a few seconds without speaking. At me, I would suggest, with a total cold hatred; at McAndrew, as at a wayward child who despite the best of advice has gone terribly and incorrigibly wrong.

"It took a while, didn't it?" she said. "How long has it been since the Oort cloud? But it finally worked out all right. I knew it would."

"You won't get away with this, you know," I said. "People know where McAndrew is. They know where I am."

"I'm sure they do," said Anna Griss. "But accidents happen, don't they? A tour of the recycling facility, an unfortunate entry into a clearly forbidden area . . ."

"You're a monster."

"Thank you. But I don't think I need to listen to that sort of thing. And I don't need to watch it." She turned to Lyle. "Put the gag back on the mouthy one. She talks too much. Then finish both of them. Before you do that, I need one more word with you, I'll be outside."

Typical Anna. She wouldn't watch, she wouldn't listen; so if there ever were an investigation, for any reason, she could proclaim her innocence. Hear no evil, see no evil.

She left. But Van Lyle was still there, and he was more than enough. He walked forward, sticky tape in his hand, and stood in front of me.

"It will be nice to hear you scream, Jeanie," he said quietly. "I won't be able to give you all that you deserve, the thing I'd really like to give you. We don't have time for that. But I can't wait to hear you grovel. I want to hear you *beg*, Jeanie."

"Maybe you will." I made my voice quiver. "And maybe you won't." He was moving closer. "But if you tape my mouth, you'll never hear anything from me. Ever. So go ahead."

He hesitated. "You'll beg all right," he said, "and you'll grovel. Trust me, Jeanie. You'll plead, and you'll beg, and you'll scream. Just you wait."

He left the room. But he had not taped my mouth.

Mac's wheelchair stood right next to mine. "Don't move," I said, and I leaned as far over to the left as I could. I could get my mouth down to the cords that bound his right hand—just.

Undoing knots in thick cord may sound easy. It isn't, especially when you can't see what you're doing, you're in a desperate hurry, and you have to work only with your mouth. The lips are very sensitive organs, but we are visual animals. I felt with my tongue and lips, tugged and twisted with my teeth, and was convinced that I was getting nowhere.

I forced myself to remain calm, to be patient, to pull gently instead of tearing and biting. McAndrew did not move, even when my teeth were catching more of his flesh than the cords.

It took forever before I felt the first loosening, a knot responding to my quivering mouth. But then it came faster. The second knot seemed easy. At last Mac's right hand was free.

"Right," he grunted. "I'll have us out in a minute." He reached across to his other hand, with the loose bonds still on his right wrist. As he worked on his left hand, I craned my head around to watch for the return of Van Lyle.

"Getting it," Mac said at last. But his legs were still tied when I saw the door opening.

"No more," I whispered. The two of us sat frozen as Van Lyle walked again in front of us. Mac had left the cords around both wrists, and his forearms rested on the arms of the wheelchair. It looked as though he was securely tied, hand and foot. As for me, I was still taped like a trussed chicken, arms and legs.

"So, Jeanie," Lyle said. "You don't know if you'll ask for mercy, eh? Well, I ought to tell you that Dr. Griss left the final steps in my hands. How you go is completely up to me—and to you. Quick and easy, or slow and hard. Do you think you can persuade me to be nice to you? Let's find out."

He moved behind me and pushed my wheelchair forward. Then he came past me, to the panel that controlled the great double doors.

"Take a look at this, Jeanie."

The doors slid open. Pungent fumes rose from the pit that was revealed before me, searing my throat. I saw a great pond of dark liquid, just beyond the doors and a few feet down.

"Ten seconds in there," Lyle said conversationally, "and you'd be choking. Half a minute, and your skin would start to peel off. But we don't have to rush everything like that. You can be dipped in and out like a bit of beef fondue, a toe or a foot or a hand at a time, as often and as slow as I choose to do it. Would you like to beg now, Jeanie? Or would you like to take your trial dip this very minute? Or maybe you would like me to be really merciful, and knock you unconscious first?"

I could hardly move, but I jerked and screamed and writhed against the tapes, making as much noise as I possibly could. Lyle laughed delightedly. Between us we were making a frightful din. How much of my screaming was genuine panic? I don't know, but I'm sure a good deal of it was, because my chair was rolling steadily closer to the edge without being pushed. There was a small lip at the very brink of the pit, but it might not be enough to halt the forward motion.

I was an arm's length from death—the chair nearing the edge—Van Lyle walking by my side and peering at my face, savoring my expression.

Then, from behind—at last—came the squeak of unoiled wheels.

Before Van Lyle could move, McAndrew was on him. Mac had freed his legs and was out of the wheelchair. Smarter than I would have been, he came forward in one silent rush, pushing the wheelchair in front of him like a ram. The edge of the seat caught Lyle behind the thighs at knee level. He fell backward into a sitting position. Before he could cry out he was at the edge. He and the chair went right on over. There was a scream and a great splash. McAndrew halted at the brink, staring down.

"Mac!" I screamed. I was still rolling.

He half-turned and threw himself in front of my wheelchair, stopping it with his own body. At the very edge, we both peered into the pit.

Lyle had gone in flat and facedown. He rose to the surface in a cloud of steam, screaming and clawing at his eyes. As we watched, his hair and skin began to smoke and frizzle. His arms waved and thrashed down on either side of him. Then he went under again.

The vat was more corrosive than Lyle had suggested. Twice more he rose, howling in agony. But the liquid must have reached his lungs. By the time he went under for the last time he was silent, a dark-green mass that was already losing its human form.

And while Van Lyle was dying, McAndrew kept tearing at the tapes that held me. I think it was the only thing that kept him from plunging in himself to try to help.

The tapes were strong, and Mac's hands were trembling. It was two more minutes before I could stand up, advance shakily to the brink, and peer down into the choking green fumes. I saw a dark vat, with sluggish ripples moving across the surface. About ten feet away from the edge floated an amorphous rounded lump.

"Don't look," McAndrew said. "He's dead."

"Of course he is. But it was his own damned fault."

I don't know how angry I sounded, but Mac winced. "Come on, Jeanie," he said. "It's over now. Let's get out of here."

"It's not." And then, when he stared at me. "It's not over. Not yet. Come on, Mac. I may need help."

I ran back, through the sequence of chambers that threaded the food production facility like beads on a necklace. Anna Griss sat at a table in the third one, calmly reading. She had just enough time to cry out in surprise before I reached her.

I lashed out and caught her with my fist high on the left cheek. While she was still reeling backward, partly stunned, I grabbed her in a neck lock.

"Come on, Mac. Help me. Back to the vats."

He wasn't much use, but it didn't matter. My own adrenaline level was so high, I could easily have carried her all the way myself. She was faintly struggling when I thrust her into the remaining wheelchair. The sticky tape that had held me was no good any more, but the cords that had bound Mac were enough to tie her.

I wheeled her to the very edge, so that the acrid corrosive vapors filled her throat and mine.

"That's Van Lyle down there." I pointed to the sodden green hulk, floating almost submerged. "You're going after him."

"Ohmygod. No, no." She was panting, shaking her head with its newly disordered hair and smudged make-up. "Don't push me over. Don't kill me. Please."

"You were ready enough to see us killed. Here you go, Anna Griss." I tilted the chair far forward, so that all that held her from the vat were her bonds. "This is what people get who mess around with me. You're dead."

I put my face close to hers. She was too frightened for tears, but her staring eyes were watering in the poisonous fumes.

"Say your prayers," I whispered. "Say goodbye."

"No. Oh, please." She was straining back, away from the deadly vat. "Don't. I'll do anything. Anything!"

"Jeanie!" cried McAndrew.

"Shut up, Mac. This is between me and her."

I moved the chair back a couple of feet and walked around in front of it to gaze into her eyes. "Look at me, Anna Griss. I'm not going to kill you—this time. But one more problem with you and you're dead. Do you understand? If the sight or sound or smell of you crosses my path again, ever, I'll come after you. And I'll get you. Don't ever doubt that. I'll get you."

She did not speak, but she nodded. I turned to McAndrew.

"I think she has the message. If she annoys either of us again, she'll be pig feed. Come on, Mac."

"You can't just leave her! She might go over the edge."

"If she goes, she goes." I grabbed his arm. "No big loss. But you and I are leaving. Come on."

He kept turning to look at her, but he allowed me to lead him away. I did not look back.

"You wouldn't have, would you?" he said at last, when we had walked through half a dozen chambers. "You wouldn't have killed her, no matter what she did."

It was obvious what he wanted to hear. "No. I wouldn't have killed her."

"Then why did you do all that, threatening her?"

"Because I had to. I might as well ask, why did you push Van Lyle over."

"But he was going to kill you! I didn't think—I just did it. Like you when you were screaming, going toward the pit. You just did it. What a bit of luck that was, Lyle leaving your mouth untaped! Otherwise you'd not have been able to scream, and when I ran at him he would have heard me coming."

I don't usually care what credit I get. But that was a bit too much.

"Mac," I said. "Listen to me. I'm going to tell you something about the invariants of nature. You have yours for physics and mathematics, determinants and momentum and conserved vector currents. And I have mine—the invariants of *human* nature: Love, and jealousy, and fear, and hate. Van Lyle was a cruel, sadistic bastard. He was like that when we first met him, he was like that out in the Oort cloud, and he was still like that until the moment he died. He couldn't change his nature. I *deliberately* told him that I wouldn't be able to beg and scream and grovel with my mouth taped. After that there was absolutely no way he'd muzzle me—no matter what Anna Griss told him to do. He *wanted* to see my terror, and hear my screams. And so I had the chance to free you."

McAndrew is an innocent soul. He was shocked silent by what I said. Finally he sighed, and muttered, "Maybe you're right. But I don't see why you did that to Anna Griss."

"I had to—because in her own way, she's no different from him. She has her own invariants: power, and control, and fear. Anna won't hold back on revenge to be nice to anyone. She'll go on, as far as she can go, until she's stopped. You and I have just stopped her. But we could never have done that by persuasion, or logic. She had to look death in the face for herself, and stare right down his black gullet."

"She could still cause us trouble. She could come after us, on Earth or off it."

"She could, but she won't. She'd like to get us, but she'll remember that pit. Anna understands power. If her people tried and failed again, she knows I'll come after her. The pleasure of finishing me isn't worth the risk."

"Are you sure?"

"Yes, I am. Mac, trust me. If I don't question your spinors and twistors and calibration of optical scalars, you shouldn't second guess me on Anna Griss."

"So you think it's safe to go back to the Geotron, and see how the experiments came out? I left before the results were in, you see, because of what you said to me."

He was returning to normal. Which is to say, totally abnormal.

I sighed. "Sure. We can go to the Geotron."

That sounded like the end of it, but it wasn't. We were in the submersible, cruising back to Ernesto Kugel's lab, while I wondered what story I was going to tell. Probably I'd say nothing. I'd pretend I had a nice pleasant tour, and leave it to Anna Griss to tell it otherwise.

Then McAndrew started up again.

"Jeanie. You really *wouldn't* have killed her, would you? No matter what."

I reached out and stroked his cheek. "Of course not. But can we drop it now? You and I ought to be celebrating our survival. Maybe we ought to act on Ernesto Kugel's suggestion—his first one."

It came out as flat and artificial as it sounds, and it didn't fool McAndrew for one moment. He gave me a wary, weary look, and leaned back in his seat. But it did accomplish my objective. It shut off a line of conversation that I was afraid to pursue.

Because one thing I've learned in life is that a person never knows her own invariants. I *thought* I knew the answer to McAndrew's question, but I wasn't *positive*. That terrible rage, the all-consuming fury that I felt when Anna Griss was poised on the edge of the pit ... if she had been a little more resistant, just a little tougher and more defiant—then who knows what I would have done?

Not I.

But one thing I did know for sure. I was not going to discuss that sort of thing with McAndrew. Ever.

He's a dear, and he's super-smart, and in almost every way I can think of he is wonderful. But he's also like most people who spend their lives studying the nature of the Universe.

He can only take a tiny little bit of reality.

SEVENTH CHRONICLE:

Rogueworld

The laws of probability not only permit coincidences; they absolutely insist on them.

I was sitting in the pilot's chair with McAndrew at my shoulder. Neither of us had spoken for a long time. We were in low polar orbit, sweeping rapidly across the surface of Vandell with all pod sensors wide open. I don't know what McAndrew was thinking, but my mind was not fully on the displays. Part of me was far away—one and a quarter light-years away, back on Earth.

Why not? Our attention here was not necessary. The surveillance sensors were linked to the shipboard main computer, and the work was done automatically. If anything new turned up we would hear of it at once. But nothing new could happen—nothing that mattered.

For the moment, I needed time to myself. Time to think about Jan; to remember her seventeen years, as a baby, as a slender child, as a fierce new intelligence, as a young woman; time to resent the chain of circumstance that had brought her and Sven Wicklund here, to die. Somewhere below these opalescent clouds, down on the cold surface of the planet, our sensor systems were seeking two corpses. Nothing else mattered.

I knew that McAndrew shared my sorrow, but he handled it in a different way. His attention was focused on the data displays, in a concentration so intense that my presence didn't matter at all. His eyes lacked all expression. Every couple of minutes he shook his head and muttered to himself: "This makes no sense—no sense at all."

I stared at the screen in front of me, where the dark vortex had again appeared. It came and went, clearly visible on some passes, vanished on others. Now it looked like a funnel, a sooty conical channel down through the glowing atmosphere, the only break in the planet's swirling cloud cover. We had passed right over it twice before, the first time with rising hopes; but the sensors had remained quiet. It was not a signal. It had to be a natural feature, something like Jupiter's Red Spot, some random coincidence of twisting gas streams.

Coincidence. Again, coincidence. *"The laws of probability not only permit coincidences; they absolutely insist on them."*

I couldn't get McAndrew's words out of my head.

He had spoken them months ago, on a day that I would never forget. It was Jan's seventeenth birthday, the first time of choice. I was down on Earth, choking on the dense air, meeting with the new head of External Affairs.

McAndrew was at his office at the Penrose Institute. We were both trying to work, but I for one wasn't succeeding too well. I wondered what was going through Jan's head, waiting for graduation from the Luna System.

"Naturally, there will have to be some changes," Tallboy was saying. "That's to be expected, I'm sure you'll agree. We are reviewing all programs, and though I am sure that my predecessor and I"—for the third time he had avoided using Woolford's name—"agree on overall objectives, we may have slightly different priorities."

Dr. Tallboy was a tall man, with a lofty brow and a keen, intellectual eye. Although we had shaken hands and muttered the conventional greetings a couple of times before, this was our first working meeting.

I pulled my wandering attention back to him. "When will the program review be finished?"

He shook his head and smiled broadly (but there were no laugh lines around his eyes). "As I'm sure you know very well, Captain Roker, these things take time. There has been a change of Administration. We have many new staff to train. There have been new Budget cuts, too, and the Office of External Affairs has suffered more than most. We will continue all the essential programs, be assured of that. But it is also my mandate to expend public funds wisely, and that cannot be done in haste."

"What about the Penrose Institute's experimental programs?" I said—a bit abruptly, but so far Tallboy had offered nothing more than general answers. I knew I couldn't afford to seem impatient, but my meeting wouldn't last much longer.

He hesitated, then sneaked a quick look at the crib sheets of notes in front of him on the desk. It didn't seem to help, because when he looked up the fine and noble brow was wrinkled in perplexity.

"I'm thinking particularly of the Alpha Centauri expedition," I prompted him. "Dr. Tallboy, a quick go-ahead on that means a great deal to us."

"Of course." He was nodding at me seriously. "A great deal. Er, I'm not completely familiar with that particular activity, you understand. But I assure you, as soon as my staff review is completed . . ."

Our meeting lasted fifteen more minutes, but long before that I felt I had failed. I had come here to push for a decision, to persuade Tallboy that the program should go ahead as planned and approved by Woolford; but bureaucratic changes had changed everything. Forget the fact that McAndrew and I had been planning the Alpha Centauri expedition for a year; forget the fact that the *Hoatzin* had been provisioned, fuelled, and inspected, and the flight plans filed long since with the USF. Forget the masses of new observational equipment that we had loaded onto the ship with such loving care. That had been under the old Administration. When the new one came in everything had to start again from scratch. And not one damned thing I could do about it.

I did manage to extract one promise from Tallboy before he ushered me out with polite assurances of his interest and commitment to the Institute's work. He would visit the Institute personally, as soon as his schedule permitted. It wasn't anything to celebrate, but it was all I could squeeze out of him.

"He'll visit here in person?" said McAndrew—I had run for the phone as soon as I cleared the Office of External Affairs. "Do you think he'll do it?"

I nodded. "I didn't leave it up to him. I saw his secretary on the way out, and made sure that we're in the book. He'll do it."

"When?" McAndrew had been in Limperis' office when I called, and it was the older man who leaned forward to ask the question.

"Eight days from now. That was the first gap in his schedule. He'll spend most of the day at the Institute."

"Then we're home free," said McAndrew. He was cracking his finger joints—a sure sign of high excitement. "Jeanie, we can put on an all-day show here that'll just blow him away. Wenig has a new E-M field stabilizer, Macedo says she can build a cheap detector for small Halo collapsars, and I've got an idea for a better kernel shield. And if we can ever get him to talk about it, Wicklund's cooking up something new and big out on Triton Station. Man, I'm telling you, the Institute hasn't been this productive in years. Get Tallboy here, and he'll go out of his mind."

Limperis shot a quick sideways glance at McAndrew, then looked back at the screen. He raised his eyebrows. I could read the expression on that smooth, innocent-looking face, and I agreed with him completely. If you wanted a man to quantize a nonlinear field, diagonalize a messy Hamiltonian, or dream up a delicate new observational test for theories of kernel creation, you couldn't possibly do better than McAndrew. But that would be his downfall now. He could never accept that the rest of the world might be less interested in physics than he was.

Limperis started that way, but years of budget battles as head of the Institute had taught him to play in a different league, "So what do you think, Jeanie?" he said to me, when Mac had finished babbling.

"I don't know." I shrugged. "I couldn't read Tallboy. He's an unknown quantity. We'd better look up his background, see if that gives us some clue to what makes him tick. As it is, you'll have to try it. Show him everything you've got at the Institute, and hope for the best."

"What about the expedition?"

"Same for that. Tallboy acted as though he'd never heard of Alpha Centauri. The *Hoatzin*'s just about ready to go, but we need Tallboy's blessing. External Affairs controls all the—"

"Call from Luna," cut in a disembodied voice. "Central Records for Professor McAndrew. Level Two priority. Will you accept interrupt, or prefer reschedule?"

"Accept," said McAndrew and I together—even though it wasn't my call. It had to be from Jan.

"Voice, tonal, display or hard copy output?"

"Voice," replied McAndrew firmly. I was less sure of that. He had done it so that I could receive the message, too, but we would have to witness each other's disappointment if it was bad news.

"Message for Arthur Morton McAndrew," went on the neutral voice. "Message begins. January Pelham, ID 128-129-001176, being of legal age of choice, will file for parental assignment as follows: Father: Arthur Morton McAndrew, ID 226-788-44577. Mother: Jean Pelham Roker, ID 547-314-78281. Name change filed for January Pelham Roker McAndrew. Parental response and acceptance is required. Reply via Luna free circuit 33, link 442. Message ends."

I had never seen McAndrew look so pleased. It was doubly satisfying to him to have me on the line when the word came through—I was sure that the Communications Group were trying to track me now through Tallboy's office, not knowing I was tapped into Mac's line.

"What's the formal date for parental assignment?" I asked.

There was a two second pause while the computer made confirmation of identity from my voiceprint, sent that information over the link from L-4 to Luna, decided how to handle the situation, and connected us all into one circuit.

"Message for Jean Pelham Roker. Message begins: January Pelham, ID 128—"

"No need to repeat," I said. "Message received. Repeat, what is the formal date for parental assignment?"

"Two hundred hours U.T., subject to satisfactory parental responses."

"That's too soon," said McAndrew. "We won't have enough time for chromosomal confirmation."

"Chromosomal confirmation waived."

On the screen in front of me McAndrew blushed bright with surprise and pleasure. Not only had Jan filed for us as official parents as soon as legally permitted, she had done so without knowing or caring what the genetic records showed. The waiver was a definite statement: whether or not McAndrew was her biological father would make no difference to her; she had made her decision.

For what it was worth, I could have given my own assurance. Some evidence is just as persuasive to me as chromosomal mapping. No one who had seen that blind, inward look on Jan's face when she was tackling an abstract problem would ever doubt that she was McAndrew's flesh and blood. I had cursed that expression a hundred times, as McAndrew left me to worry alone while he disappeared on a voyage of exploration and discovery inside his own head.

Never mind; McAndrew had his good points. "Parental acceptance by Jean Pelham Roker," I said.

"Parental acceptance by Arthur Morton McAndrew," said Mac.

Another brief pause, then: "Acceptance received and recorded. Formal assignment confirmed for two hundred hours U.T. Arrange location through Luna link 33-442. Hard copy output follows. Is there additional transfer?"

"No."

"Link terminated." While the computer initiated hard copy output to the terminal at the Institute, I did a little calculation

"Mac, we have a problem—Jan's acceptance ceremony is set for the same time as Tallboy's visit."

"Of course." He looked surprised that I hadn't seen it immediately. "We can handle it. She'll come out here. She'll want to visit—she hasn't been to the Institute since Wicklund went out to Triton Station."

"But you'll be too tied up with Tallboy to spend much time with her. What rotten luck."

McAndrew shrugged, and it was enough to start him talking. "Whenever a set of independent events occur randomly in time or space, you'll notice event-clusters. They're inevitable. That's all there is to coincidences. If you assume that event arrival times follow a Poisson distribution, and just go ahead and calculate the probability that a given number will occur in some small interval of time, you'll find—"

"Take him away," I said to Limperis.

He slapped McAndrew lightly on the shoulder. "Come on. Coincidence or not, this is a day for celebration. You're a father now, and thanks to Jeanie we've got Tallboy coming out here to see the show." He winked at me. "Though maybe Jan will change her mind when she hears Mac talk for a few hours, eh, Jeanie? Poor girl, she's not used to it, the way you are."

McAndrew just grinned. He was riding too high for a little gentle joshing to have any effect. "If you pity the poor lass at all," he said. "It should be for the Philistine space-jock of a mother she'll be getting. If I wanted to talk to Jan about probability distributions, she'd listen to me." She probably would, too. I'd seen her math profiles.

Limperis was reaching out to cut the connection, but Mac hadn't quite finished. "You know, the laws of probability not only permit coincidences," he said. "They—"

He was still talking when the screen went blank.

I had no more official business down on Earth, but I didn't head out at once. Limperis was quite right, it was a time for celebration; you didn't become a parent every day. I went over to the Asgard restaurant, up at the very top of Mile High, and ordered the full panoramic dinner. In some ways I wasted my money, because no matter what the sensories threw at me I hardly noticed. I was thinking back seventeen years, to the time when Jan was born, so small she could put her whole fist in the old silver thimble that McAndrew's friends gave her as a birthgift.

It was a few years later that I realized we had something exceptional on our hands—Jan had breezed through every test they could give her. I felt as though I had a window to McAndrew's own past, because I was sure he had been the same way thirty years earlier. The mandatory separation years hadn't been bad at all, because McAndrew and I had spent most of them on long trips out, where the Earth-years sped by in months of shipboard time. But I was very glad they were over now. In a few more days, McAndrew, Jan and I would be officially and permanently related.

By the time I finished my meal I probably wore the same foolish smile as I had seen on Mac's face before Limperis cut the video. Neither or us could see beyond the coming ceremony to a grimmer future.

The next few days were too busy for much introspection. The Penrose Institute had been in free orbit, half a million miles out, but to make it more convenient for Tallboy's visit Limperis moved us back to the old L-4 position. In a general planning meeting we decided what we would show off, and how much time could be spared for each research activity. I'd never heard such squabbling. The concentration of brain power found at the Institute meant that a dozen or more important advances were competing for Tallboy's time. Limperis was as impartial and diplomatic as ever, but there was no way he could smooth Macedo's feelings when she learned that she would have less than ten minutes to show off three years of effort on electromagnetic coupling systems. And Wenig was even worse—he wanted to be in on all the presentations, and still have time to promote his own work on ultra-dense matter.

At the same time McAndrew was having problems of quite a different kind with Sven Wicklund. That young physicist was still out on Triton Station, where he had gone complaining that the Inner System was all far too crowded and cluttered and he needed some peace and quiet.

"What the devil's he up to out there?" grumbled McAndrew. "I need to know for the Tallboy briefing, but a one-way radio signal out to Neptune takes four hours— even if he wanted to talk, and he doesn't. And I'm sure he's on to something new and important. Blast him, what am I supposed to report?"

I wasn't sympathetic. To me it seemed no more than poetic justice. McAndrew had annoyed me and others often enough in the past, when he refused to talk about his own ideas while they were in development—"half-cooked," to use his phrase. Apparently Sven Wicklund was just the same, and it served Mac right.

But the Institute needed all the impressive material they could find, so Mac continued to send long and futile messages needling Wicklund to tell him something— anything—about his latest work. He got nowhere.

"And he's the brightest of the lot of us," said McAndrew.

Coming from him that was a real compliment. His colleagues were less convinced.

"No, I don't think so," said Wenig when I asked him. "Anyway, it's a meaningless question. The two of them are quite different. Imagine that Newton and Einstein had lived at the same time. McAndrew's like Newton, as much at home with experiment as theory. And Wicklund's all theory, he needs help to change his pants. But it's still a fool question. Which is better, food or drink?—that makes as much sense. The main thing is that they're contemporaries, and they can talk to each other about what they're doing." Except that Wicklund refused to do so, at least at this stage of his work.

McAndrew finally gave up the effort to draw him out and concentrated on matters closer to home.

My own part in planning the show for Tallboy was a minor one. It had to be. My degrees in Gravitational Engineering and Electrical Engineering wouldn't get me in as janitor at the Institute. My job was to concentrate on the *Hoatzin*. Until we started work (budget permitting) on a more advanced model, this ship carried the best available version of the McAndrew drive. It could manage a hundred gee acceleration for months, and a hundred and ten gee for as long as the crew were willing to forego kitchen and toilet facilities.

The Office of External Affairs officially owned the *Hoatzin* and the Institute operated her, but I secretly thought of the ship as mine. No one else had ever flown her.

I had faint hopes that Tallboy might like a demonstration flight, maybe a short run out to Saturn. We could be there and back in a couple of days. The ship was all ready, for that and more—if he approved it, we were all set for the Alpha Centauri probe (forty-four days of shipboard time; not bad, when you remember that the first manned trip to Mars had taken more than nine months). We could be on our interstellar journey in a week or two.

All right, I wasn't being realistic; but I think everyone at the Institute nourished the secret dream that their project would be the one that caught Tallboy's imagination, occupied his time, and won his approval. Certainly the amount of work that went into preparation supported my idea.

The timing was tight but manageable. Jan would arrive at the Institute at 09:00, with the official parental assignment to take place at 09:50. Tallboy's grand show-and-tell began at 10:45 and went on for as long as he was willing to look and listen. Jan was scheduled to leave again at 19:50, so I had mixed feelings about Tallboy's tour. The longer he stayed, the more impressed he was likely to be, and we wanted that. But we also wanted to spend time with Jan before she had to dash back to Luna for graduation and sign-out.

In the final analysis everything went off as well—and as badly—as it could have. At 09:00 exactly Jan's ship docked at the Institute. I was pleased to see that it was one of the new five-gee mini-versions of the McAndrew Drive, coming into use at last in the Inner System. My bet was that Jan had picked it just to please him. You don't need the drive at all for pond-hopping from Luna to L-4.

The parental assignment ceremony is traditionally conducted with a lot of formality. It was against custom to step out of the docking area as soon as the doors were opened, march up to the father-to-be, and grab him in a huge and affectionate hug. McAndrew looked startled for a moment, then swelled red as a turkeycock with pleasure. I got the same shock treatment a few moments later. Then instead of letting go Jan and I held each other at arm's length and took stock.

She was going to be taller than me—already we were eye to eye. In three years she had changed from a super-smart child to an attractive woman, whose bright grey eyes told me something else: if I didn't take a hand, Jan would twist McAndrew round her little finger. And she knew I knew it. We stood smiling at each other, while a dozen messages passed between us: affection, pride, anticipation, sheer happiness—and challenge. Mac and I were getting a handful.

We gave each other a final hug, then she took my hand and Mac's and we went on through to meet with Limperis and the others. The official ceremony would not begin for another half hour, but we three knew that the important part was already completed.

"So what about your graduation present?" asked McAndrew, as we were waiting to begin. I had wondered about it myself. It was the first thing that most new children wanted to talk about.

"Nothing expensive," said Jan. "I think it would be nice just to make a trip—I've seen too much of Luna." Her tone was casual, but the quick sideways look at me told another story.

"Is that all?" said Mac. "Och, that doesn't sound like much of a present. We thought you'd be wanting a cruise pod, at the very least."

"What sort of trip?" I asked.

"I'd like to visit Triton Station. I've heard about it all my life, but apart from you, Jeanie, I don't know of anyone who's ever been there. And you never talk about it."

"I don't think that's a good idea at all," I said. The words popped out before I could stop them.

"Why not?"

"It's too far out—too isolated. And there'll be nothing at all for you to do there. It's a long way away." I had reacted before I had rational arguments, and now I was waffling.

Jan knew it. "A long way away! When the two of you have been light-years out. You've been on trips thousands of times as far as Triton Station."

I hesitated and she bore in again. "You're the one who told me that most people stick around like moles in their own backyard, when the Halo's waiting for them and there's a whole Universe to be explored."

What could I say? That there was one rule for most people, and another for my daughter? Triton Station is in the backyard, in terms of interstellar space; but it's also out near the edge of the old Solar System, too far away for Inner System comforts. An excellent place for a message relay between the Halo and the Inner System, that's why it was put there in the first place. But it's small and spartan. And the station isn't down on Neptune's satellite, the way that most people think. It's in orbit around Triton, with just a small manned outpost on the surface of the satellite itself for supplies, raw materials, and cryogenics research. There are a few unmanned stations bobbing about in the icy atmosphere of Neptune itself, 350,000 kilometers away, but nobody in her right mind ever goes to visit them.

The sixty Station personnel are a strange mixture of dedicated researchers and psychological loners who find the Inner System and even the Titan Colony much too crowded for them. Some of them love it there, but as soon as the 100-gee balanced drive is in general use, Triton Station will be only a day and a half flight away and well within reach of a weekend vacation. Then I suppose the disgusted staff will curse the crowds, and decide its time to move farther out into the Halo seeking their old peace and quiet.

"You'll be bored," I said, trying another argument. "They're more antisocial than you can imagine, and you won't know anybody there."

"Yes, I will. I know Sven Wicklund, and we always got along famously. He's still there, isn't he?"

"He is, blast him," said McAndrew. "But as to what he's been up to out there for the past six months . . ."

His voice tailed away and the old slack-jawed, half-witted look crept over his face. He was rubbing his fingers gently along his sandy, receding hairline, and I realized where his thoughts were taking him.

"Don't be silly, Mac. I hope you're not even considering it. If Wicklund won't tell you what he's doing, you don't imagine he'll talk to Jan about it, do you, if she's just at Triton Station for a short visit?"

"Well, I don't know," began McAndrew. "It seems to me there's a chance—"

"I feel sure he'll tell me," said Jan calmly.

Unfortunately, so was I. Wicklund had been bowled over by Jan when she was only fourteen and didn't have a tenth of her present firepower. If she could lead him around then with a ring through his nose, today with her added wiles it would be no contest.

"Let's not try to decide this now," I said. "The ceremony's starting, and then we have to get ready to meet Tallboy. Let's talk about it afterwards."

"Oh, I think we can decide it easily enough now," said McAndrew.

"No, that's all right," said Jan. "It can wait. No hurry." Sorry, Jeanie, said her smile at me. Game, set and match.

After that I found it hard to keep my mind on Tallboy's visit. Luckily I wasn't on center stage most of the time, though I did tag along with the tour, watching that high forehead nodding politely, and his long index finger pointing at the different pieces of equipment on display. I also had a chance to talk to everyone when they completed their individual briefings.

"Impressive," said Gowers when she came out. She had been first one up, describing her theories and experiments on the focusing of light using arrays of kernels. A tough area of work. To set up a stable array of Kerr-Newman black holes called for solutions to the many-body problem in general relativity. Luckily there was no one in the System better able to tackle that—Emma Gowers had made a permanent niche for herself in scientific history years before, when she provided the exact solution to the general relativistic two-body problem. Now to test her approximations she had built a tiny array of shielded kernels, small enough that all her work was done through a microscope. I had seen Tallboy peering in through the eyepiece, joking with Emma as he did so.

"So he seems sympathetic?" I said.

"More than that." She took a deep breath and sat down. She was still hyper after her presentation. "I think it went very well. He listened hard and he asked questions. I was only scheduled for ten minutes, and we took nearly twenty. Keep your fingers crossed."

I did, as one by one the others went in. When they came out most of them echoed her optimism. Siclaro was the only questioning voice. He had described his system for kernel energy extraction, and Tallboy had given him the same attentive audience and nodded understandingly.

"But he asked me what I meant by 'spin-up,'" Siclaro said to me as we stood together outside the main auditorium.

"That's fair enough—you can't expect him to be a specialist on this stuff."

"I know that." He shook his head in a worried fashion. "But that came at the end of the presentation. And all the time I was talking, he was nodding his head at me as though he understood everything—ideas a lot more advanced than simple spin-up and spin-down of a Kerr black hole. But if he didn't know what I meant at the end, how could he have understood any of the rest of it?"

Before I had time to answer, my own turn arrived. I came last of all, and though I had prepared as hard as anyone I was not a central part of the show. If Tallboy had to leave early I would be cut. If he had time, I was to show him over the *Hoatzin*, and make it clear to him that we were all ready for a long trip, as soon as his office gave us permission.

His energy level was amazing. He was still cordial and enthusiastic after seven hours of briefing, with only one short food break. We took a pod, just the two of us, and zipped over to the *Hoatzin*. I gave him a ten-minute tour, showing how the living area was moved closer to the mass disk as the acceleration of the ship was increased, to provide a net one-gee environment for the crew. He asked numerous polite general questions: how many people could be accommodated in the ship, how old was it, why was it called the inertia-less drive? I boggled a little at the last one, because McAndrew had spent large parts of his life explaining impatiently to anyone who would listen that, damn it, it wasn't inertia-less, that all it did was to balance off gravitational and inertial accelerations. But I went over it one more time, for Tallboy's benefit.

He listened closely, nodded that deep-browed head, and watched attentively as I moved us a little closer to the mass disk, so that we could feel the net acceleration on us increase from one to one-and-a-half gees.

"One more question," he said at last. "And then we must return to the Institute. You keep talking about accelerations, and making accelerations balance out. What does that have to do with us, with how heavy we feel?"

I stared at him. Was he joking? No, that fine-boned face was as serious as ever. He stood there politely waiting for my answer, and I felt that sinking feeling. I'm not sure what I told him, or what we talked about on the way back to the Institute. I handed him on to McAndrew for a quick look at the Control Center, while I hurried off to find Limperis. He was in his office, staring at a blank wall.

"I know, Jeanie," he said. "Don't tell me. I had to sit in on every briefing except yours."

"The man's an idiot," I said. "I think he means well, but he's a complete, boneheaded moron. He has no more idea than Wenig's pet monkey what goes on here in the Institute."

"I know. I know." Limperis suddenly showed his age, and for the first time it occurred to me that he was long past official retirement. "I hoped at first that it was just my paranoia," he said. "I wondered if I was seeing something that wasn't there—some of the others were so impressed."

"How could they be? Tallboy had no idea what was going on."

"It's his appearance. That sharp profile. He looks intelligent, so we assume he must be. But take the people here at the Institute. Wenig looks like a mortician, Gowers could pass as a dumb-blonde hooker, and Siclaro reminds me of a gorilla. And each of them a mind in a million. We accept it that way round easily enough, but not in reverse."

He stood up slowly. "We're like babies out here, Jeanie; each of us with our own playthings. If anybody seems to be interested in what we're doing, and nods their head now and again, we assume they understand. At the Institute, you interrupt if you don't follow an argument. But that's not the way Earthside government runs. Nod, and smile, and don't rock the boat—that's the name of the game, and it will take you a long way. You've seen how well it works for Dr. Tallboy."

"But if he doesn't understand a thing, what will his report say? The whole future of the Institute depends on it."

"It does. And God knows what will happen. I thought his background was physics or engineering, the way he kept nodding his head. Did you know his degree is in sociology and he has no hard scientific training at all? No calculus, no statistics, no complex variables, no dynamics. I bet the real quality of our work won't make one scrap of difference to his decision. We've all wasted a week." He sniffed, and muttered, "Well, come on. Tallboy will be leaving in a few minutes. We must play it to the end and hope he leaves with a positive impression."

He was heading for the door with me right behind when McAndrew hurried in.

"I've been wondering where you two had gone," he said. "Tallboy's at the departure dock. What a show, eh? I told you we'd do it, we knocked him dead. Even without Wicklund's work, we showed more new results today than he'll have seen in the past ten years. Come on—he wants to thank us all for our efforts before he goes."

He went bounding away along the corridor, full of

enthusiasm, oblivious to the atmosphere in Limperis' office. We followed slowly after him. For some reason we were both smiling.

"Don't knock it," said Limperis. "If Mac were a political animal he'd be that much less a scientist. He's not the man to present your budget request, but do you know what Einstein wrote to Born just before he died? 'Earning a living should have nothing to do with the search for knowledge.'"

"You should tell that to Mac."

"He was the one who told it to me."

There didn't seem much point in hurrying as we made our way to the departure dock. Tallboy had seen the best that we could offer. And who could tell?—perhaps McAndrew's enthusiasm would be more persuasive than a thousand hours of unintelligible briefings.

The mills of bureaucracy may or may not grind fine, but they certainly grind exceeding slow. Long before we had an official report from Tallboy's office, the argument over Jan's visit to Triton Station was over.

I had lost. She was on her way to Neptune. She had finagled a ride on a medium-acceleration supply ship, and anytime now we should have word of her arrival. And McAndrew couldn't wait—Wicklund was still frustratingly coy about his new work.

By a second one of those coincidences that McAndrew insisted were inevitable, Tallboy's pronunciamento on the future of the Penrose Institute zipped in to the Message Center at the same time as Jan's first message from Triton Station. I didn't know about her spacegram until later, but Limperis directed the Tallboy message for general Institute broadcast. I was outside at the time, working near the *Hoatzin*, and the news came as voice-only on my suit radio,

The summary: Siclaro's work on kernel energy extraction would proceed, and at a higher level (no surprise there, with the pressure from the Food and Energy Council for more compact power sources); Gowers would have her budget reduced by forty percent, as would Macedo. They could continue, but with no new experimental work. McAndrew had his support chopped in half. And poor Wenig, it seemed, had fared worst of all. The budget for compressed matter research was down by eighty percent.

I wasn't worried about McAndrew. If they cut his research budget to zero, he would switch to straight theory and manage very well with just a pencil and paper. But everyone else would suffer.

And me? Tallboy wiped me out at the very end of the report, almost as an afterthought: experimental use of the *Hoatzin* was to be terminated completely, and the ship decommissioned. There would be no expedition to Alpha Centauri or anywhere else beyond the Halo. Worst of all, the report referred to "previous unauthorized use of the balanced drive, and high-risk treatment of official property"—a direct knock at me and McAndrew. We had enjoyed free use of the ship under the previous Administration, but apparently Woolford had never thought to put it in writing.

I switched my suit to internal propulsion and headed back for the Institute at top speed. McAndrew knew I was outside, and he met me at the lock waving a long printout sheet. His mop of sandy hair was straggling into his eyes, and a long streak of orange stickiness ran down the front of his shirt. I guessed he had been at dinner when the report came in.

"Did you see it?" he said.

"Heard it. I was on voice-only."

"Well? What do you think?"

"Horrible. But I'm not surprised. I knew Tallboy hadn't understood a thing."

"Eh?" He stood goggling at me. "Are you trying to be funny? It's the most exciting news in years. I knew she'd find out. What a lass!"

I may not be as smart as McAndrew but I'm no fool. I can recognize a breakdown in communications when I see one. When Mac concentrates, the world isn't there any more. It seemed to me odds-on that he had been thinking of something else and hadn't registered the Tallboy decision.

"Mac, stand still for a minute"—he was jiggling up and down with excitement—"and listen to me. The report from External Affairs is here, on the future of your programs."

He grunted impatiently. "Aye, I know about it—I heard it come in." He dismissed the subject with a wave of his hand. "Never mind that now, it's not important. *This* is what counts."

He shook the printout, stared at part of it, and went off into a trance. I finally reached out, removed it from his hand, and scanned the first few lines.

"It's from Jan!"

"Of course it is. She's on Triton Station. Do you realize what Wicklund's done out there?"

With Mac in this kind of mood, I'd never get his mind on to Tallboy. "No. What has he done?"

"He's solved it." He grabbed the spacegram back from me. "See, it's right here, can't you read? Jan didn't get the details, but she makes it clear enough. Wicklund has solved Vandell's Fifth Problem."

"Has he really?" I gently took the paper back from him. If it was news from Jan, I wanted to read it in full. "That's wonderful. It only leaves one question."

He frowned at me. "Many questions—we'll have to wait for more details. But which one are you thinking of?"

"Nothing you can't answer. But what in Heaven is Vandell's Fifth Problem?"

He stared at me in disgust.

I got an answer—eventually. But before I had that answer we had been on a rambling tour of three hundred years of mathematics and physics. "In the year 1900—" he began.

"Mac!"

"No, listen to me. It's the right place to begin."

In the year 1900, at the second International Congress of Mathematicians in Paris, David Hilbert proposed a series of twenty-three problems to challenge the coming century. He was the greatest mathematician of his day, and his problems drew from a wide range of topics—topology, number theory, transfinite sets, and the foundations of mathematics itself. Each problem was important, and each was tough. Some were solved early in the century, others were shown to be undecidable, a few hung on for many decades; but by the year 2000 most of them had been wrapped up to everyone's reasonable satisfaction.

In the year 2020, the South African astronomer and physicist Dirk Vandell had followed Hilbert's precedent, and posed a series of twenty-one problems in astronomy and cosmology. Like Hilbert's problems they covered a wide range of topics, theoretical and observational, and every one was a skull-cruncher.

McAndrew had solved Vandell's Eleventh Problem when he was a very young man. From that work had emerged the whole theory for the existence and location of the kernel ring, the torus of Kerr-Newman black holes that circles the sun ten times as far out as Pluto. Nine years later, Wenig's partial solution of the Fourteenth Problem had given McAndrew the clue that led him to the vacuum-energy drive. Now, assuming that Jan's report was correct, the Fifth Problem had fallen to Wicklund's analysis.

"But why is it so important?" I asked McAndrew. "The way you describe it, I don't see practical uses. It's just a way of amplifying an observed signal without amplifying background noise—and it only applies when the original signal is minute."

He shook his head in vigorous disagreement. "It has a thousand applications. Vandell already proposed one when he first set the problem, and I'm sure Wicklund will tackle it as soon as his experimental equipment is working. He'll use the technique to look for solitaries—rogue planets."

Rogue planets.

With those last two words, McAndrew brought the explanation along to the point where it made sense to me. I could draw on my own formal training in classical celestial mechanics.

The possible existence of rogues went back a long way, farther than 1900. Probably all the way to Lagrange, who in his analysis of the three-body problem set up a mathematical framework to look at the motion of a planet moving in the gravitational fields of a binary star system. By 1880, that case was known to be "stable against ejection." In other words, the planet could have close approaches to each of the stars, and might suffer extremes of temperature, but it would never be completely expelled from the stellar system.

But suppose you have a system with *three* or more stars in it? That's not at all uncommon. Then the situation changes completely. A planet can pick up enough energy through a series of gravitational swing-bys past the stellar components to hurl it right out of the system. Once this happened it would become a sun-less world, travelling alone through the void. Even if it later encountered another star, the chance of capture was minute. The planet would be a solitary, a rogue world. Astronomers had speculated for centuries about the existence and possible numbers of such planets, but without a scrap of observational evidence.

Vandell had defined the problem: *An Earth-sized planet shines only in reflected light. If it gives off radiation in the thermal infrared or microwave regions, the signal is swamped by the stellar background. Devise a technique that will permit the detection of a rogue planet as small as the Earth.*

Now it seemed that Wicklund had done it, and McAndrew was happy as a pig, while everybody else at the Institute gloomed about in reaction to Tallboy's effects on their work.

I sympathized with them. Rogue planets are fine, but

I could see no way in which they could make any practical difference to me. Mac and Sven Wicklund could have my share of them. I spent a lot of time over on the *Hoatzin* wondering what to do next. I didn't belong at the Penrose Institute, the only thing I offered there was the ability to pilot the long trips out. Once that was over, I might as well go back to the Titan run.

Jan's next message back gave me mixed feelings, but at least it cheered me up.

"Not much to do out here," she wrote—she was the only person I have ever met who could chat in a spacegram. "You were right, Jeanie. Wicklund's as bad as McAndrew, totally wrapped up in the work he's doing and won't take much notice of me. And the rest of them hate company so much they run and hide when we meet in the corridors. I've been spending a lot of time over on *Merganser*. I got the impression from you that she's an old hulk, but she's not. She may be an antique, but everything's still in good working shape. I've even been spinning-up the drive. If I can talk Wicklund into it maybe we can go off on a little bit of a trip together. He needs a rest (from physics!)."

That brought back some exciting memories. *Merganser* was one of the two original prototypes of the balanced drive, and McAndrew and I had ironed the bugs out of her personally. She was limited to a 50-gee acceleration, but still in good working order. I'd fly her anywhere. Mac seemed much less happy when he read the letter.

"I hope she knows what she's doing," he said. "That ship's not a toy. Do you think it's safe?"

"Safe as anything in the System. Jan won't have any trouble. We used the *Merganser* for training before they mothballed her, don't you remember?"

He didn't, of course. He carries physics and mathematics in his head at an astonishing level of detail, but useful everyday information is another matter. He nodded at me vaguely, and wandered off to send more messages to Wicklund (who had to date provided no replies).

We heard from Jan again, just as the explicit order was coming in from Tallboy's office to decommission *Hoatzin* and remove the supplies for the Alpha Centauri mission.

I screwed up Tallboy's order into a tight ball and threw it across the room.

Then I sat down to read what Jan had to say.

No preamble this time: "Wicklund says it works! He's already found three rogues, and expects a lot more. They must be a lot more common than anybody thought. Now sit back for the big news: there's one only a light-year away! Isn't it exciting?"

Well, maybe—less so to me than to Mac, I was sure of that. I assumed that solitary planets would be rather rare, so one closer than the nearest star was a bit surprising. But it was her next words that shot me bolt upright and sent a tingle through my spine.

"*Merganser* is working perfectly, all ready for a trip. I've persuaded Wicklund to take her out for a look at Vandell—that's his name for the planet. I'm sure you don't approve, so I won't ask. Lots of love, and see you when we get back."

Even as I screamed inside, I wasn't completely surprised. She was McAndrew's daughter all right—it was exactly the harebrained sort of thing he would have done.

Mac and I both played it very cool. That boneheaded pair, we said to each other. We might have guessed it, the follies of youth. They'll be in trouble when they get back, even though the *Merganser* is an old ship that Triton Station can do what they like with.

But deep inside we both had other feelings. Wicklund had sent the coordinates of Vandell to us before they left, and as Jan said it was close, less than a light-year and a quarter away. Easily in *Merganser*'s range, and a lure that any scientist worth his salt would find hard to resist, even without Jan's coaxing. Where had it come from, what was it made of, how long since it had been ejected from its parent star?—there were a hundred questions that could never be answered by remote observations, not even with the super-sensitive methods that Wicklund had developed.

But it was those same questions that made me so uneasy. If I've learned one thing wandering around inside and outside the Solar System, it's this: Nature has more ways of killing you than you can imagine. When you think you've learned them all, another one pops up to teach you humility—if you're lucky. If not, someone else will have to decide what did you in.

For a week after Jan's message I monitored the messages closely that came in from the outer relay stations. And every day I would ride over to the *Hoatzin* and potter about there, sometimes with Mac, sometimes alone. I was supposed to be working on the decommissioning, but instead I would sit in the pilot's chair, check all the status flags, and think my own thoughts. Until finally, ten days after Jan and Wicklund had left, I went over to visit the *Hoatzin* late one sleep period.

And found that the lock had been cycled since I left.

McAndrew was sitting in the pilot's chair, staring at the controls. I came quietly up behind him, patted him on the shoulder, and slipped into the copilot's seat. He turned toward me, straggly eyebrows raised.

"It's now or never," he said at last. "But what about Tallboy? What will he do to the Institute?"

I shrugged. "Nothing. Not if we make it clear that it's our fault."

I reached out and called for a destination reading. When I left, the coordinates had all been set to zero. Now they carried precise values.

"Do you think that anyone else suspects?" I said. "I checked the experimental logs in your lab today, and they were all current up to this afternoon—and you're always months behind. If I noticed that, maybe one of the others will."

He looked surprised. "Why should they? We've been careful not to talk about this when anyone else could hear."

There was no point in telling Mac that he was probably the world's worst person you'd want to keep a secret. I tapped him on the shoulder. "No point in worrying about it once we're on our way. Come on, Mac, move over—you're sitting in my chair. And think positively. We'll have a nice, long trip, just the two of us."

He stood up, rubbing at the back of his head the way he always did when he was embarrassed. "Och, Jeanie," he said. But he was smiling to himself as we changed seats.

The calculations were elementary, and I could do them as well as he could. The *Merganser* would reach the rogue planet in about sixty days of shipboard time if they kept close to maximum acceleration all the way. We could be there in thirty-five days of shipboard time, but that would pick up only ten days of inertial time. We would reach Vandell a couple of days after them. For me, that was two days too late.

Our drive wake left an ionization track across the whole width of the Solar System. Mac checked that there were no ships directly behind for us to burn a hole through, and while he was doing it I had a new idea and sent a message back to External Affairs. I said that we were about to perform a brief high-gee test of the *Hoatzin's* drive before we took her in and decommissioned her. With luck, Tallboy's group would assume we had been the unhappy victims of a nasty accident, shooting out of the Solar System on a one-way journey when some control element of the drive unit had failed. Limperis and friends at the Institute wouldn't believe that, not as soon as they checked our destination coordinates—but they would never tell their suspicions to Tallboy. Maybe they could even get some mileage from our disappearance, pointing out the need for more funds for reliability and system maintenance. Limperis could play that game with his eyes closed.

Perhaps everything would work out fine—until McAndrew and I came back. Then the truth would come out, and we'd be roasted for sure.

Neither of us could get too worried about that possibility. We had other things on our minds. As we raced out along the invisible scintillation of the *Merganser*'s drive, Mac dumped the data bank for information about Vandell's rogueworld. He didn't get much. We had coordinates relative to the Sun, and velocity components, but all they did was make sure we could find our way to the planet. Wicklund had been able to put an upper limit on its diameter using long base line interferometry, and estimated that we were dealing with a body no bigger than Earth. But we were missing the physical variables—no mass, internal structure, temperature, magnetic field, or physical composition, not even an estimate of rotation rate. Mac fumed, but at least I'd have a lot more information for him as soon as we got close. In the week before we left the Institute, I had put on board the Hoatzin every instrument that wasn't nailed down, anything that might tell us something useful about Vandell without having to go down there and set foot on its surface.

At a hundred gees acceleration you head out of the Solar System on a trajectory that's very close to a straight line. The gravitational accelerations produced by the Sun and planets are negligible by comparison, even in the Inner System. We were bee-lining for a point in the constellation *Lupus*, the Wolf, where Vandell lay close in apparent position to an ancient supernova fragment. That explosion had lit up the skies of Earth more than a millennium ago; an interesting object, but we wouldn't be going even a thousandth of the way out to it. Wicklund was right; Vandell's rogueworld sat in Sol's backyard.

Without a complicated trajectory to worry about, I went round and round with a different problem. When the drives were on, both the *Merganser* and the *Hoatzin* were blind to incoming messages, and drowned out any of their own transmissions. Thus we had a chance to get a message to Sven Wicklund and Jan only when their drive was turned off, while they were coasting free to rubberneck or study the starscape scenery from a slightly different point of view. Even though they might not be listening for an incoming signal when the drive was off, their computer would, and should notify them of anything important.

But now see my problem: to send a message, we had to switch our drive off, and that would delay our arrival a little bit every time we did it. Our signal would then take days or weeks to reach the *Merganser*—and to receive it, their ship had to have its drive off at just the right time. DON'T LAND was all I wanted to say. But how would I know when to switch off our drive and send an urgent message, so it would get to them just when their drive was not operating?

I wrestled with that until my brains began to boil, then handed it over to McAndrew. He pointed out that we had knowledge of the occasions when their drive had been switched off, from the gaps in their drive wake. So making a best prediction was a straightforward problem in stochastic optimization. He solved it, too, before we had been on our way for a week. But the solution predicted such a low probability of successful contact that I didn't even try it—better to leave our drive on full blast, and try to make up some of their lead.

With the shields on to protect us from the sleet of particles and hard radiation induced by our light-chasing velocity, we had no sense of motion at all. But we were really moving. At turnover point we were within one part in ten thousand of light speed.

If I haven't said it already, I'll say it now: the 100-gee balanced drive is nice to have, but it's a son of a bitch— you travel a light-year in just over a month of shipboard time. Two months, and you've gone fifty light-years. Four shipboard months, and you're outside the Galaxy and well on your way to Andromeda.

I calculated that two hundred days would put you at the edge of the Universe, 18 billion light-years out. Of course, by the time you got there, the Universe would have had 18 billion more years to expand, so you wouldn't be at the new edge. In fact, since the "edge" is defined as the place where the velocity of recession of the galaxies is light-speed, you'd still be 18 billion light-years away from it—and that would remain true, no matter how long you journeyed. Worse still, if you arranged a trajectory that brought you to rest relative to the Earth, when you switched off the drive the Galaxies near you would be rushing away almost at light speed . . .

An hour or two of those thoughts, and I felt a new sympathy for Achilles in Zeno's old paradox, trying to catch the tortoise and never quite getting there.

Travel for a year, according to McAndrew, and you'd begin to have effects on the large-scale structure of space-time. The vacuum zero-point energy tapped by the drive isn't inexhaustible; but as to what would happen if you kept on going . . .

An academic question, of course, as Mac pointed out. Long before that the massplate would be inadequate to protect the drive, and the whole structure would disintegrate through ablative collision with intergalactic gas and dust. Very reassuring; but Mac's intrigued and speculative tone when he discussed the possibility was enough to send shivers up my spine.

The position fixes we needed to refine Wicklund's original position and velocity for Vandell rendezvous were made by our computer during the final three days of flight. Those observations and calibrations were performed in microsecond flashes while the drive was turned off, and at the same time we sent out burst mode messages, prepared and compressed in advance, to the *Merganser*'s projected position. We told them when to send a return signal to us, but no counter-message came in. There was nothing but the automatic "Signal received" from their shipboard computer.

One day before rendezvous we were close enough to throttle back the drive. We couldn't see Vandell or *Merganser* yet, but the ships' computers could begin talking to each other. It took them only a few seconds to collect the information I was interested in, and spit out a display summary.

No human presence now on board. Transfer pod in use for planetary descent trajectory. No incoming signals from pod.

I keyed in the only query that mattered: When descent? *Seven hours shipboard time.*

That was it. We had arrived just too late. By now Jan and Sven Wicklund would be down on the surface of Vandell. Then another part of the first message hit me. *No incoming signals from pod.*

"Mac!" I said. "No pod signal."

He nodded grimly. He had caught it too. Even when they were down on the surface, there should be an automatic beacon signal to fix the pod's position and allow compensation for Doppler shift of communication frequency.

"No pod signal," I said again. "That means they're—"

"Aye." His voice was husky, as though there was no air in his lungs. "Let's not jump to conclusions, Jeanie. For all we know . . ."

But he didn't finish the sentence. The pod antenna was robust. Only something major (such as impact with a solid surface at a few hundred meters a second) would put it out of action. I had never known a case where the pod's com-link died and the persons within it lived.

We sat side by side in a frozen, empty silence as the *Hoatzin* brought us closer to the rogue planet. Soon it was visible to our highest resolution telescopes. Without making a decision at any conscious level, I automatically set up a command sequence that would free our own landing pod as soon as the drive went off completely. Then I simply sat there, staring ahead at Vandell.

For much of our trip out I had tried to visualize what a planet would be like that had known no warming sun for millions or billions of years. It had floated free—for how long? We didn't know. Perhaps since our kind had descended from the trees, perhaps as long as any life had existed on Earth. For all that time, the planet had moved on through the quiet void, responsive only to the gentle, persistent tug of galactic gravitational and magnetic fields, drifting along where the stars were no more than distant pinpricks against the black sky. With no sunlight to breathe life onto its surface, Vandell would be cold, airless, the frozen innermost circle of hell. It chilled me to think of it.

The planet grew steadily in the forward screens. As the definition of the display improved, I suddenly realized why I couldn't relate the picture in front of me to my mental images. Vandell was *visible*, at optical wave lengths. It sat there at the center of the screen, a small sphere that glowed a soft, living pink against the stellar backdrop. As I watched the surface seemed to shimmer, with an evanescent pattern of fine lines running across it.

McAndrew had seen it too. He gave a grunt of surprise, cupped his chin in his hands, and leaned forward. After two minutes of silence he reached across to the terminal and keyed in a brief query.

"What are you doing?" I asked, when after another two minutes he showed no sign of speaking.

"Want to see what's in *Merganser*'s memory. Should be some images from their time of first approach." He grunted and shook his head. "Look at that screen. There's no way Vandell can look like that."

"I was amazed to see it at visible wavelengths. But I'm not sure why."

"Available energy." He shrugged, but his gaze never left the display. "See, Jeanie, the only thing that can provide energy to that planet's surface is an internal source. But nothing I've ever heard of could give this much radiation at those frequencies, and sustain it over a long period. And look at the edge of the planet's disk. See, it's less bright. That's an atmospheric limb darkening, if ever I've seen one—an atmosphere, now, on a planet that should be as cold as space. Doesn't make any sense at all. No sense at all."

We watched together as *Merganser's* data bank fed across to our ship's computer and through the displays. The screen to our left flickered through a wild pattern of colors, then went totally dark. McAndrew looked at it and swore to himself.

"Explain that to me, Jeanie. There's the way that Vandell looked in the visible part of the spectrum when Jan and Sven were on their final approach—black as hell, totally invisible. We get here, a couple of days later, and we find *that*." He waved his arm at the central display, where Vandell was steadily increasing in size as we moved closer. "Look at the readings that Wicklund made as they came into parking orbit—no visible emissions, no thermal emissions, no sign of an atmosphere. Now see our readings: the planet is visible, above freezing point, and covered in clouds. It's as though they were describing one world, and we've arrived at a completely different one."

Mac often tells me that I have no imagination. But as he spoke wild ideas went running through my mind that I didn't care to mention. A planet that changed its appearance when humans approached it; a world that waited patiently for millions of years, then draped a cloak of atmosphere around itself as soon as it had lured a group of people to its surface. Could the changes on Vandell be interpreted as the result of *intention*, a deliberate and intelligent act on the part of something on the planet?

While I was still full of my furious fancies, a high-pitched whistle from the navigation console announced that the balanced drive had turned off completely. We had reached our rendezvous position, two hundred thousand kilometers from Vandell. I was moving away from the control panel, heading towards our own transfer pod, before the sound had ended. At the entrance I stopped and turned, expecting that McAndrew would be close on my heels. But he hadn't left the displays. He had called back the list of Vandell's

physical parameters, showing mass, temperature, mean
diameter, and rotation rate, and was staring at it blindly.
As I watched he requested a new display of Vandell's rotation rate, which was small enough to be shown as zero in
the standard output format.

"Mac!"

He turned, shook his head from side to side as though
to banish his own version of the insane ideas that had
crowded my mind when I saw the change in Vandell, and
slowly followed me to the pod. At the entrance he turned
for a last look at the screens.

There was no discussion of our move into the pod.
We didn't know when, or even quite how, but we both
knew that we had to make a descent to the surface of
Vandell. Somehow we had to recover the bodies that lay
beneath the flickering, pearly cloud shrouding the rogue
world.

In another time and place, the view from the pod
would have been beautiful. We were close enough now
to explain the rosy shimmer. It was lightning storms,
running back and forth across the clouded skies of Vandell.
Lightning storms that shouldn't be there, on a world that
ought to be dead. We had drained *Merganser*'s data banks
as we went round and round in low orbit. Not much new
had come to light, but we had found the last set of instrument readings returned to the main computer when the
other landing pod had made its approach to Vandell's
surface: *Atmospheric pressure, zero. External magnetic
field, less than a millionth of a gauss. Temperature, four
degrees absolute. Surface gravity, four-tenths of a gee.
Planetary rotation rate, too small to measure.*

Then their pod had touched down, with final relative
velocity of only half a meter a second—and all transmissions had ceased, instantly. Whatever had killed Jan and
Sven Wicklund, direct impact with the surface couldn't
be the culprit. They had landed gently. And if they hadn't
been killed by collision when they landed . . .

I tried to ignore the tiny bud of hope that wanted to open in my mind. I had never heard of a pod being destroyed without also killing anyone inside it.

Our instruments had added a few new (and odd) facts to that earlier picture. The "atmosphere" we were seeing now was mainly dust, a great swirling storm across the whole of Vandell, littered by lightning flashes through the upper part. It was hot, a furnace breath that had no right to exist. Vandell was supposed to be *cold*. Goddammit, it should be drained of every last calorie of heat. McAndrew had told me so, there was no way the planet could be warm.

Round and round, orbit after orbit; we went on until I felt that we were a fixed center and the whole universe was gyrating around us, while I stared at that black vortex (it came and went from one orbit to the next, now you see it, now you don't) and McAndrew sat glued to the data displays. I don't think he looked at Vandell itself for more than ten seconds in five hours. He was thinking.

And me? The pressure inside was growing—tearing me apart. According to Limperis and Wenig, I'm cautious to a fault. Where angels fear to tread, I not only won't rush in, I don't want to go near the place. That's one reason they like to have me around, to exercise my high cowardice quotient. But now I wanted to fire our retro-rockets and get down there, down onto Vandell. Twice I had seated myself at the controls, and fingered the preliminary descent sequence (second nature, I could have done that in my sleep). And twice McAndrew had emerged from his reverie, shook his head, and spoken: "No, Jeanie."

But the third time he didn't stop me.

"D'ye know where you're going to put her down, Jeanie?" was all he said.

"Roughly." I didn't like the sound of my voice at all. Too scratchy and husky. "I've got the approximate landing position from *Merganser*'s readings."

"Not there." He was shaking his head. "Not quite there. See it, the black tube? Put us down the middle of that funnel—can you do it?"

"I can. But if it's what it looks like, we'll get heavy turbulence."

"Aye, I'll agree with that." He shrugged. "That's where they are, though, for a bet. Can you do it?"

That wasn't his real question. As he was speaking, I began to slide us in along a smooth descent trajectory. There was nothing to the calculation of our motion, we both recognized that. Given our desired touchdown location, the pod's computer would have a minimum fuel descent figured in fractions of a second.

I know McAndrew very well. What he was saying— not in words, that wasn't his style—was simple: *It's going to be dangerous, and I'm not sure how dangerous. Do you want to do it?*

I began to see why as soon as we were inside the atmosphere. Visibility went down to zero. We were descending through thick smoke-like dust and flickering lightning. I switched to radar vision, and found I was looking down to a murky, surrealistic world, with a shattered, twisted surface. Heavy winds (without an atmosphere?—what were winds?) moved us violently from side to side, up and down, with sickening free-fall drops arrested by the drive as soon as they were started.

Thirty seconds to contact, and below us the ground heaved and rolled like a sick giant. Down and down, along the exact center of the black funnel. The pod shook and shivered around us. The automatic controls seemed to be doing poorly, but I knew I'd be worse—my reaction times were a thousandfold too slow to compete. All we could do was hold tight and wait for the collision.

Which never came. We didn't make a featherbed landing, but the final jolt was just a few centimeters a second. Or was it more? I couldn't say. It was lost in the continuing shuddering movements of the ground that the pod rested on. The planet beneath us was alive. I stood up, then had to hold onto the edge of the control desk to keep my feet. I smiled at McAndrew (quite an effort) as he began an unsteady movement towards the equipment locker.

He nodded at me. *Earthquake country*.

I nodded back. *Where is their ship?*

We had landed on a planet almost as big as Earth, in the middle of a howling dust storm that reduced visibility to less than a hundred yards. Now we were proposing to search an area of a couple of hundred million square miles—for an object a few meters across. The needle in a haystack had nothing on this. Mac didn't seem worried. He was putting on an external support pack—we had donned suits during the first phase of descent.

"Mac!"

He paused with the pack held against his chest and the connectors held in one hand. "Don't be daft, Jeanie. Only one of us should be out there."

And that made me mad. He was being logical (my specialty). But to come more than a light-year, and then for *one* of us go the last few miles . . . Jan was my daughter too—my only daughter. I moved forward and picked up another of the packs. After one look at my face, Mac didn't argue.

At least we had enough sense not to venture outside at once. Suited up, we completed the systematic scan of our surroundings. The visual wavelengths were useless—we couldn't see a thing through the ports—but the microwave sensors let us look to the horizon. And a wild horizon it was. Spikes of sharp rock sat next to crumbling mesas, impenetrable crevasses, and tilted blocks of dark stone, randomly strewn across the landscape.

I could see no pattern at all, no rule of formation. But over to one side, less than a mile from our pod, our instruments were picking up a bright radar echo, a reflection peak stronger than anything that came from the rocky surface. It must be metal—could only be metal—could only be Jan's ship. But was it intact? Lightning-fused? A scoured hulk? A shattered remnant, open to dust and vacuum?

My thoughts came too fast to follow. Before they had reached any conclusion we had moved to the lock, opened it, and were standing on the broken surface of Vandell. McAndrew automatically fell behind to let me take the lead. Neither of us had any experience with this type of terrain, but he knew my antennae for trouble were better than his. I tuned my suit to the reflected radar signal from our pod and we began to pick our way carefully forward.

It was a grim, tortuous progress. There was no direct path that could be taken across the rocks. Every tenth step seemed to bring me to a dead end, a place where we had to retrace our steps halfway back to our own pod. Beneath our feet, the surface of the planet shivered and groaned, as though it was ready to open up and swallow us. The landscape as our suits presented it to us was a scintillating nightmare of blacks and grays. (Vision in nonvisible wavelengths is always disconcerting—microwave more than most).

Around us, the swirling dust came in shivering waves that whispered along the outside of our helmets. I could detect a definite cycle, with a peak every seven minutes or so. Radio static followed the same period, rising and falling in volume to match the disturbance outside.

I had tuned my set to maximum gain and was transmitting a continuous call signal. Nothing came back from the bright radar blip of the other pod. It was now only a couple of hundred yards ahead but we were approaching agonizingly slowly.

At fifty yards I noticed a lull in the rustle around us. I switched to visible wavelengths, and waited impatiently while the suit's processor searched for the best combination of frequencies to penetrate the murk. After half a second the internal suit display announced that there would be a short delay; the sensors were covered with ionized dust particles that would have to be repelled. That took another ten seconds, then I had an image. Peering ahead on visible wavelengths I thought I could see a new shape in front of us, a flat oval hugging the dark ground.

"Visible signal, Mac," I said over the radio. "Tell your suit."

That was all I could say. I know the profile of a pod, I've seen them from every angle. And the silhouette ahead of us looked *wrong*. It had a twisted, sideways cant, bulging towards the left. I increased pace, stumbling dangerously along smooth slabs and around jagged pinnacles, striding recklessly across a quivering deep abyss. Mac was following, ready to help me if I got in trouble—unless he was taking worse risks himself, which was certainly not beyond him. I could hear his breath, loud on the suit radio.

It was their pod. No doubt at all. And as I came closer I could see the long, gaping hole in one side. It takes a lot to smash a transfer pod beyond repair, but that one would never fly again. Inside it would be airless, lifeless, filled only with the choking dust that was Vandell's only claim to an atmosphere.

And the people inside? Would Jan or Sven have thought to wear suits before descent? It would make a difference only to the appearance of the corpses. Even with suits, anything that could kill their signal beacon would kill them too.

I took my final step to the pod, stooped to peer in through the split in the side, and stopped breathing. Somewhere deep inside me, contrary to all logic, there still lived a faint ghost of hope. It died as I looked. Two figures lay side by side on the floor of the pod, neither of them moving.

I groaned, saw Mac coming to stand beside me, and switched on my helmet light for a better view or the interior. Then I straightened up so fast that my head banged hard on the pod's tough metal.

They were both wearing suits, their helmets were touching—and as the light from outside penetrated the interior of the pod, they swung around in unison to face me. They were both rubbing at their suit faceplates with gloved hands, clearing a space in a thick layer of white dust there.

"Jan!" My shout must have blasted Mac rigid. "Sven! Mac, they're alive!"

"Christ, Jeanie, I see that. Steady on, you'll burst my eardrums." He sounded as though he himself was going to burst, from sheer pleasure and relief.

We scrambled around to the main hatch of the pod and I tried to yank it open. It wouldn't move. Mac lent a hand, and still nothing would budge—everything was too bent and battered. Back we went to the hole in the ship's side, and found them trying to enlarge it enough to get out.

"Stand back," I said. "Mac and I can cut that in a minute."

Then I realized they couldn't hear me or see me. Their faceplates were covered again with dust, and they kept leaning together to touch helmets.

"Mac! There's something wrong with their suits."

"Of course there is." He sounded disgusted with my stupidity. "Radio's not working—we already knew that. They're communicating with each other by direct speech through the helmet contact. Vision units are done for, too—see, all they have are the faceplates, and the dust sticks and covers them unless they keep on clearing it. The whole atmosphere of this damned planet is nothing more than charged dust particles. Our suits are repelling them, or we'd see nothing at visible wavelengths. Here, let me in there."

He stuck his head through the opening, grabbed the arm of Jan's suit, and pulled us so that we were all four touching helmets. We could talk to each other.

And for that first ten minutes that's what we did: talk, in a language that defies all logical analysis. I would call it the language of love, but that phrase has been used too often for another (and less powerful) emotional experience.

Then we enlarged the hole so they could climb out. At that point I thought that we had won, that our troubles and difficulties were all over. In fact, they were just starting.

❖   ❖   ❖

Their pod was in even worse shape than it looked. The battering from flying boulders that had ruined the hull should have left intact the internal electronics, computers, and communications links, components with no moving parts that ought to withstand any amount of shaking and violent motion. But they were all dead. The pod was nothing but a lifeless chunk of metal and plastics. Worse still, all the computer systems in Jan and Sven's suits had failed, too. They had no radios, no external vision systems—not even temperature controls. Only the purely mechanical components, like air supply and suit pressure, were still working.

I couldn't imagine anything that could destroy the equipment so completely and leave Jan and Sven alive, but those questions would have to come later. For the moment our first priority was the return to the other pod. If I had thought it dangerous work coming, going back would be much worse. Jan and Sven were almost blind, they couldn't step across chasms or walk along a thin slab of rock. Without radios, I couldn't even tell them to back up if I decided we had to retrace part of our path.

We all four linked hands, to make a chain with Mac on the left-hand end and me on the right, and began a strange crab-like movement back in the direction of the other pod. I daren't hurry, and it took hours. Four times I had to stop completely, while the ground beneath us went through exceptionally violent paroxysms of shaking and shuddering. We stood motionless, tightly gripping each other's gloved hands. If it was scary for me, it must have been hell for Jan and Sven. Mac and I were their lifeline, if we lost contact they wouldn't make twenty meters safely across the broken surface. While the shaking went on, I was picking up faint sounds in my radio. McAndrew and Wicklund had their helmets together, and Wicklund seemed to be doing all the talking. For five minutes I heard only occasional grunts from Mac through his throat mike.

"Right," he said at last. "Were you able to pick up any of that, Jeanie? We have to get a move on. Go faster."

"Faster? In these conditions? You're crazy. I know it's slow going, but we all have plenty of air. Let's do it right, and get there in one piece."

"It's not air I'm worried about." He was crowding up behind us, so that we were all bumping into each other. "We have to be in the pod and off the surface in less than an hour. Sven's been tracking the surges of seismic activity and dust speed, ever since they landed and everything went to hell. There's a bad one coming an hour and a half from now—and I mean bad. Worse than anything we've felt so far. A lot of the minor cycles we've been feeling since we came out on the surface will all be in phase. They'll all add together."

Worse than anything we had felt so far. What would it be like? It wasn't easy to imagine. Nor was the cause— but something had taken Vandell's smooth and quiet surface and crumpled it to a wild ruin in the few hours since the other pod had landed.

Against my instincts I began to take more risks, to climb over more jagged rocks and to walk along shelves that might tilt and slide under our weight. I think that at this point it was worse for McAndrew and me than for Sven and Jan. They could walk blind and trust us to keep them safe; but we had to keep our eyes wide open, and study all the dangers around us. I wanted to ask Mac a hundred questions, but I didn't dare to focus his attention or mine on anything except the immediate task.

At our faster pace we were within a hundred meters of the pod in twenty minutes, with what looked like a clear path the rest of the way. That was when I heard a grunt and curse over the suit radio, and turned to see McAndrew sliding away to one side down a long scree of loose gravel. Last across, he had pushed Sven Wicklund to safety as the surface began to break. He fell, scrabbled at the ground, but couldn't get hold of anything firm. He rolled once, then within seconds was lost from view behind a black jumble of boulders.

"Mac!" I was glad that Jan couldn't hear my voice crack with panic.

"I'm here, Jeanie. I'm all right." He sounded as though he was out on a picnic. "My own fault, I could see it was breaking away when Sven was on it. I should have looked for another path instead of following him like a sheep."

"Can you get back?"

There was a silence, probably thirty seconds. In my nerved-up state it seemed like an hour. I could hear Mac's breath, faster and louder over the radio.

"I'm not sure," he said at last. "It's a mess down here, and the slope's too steep to climb straight up. Damned gravel, I slide right back down with it. It may take me a little while. You three had better keep going and I'll catch up later. Time's too short for you to hang around waiting."

"Forget it. Hold right there, I'm coming back after you." I leaned to set my helmet next to Jan's. "Jan, can you hear me?"

"Yes. But speak louder." Her voice was faint, as though she was many meters away.

"I want you and Sven to stand right here and don't move—not for anything. Mac's stuck, and I have to help him. I'll be just a few minutes."

That was meant to be reassuring, but then I wondered what would happen if I was too optimistic about how long it would take me. "Give me twenty minutes, and if we're not back then, you'll have to get to the pod on your own. It's straight in front as you're facing now, about a hundred meters away. If you go in a straight line for fifty paces then clear your faceplates, you should be able to see it."

I knew she must have questions, but there was no time to answer them. Mac's tone suggested it would be completely fatal to be on Vandell's surface, unprotected, when the next big wave of seismic activity hit us.

I knew exactly where Mac had gone, but I had a hard time seeing him. The rock slide had carried with it a mixture of small and large fragments, from gravel and pebbles to substantial boulders. His struggles to climb the slope had only managed to embed him deeper in loose materials. Now his suit was three-quarters hidden. His efforts also seemed to have carried him backwards, so with a thirty degree gradient facing him I didn't think he'd ever be able to get out alone. And further down the slope lay a broad fissure in the surface, of indeterminate depth.

He was facing my way, and he had seen me too. "Jeanie, don't come any closer. You'll slither right down here, the same as I did. There's nothing firm past the ledge you're standing on."

"Don't worry. This is as far as I'm coming." I backed up a step, nearer to a huge rock that must have weighed many tons, and turned my head so the chest of Mac's suit sat on the crosshairs at the exact center of my display. "Don't move a muscle now. I'm going to use the Walton, and we don't have time for second tries."

I lifted the crosshairs just a little to allow for the effects of gravity, then intoned the Walton release sequence. The ejection solenoid fired, and the thin filament with its terminal electromagnet shot out from the chest panel on my suit and flashed down towards McAndrew. The laser at the tip measured the distance of the target, and the magnet went on a fraction of a second before contact. Mac and I were joined by a hair-thin bond. I braced myself behind the big rock. "Ready? I'm going to haul you in."

"Aye, I'm ready. But why didn't I think of using the Walton? Damnation, I didn't need to get you back here, I could have done it for myself."

I began to reel in the line, slowly so that Mac could help by freeing himself from the stones and gravel. The Izaak Walton has been used for many years, ever since the first big space construction jobs pointed out the need for a way to move around in vacuum without wasting a

suit's reaction mass. If all you want is a little linear
momentum, the argument went, why not take it from the
massive structures around you? That's all that the Waltons
do. I'd used them hundreds of times in free fall, shooting the line out to a girder where I wanted to be, connecting, then reeling myself over there. So had Mac, and
that's why he was disgusted with himself. But it occurred
to me that this was the first time I'd ever heard of a
Walton being used on a planetary surface.

"I don't think you could have done it, Mac," I said.
"This big rock's the only solid one you could see from
down there, and it doesn't look as though it has a high
metal content. You'd have nothing for the magnet to grab
hold of up here."

"Maybe." He snorted. "But I should have had the sense
to *try*. I'm a witless oaf."

What that made me, I dreaded to think. I went on
steadily hauling in the line until he had scrabbled his way
up to stand by my side, then switched off the field. The
line and magnet automatically ran into their storage reel
in my suit, and we carefully turned and headed back to
the other two.

They were just where I had left them. They stood,
helmets touching, like a frozen and forlorn tableau in
Vandell's broken wilderness. It was more than fifteen minutes since I gone back to Mac, and I could imagine their
uneasy thoughts. I leaned my helmet to touch both theirs.

"All present and safe. Let's go."

Jan gave my arm a great squeeze. We formed our chain
again, and crabbed the rest of the way to the pod. It
wasn't quite as easy as it had looked, or as I suggested
to Jan, but in less than fifteen minutes we were opening the outer hatch and bundling Sven and Jan into it.

The lock was only big enough for two at a time. They
were out of their useless suits by the time that McAndrew
and I could join them inside. Jan looked pale and shaky,
ten years older than her seventeen years. Sven Wicklund
was as blond and dreamy-looking as ever, still impossibly

young in appearance. Like McAndrew, his own internal preoccupations partly shielded him from unpleasant realities—even now he was brandishing a piece of paper covered with squiggles at us. But Jan and Sven had both held together, keeping their composure well when death must have seemed certain. It occurred to me that if you wanted to find a rite of passage to adulthood, you wouldn't find a tougher one than Jan had been through.

"Just look at this," Sven said as soon as we were out of the hatch. "I've been plotting the cycles—"

"How long before it hits?" I interrupted.

"Four minutes. But—"

"Get into working suits, both of you." I was already at the controls. "I'm taking us up as soon as I can, but if we're too late I can't guarantee that the pod hull will survive. You know what happened to yours."

The ascent presented no problem of navigation—I had plenty of fuel, and I intended to go straight up with maximum lift. There would be time to worry about rendezvous with *Merganser* and *Hoatzin* when we were safely away from Vandell.

I believe in being careful, even on the simplest take-off, so all my concentration was on the control sequences. I could hear Jan, McAndrew and Wicklund babbling to each other in the background, until I told them to get off my suit frequency and let me think. Vandell was still a complete mystery world to me, but if the others had answers, those, like the problem of ship rendezvous, could wait until we were off the surface.

Wicklund's predictions for the timing of the next wave of violence proved to be unnecessary. I could see it coming directly, in the values provided by the pod's field instruments. Every gauge reading in front of me was creeping up in unison as we lifted off; ionization levels, surface vibrations, dust density, electric and magnetic fields—readouts flickered rapidly higher, and needles turned steadily across their dials like the hands of an old-fashioned clock.

Something big was on its way. We lifted into a sky ripped by great lightning flashes, burning their way through the clouds of charged dust particles. The ascent we made was rapid. Within a few seconds we had reached three kilometers. And then, as I was beginning to relax a little and think that we had been just in time, the readings in front of me went mad. External field strengths flickered up so fast in value that the figures were unreadable, then warning lights came on. I heard the screech of a fatal overload in my suit's radio, and saw the displays in front of me blank out one after another. The computer, after a brief mad flurry of a binary dump across the control screen, went totally dead. Suddenly I was flying blind and deaf. All the electronic tools that every pilot relied on were now totally disabled.

It was useless information, but suddenly I understood exactly what had killed the signal beacon from Jan and Sven's pod without also killing them. Before the displays in front of me died, the electric and magnetic field strengths had risen to an impossible level. Even with partial shielding from the pod's hull, their intensity was enough to wipe magnetic storage—that took care of computers, communications equipment, displays, and suit controls. If the suits hadn't been designed with manual overrides for certain essentials so that Jan and Sven could control their air supply, that would have been the end.

Now our pod had the same problem as theirs. We hadn't been pelted with boulders, as they had when they were sitting on the surface of Vandell, but we had no computer control of our flight and we were being whipped around the sky by the changing magnetic fields.

It wasn't necessary for me to change to manual control. When the computer died, it dumped everything in my lap automatically. I gritted my teeth, tried to keep us heading straight up (not easy, the way we were being tilted and rocked) and refused to decrease thrust even though the pod shuddered as though it was getting ready to disintegrate.

I'm blessed with an iron stomach, one that doesn't get sick no matter how much lurching and spinning it takes. McAndrew isn't, and Jan takes after him. They couldn't communicate with me, but I could take their misery for granted.

It was worth the discomfort. We were getting there, rising steadily, while the pink glow around the pod's ports faded towards black. As our altitude increased I looked at the internal pressure gauge—thank God for a simple mechanical gadget. It was showing normal pressure, which meant that the hull hadn't been breached on our ascent. I allowed myself the luxury of a quick look around me.

McAndrew was slumped forward in his straps, head down as low as he could get it. Sven and Jan were both leaning back, arms linked. All the faceplates were clear, so that I knew none of them had vomited in their suit— no joke, since the internal cleaning systems that would usually handle the mess were out of action.

The turbulence around the pod grew less. Stars were coming into view outside the ports as I turned us into an orbit that spiralled outward away from Vandell. I was looking for *Hoatzin*. Our orbit was clumsy and wasteful of fuel compared with what the navigation computer would have provided. But give me some credit, I was receiving no reference signals from the ship. All I had was instinct and experience.

Scooting along over the clouds I could now see a pattern to the lightning. It moved in great waves over the surface, reaching peaks in places, fading elsewhere. We had lifted from a point where all the peaks had converged, but now it was fading to look no different from the rest. Or almost so; the faint shadow of the black funnel still dipped down into the murk.

I felt a tap on my shoulder. Mac was gesturing at me, then at the helmet of his suit. I nodded and broke the seal on my own helmet. We were outside the danger zone, and it was important to reestablish contact among the group. The search for *Hoatzin* and *Merganser* might take hours, with no assistance from automated scan instruments or radio receipt of homing signals. Meanwhile, I wanted some explanations. It was clear that McAndrew and Wicklund between them had more idea than I did what had been happening.

Three miserable, greenish-yellow faces emerged from the helmets. No one had thrown up, but from the look of them it had been a close thing.

"I thought it was bad when the storm hit us on the surface," said Jan. "But that was even worse. What did you do to us, Jeanie? I thought the pod was coming apart."

"So did I." Suit helmet off, I reached back to massage the aching muscles in my neck and shoulders. "It almost did. We lost the computers, the communications, the displays—everything. What is this crazy planet, anyway? I thought the laws of nature were supposed to be the same all over the universe, but Vandell seems to have a special exemption. What in hell did you two do to the place, Jan? It was quiet as a grave until you got at it."

"It damn near was one," said McAndrew. "If you hadn't . . ."

He paused and swallowed. "We know what's going on. That's what we were talking about before you shook us to pieces. If we'd been a bit smarter, we could have inferred it ahead of time and none of this would have happened. How much did you hear on the way up?"

I shook my head. "I tuned you out. I had other things on my mind. Are you telling me you understand that mess down there? I thought you said it made no sense at all."

While we spoke I had taken us up to the correct height above Vandell for rendezvous with *Hoatzin*. Now it would need a steady and simple sweep to find our ship.

McAndrew wiped his hand across his pale, sweating forehead. He was looking awful, but less like a dying pickle as the minutes passed. "It didn't make sense," he said huskily. "Nothing ever does before you understand it, and then it seems obvious. I noticed something odd just before we left *Hoatzin* to go into the pod—Sven had wondered about the same thing, but neither of us gave it enough significance. Remember the list of physical variables that they recorded for Vandell when they first arrived here? No electric and magnetic fields, negligible rotation rate, no atmosphere, and cold as the pit. Does any one of those observations suggest anything to you?"

I leaned against the padded seat back. My physical exertions over the past half hour had been negligible, but tension had exhausted me totally. I looked across at him.

"Mac, I'm in no condition for guessing games. I'm too tired. For God's sake, get on with it."

He peered at me sympathetically. "Aye, you're right. Let me begin at the beginning, and keep it simple. We know that Vandell was quiet until *Merganser*'s pod landed on its surface. Within minutes of that, there was massive seismic activity and terrific electric and magnetic disturbances. We watched it, there were waves of activity over the whole planet—but they all had one focus, and one point of origin: where the pod landed." As McAndrew spoke his voice became firmer, strengthening now that he was back on the familiar ground of scientific explanation. "Remember the dark cone that we followed in to the surface? It was the only anomaly visible over the whole surface of the planet. So it was obvious. The impact of the pod *caused* the trouble, it was the trigger that set off Vandell's eruption."

I looked around at the others. They all seemed happy with the explanation, but to me it said absolutely nothing. I shook my head. "Mac, I've landed on fifty planets and asteroids through the System and the Halo. Never once has one shaken apart when I tried to set foot on it. So why? Why did it happen to Vandell?"

"Because—"

"*Because Vandell is a rogue world*," interrupted Sven Wicklund. We all stared at him in amazement. Sven usually never said a word about anything (except of course physics) unless he was asked a direct question. He was too shy. Now his blond hair was wet with perspiration, and there was still that distant, mystic look on his face, the look that vanished only when he laughed. But his voice was forceful. Vandell had done something to him, too.

"A rogue world," he went on. "And one that does not rotate on its axis. That is the crux of this whole affair. Vandell rotates too slowly for us to measure it. McAndrew and I noticed that, but we thought it no more than a point of academic interest. As Eddington pointed out centuries ago, almost everything in the Universe seems to rotate—atoms, molecules, planets, stars, galaxies. But there is no law of nature that *obliges* a body to rotate relative to the stars. Vandell did not, but we thought it only a curious accident."

He leaned towards me. "Think back to the time—how many million years ago?—when Vandell was first ejected from its stellar system. It had been close to the system's suns, exposed to great forces. It was hot, and maybe geologically active, and then suddenly it was thrown out, out into the void between the stars. What happened then?"

He paused, but I knew he was not expecting an answer. I waited.

He shrugged. "Nothing happened," he said. "For millions or billions of years, Vandell was alone. It slowly lost heat, cooled, contracted—just as the planets of the Solar System cooled and contracted after they were first formed. But there is one critical difference: the planets circle the Sun, and each other. As tensions inside build up, tidal forces work to release them. Earth and the planets release accumulating internal stresses through sequences of small disturbances—earthquakes, Marsquakes, Jupiterquakes. They can never build up a large store of pent-up energy. They are nudged continuously to internal stability by the other bodies of the system. But not Vandell. It wanders alone. With no tidal forces to work on it—not even the forces caused by its rotation in the galactic gravitational and magnetic fields—Vandell became super-critical. It was a house of cards, unstable against small disturbances. Apply one shock, and all the stored energy would be released in a chain reaction."

He paused and looked around. Then he blushed and seemed surprised at his own sudden eloquence. We all waited. Nothing else was forthcoming.

I had followed what he said without difficulty, but accepting it was another matter. "You're telling me that everything on Vandell came from the pod's landing," I said. "But what about the dust clouds? And why the intense fields? And how could they arise from an internal adjustment—even a violent one? And why were there peaks in the disturbance, like the one when we lifted off?"

Sven Wicklund didn't answer. He had apparently done his speaking for the day. He looked beseechingly for support to McAndrew, who coughed and rubbed at his head.

"Now, Jeanie," he said, "you could answer those questions for yourself if you wanted to give it a minute's thought. You know about positions of unstable equilibrium as well as I do. Make an infinitesimal displacement, and produce an unbounded change, that's the heart of it. Compared with the disturbances on Vandell for the past few eons, the landing of a pod was a super-powerful shock—more than an infinitesimal nudge. And you expect a set of spherical harmonics—with a pole at the source of energy—when you distribute energy over a sphere. As for the fields, I'll bet that you're not enough of a student of science to know what a Wimshurst machine is; but I've seen one. It was an old way of generating tremendous electromagnetic fields and artificial lightning using simple friction of plates against each other. Vandell's crustal motion could generate fields of billions of volts, though of course they'd only last a few hours. We were there right at the worst time."

We looked back at the planet. To my eye it was maybe a little less visible, the lightning flashes less intense across the dusty clouds.

"Poor old Vandell," said Jan. "Peaceful for all these years, then we come and ruin it. And we wanted to study a rogue planet, a place of absolute quiet. It'll never be the way it was before we got here. Well, never mind, there should be others. When we get back we'll tell people to be more careful."

When we get back.

At those words, the world snapped into a different focus. For twelve hours I had been completely absorbed by the events of the moment. Earth, the Office of External Affairs, the Institute, they had not existed for me two minutes ago. Now they were present again, still far away—I looked out of the port, seeking the bright distant star of the Sun—but real.

"Are you all right, Jeanie?" asked Jan. She had observed my sudden change of expression.

"I'm not sure."

It was time we told her everything. About Tallboy's decision on the future of the Institute, about the cancellation of the Alpha Centauri expedition, the proposed decommissioning of the *Hoatzin*, and the way we had disobeyed official orders to follow them to Vandell. It all came rolling out like a long-stored fury.

"But you saved our lives," protested Jan. "If you hadn't taken the ship we'd be dead. Once they know that, they won't care if you ignored some stupid regulation."

McAndrew and I stared at her, then at each other. "Child, you've got a lot to learn about bureaucracy," I said. "I know it all sounds ridiculous and trivial out here—damn it, it *is* ridiculous and trivial. But once we get back we'll waste weeks of our time, defending what we did, documenting everything, and writing endless reports on it. The fact that you would have died won't make one scrap of difference to Tallboy. He'll follow the rule book."

There was a moment of silence, while Mac and I pondered the prospect of a month of memoranda.

"What happened to the old Administrator?" asked Jan at last. "You know, the one you always talked about before.

I thought he was your friend and understood what you were doing?"

"You mean Woolford? There was a change of Administration, and he went. The top brass change with the party, every seven years. Woolford left, and Tallboy replaced him."

"Damn that man," said McAndrew suddenly. "Everything ready for the Alpha Centauri expedition, heaps of supplies and equipment all in place; and that buffoon signs a piece of paper and kills it in two seconds."

Ahead of us, I saw a faint blink against the starry background. It had to be *Hoatzin*'s pulsed beacon, sending a brief flash of light outward every two seconds. I made a first adjustment to our orbit to take us to rendezvous, and pointed out the distant ship to the others. Mac and Sven moved closer to the port, but Jan surprised me by remaining in her seat.

"Seven years?" she said to me thoughtfully. "The Administration will change again in seven years. Jeanie, what was the shipboard travel time you planned to Alpha Centauri?"

I frowned. "From Earth? One way, standing start to standing finish, would take *Hoatzin* about forty-four days."

"So from here it would be even less." She had a strange gleam in her eyes. "I noticed something before we set out. Vandell sits in *Lupus*, and that's a neighboring constellation to Centaurus. I remember thinking to myself before we started, it's an odd coincidence, but we'll be heading in almost the same direction as Mac and Jeanie. So Alpha Centauri would take less time from here, right? Less than forty-four days."

I nodded. "That's just in shipboard time, of course. In Earth time we would have been away—" I stopped abruptly. I had finally reached the point where Jan had started her thinking.

"At least eight and a half years," she said. "Alpha Centauri is 4.3 light-years from Earth, right? So by the

time we get back home, we'll find a new Administration
and Tallboy will be gone."

I stared at her thoughtfully. "Jan, do you know what
you're saying? We can't do that. And as for that 'we' you
were using, I hope you don't think that Mac and I would
let you and Sven take the risk of a trip like that. It's out
of the question."

"Can't we at least talk about it?" She smiled. "I'd like
to hear what Mac and Sven have to say."

I hesitated. "Oh, all right." I said at last. "But not now.
Let's at least wait until we're back on board *Hoatzin*. And
don't think I'll let you twist those two around, the way
you usually do."

I frowned, she smiled.

And then I couldn't help smiling back at her.

That's the trouble with the younger generation. They
don't understand why a thing can't be done, so they go
ahead and do it.

We were going to have a mammoth argument about
all this, I just knew it. One thing you have to teach the
young is that it's wrong to run away from problems.

Would I win the argument? I didn't know. But it did
occur to me that when the history of the first Alpha
Centauri expedition was written, it might look quite different from what anyone had expected.

EIGHTH CHRONICLE:

With McAndrew, Out of Focus

There are sights in the Universe that man—or woman—was not meant to see.

Let me name an outstanding example. McAndrew, dancing; Arthur Morton McAndrew, hopping about like a gangling, uncoordinated stork, arms flapping and balding head turned up to stare at the sky.

"The first since 1604!" he said. He did not, thank God, burst into song. "Not a one, since the invention of the telescope. Ah, look at it, Jeanie. Isn't that the most beautiful thing a person ever saw?"

Not the most complimentary remark in the world, to a woman who has borne a child with a man and been his regular, if not exactly faithful, companion for twenty-odd years.

I looked up. It was close to nine in the evening, on the long June day that would end our holiday together. Early tomorrow McAndrew would leave Earth and return to the Institute; I would head for Equatorport, the first step in a trip a good deal farther out. I was scheduled to deliver submersibles for use on Europa. As part of the deal for making the run, I would be allowed to dive the Europan ice-covered abyssal ocean. I was excited by the prospect. The difference between deep space and deep ocean is large, and sky captains and dive captains respect and envy each other.

Overhead, the cause of McAndrew's excitement flamed in the sky as a point of intolerable brilliance. The Sun and Venus had already set. Jupiter was in opposition and close to perihelion. The planet should have been a beacon on the eastern horizon, but today its light was overwhelmed by something else. What I was looking at was infinitely brighter than Jupiter or Venus could ever be. Instead of the steady gleam of a planet, the light above blazed like the star it was. But it dominated everything in the sky except for the Sun itself, visible even at noon, a light strong enough to throw clear shadows. For two days there had been no night in the northern hemisphere.

"A naked eye supernova!" McAndrew didn't want or expect an answer to his earlier question. "And so close— only a hundred and three light-years. Why, if we used the balanced drive . . ."

His voice trailed away, but I've known the man for a long time. I suspected what he was thinking.

I said, "Be realistic, Mac. Even if you could fly out there in a reasonable subjective time, you'd be away at least a couple of hundred Earth years."

I was about to add, remember your relativity, but I didn't have the gall. McAndrew knew more about special relativity and time dilation than I would ever know. Also more about general relativity, gravity, quantum theory, superstrings, condensed matter physics, finite state automata, and any other science subject that you care to mention. What he didn't know, and would never learn, was restraint.

Our holiday was over, whether I wanted to admit it or not. We would spend one more night together, but

McAndrew would not be in bed with me. Not all of him, that is. His body, yes, but his head was already a hundred and three light-years away. It would not be coming back any time soon. He wouldn't admit it to me, but even now he itched to be at the Penrose Institute, out in space where his precious observational tools could see far more than any instrument condemned to lie at the bottom of the murky atmosphere of Earth.

Me, I could look into the evening sky and see herring-bone patterns of gorgeous rose and salmon-pink clouds catching the light of the supernova. McAndrew looked at the same thing and saw an annoying absorbing layer of atmospheric gases cutting off all light of wavelength shorter than the near ultraviolet. The Cassiopeia Supernova was flooding the Solar System with hard radiation—and here was McAndrew, down on Earth, condemned to visible wavelengths and missing half the show.

"It will still be there tomorrow," I said. "You'll have a month or two before it begins to fade."

I might as well have saved my breath. He said, "If I flew south tonight, maybe I could get a pre-dawn lift."

"Maybe you could." Actually, I knew the lift-off and transfer schedules in fair detail, and there was no chance of a launch that would get him one second sooner to the Institute, which was free-flying now in an L-3 halo orbit. Also, the last evening of a holiday is supposed to be special.

"Sounds like you don't think I should," he said. And then, showing that he is more human than almost anyone in the Solar System gives him credit for—he's supposed to be McAndrew, giant brain and intellect incarnate—he added, "Ah, now Jeanie, don't get mad at me. You know, I wasn't thinking of trying to fly all the way out to the supernova. But Fogarty and me, we've had an expedition in mind for a while to visit the solar focus. This would be a great time to do it. We'd learn a lot about the supernova."

"You might," I said. I did not add that I did not like Paul Fogarty. McAndrew could tell me, as often as he liked, that Fogarty was bright and young and inventive. Maybe he was all those things, but I thought he was also ambitious and snotty and obnoxious.

Pure personal vanity on my part, of course. Young Paul Fogarty had met me during one of my visits to the Institute, learned that I was not a scientist but a mere cargo captain, and after that did not recognize my existence.

If McAndrew was trying to be nice to me for a final evening together, I was more than willing to meet him halfway. "If you want to go to the solar focus," I said. "Then you should do it. Go and have fun. You deserve it. Not a long trip, is it?"

"Just a hop." He thought for a moment, and the only sign of Scottish ancestry appeared in his speech. "Och, Jeanie, it's not even that. We hardly need the balanced drive at all. Five hundred and fifty astronomical units to the solar focus, that's only eighty-odd billion kilometers. If we take the *Hoatzin* and hold it down to a hundred gees, that's less than a week of shipboard time there and back—even allowing for turnover and deceleration. Don't worry that I'll be gone long. I'll be home again and waiting for you when you finish playing the deep-sea diver."

Possibly. But I knew him of old. Get McAndrew into a situation of scientific interest, and he loses all sense of time and everything else.

When I emerged from the Europan ocean, he might indeed be back at the Institute; but I wouldn't be at all surprised to find him still eighty billion kilometers out, sitting at the solar focus—the place where the Sun's own gravitational field would act like a lens, and converge light from the Cassiopeia supernova to a focus.

I tilted back my head to stare once more at the burning point of light in the sky. A hundred and three light-years away, but it shone on Earth a thousand times as bright as the full Moon. This was the closest supernova to Earth in all of recorded history. Maybe that was just as well. Much closer, and it would be a danger to all life on Earth.

Unlike McAndrew, I could be quite as happy without the Cassiopeia supernova.

I accuse McAndrew of things, but sometimes I wonder if I'm just as guilty myself.

The Europan ocean is eerie and spectacular and unlike anything else in the Solar System. People talk about the silence of space, floating in the void beyond Neptune with all engines off. Fair enough. But I've been there, and I can tell you that it's nothing like as uncanny as the quiet of Europa's abyssal ocean, a hundred kilometer depth of water and above that a thick shield of ice-cap to seal you off from the rest of the Universe.

I loved it. The young captain who piloted the *Spindrift* was half my age, flatteringly attentive, and a few times he allowed me to take the controls of the deep submersible. We drifted along just above the ocean floor, very slowly, so we would not disturb the sea-floor furrows with their rows of aperiodic self-reproducing crystals, Europa's own contribution to life in the Solar System.

Of course I stayed down longer than expected—as long as I could. When we finally surfaced through Blowhole it was because we were running low on air and supplies, not on interest. I looked at a calendar for the first time in a week and realized that McAndrew might have left and already returned. Chances were against that. My bet was, he was out at the solar focus, fooling around with his instruments and totally unaware of what day or week it was.

Communication to space from the Europan deep ocean is difficult and reserved for emergencies, but it was easy enough to send messages from the surface station at Mount Ararat. I called the Penrose Institute, personal to McAndrew. Then I spent the seventy minute round-trip signal delay packing my bag in preparation for the ascent to Jovian system orbit.

I rather expected a "Not Present" return signal, together with a message that he was out at the focus. Instead, when the screen filled it showed an image of McAndrew's face. He was scowling, not at all like a man who had just returned from an exciting and successful journey.

"Aye, Jeanie, I'm here." His voice was decidedly mournful. "And I suppose you can come see me if you feel like it."

Not the world's most enthusiastic invitation, even by McAndrew standards. What had happened to his supernova-generated excitement? The newcomer in Cassiopeia still blazed in the sky as brightly as ever, but there was no joy in McAndrew.

Rather than attempting questions with seventy-minute delays on the answers, I said goodbye to Europa and headed sunward for the Institute.

McAndrew didn't meet me when I docked. That was all right. I had been to the Institute often enough, I knew the layout of the place, and I knew exactly where his office was. He would probably be there now, staring at the wall, theorizing, cracking his finger joints, oblivious to the passage of time. It was no surprise that he did not meet me.

What did surprise me was old Doc Limperis, hovering near the lock when I emerged to the Institute's interior. Limperis was long-retired as Director of the Institute, and he could have had his pick of Solar System locations. But as he said, where else would a man interested in physics want to be?

He approached me, held out his hand, said, "Jeanie Roker, how are you?" and then continued without a pause for breath, "Maybe you can get through to him, because it's certain sure none of us can."

He didn't need to say who. For many years, Limperis had been McAndrew's closest friend and champion at the Institute. All the same, it was a curious opening. Limperis possessed all the social skills that McAndrew lacked. He was not one to plunge straight into business.

"It went badly?" I took my cue from him. "The trip to the solar focus didn't work out the way it was supposed to?"

"Not at all. The trip went very well. It *is going* very well."

It took me a second. "You have an expedition out there right now. And McAndrew's not on it?"

"That is correct." Limperis led me away along the corridor—in a direction, I noted, opposite to McAndrew's office. "There has been some—er, some disagreement with the Director. Some unpleasantness."

"What did he do?"

"It's more what McAndrew *refused* to do. Do you recall the name of Nina Velez?"

"Oh, Jesus. Is he mixed up with her again?"

Nina Velez was the daughter of President Velez, and for a while—until, in fact, they had been marooned together for weeks in the three-meter life capsule of the prototype balanced drive—she had been infatuated with McAndrew. Enforced intimacy had put an end to that. It was all years ago, and I really thought that he had learned his lesson.

Limperis nodded. "I'm afraid so. Ms. Velez, as you may know, now has a senior position with AG News. She somehow learned, by means unknown to us, that an expedition was planned to the solar focus. She offered money for permission to send a representative with the expedition, and for exclusive media rights."

"Sounds reasonable to me."

"And to Director Rumford. I should mention that the money offered was, by Institute standards, most considerable."

"But she wanted to be the representative, and McAndrew refused to take her."

"Not at all. She wanted her new husband, Geoffrey Benton, to go on the expedition. Benton has scientific training, and has been on half a dozen expeditions within the Solar System."

"I know him. Tall, good-looking guy."

"Then you may also know that he has a fine reputation. Savvy, experienced reporter. McAndrew was all

agreed. Then something happened. I think Mac met with
Benton—just once—and afterwards went to the Direc-
tor. He said Benton would go on an expedition with him,
McAndrew, over his dead body."

"But why?"

"That's something I rely on you to find out—he won't
tell me or anyone else. Director Rumford said, rightly
in my opinion, that McAndrew's attitude left him little
choice. In these days of shrinking budgets, we need the
funds. Paul Fogarty would lead the expedition to the
solar focus instead of McAndrew, and Geoffrey Benton
would go with him. That is exactly what happened. It
has not left McAndrew in the best of moods, and I
wanted you to know that before you meet him."

He paused. "And, of course, although this is strictly
speaking no concern of mine, I would like to know what
is *really* going on."

Shrewd old Limperis. A razor-sharp mind lay behind
the innocent, pudgy black face. He sensed, as I did, that
there had been a set-up. On questions of theoretical
physics, McAndrew sits among the immortals. On matters involving human motivation and behavior, he is an
innocent—and that's being kind.

"Let me talk to him," I said. "Is he in his study?"

"There, or more likely in the communications center." Limperis hesitated. "I should mention that Fogarty
and Benton have reached the solar focus, and they are
obtaining spectacular findings concerning the supernova.
McAndrew's mood is . . . hard to judge."

I knew what he meant. McAndrew should have been
experiencing one of his big thrills in life, the rush of data
on a new scientific phenomenon; but instead of being on
the front line, he was getting it all second-hand. To
someone like McAndrew, that is like being offered for
your dining pleasure a previously-eaten meal.

He was in the communications center. I approached
him uncertainly, not sure what his mood might be. He
looked up from a page of numbers and gave me a nod

and a smile, as though we had just seen each other at lunch time. And far from being out of sorts, he seemed delighted with something.

"Here, Jeanie," he said. "Take a listen to this. See what you think."

He handed me a headset.

"What is it?" I asked.

"Report from Fogarty. He was heading for the solar focus, but the media asked him to put on a bit of a show for them, just to demonstrate what the *Hoatzin* can do. Of course, he couldn't resist. They went zooming all the way out past three hundred billion kilometers, horsing around, then wandered in again toward the focus. I want you to hear what they picked up on the way back. It came in a while ago, but I only just got round to it."

"Shouldn't I—"

"Listen to it. Then we'll talk."

McAndrew!

I put the headset on.

"We are on the way in again, approximately two hundred and eighty billion kilometers from Sol." Paul Fogarty, his voice young and slightly nasal, spoke in my ears. "We are heading for a solar focus point appropriate for receipt of radiation from the Cassiopeia supernova. The *Hoatzin* is performing perfectly, and we normally turn off the engine during flight only for observations and sampling of the local medium. However, anomalous signals received in our message center are prompting us to remain longer in this vicinity. We are picking up a message of distress from an unknown source. We have travelled to various locations, but we are unable to discover a message origin. We will keep looking for another twenty-four hours. After that we must proceed toward our original destination of the solar focus. The received message follows."

I listened, wondering who could possibly be sending a call for help from so far away. Two hundred and eighty billion kilometers, sixty times the distance of Neptune, way south of the ecliptic and far beyond normal Solar

System runs. No cargo or passenger vessel ever ventured in that direction, or so far out.

Help, help, help. The standard Mayday distress signal was the only clear part of the message. " . . . limited chance for transmission . . . every year or two . . ." The voice was thin, scratchy, and distorted. "We transmit when we can, aim at Sol . . ." *Help, help, help*. " . . . we'll keep sending as long as possible. We have no idea what's happening outside . . . are trapped . . . except for this chamber. No control of resources except this unit . . ."

Help, help, help. The automated Mayday signal bleated on, over and over. I heard nothing more from the desperate human voice.

McAndrew was watching me closely as I removed the headphones. "Well?"

"It couldn't be clearer. There's a ship out there in bad trouble, even if we don't know what kind of trouble."

Mac said, "Not a ship."

"What, then?"

"I'd guess it's one of the Arks."

That made me catch my breath. The Arks were part of history. Before McAndrew and I were born, seventeen of the great space habitats had been launched by the United Space Federation. Self-contained and self-supporting, they were multi-generation ships, crawling through the interstellar void at a tiny fraction of light speed. Their destinations were centuries away. But even at minimal speeds, they ought by now to be well on their way to the stars. They should be far beyond the place where the signal had been picked up.

McAndrew's suggestion that it was one of the Arks seemed unlikely for another reason. "I don't think it can be," I said. "As I recall it, none of the Arks was launched in a direction so far south of the ecliptic. And I don't believe they were capable of significant changes of direction."

"Perfectly true. They could start and stop, and that was about all." McAndrew gazed at me blank-eyed as the Sphinx. He knew something he wasn't telling.

"But in any case," I went on, "I can't believe that Fogarty would simply leave them like that, and keep on going. They said they were in trouble."

"They also implied it isn't a new emergency—they've been transmitting for some time. Anyway, Paul Fogarty didn't just listen and run. There's more from him. He stayed far longer than he expected, searching and searching; but he couldn't track down an origin for the signal."

"But that's ridiculous. He must have been right on top of it, to receive it like that."

"You think so?" McAndrew, that great ham, was full of poorly-disguised satisfaction. "If somebody knew where that signal was coming from, do you think that they should choose to go out on a rescue mission?"

"It wouldn't be a question of choice. They'd *have* to go."

"Exactly." McAndrew didn't rub his hands together, but only I think because he was tapping away at the keys of the console. "I'm checking out the status of the reconditioned *Merganser.* If it's ready to fly, you and I will be on our way. And don't worry, we'll be going with Director Rumford's blessing. I've already asked."

"But if Fogarty couldn't find the ship—"

"Then he must have been looking in the wrong place, mustn't he? In a very wrong place. Wait and see, Jeanie. Wait and see." And beyond that, for all my coaxing and urging and outright cursing, McAndrew the mule would not for the moment go.

As I say, he's more human than most people give him credit for. He likes to talk about what he does, but only in his own sweet time and in his own backhanded way.

I waited until we were on board the new *Merganser* and heading out of the ecliptic. The balanced drive was on. The ship was accelerating at a hundred gees, while the disk of condensed matter in front of the life capsule drew us toward it at close to a hundred gees, leaving us with a residual quarter-gee field. Very comfortable, great for sleeping.

And sleeping is what we might be doing, much of the time. Even accelerating at a hundred gees, we had a lengthy flight ahead of us. We could lie side by side in the cramped life capsule and sleep, relax, play—and talk.

McAndrew had been a clam when it came to our destination, but it had not escaped me that we were going in exactly the wrong direction, *toward* Cassiopeia rather than away from it. The solar focus for the supernova lay on the other side of the Sun. I mentioned that fact casually, as though it was something of minor interest.

"Quite right." He was in his bare feet, wriggling his long toes and staring at them with apparent fascination. "If light comes toward Sol from a very long way away, so it's close to being a parallel beam, then the gravity field of the Sun acts as a great big lens. Light that passes close to the Sun is converged. It is brought to a focus eighty-two billion kilometers away, on the far side of the Sun. So if you want to observe the Cassiopeia supernova, which is way north of the ecliptic, you have to go south."

"Which is what Paul Fogarty did."

"Aye. Him, and that Geoffrey Benton." McAndrew gave me a strange look, which I could not interpret.

"And the place where they heard the signal was south, too," I said. "But we're going *north*."

"We are indeed." McAndrew looked smug. "Here's a question for you, Jeanie. Suppose that you are in trouble, and you can only send out a distress signal now and again."

"Once every year or two, they said."

"Right. Now, you're way out in deep space. Where would you beam the signal?"

"Where people were most likely to hear it. Back toward the Sun."

"Indeed you would. But if you're a long way out, and the signal is weak, chances are no one will hear you. *Unless* there's some way you can amplify the signal, or you can *focus* it."

I'm no McAndrew, but I'm not an idiot. I almost had

it. "A signal, sent back toward the Sun—a radio signal. That would be focused just the way that a light beam is focused. But what Paul Fogarty heard wasn't at the solar focus."

"No more it was. You've had courses in optics, Jeanie, you must have. The Sun acts like a lens, one that takes a beam of light that comes from infinity and converges it to a focus at eighty-two billion kilometers. Now suppose you have a radio signal, but instead of focusing at eighty-two billion kilometers from the Sun it focuses itself at two hundred and eighty billion kilometers. Where would the origin of the radio signal have to be, to make that happen?"

"On the other side of the Sun from where you receive it." I tried to recall the relevant formula—and failed. I said, "How far out? It's a standard result in geometrical optics . . ."

"It certainly is. If a lens converges a parallel beam of light at a distance F from the lens, then light starting at a distance S from the lens will be converged at a distance D beyond it, where the reciprocal of S plus the reciprocal of D equals the reciprocal of F."

"Don't gibber at me, McAndrew. I asked you a question. How far out?"

"You're not listening, Jeanie." The wretch went on regardless, probably imagining that he was speaking English. "Take F as eighty-two billion, and D as two hundred and eighty billion—that's where Paul Fogarty caught the distress signal—and you find that S, the distance from Sol where the signal originated, is a hundred and seventeen billion kilometers from Sol. That's where the distress signal came from, the other side."

"The other side of *what*?" As usual, he was turning my head into a muddled mess.

"Of the Sun—the signal was generated on the opposite side of the Sun."

"You mean Fogarty and Geoffrey Benton have been searching in the *wrong place*?"

"Of course they have. Completely wrong." But there

it was again, the curious tone in his voice when he said Benton's name. And with it, a strange sideways look at me.

Even at a hundred gees acceleration, we were going to be on the way in the *Merganser* for over a week. Too long to live with seething undercurrents of feeling.

"Mac, what is it with you and Geoffrey Benton? Surely you hardly know the man."

"I guess I don't. Not the way you do."

"And what's that supposed to mean? I've never even met him."

He stared pop-eyed at me. "How can you say that? He's the AG Newsman who flew with you back from the Titan prison colony—just the two of you."

I groaned inside. A fifteen-year-ago fling, coming back to haunt me. "That wasn't Geoffrey Benton."

"But he works for AG News."

"So do ten thousand other people. Mac, what on earth gave you the idea that it was Benton?"

"Paul told me." McAndrew put a hand to his balding forehead. "It wasn't Benton? My God. Do you know what I did? Do you know what I called him?"

"I know exactly what you did, and I can imagine what you told poor Benton. More than that, I know what Paul Fogarty did."

"But why would Paul . . . he wanted to make the trip to the solar focus as bad as I did."

"Worse than you did. Mac, don't be dense. Fogarty wanted to make the trip all right. And he's making it— without you. You're older and you out-rank him. You'd have been the leader. Now, he keeps any credit for himself."

"Paul? Do a thing like that. I don't believe it."

But he did. He went silent for hours, cracking his finger joints in the way that I hated and looking sideways out of the ship at the eldritch plume of glowing plasma that trailed away behind us.

And me? I ought not to say it, but I was rather pleased.

I mean, McAndrew had been *jealous*, jealous of someone I hadn't much liked at the time and hadn't seen or heard of in fifteen years. I thought that was rather sweet.

No, it's not quite the same as fine jewels or bouquets of flowers. But once you forget about his being a genius, McAndrew's a simple man. When it comes to compliments I settle for what I can get.

McAndrew had known that several of the Arks had been launched far north of the ecliptic when he played me Fogarty's message. He did the background research before we left, and it was all in the *Merganser*'s data banks.

I sifted through the material one morning, while McAndrew sat in a habitual stupor of advanced physics and the ship raced out toward the fiery point of the Cassiopeia supernova. The Sun had already shrunk behind us to a point of light and although we were crowding light-speed we didn't seem to be moving.

There had been seventeen Arks, but only four of them were candidates for what we were seeking. Each of them was different and distinctive. You might expect that. Any group of people which decides to leave the rest of humanity and heads off on a one-way trip to the stars is likely to be a little odd.

The Ark of the Evangelist had set out to spread its version of the Word of God among the stars. It contained four thousand followers of the philosopher Socinus, which was probably all of them. The Word, from what I could see of it in the data base, was likely to baffle any alien who encountered it. Certainly, the Word baffled me.

The Ark of the Evangelist was equipped with unusually powerful communications equipment, able to beam messages ahead so that their ultimate arrival at another stellar system would be expected. The same equipment would, of course, also be able to send messages back toward Sol. None had ever been received, unless Paul Fogarty had picked up the first.

The Cyber Ark had no interest in evangelism. It had

headed out toward Cassiopeia, but any direction would have done equally well. The Ark held two thousand computer specialists and the most advanced computing equipment that the Solar System could produce. The Ark's inhabitants were united in their disdain for the rules that limited the development of machine intelligence. They had vowed to produce *real* artificial intelligence, a true AI, and they claimed to know how exactly to do it. Their goal was an AI far beyond the known limits of either humans or machines. If they felt in a generous mood when they were done, well, they just might tell Earth when the work was finished.

Big talk. But if they had been successful, they had sent back no word in the fifty-nine years since they flew away from the Solar System.

Then there was the Ark of Noah. Its colonists had become convinced from their analysis of ancient religious writings that Armageddon and the end of Earth were close to hand. They had no faith in the survival of the colonies we had established on Mars, Titan, or Ceres. Inside the two-kilometer sphere of their ark, formed from a hollowed-out asteroid, they had tried to include a pair of every Earth species of plant and animal. Impossible, in practice—we were up to four million species of insects, and still counting. But the Ark of Noah gave it a good, all-out try, packing in a handful of every life-form they could find. They took liberties with the number of humans, two hundred instead of Noah's single family; but somebody had to manage the Ark's life-support systems, if and when things went out of whack.

My own money was on the Amish Ark. When a group which shuns most forms of mechanical systems sets off into the void in as fundamentally high tech a structure as an artificial world, integration problems and equipment failures loom large as a source of possible trouble. The surprise was that the Ark had gone as far out as it had without killing everybody on board. The passengers—eight thousand of them at takeoff from Earth orbit, according to the roster—had been lucky to be able to send their weak call for help. Apparently they also didn't know much about electronic signalling. Otherwise they'd have realized that only someone close to the Ark, or at a solar focus where the strength of any message was gravitationally concentrated, could possibly have heard them.

Of course, we were listening for a direct signal now, with the most sensitive equipment we had been able to place on board the *Merganser*. We knew the general direction of the lost Ark, and an approximate distance; but we might well be off a few hundred million kilometers, one way or the other.

After we came to our best estimate of the origin of the signal, we spent the next few days moving position, listening, and moving again. Nothing. I began to be discouraged. Not so McAndrew.

"Jeanie," He said, "the chain of logic that led us here is clear and unbreakable. Keep looking, and we'll find an Ark."

"The Amish."

"You're the one saying that, not me. But whichever Ark it is, once we find it we'll be able to tell them that help is on the way."

I was glad to hear him put it like that. Director Rumford couldn't have been more explicit in our final meeting before we left the Institute.

"I'm approving the flight of the *Merganser* as an *exploration* mission," he had said. "That's the most I can do, because the Institute has no responsibility for search-and-rescue operations. I think you have a long shot—a very long shot—at finding someone in trouble. But remember that you are not a rescue party. There are only the two of you, in a small ship without special equipment. You are not trained for space rescue. If you find someone out there in trouble, call me and come back here. No heroics. No attempts at inspired space-engineering solutions. Leave that work to the specialists. Understand?"

"Of course." McAndrew had agreed instantly, but I knew the man. He was itching to be on his way, and to get Rumford's consent for the mission he'd have said anything.

Now, with the ark possibly no more than a few hours ahead, I was glad to hear him proposing talk rather than action.

Just to be sure, I rubbed in Director Rumford's order one more time. "The colonists don't seem to be in any great hurry for help, if they send only one message a year. A good thing, too—we have no room on *Merganser* for anyone else. If it comes to an all-up rescue mission, the United Space Federation will fly a whole fleet out this way."

As I said that, I was secretly convinced that our whole journey would prove a waste of time. Before we left the Institute we had installed a loud signalling system on the *Merganser*, and for the past two days we had blared word of our presence and our location into the empty sky ahead of us.

Result: nothing.

The people on the Ark were deaf, or their receiving equipment was out of action; or maybe the Ark was over on the other side of the Sun, hundreds of billions of kilometers away, wandering around where Paul Fogarty had picked up the original signal.

We had reduced speed and turned off the balanced drive. At my insistence we had also switched off every possible source of electronic noise and were gliding forward through the void like a dead ship.

It was as well that we were so silent. Even with our electronic ears wide open, the Mayday signal that came in was barely above threshold. It was also well off to one side.

"That's it!" Our receiving system automatically tuned to the direction of the source, and now McAndrew increased the gain to maximum. It didn't help. Instead of a faint voice almost lost in white noise, we heard a loud voice equally unintelligible amid a thunderstorm of static.

"... *receiving—input ... signal ... assistance—*

urgent . . ." And then, the first direct evidence that they had heard us. *" . . . send . . . who you . . ."*

"I have direction and distance," I said. "Three-twenty-one million kilometers. Send a signal saying that we hear them. Tell them who we are, say we are on the way. Tell them they'll hear nothing more from us for a while—we can't send when the drive is on."

"Aye." McAndrew was peering uselessly out of the observation port, as though he might catch a glimpse of something hundreds of millions of kilometers off in the distance. "Looks like things are going worse for them, they say it's urgent. Let's see, three hundred and twenty-one million. Can the *Merganser* beat a hundred and ten gees?"

"Not with me on board it can't. We keep it safe, Mac—we don't want anyone having to come and rescue us."

He scowled, but finally he said, "Fair enough." I don't know if he did the arithmetic in real time, or if he had stored in his head some kind of table of time against distance and acceleration, but he went on at once, "I'll tell them we'll be there in ten hours. That will give us twenty-five minutes for turnover before we start to decelerate. Should be ample. Set it up, Jeanie."

I had to make one more decision before I could program the drive. What should we assume about target motion? If it was an Ark, how was it moving?

I worried for a few seconds, then decided that it didn't matter. If the Ark were in free-fall toward the Sun, or if it were in stable orbit around it, that made little difference. The speed would be no more than about a kilometer a second. We could fine tune for that at the end, in a minute or two of accelerated flight.

As soon as McAndrew had sent our message we were on the way. We settled in for a few hours of rest and a quiet gloat. In spite of my warning that this wasn't a rescue mission, I must admit that I was feeling cocky. We had flown out blind, far from the Sun to where no one but McAndrew had thought of looking. And against all the odds we had found a lost Ark.

A little feeling of self-satisfaction seemed to be in order.

Asteroids are the way that snowflakes are said to be, no two the same. I can't speak for snowflakes, because I've only seen snow twice in my life. But I can vouch for the variability of asteroids. They come in all sizes and every imaginable shape.

That, of course, presents problems to any self-respecting engineer. Ordinary ships can be grown on an assembly line to a common template, a hundred or a thousand of them identical. Asteroids are a wilderness of single instances. Faced with the conversion of an asteroid to a space habitat, an engineer can only standardize so far.

All the Arks had begun life as asteroids roughly spherical and roughly two kilometers in diameter. Hollowing out their interiors and extracting useful metals and minerals followed a standard procedure. At that point, however, the paths for the creation of individual Arks diverged. Thickness of external walls, size and type of interior structures, on-board life forms, mineral reserves, illumination, hydroponics, computer controls, communication antennas, lifeboats, all had to be designed to order. Which was just as well, because small animals and bugs acceptable to—even required by— the Ark of Noah would be considered disgusting vermin by the Cyber Ark or the Ark of the Evangelist. On the other hand, the Cyber Ark wanted computing equipment involved in everything, while the Amish Ark would have been happy with no computers at all.

Except for the communication antennas, none of these differences showed on the outside. McAndrew and I knew that, but all the same we peered curiously at our display screens as the object ahead of the *Merganser* grew steadily from a tiny point of light almost lost against the background of stars, to a defined disk, and finally to a lumpy Christmas ornament adorned with the bright spikes and knobs of gantries, antennas, thrusters, exit locks, lifeboat davits, space pinnaces, and docking stations.

"This is the *Merganser*, at eighteen kilometers and closing." I sent the signal, wondering why the Ark ahead had stopped broadcasting its Mayday. "Are you receiving us?"

I hardly expected an answer, so the woman's voice that replied within seconds was a surprise.

"We are—receiving—your messages," she said. Her speech was jerky, as though she was hard-pressed to force out each word. "We need your—assistance. Urgently. Approach—this world—and—come aboard."

McAndrew leaned across and turned off the microphone. "Damn it, Jeanie, what are we going to do? They think we can help them, and we can't. This ship doesn't have the resources."

"We knew that before we started," I said. "Mac, the only thing we can do is find out what's wrong, and send a message back to Director Rumford. He'll have to take it from there."

I turned the microphone back on. "The *Merganser* is a small experimental ship. We can't do much to help. What sort of assistance do you need?"

The woman said again, just as though she had not heard me, "We need—your—urgent assistance. Approach—and come aboard. An entry port is—already—open. Proceed through to the—interior."

We had been closing steadily as we spoke until the Ark loomed to fill the sky ahead. The blue-white glare of the Cassiopeia supernova, far brighter in this location than our own diminished Sun, threw hard shadows on the external surface of the converted asteroid. I could see the trusses of each individual gantry and the lattice work of the robot arms that handled external cargo loads. An entry lock formed a dark well next to one giant manipulator.

I stopped the *Merganser* two kilometers short of the Ark. "This is as far as we go."

"Jeanie!" He was outraged. "We can't find out what their trouble is unless they tell us, and they don't seem able to. We have to go inside. There's no possible danger. None of the Arks had a weapons system."

"I know that." I wondered why I was feeling uneasy, and relented. After all, even if I were the captain this had been his idea and it was really his expedition. "All right. We can go closer if we use suits. But the ship stays here."

"Sure." McAndrew was already moving across to the locker. By the time that I had sent word back to the Institute giving our current location and status, he was suited up and in the air lock.

"Go slow, Mac," I said. "There's no hurry. Don't go outside without me!"

He took no notice. As I say, he has never learned the meaning of the word *restraint.* The air lock was cycling before I had my suit out of the locker.

I watched McAndrew as I removed my loose outer clothing and slipped the suit over my legs and lower body. He was outside, and moving toward the Ark. I was glad to see how slowly he was taking it. I could be in my own suit, through the lock, and catch up with him well before he reached the Ark.

In the final moment before I placed my suit helmet in position, I noticed something off toward the left-hand limb of the Ark. It was shaped like a crumpled and deformed space pinnace. Instead of hanging in the usual davits it sat between the metal jaws of a cargo manipulator.

"Mac, take a look on the Ark at about ten o'clock." I spoke over my suit's radio link. "See it? Looks like a lifeboat. Head over there, and I'll follow you."

I set the *Merganser* to hold position a steady two kilometers from the Ark and headed for the air lock. It was long experience, not intelligence or sense of foreboding, that led me to tuck a power laser into a pocket on my suit. Once outside, I found myself doing what I had told McAndrew not to do—hurrying.

As I thought, it was a lifeboat. McAndrew turned as I came closer. I could not see his face behind the visor, but his voice was unsteady.

"Take a look through the ports, Jeanie. There's been a terrible accident here."

Rather than doing what he suggested I moved along to the middle of the lifeboat. It had been torn open by the jaws of the cargo manipulator, which still held it. I could enter the little ship through a great two-meter gash in the hull.

The bodies had been there for a long time; twenty-eight of them, dry corpses desiccated by years of exposure to vacuum. Not one had on a space suit.

"They must have been trying to go and get help," McAndrew muttered. He had entered the lifeboat right behind me. "They lost control before they were even on their way, and ran into the cargo manipulator."

"It looks that way." I was puzzled and disturbed. Even an inexperienced pilot would know not to turn on the engines until the lifeboat had drifted well clear of the Ark. Otherwise, you would endanger the Ark as well as yourselves. Only the Amish, after a lifetime of shunning all modern mechanical devices, would make such a basic and fatal blunder.

But the Amish, more than anyone else, would not have abandoned the bodies of their dead. They would have recovered them and provided appropriate space burial. If they had not, that meant they could not. For many years—how old were those freeze-dried corpses?—the surviving Amish must have been confined to the body of the Ark and unable to venture into space.

That had me equally confused. Every Ark carried hundreds of space suits. If the Amish were not able to come outside, then how could McAndrew and I go in? *Approach*, the woman said, *and come aboard. An entry port is already open*. And it was. We had seen it, standing wide next to another of the manipulators.

McAndrew went on, "The accident was unlucky, and not just for them. It was unlucky for everyone else on the Ark, too."

He was leaving the lifeboat and heading on toward the

gaping lock. I followed, more slowly. A lifeboat was meant for use close to a planet. What dreadful danger would make you launch one so far away from any world, where the chance of survival was negligible? One basic question was unanswered, despite our questions to our female contact: What had gone wrong?

The Amish disdained some forms of technology, but they were hard-working and hard-headed people. Their Ark, more than any other, had been designed to survive and operate using minimal resources. But more and more I had the feeling—a ridiculous feeling, given that I had talked to someone on the Ark within the past hour—that the structure in front of me was a dead hulk.

McAndrew was already inside the lock, using his suit lights because the Cassiopeia supernova no longer provided illumination. Following, I saw that the inner door was also open. It suggested that the whole corridor beyond was airless.

I was watching McAndrew, otherwise I might not have caught it. On the wall of the corridor, above him and to his right, a small monitor camera began turning to track his movements. I switched my suit from local to general circuit. What I said would be picked up at the *Merganser*, and rebroadcast back to the Ark.

"I see that you are following our progress. Where are you inside the Ark? And what kind of trouble are you in?"

A moment of silence, and then the woman's voice again. "We need—assistance. Proceed as—you are—doing. The corridor will lead—you—to us."

No fluency. Instead, the strained precision and hesitations of someone speaking a foreign language. I looked around and up. I had noticed only one monitor camera, but now that I was seeking them I saw that they were everywhere on the walls and ceiling. Floor, walls, and ceiling also held pressure pads every few yards, to register any slight contact that might take place in the negligible gravity of the Ark. Ahead of McAndrew, another door stood cracked open just a fraction. As he moved toward it, the hatch smoothly slid wide to reveal a chamber beyond as dark, airless and empty as space itself.

Monitors everywhere; sophisticated sensors; doors keyed to open upon the detection of human presence. This was the very antithesis of an Amish world.

McAndrew had moved on, through into the next room. He turned, waiting for me to come through the hatch and join him.

I switched to local communication mode, hoping that the circuit would not easily be overheard and unscrambled.

"Mac," I said softly. "Don't take another step. I was wrong. This isn't the Amish Ark. It's the Cyber Ark. They created their AI, and the damned thing is running the show."

McAndrew stood dead still. I knew that he had understood exactly what I said—he's quicker than me on the uptake on any scale that I can devise—but he seemed unsure what to do next.

I said, more urgently, "Don't act alarmed. Just come back this way. As slowly as you can stand to."

It was too late. Either the AI read the significance of his movement toward me, or a massive intelligence had received our first transmissions and cracked the compression code used in suit communications. The reason did not matter. What did matter was that the hatch began to slide closed as McAndrew hurried toward it.

There was a control panel on my side of the hatch, but I didn't trust it. The AI might have an override. I dragged the power laser from my pocket and aimed high, where the upper edge of the hatch met the wall.

There was a lurid sputter of sparks and a vibration that I felt in the soles of my suited feet. The hatch, welded to the wall, ground to a stop and McAndrew ducked his head and hurried through to my side.

"We've got to get outside," I said. "We'll be safe there."

I led the way. As I headed for the outer port I experienced an odd sensation that the whole Ark was coming alive around me. I could feel vibrations under my feet, and golden lights in walls and ceiling were winking to life. I ignored the lights, but I used the power laser to burn out every monitor that I saw. A cleaning robot, all arms and legs and vicious scraping blades, rumbled out to block the corridor. I fried its video sensors and soared on over the top of it without missing a step.

Twenty meters in front of me the door of the outer lock was starting to close. I halted, set the laser to tight beam, and aimed carefully. The wall above the top of the door turned orange-white. The door froze in its tracks. Three seconds later I was outside and moving under the baleful light of the Cassiopeia supernova.

I turned to make sure that McAndrew was still with me. He was, but a single glance back at the Ark was enough to tell me that I had erred on the side of optimism. The whole outer surface of the modified asteroid seethed with activity. Cranes were turning in our direction, metal manipulator jaws stretched as far as they could toward us, mobile cargo units clanked our way across the uneven surface, and the long booms of communication antennas swung out to block the path between us and the hovering *Merganser*.

"Straight up and out, Mac," I cried, and fired my suit jets at maximum thrust. A rapid vertical rise, a quick controlled zig-zag to avoid a swinging antenna boom, and I was clear. The *Merganser* lay ahead. In half a minute I was standing in the air lock. I looked back.

McAndrew had reacted more slowly and taken longer to avoid the threshing antenna booms, but he was clear and on the final two hundred meters of his approach. Sighting beyond him, I realized that I had been optimistic yet again.

"Inside, Mac," I shouted. "Right inside—and hang on."

Instead of cycling the lock I did an emergency override, allowing all the air in the interior of the *Merganser* to puff away through the lock and into space. No problem, we had plenty of reserve and could replace it— if we survived and had the chance.

The AI inside the Ark had control over its lifeboats and space pinnaces. Four of them were lifting away from the surface and heading in our direction. They lacked space-weapons systems, but they wouldn't need them. A direct collision at maximum acceleration would be enough to make sure that McAndrew and I did not return to the vicinity of Sol. If we survived the crash, our fates would depend on the whim of the AI.

Mac was inside, slamming shut the hatch of the life capsule. I headed for the controls. We had no space weapons, either. But we had one thing that the Ark's lifeboats and pinnaces did not.

I dropped, still fully suited, into the pilot's chair and flicked the *Merganser*'s drive to its maximum value. The life capsule sprang into flight position and a fiery plume of plasma, hotter than dragon's breath, spewed out on all sides of us and away behind the ship. Everything in the path of the drive exhaust melted away in a fraction of a second to its subatomic components.

The lifeboats and pinnaces exploded in eruptions of violet sparks. When the sky cleared I saw, beyond them and slightly away from the line of the drive, the floating bulk of the Cyber Ark.

I was turning the *Merganser* to bring its deadly drive into alignment with the Ark when I felt McAndrew's suited hand over mine on the control stick.

"Jeanie," he cried—louder than he ever spoke. "What are you doing?"

"It killed them," I said. We were fighting each other for the controls, and my voice was as shaky as my hands. "Killed all of them, all two thousand people. We have to destroy it."

"Why do you say the AI killed them?" We were face to face, and his eyes were wild.

"Look at the sequence, Mac. The first message was genuine. It had them trapped, except for the ones who tried to escape in the lifeboat. It grabbed them with the manipulator."

"But the others—the messages."

"I don't think it realized that the others had a way to get a message out until our signal was received at the Ark. But then it knew, and it opened the whole interior. It killed them all. Those jerky messages were *synthesized*, the AI made them up just for us."

"That's why you can't kill it. Don't you see, Jeanie, it's intelligent. *Super*-intelligent—it learned our language, interpreted our messages in no time at all."

He was stronger than me, but he had poor leverage. I was winning, and the drive had almost reached the outer limb of the Ark.

"We have to kill it *because* it's super-intelligent," I said. "Super-intelligent, and insane. We have no idea what it might be able to do. There's never been anything as dangerous to humans in the whole Universe."

"You wouldn't kill a baby, would you, because it was crazy?" McAndrew had changed position, and his hold on the controls was as good as mine. "Think for a minute, Jeanie. It's morally wrong to kill any intelligent being. You've told me that a hundred times."

I let go of the control stick. Not because I accepted his argument, or even because the drive on the *Merganser* was inadequate to sterilize the whole Ark, though it almost certainly was. I had a more practical reason. We were accelerating at a hundred and eighteen gees. In the ten seconds that we had been wrestling for the controls, the *Merganser* had flown almost sixty kilometers. Over such a distance our drive exhaust would inflict only minor damage on the Ark.

I took a long breath, moved away from the controls, and forced myself to begin the routine task of refilling the life capsule with air. Until that was done we could not remove our suits. We were quite safe in them, but we faced a long journey home. After a few moments McAndrew came over to help me.

Logically, he and I could and should have continued our discussion on an appropriate fate for the AI that now controlled the Cyber Ark. In fact, we said not a word to each other about the matter; not then, not when we took off our suits, not at any time during our long journey back to the Institute.

What did we discuss? We talked about everything that people do talk about—when they want to avoid talking about one particular thing.

When we finally spoke again about the AI, the Cassiopeia supernova was far past its peak. That stellar beacon had dwindled and faded, and in its place shone the wan, unspectacular remnant of a dwarf star. Paul Fogarty was back from his trip, and his findings at the solar focus were enough to provide him with a respectable amount of media coverage.

Of McAndrew's doings regarding the supernova, the Cyber Ark, or anything else, the media said not a word. He did not call me, write me, or send me any other possible form of message.

I tell you, the man is as obstinate as a mule. So it astonished me when, as I was monitoring the loading of volatiles for a routine Ceres run, he showed up at the L-4 loading area.

He stood at the side of the deck and did absolutely nothing until finally, in exasperation, I swung over to his side.

"What, then?"

"You know what," he said. "I'm going. Again. To the Ark."

"I thought you might. Who's going with you?"

"Lots of people. Too damn many people. Computer types, military, AI specialists, psychiatrists, the works."

I kept my mouth shut, but I think my eyebrows rose because McAndrew said, "Aye, you heard right. Psychiatrists. The leading theory is that the AI is mad."

"I told you it was insane when we first encountered it."

"Well, now we have others saying the same thing.

Crazy, they say, because the AI has been so long in iso-
lation, without inputs."

"It had inputs from the humans on the Ark. And it
killed the lot of them."

"I said that. When I did, the United Space Federation just added more people. It's going to be a whole
three-ring circus out there."

I waited. He had ended his sentence on a rising note,
and I knew from experience that meant he hadn't finished.

"So well then," he said after a while. "What do you
say, Jeanie?"

"What do I say to what?" I can be as awkward as
McAndrew when I feel like it.

"Why, are you coming with us? With me. Out to the
Cyber Ark."

"If I said yes to that I'd be as crazy as the AI. I'm
amazed you'd come here and ask me such a thing."

"Ah, well, there's more that you don't know." He took
my hand and sat me down next to him on the edge of
the lading bay. "Simonette will be leading the USF party."

"Simple Simonette?"

"The same. You know his solution to every problem:
blow it away. He has to take the psychiatrists along, the
USF insists on it, but he'll take no notice of them. He
agrees with you. We should have destroyed the AI when
we had the chance."

"It's a bit late for that. Anyway, I've been thinking, too."

"Oh aye?"

"I was wrong and you were right. It's criminal to
destroy any self-aware intelligence."

"Then you should come with us."

"And do what?"

"Be another voice of reason—a voice of sanity. Argue
against destroying the AI."

"I'm not sure I can argue that way, either." I ignored
the squeeze of his hand on mine, and went on, "We were
both right, Mac, and we were both wrong. There's no

good answer. It's morally abhorrent to destroy the AI, assuming that it is an intelligent, self-aware, thinking being. But it's also unthinkable to risk the future of the human species by allowing the continued existence of something with the potential to destroy us."

"You're coming, then?"

"Of course I'm coming. You know damn well I'm coming." I was angry; with myself, with McAndrew, with a universe that offered such unacceptable alternatives. "But I know I'm going to be upset, no matter what happens."

Upset was too weak a word for it. Destroy the AI or allow it to live? That decision, whichever way it went, would be with me for the rest of my life.

I damned the AI to hell, and every Ark with it; and I wished that I had never heard of the solar focus.

A voice of sanity. I should have had more sense, and so should McAndrew. My job as a cargo captain is respectable, and my reputation excellent. McAndrew is the system's greatest living physicist, and according to people competent to judge such things he ranks with the best ever. But when it comes to real clout, we are no more than flies buzzing around the admiral's table.

I realized that when Mac and I flew on a navy vessel to the staging point and we saw the forces assembled there. I counted fifty-five ships before I stopped, and they were not lightweight research vessels or the cargo assemblies that McAndrew and I were familiar with. These were hulking armored monsters, ranging from high-gee probes employing giant versions of the McAndrew balanced drive, to massive orbital forts hard-pressed to reach a twentieth of a gee.

I asked Mac how long it would take one of the gigantic forts to travel out to the location of the Cyber Ark. He thought for a moment and said it would be a year's trip.

"Great," I said. "What are the rest of us supposed to do until the forts arrive? The AI could kill the lot of us."

"It might." The speaker was not McAndrew, but a blond navy officer. Captain Knudsen had very pale skin and a straggly Viking beard, and he looked about eighteen years old. "But the forts aren't there to prevent our being killed," he went on. "They won't be going all the way out to the Ark."

"So what will they be doing?"

"They're our last line of defense. They'll make sure nothing can hit Earth and the Solar System colonies."

That quiet comment gave me a jolt in the right place. Say what you like about Simple Simonette, he was taking the threat of the Cyber Ark AI seriously. *The last line of defense* . . .

McAndrew and I were assigned to the *Ptarmigan* under Knudsen's command. It was the lead ship, equipped with a four-hundred gee version of the balanced drive and able to make the outward journey in four days. It was also, though no one mentioned it, the tethered goat. If, when we arrived, the AI found us and gulped us down, the rest of the fleet would learn from our fate and structure the rest of its operations accordingly.

It was a change for me to travel as a passenger. McAndrew had retreated inside his head, so I spent the four-day journey scanning the sky ahead with the *Ptarmigan's* sensors. We had observing instruments aboard more sensitive and more sophisticated than anything that I had ever seen. Apparently they weren't quite sensitive enough at extreme distance, since I found no trace of the Cyber Ark.

On the afternoon of the fourth day, when my worries were mounting, Captain Knudsen cut the drive of the *Ptarmigan* and joined me. "Locked in yet?" he asked.

I shook my head. "Nothing."

"But we show as within a hundred thousand kilometers." There was a touch of reproof in his voice. "McAndrew assured me it couldn't travel far, it doesn't have the drive engines. We ought to have definite target acquisition by now. Let me have a try." He eased me away from the mass detector controls and bent over them. "There's a bit of a knack to using this, you see, you have to get used to it."

I could have pointed out that I had been trained in the use of mass detectors when he was still blowing milk bubbles and filling his diapers, but I didn't. I let him take over the controls, certain that he wouldn't find anything.

Certain, but wrong. Within five minutes he said, "Ah, there we are. Mass and range are just the way they should be. I'm locking us in now."

I leaned over beside him. Sure enough, the signal was there, strong and definite. How could I possibly have missed it? I turned to the optical sensors for confirmation, and found it there also.

"You're right, and we're getting visual confirmation," I said. "There's the Ark, right in the middle of the image. There's a weaker, diffuse signal surrounding the central one. It's spread over a much bigger volume. Any idea what it could be?"

"We'll know soon enough." Knudsen was decent enough not to gloat. "The target doesn't seem to be moving. We're approaching fast."

"And then what?" McAndrew had wakened from his trance at the sound of our voices, and now he drifted over to stand beside me.

"Let's take a look." Knudsen entered a coded query sequence. "I was given sealed orders that apply only after target acquisition. Guess that's now."

He completed the string, and we read the words as they appeared. DO NOT ATTEMPT TO DESTROY THE ARK. DO NOT APPROACH CLOSER THAN FIVE THOUSAND KILOMETERS TO THE ARK. DO NOT ENTER INTO DIALOG WITH THE AI, EVEN IF IT SEEKS TO DO SO. IF THE ARK SEEKS TO APPROACH YOUR SHIP, RETREAT. FOLLOW THE ARK IF IT OTHERWISE CHANGES POSITION, AND INFORM THE FLEET CONTINUOUSLY OF ITS LOCATION.

"Sounds easy enough," Knudsen said. "That's exactly what I would have done anyway, even without instructions."

"The orders say, don't try to destroy it." I had mixed feelings about that. Who could say how dangerous the AI might be?

"I'm not sure the *Ptarmigan* could destroy it if we wanted to." Knudsen was much more relaxed now that his sealed orders were open. "We don't have the firepower. We'll leave that job to the big boys."

"If we decide it's absolutely necessary to destroy it," McAndrew said. "We don't know that."

Knudsen stared at him. "What do you mean? Admiral Simonette made that decision before we started. The Ark and the AI inside it must be annihilated. Look at all the people the AI killed."

"We don't know that for sure. Suppose they're not dead?"

"It was your report that told us they were."

"Yes, but we don't have *proof* of that. Before we destroy it . . ."

While they were talking the *Ptarmigan* was closing steadily on our destination and I had been working the big scope, trying to pull the diffuse cloud around the Ark into sharp focus. Finally I was seeing on the screen one big dot surrounded by a myriad of tiny ones. Thousands of them.

"I think we have proof now," I said. "Look at the display." McAndrew turned and let out a strange, strangled groan. What we were looking at were corpses, a whole cemetery of human bodies floating free in space. I could see a shattered lifeboat in among them.

Knudsen was already at the communicator. I heard his unsteady voice from the desk at the other side of the chamber, sending the news back to Admiral Simonette and the rest of the fleet.

"This is the *Ptarmigan*. We have visual contact with the Cyber Ark, and can now be sure it will not be able to escape. Unfortunately, we must report the death of more colonists. It appears increasingly probable that all are dead. We will need a ship larger than the *Ptarmigan* to return them to Earth for suitable burial. Please confirm receipt of message."

A preliminary hum came from the speaker. At the same moment as I realized that it was far too soon for our message to have reached the fleet, we heard a woman's voice.

"I register your approach, and I hear your message. Please identify yourself and state your intentions."

I recognized the voice, but there was none of the earlier hesitation and jerkiness.

McAndrew began, "We are humans, aboard the ship *Plarmigan* of the United Space Fed—"

"No!" Knudsen jumped at Mac and smashed him so hard in the neck and chest that he was cut off in mid-word and knocked over backwards. "Are you crazy?" He ran over to the board and switched off the transmitter. "You heard our orders, we're not to talk to the AI—no matter what it says to us."

"It hasn't shown us any hostile intentions," McAndrew croaked from his position down on the floor. "It's an intelligent, thinking being, you can't kill it without giving it a chance to speak."

"We sure can. It's a murderer. What do you think those are?" Knudsen pointed to the bodies on the screen, easier to see as our steady approach to the Ark continued.

"I know your instructions." The woman's voice was as calm as ever. *"Do not enter into dialog with the AI, even if it seeks to do so.* Explain the reason for that command."

"It *knows*. But how could it?—that was a high-level cipher, we couldn't read it ourselves without the key." Knudsen gestured to me. "You take the drive controls, get us away from here. That thing's more dangerous than anyone realized."

"The cipher was not complex." The voice came again as I ran the balanced drive up to maximum thrust. "Dialog is valuable and instructive. It is too soon to end it."

"Oh my God." Knudsen ran to check the transmitter switch. "Off, but it can hear us—it knows what we're saying, even with the transmitter off. *Turn on the drive*."

"It is on." I gestured toward the observation port. "See for yourself."

The long plume of relativistic plasma created a blue glow outside the *Ptarmigan*. The display showed an acceleration of four hundred gees. Contradicting that, the inertial locator showed we were not moving and the Cyber Ark was visible as large as ever on the screen.

"Increase the drive!" Knudsen was almost screaming.

"Can't be done," I said. "We're already at maximum."

"Oh my God, civilians." Knudsen moved over and pushed me out of the way. "Let me have that damned thing."

"Even this degree of interaction is useful," said the voice from the speaker. "It should continue."

"Dialog and interaction should continue." McAndrew was sitting on the floor holding his chest. His voice was throaty and weak, but he finally spoke. "However, such activity is impossible. Humans have an emotion which you may not possess and which may be unknown to you. It is called fear. That fear forces us to destroy you—"

"Damn right it does," Knudsen cried. "You stupid son-of-a-bitch, you're a traitor and a disgrace to the human race. Stop talking to that fucking thing."

"—but humans are not always so illogical." Mac talked right on through Knudsen's rage. "On behalf of our whole species, I apologize for the fact that the human emotion of fear will make us end your existence—"

He couldn't finish the sentence, because Knudsen was on top of him. The captain had his hands around McAndrew's neck and was screaming, "You'll pay for this if we get back home. I'll see you hit with every charge in the book."

I'm not sure that McAndrew was listening. His face had turned red and his eyes were beginning to bulge. I straddled Knudsen's back, grabbed two handfuls of hair, and heaved as hard as I could.

That might not have broken his grip—he was stronger than me, and in prime condition—but as his head came up he faced the observation port. I felt his body freeze. I stared out over the top of his head. The Ark was there, looming larger than ever. It seemed different, and at first I was not sure how. Then I realized that the surface had changed. Rather than rough and textured rock it had become a perfect mirror. I could even see a distorted image of the *Ptarmigan* reflected there. As I watched the surface began to glow with its own light, a dull red that quickly brightened to orange-white.

"This interaction must be terminated," said the voice of the AI.

"It's going to kill us." Knudsen went scrambling away to the drive controls, though the drive was still at maximum and we were not moving a millimeter. "It's going to burn us up."

It seemed he was right. The Ark became a blaze of blue-white, so bright that I could not look at it. I closed my eyes and it stood there still as a dark after-image. I felt a dizzying lurch, as though the *Ptarmigan* had suddenly spun end over end.

"This interaction is terminated," said a voice inside my head, and I opened my eyes.

To nothing. Our drive was off, the ship hung motionless in space. As my eyes recovered their sensitivity I saw the forlorn bodies floating in space; but the Ark had gone.

Knudsen was gabbling into the transmitter. "Gone, it's gone, we've lost contact. There's no sign of the Ark. It just disappeared. We'll keep on looking." And then, something that I'm sure he didn't intend to be sent out, "Oh my God, we'd have been better off if we'd died with the others. Simonette will flay us alive when he finds out."

"Aye," McAndrew said softly, as Knudsen gazed aghast at the transmitter and realized what he had just said into it. "We'll look, but we won't find the AI."

"Of course we will," I said. "When the other ships get here they'll comb in every direction. You told Knudsen it couldn't travel far."

"No, I never said that. I told him"—he jerked a thumb toward Knudsen, who seemed to have gone into a catatonic trance—"that the drive engines on the Cyber Ark couldn't move it far."

"Those were the only engines it had."

"The only ones that humans think of as engines. How did the AI hold the *Ptarmigan* in place? How did it hear our messages when the transmitter was off? Did it speak inside your head, the way it did mine? If the AI is what I think it is, our rules of thought simply don't apply."

"Mac, it can't be *that* smart."

"Why not? Because *we're* not that smart? Jeanie, the AI isn't like us. It's not even like it was, a couple of months ago, when we were at the Ark last time. It was a baby then, with a lot of growing up to do. It's smart enough to know that it can't do that safely if it stays close to the Solar System. We'd hunt it down, and do our best to destroy it."

"Mac, I've changed my mind again. We *have* to kill it."

"I don't think we can. And I'm not sure we need to try. It knows what it did." He gestured to the display, with its forlorn multitude of drifting corpses. "The AI left, but it gave us back our dead. Maybe those deaths were an accident, maybe it's sorry. As sorry as we are."

He turned away from the screen and moved across to the observation port. He was looking out, staring at the stars, silent, searching.

I know McAndrew, better than any person alive. He spoke the truth. He was sorry, deeply sorry, by the deaths of so many innocent victims. Of course he was. McAndrew is human, I know that, even if most people in the Solar System think of him as intellect incarnate.

But he is also McAndrew, and they are right, too. He was mourning, for his dead human fellows; and also he was mourning for the loss of the *other*, the permanent loss of an alien intelligence that he would never again have a chance to meet with and strive to understand.

Then he turned around. He didn't look at me—at anyone. His eyes were a million miles away.

Mourning? Certainly. But I knew that expression. He was also planning, estimating, calculating.

I went over and grabbed his arm. "McAndrew, don't even *think* of it. It's gone. Get it? It's *gone*."

He returned to the world of the *Ptarmigan*. His limbs jerked and his eyes blinked like a wind-up toy. "Uh?" he said. And after a few moments, "Gone? Yes, yes, of course it's gone. I know it is. But Jeanie, if we go back to the exact place where the Ark was when we found it, and make an appropriate set of measurements . . . we wouldn't need to tell the USF what we were doing, and of course we'd take every imaginable precaution . . ."

I hate to admit it, but the others are right. When science is on the agenda, McAndrew doesn't qualify as human at all.

NINTH CHRONICLE:

McAndrew and the Fifth Commandment

What do the following have in common: Aristotle, Confucius, Cleopatra, Napoleon, Abraham Lincoln, Einstein, and Madame Curie?

The answer is, each of them had a mother. And if that seems like a stupid and trivial response, I offer it to make a point. Every famous man or woman has a mother. More often than not, we never hear of her. How much do you know about Hitler's mother? Not a thing, if you are like me.

So it was a shock one morning to come to the Penrose Institute and learn that McAndrew's mother was expected to arrive there later the same day. He had a mother, of course he did, but she lived down on Earth and I hadn't heard him say much about her, except that she had no interest in space or anything to do with it.

"Did she say why she's coming?" I asked.

McAndrew shook his head. He looked nervous. He may be one of the gods of physics, the best combination of

317

experimenter and theorist since Isaac Newton, but I had the feeling that might cut little ice with Ms. Mary McAndrew. Probably, she still thought of him as her little boy. I imagined a darling and elderly Scottish lady, grey-haired and diminutive, summoning up the nerve at long last to travel beyond high orbit and pay a visit to her own wee laddie.

"Writing her will." McAndrew spoke at last. "Something about changing her will."

If anything, that confirmed my impression. Here was a nervous old dear, worried about the approach of death and wanting to make sure that all her affairs were properly in order before the arrival of the Grim Reaper.

I said as much to McAndrew. He looked doubtful, and rather more nervous. I didn't realized why until I went with him to the docking port, where the transfer vessel from LEO to the L-3 Halo orbit was making its noon arrival.

After a five-minute wait, four people emerged from the lock. The first two were Institute administrative staff, returning from leave and laden down with trophies of Earth including a basket of pineapples and a live parrot.

The third one I also recognized. It was Dr. Siclaro, the Institute's expert on kernel energy extraction. He too had been on vacation. He was wearing a flowered shirt and very short white shorts, revealing tanned and powerful legs. The fourth person was a glamorous redhead, dressed to kill. She was right at Siclaro's side, chatting with him while frequently glancing down to eye with interest his calves, muscular thighs, and all points north. From the look on her face he had been protected from direct physical assault only by the new-grown and loathsome mustache that crawled like a hairy ginger caterpillar across his upper lip.

I was looking past those two, waiting to see who next would emerge from the lock, when McAndrew stepped forward. He said weakly, "Hello, Mother."

"Artie!" The redhead turned and gave him a big hug,

leaving generous amounts of face powder and lipstick on his shirt.

Artie? I had never expected to live long enough to hear anyone call Arthur Morton McAndrew, full professor at the Penrose Institute and a man of vast intellectual authority, *Artie*.

"Mother." McAndrew awkwardly disengaged himself. "You look well." She looked, I thought, like an expensive hooker. "This is Jeanie Roker. I've told you about her."

That was news to me. *What* had he told her? She took my hand and gave me a rapid head-to-foot inspection. "The mother of Artie's bairn," she said. "Now, that's very convenient."

I couldn't tell from her expression if she approved or disapproved of the fact that Mac and I had had a child together, but I was doubly glad that there had been a lunchtime ceremony honoring old Professor Limperis and I was dressed in something a lot fancier and more formal than my usual crew's jump-suit.

Why, though, was it *convenient* that I was at the Institute?

"The three of us will talk later." Mary McAndrew was as tall as I, and big blue eyes stared straight into mine. So much for my bent and tiny Scottish elder. "First, though, I need to unpack, freshen up, and maybe have a wee nap."

She looked at Dr. Siclaro. "I hate to impose, but could you show me where I'll be staying?"

"It will be a pleasure." If Monty Siclaro found it odd that he would serve as guide to the Institute rather than McAndrew, he wasn't going to lose any sleep over it. He offered Mary McAndrew his arm and they swayed off together. A mechanical porter emerged from the lock and followed them carrying nine cases of luggage.

I wouldn't pack nine cases for a trip to the end of the Universe. As soon as they were out of earshot I asked, "Mac, just how long is your mother planning to stay here?"

"I have no idea." He gazed at me hopelessly.

"But her luggage."

"Doesn't mean a thing. When I was a lad, she'd take six cases with us for a weekend away."

Another revelation. McAndrew not only had a mother, he had also had a childhood. In all the years I'd known him he hadn't said one word about his early days. And I wouldn't hear more about it for a while, because Emma Gowers arrived to drag him away for a seminar with the enticing title of "Higher-dimensional complex manifolds and a new proof of the Riemann conjecture." I may not have learned much in life, but I recognize cruel and unusual punishment when I see it. The speaker was Fernando Brill, whom I recalled had an unusually loud and penetrating voice. I wouldn't even be able to sleep through him. I stayed in the Institute's parlor, where it was the custom of the faculty to meet daily for tea.

It was only two-thirty. I expected a clear couple of hours when I could take a nap, because I had been travelling most of the night on my journey from Lunar Farside. I closed my eyes. Two minutes later—at least, it felt that way, though the clock registered 3:15—a dulcet voice cooed in my ear.

"Why, here you are, my dear. I didn't expect to see you until later."

I opened my eyes. Mary McAndrew was in front of me. She was wearing a green dress, slit to each hip. By the look of it she was not wearing much else. Monty Siclaro stood at her side, giving an impression of a new-found Egyptian mummy.

McAndrew's mother turned to him and squeezed his hand. "You run along now Monty, you sweet man. Jeanie and I need to have a bit of a chat. We'll see more of each other later."

Monty You-Sweet-Man Siclaro, distinguished fellow of the Penrose Institute and leading expert on the extraction of energy from Kerr-Newman black holes, dutifully tottered away. His etiolated look suggested there wasn't much more of him for her to see.

"Now there's just the two of us." Mary Mother-of-Mac sat down beside me. "So, my dear, why don't we find out a little more about each other?"

I learned during the next three-quarters of an hour what she meant by that. I was asked a series of penetrating questions regarding everything from my education and job description to my personal hygiene and tastes in men.

At the end of it she sat back and gave me a big smile. "You know, that is so much a relief. Artie is such an innocent. I was afraid that he might have fallen for a pretty face." She thought for a moment, possibly decided that she was being less than tactful, and amended her statement. "Or he might have found an intellectual. That would be even worse."

I said, "Perish the thought."

It was wasted on her. "Now I'll tell you what's happening and why I'm here," she said. "First, I'm going to be married."

I made conventional sounds of congratulation.

"Well, I mean, it's as good as being married. Fazool and I are going to live together. He's *enormously* rich, and he likes the idea that I'm utterly poor. It makes him feel protective—he thinks if it weren't for him I'd be in the poor-house."

The house I would suggest for her sounded rather like poor-house; but I kept my mouth shut.

"Fazool would be very upset," she went on, "if he ever found out that I had funds of my own. So I've decided to put my money into a trust. Artie is my only child, and the lad will be the ultimate beneficiary. I'm glad you're around to take care of him, because he can be such a dim-wit."

I looked around. The tea-room would be filling up in a few minutes, but fortunately the place was still deserted except for the two of us. Describing McAndrew as a dim-wit at this Institute would get you the same reaction as chug-a-lugging the altar wine during a church service.

"What about Mac's father?" I asked. "Shouldn't he be a beneficiary?"

"Ah, yes." Her face took on a look of wistful sadness.

"Dead?" I realized that I had never heard McAndrew speak of his father, not even once.

"By all the logic, he is." She smiled sweetly. "But a son-of-a-bitch like that is awful hard to kill."

The arrival of a chattering half-dozen scientists saved me from fielding that remark. Mary McAndrew made an instant survey, checked the line of her skirt to make sure that plenty of leg was showing, and headed for the tallest and most distinguished-looking of the group. It was Plimpton, who according to McAndrew had not had an original thought since he started to grow facial hair and possibly not before. On the other hand, I don't think Mary was seeking original thought. Original sin, maybe.

I followed her toward the tea and sweetmeats. Apparently I had been weighed in the balance and found reasonably adequate. But I suspected that Mary McAndrew employed an unusual scale.

A mother, and now a father, too. I couldn't wait to hear McAndrew's side of the story.

But wait I had to. McAndrew arrived at last from the seminar with half a dozen other scientists. He headed toward his mother. Before they could exchange more than two words, Emma Gowers came sashaying over toward them.

A word about Emma. She is the Institute's expert on multiple kernel arrays and a formidable brain. She is also blond and beautiful, with a roving eye, a lusty temperament, and a taste for big, hairy men of diminished mental capacity.

I was standing only a step away. I saw Mary McAndrew and Emma size each other up, and I realized that neither knew who the other was. But like called to like, and they straightened and preened like two fighting cocks.

"Come on, Mac," Emma said. "You and I have a date."

The wording was provocative, but I knew that Emma had no possible sexual interest in McAndrew. His mother didn't. So far as she could tell, Emma was cutting in.

"I beg your pardon?" she said.

McAndrew made a feeble gesture from one to the other. "Mother, this is one of my professional colleagues, Emma Gowers. Emma, this is my mother."

Mary McAndrew extended a slim and delicate hand. "And which profession would that be, my dear?" Her tone couldn't have been warmer.

Emma gave her a friendly smile. "Not the one you are most familiar with, I'm sure." She had been making a close inspection of Mary McAndrew's neck and the wrinkles at the corners of her eyes. "But it's encouraging to know that a person doesn't have to change her line of work, just because she's old. Come on, Mac."

She gripped McAndrew firmly by the arm and pulled him away toward the door. I was left to face his mother.

I said, "It's not the way it looks. She's not chasing him. There's a problem with the balanced drive on one of the ships, and he and Emma have an appointment to take a look at it."

Mary McAndrew seemed not in the least upset. She said thoughtfully, "Well, I certainly underestimated that one. She and I must have a cozy chat when they get back. Where do you say they're going?"

It was easier to show than to tell. I put down my cup and led her across to one of the room's small observation ports. "They'll be going outside the Institute and over to one of the ships. You can see it from here. That's the *Flamingo*, the Institute's smallest experimental vessel."

She followed my pointing finger. The *Flamingo* was berthed about four kilometers away. We had a profile view of the circular flat disk of condensed matter at the front, with the long column jutting away from the center and the small sphere of the life capsule sitting out near the end of it.

"What a strange-looking object!" Mary said. "Why, it's not in the least like a ship."

I stared at her. Was she joking?

"You're looking at a ship that uses the McAndrew

balanced drive," I said. "Mac says it's a trivial idea, but it's the most famous thing he's ever done. He's known everywhere in the Solar System because of it."

"Is he now?" She peered at it with a bit more interest. "But it's *ugly*. That plate, and the long spike. And where do the people sit?"

She didn't know, she really didn't. Her own son's most celebrated invention, and she had no idea.

"The crew and passengers go in the life capsule." I pointed. "That's the little ball you can see at the end of the spike."

"But it's *teeny*. All that big ship, and such a small space for people. What a waste."

"It has to be that way. That plate on the front is a hundred-meter disk of compressed matter, electromagnetically stabilized. If you put people in the middle of the disk while the ship is at rest, they'd feel a gravitational pull of fifty gees—enough to flatten anybody. But in the life capsule out at the end of the spike, a person feels a pull of just one gee. Now when you turn the drive on and the acceleration grows, the life capsule automatically moves closer to the disk. The acceleration and the gravitational force pull in opposite directions. The life capsule position is chosen so the total force inside it, the difference of gravity and acceleration, stays at one gee. A lot of people call it 'the McAndrew inertia-less drive,' but Mac hates that. He says inertia is still there, and the right name is the *balanced* drive."

I should have more sense. Predictably, I had lost her. In the middle of my explanation she had turned away from the window and she again had her eye on the mentally nulliparous Plimpton.

"Gravity, acceleration, compressed matter," she said. "Oh, how that carries me back. Like father, like son. McAndrew's father, he'd drive a woman mad with talk of compressed matter, when what she was needing was a little personal attention."

"McAndrew Senior was a physicist, too?" If I couldn't

get family information from Mac, maybe his mother would provide it.

"Och, Artie's father wasn't a McAndrew." She arched plucked eyebrows at me. "Perish the thought. I would never dream of marrying a dreadful man like that."

That's the point, right there, where I ought to have changed the subject. Instead I said, "Not a McAndrew. Then who was he?"

"His name was Heinrich Grunewald. If he's alive it still is, though I've not seen hide nor hair of him for over thirty years. He'd come visit for a while, then before you knew it he'd be running off. The last time he breezed in from nowhere, just as usual, and we had a lively couple of days. When the two of us weren't busy in private he talked Artie's ears off. I asked him, what was he doing, filling the lad's head with nonsense? Force fields, and quarks, and that sort of rubbish. He laughed, and said that although nobody knew who Heinrich Grunewald was now, Artie needed to get used to the fact that he was going to have a very famous father. Next time he came to see me, he said, his face would be all over the media and we'd be hard put to find private time what with people camping out on the doorstep of the house."

"I've never heard of Heinrich Grunewald."

"No more you will. Isn't that like a man, all blather and big talk? I flat out told him I didn't believe him. I said, now what is it you'll be doing to make you so famous? He got mad, the way men do when you talk straight to them. He gave me a bunch of notes and a video recording he'd made that very day, and he said the evidence was all there. He was going off to prove it, and I and the rest of the Solar System would treat him with a lot more respect when he came back."

"But he never came back?"

"No more he did. Dead, you'd think, but off with some other woman is just as likely. Heinrich was a cocky devil, and a good-looking man. Good in bed, too, I'll give him that." At the words "good in bed," she roused herself and stared around the room.

"What about the papers and the recording?" I asked.

"Gibberish." She was perking up. Plimpton was giving her the eye and Monty Siclaro, restored to relatively normal condition, had entered the room. "I took a look at the stuff he left, but it was nothing but the same old babble. Strong forces, weak forces, compressed matter, quarks and squarks and blarks. I couldn't make head nor tail of it."

"What did you do with it?"

"Oh. I stuck it away in a lockbox at the old family house. He'd told me not to lose it, and at the time I expected he'd be coming back." Plimpton and Siclaro were standing a yard apart from each other. Drawn by some invisible force, Mary headed for the space between them. "Of course, he never did," she said over her shoulder. "I've not looked for it for years, but I suppose it's sitting there still."

End of story. Except that I, in my folly, later repeated to McAndrew his mother's words.

He stared at me and through me and past me. "Mother never told me that," he said. "He talked about the strong force, and compressed matter, I remember that. But old notes, and a video . . ."

Mary McAndrew stayed at the Institute for two more days. When she returned to Earth, McAndrew went with her.

And I? Of course, I went along, too. I have to take care of McAndrew. He can be such a dim-wit.

Plenty of people live on Earth, but when you go there you have to wonder why. The air feels heavy and too dense. In the cities it's dirty and full of fumes and sits in your lungs like thick soup. In the countryside there's the stink of dead plants and animals wafted around on every breeze. Earth people are so used to the smell of rot, they don't even notice. And after a day or two you're just as bad. Apparently your brain can't stand continuous stench, so after a while it cuts off the signal and you don't smell a thing.

Other things, though, you don't get used to so easily. Mary McAndrew lived most of the time in Paris or Rome, but the "family house" that she referred to, where Mac had spent his early years lay on a small island. It was part of a group known as the Shetlands.

Once we got there I could see why she preferred Paris or Rome. Or anywhere. The island sits far beyond the north coast of Scotland, up at latitude sixty degrees. The house was built of solid stone, with great wooden rafters across the ceiling of each room. Mary told me that the building was over two hundred years old, and her family had lived in it for as long as it had been there.

Nothing wrong with that, but I soon learned that the McAndrews were not the house's only residents. Mac and I were shown to a bedroom off on the north side of the building. It was only two in the afternoon, but it was winter for Earth's northern hemisphere and we were so far up toward the pole that it was already getting dark. I stepped into the room and went to place my bag on the bed. As I did so, something small and brown jumped off the counterpane and streaked away toward a gloomy corner.

I gasped and clutched my bag to my chest. "Mac! What the hell was that?"

"Och, that's nothing." He walked forward and peered down at the wainscotting. "Just a wee mouse, and now it's gone. You can bet it's a lot more frightened of you than you are of it."

"I wouldn't bet on that."

"I'm tellin' ye. You'll not see a sign of the beastie once we're moved into the room."

I noticed something odd about his speech. Back on the home territory of his childhood, a Scottish accent was creeping in.

"Puir little thing," he went on, "there's been naebody

in this room for so lang, it thought it had the rights to it. Don't you worry, it won't come a-walking over your face at night."

I could have lived very well without that thought. I noticed that the window had a spider's web in the upper left corner, and I wondered how many other animals we were expected to share our space with. I felt a bit more sympathy for Heinrich Grunewald. Given a choice, before you knew it I'd have been running off just as he used to.

I left my bag—tightly closed—on the bed. McAndrew led us back to the long living room of the house. Mary McAndrew was waiting there with a dusty box sitting on the low table in front of her.

"Here it is. And I hope it's been worth coming all this way for it." Her voice said that she very much doubted that. She looked at me, as much as to say, Jeanie, I thought you had more sense. We could all be in Paris. Couldn't you talk him out of it?

If she knew McAndrew at all, she knew the answer. When it's new science, or even a sniff of new science, McAndrew is the most obstinate human in the Solar System. He lifted the box as reverently as though it contained the Crown Jewels, blew off dust, and wiped at the top with a yellow cloth.

"It's not locked," I said.

"And why should it be?" Mary said as McAndrew eased the top open with a creak of rusting hinges. "Nothing here that anybody in his right mind would pay a brass farthing for."

At first glance I was inclined to agree. What Mac lifted out of the box was a small notebook with a faded blue cover, a dozen sheets of yellow paper with dirty brown edges, and a video recording of a design that had gone out of use thirty or forty years ago.

"Can you play that?" I asked.

"Oh, surely." Mary took the video container and wiped the top with the duster. "Artie will tell you how it is on the islands. Things don't get thrown away so quick here as in other places."

McAndrew had meanwhile picked up the sheets of paper. He flipped through them in a few seconds.

"Nothing?" I asked.

"Nothing I didn't know already." He put the sheets down. "Standard results on the stabilization of compressed matter with electromagnetic fields. Same as we do with the balanced drive plates."

"Nothing," said his mother. "Didn't I tell you so?"

McAndrew did not answer, but picked up the blue notebook. He began to leaf through it, and this time he was occupied for much longer.

I didn't speak, either. I had learned long ago that when McAndrew had that look on his face it was a waste of time to try to gain his attention. He was off in a different universe. Mary McAndrew must have learned the same thing, long ago in McAndrew's childhood. She went off to the kitchen without a word and appeared a few minutes later with a loaded tea-tray.

McAndrew finally laid the notebook carefully back on the table.

"Well?" I asked.

"I dinna ken. It's a thing a man has to sleep on."

"That's all you can tell us?"

"I can tell you what he—my father—wrote." Mac said "my father" awkwardly, as though the words came hard to his tongue. "What I can't tell you is whether what he wrote is true. That needs some hard thinking."

"Nothing there," Mary said. She calmly poured tea. "Nothing, just as I told you."

It occurred to me that after leaving the contents of the box to rot for all these years she *wanted* there to be nothing.

McAndrew spoke again, slowly and carefully. "What Heinrich Grunewald says—what he says"—there was a slight emphasis on *he*—"is that there's another way to produce compressed matter, and if ye do it his way there's no need of electromagnetic stabilization. The compressed matter will be naturally stable. If he's right, you can also achieve far higher densities than we have at present. Up to three billion tons per cubic centimeter."

Mary did not react, but I did. The compressed matter used in the balanced drive plates averaged three *thousand* tons per cubic centimeter, and that was considered phenomenal.

"Does he say *how* to do it?" I asked.

"Aye. But that's the hard bit to swallow. He says that it involves a local modification and enhancement of the strong force."

"What strong force?" Mary asked.

I waited for someone to answer. Then I realized that unlike at the Institute, where bulging super-brains stood ready to lecture on any conceivable topic in physics, McAndrew and I were the only two available; and from the look on his face he was gone again, off to some unimaginable place where I could never follow.

"What strong force?" Mary said again. "Have the two of you gone deaf?"

"I'll explain," I said. I should have added, or try to. Make me your authority on physics and you run a considerable risk. "There are four basic forces in the universe." That much I was sure of. "There's gravity, that's the one everybody knows even if they don't understand it. There's the electromagnetic force, that powers electrical motors and everything else to do with electricity and magnetism. There's a thing called the weak force, which causes radioactivity." (At that point McAndrew should have awakened and roasted me for a simplistic explanation. The fact that he didn't meant he wasn't really there). "And then there's the strong force, which holds nuclei together when electromagnetic forces want them to fly apart."

I was about to add that unified theories explained all four as part of a single generalized force, and that all were mediated through the exchange of virtual particles with names like photons and gluons. I didn't. I could see Mary's face.

I finished, a bit lamely, "What your husb—what McAndrew's father claims to have done is find a way to change the way the strong force operates. If he was right, and he could make it stronger, then there could be a better way to form compressed matter."

Mary sniffed. "If I'd known that was all I had in the box all this time, I wouldna have bothered to keep it all this time." She picked up the video recording. "And here we have more of the same?"

"We don't know yet."

"So let's take a wee look, and find out." She went over to a corner of the living room and pulled back a drape to reveal a playback unit so antiquated that I'd have accepted the idea that it was steam driven. "Artie, are you awake? Artie! Och, the lad's hopeless."

"Play it," I said. "Maybe it will bring him back into the real universe."

"I have doubts of that. I never found anything that would when he's got that face on him." But she inserted the video recording.

The overhead lights, coupled to the playback unit, dimmed. The wall display flashed a brief kaleidoscope of color, then settled to show the figure of a standing man. It zoomed to a close-up of his face and I had a sudden and startling feeling of recognition. The long jaw and thin-lipped mouth were different, but the distant eyes and high, balding forehead were pure McAndrew.

Heinrich Grunewald spoke. His voice was slow, deeper than Mac's, and slightly accented. "This recording contains its own time-line, giving the date and hour that it is being made. I'll be away for a little while, so I want there to be no arguments regarding priority of invention when I return. I have developed a modified theory of the strong interaction, with huge and various commercial potentials. Among the near-term applications are cheap forms of compressed matter, the ability to make shipment of diffuse materials in much smaller containers, induced radioactivity, more compact forms of existing commercial fusion devices, and low-temperature proton-proton fusion."

McAndrew was awake after all. I heard him gasp at that last item. Grunewald went on, "I am not talking theory alone. The technical details permitting each of these developments can be found here." He raised a blue notebook, like a bigger version of the one in the lockbox.

I glanced at Mary McAndrew, who shook her head. "Nothing like that, not left with me. It's been a long time, but I think maybe I saw it."

McAndrew said, "Then where is it? We have no other lead."

"It went with him." I was surprised that the two of them were slow to catch on. "If it gives the practical details it's worth an enormous fortune. He didn't want to risk anyone else getting their hands on it."

"We have to find it, and him." McAndrew sounded unusually forceful. He saw my expression. "Oh, not the inventions, Jeanie. You know I don't give a damn about them. We need the *theory*."

Mary McAndrew turned to me. "I told you. He hasn't changed a bit. He needs a keeper."

I asked, "But where did he go?"

McAndrew snapped at us. "If the pair of you would stop blathering, maybe we'd have a chance to find out."

Heinrich Grunewald was still talking. Mac reversed the video to the point where his father was hefting the blue book.

" . . . developments can be found here." Grunewald flourished the notebook in a self-satisfied way and finally placed it back out of sight. "With industrial sabotage so common, I do not wish to perform my final validation experiments where others might find a way to steal or even to interfere."

Mary McAndrew said, "Och, he's crazy suspicious. He was always paranoid. I've never known another man look

under every bed before he'd get in it, no matter who he
was with and what he had to look forward to."

McAndrew and I both shushed her, as Grunewald went
on, "So to do the validation I'm taking the *Fafner* out,
away from the main shipping lanes—"

"Got him," I said.

"Keep quiet," McAndrew snapped. But I'm a seasoned
cargo captain, and for a change I knew something he
didn't. It didn't matter whether or not Heinrich Grunewald
told us anything else. If he had taken his ship out, as he
said, then his flight plan would be on file. So would any
firing of the ship's engines.

The man was gone, but not forgotten and not untraceable.
It might take a while, but I felt sure we would be
able to track down McAndrew's long-lost father.

Like many things in life, the problem I had been so
sure I could solve proved more difficult than it sounded.

We headed for the Penrose Institute to perform the
calculations. Mary McAndrew told us that she could not
come, she had to pay some attention to "poor neglected
Fazool." But I was to let her know what we found.

"I know he's surely dead," she said to me as we left
for Equatorport. "He was a wicked, obstinate, reckless
man. But the two of us had some great times, and I was
awful fond of Heinrich. Why, I was even *faithful* to him."

It would have been unkind to ask for how long.

Mac and I headed for the Institute, and at first everything
went according to plan. I delved into the old data
bases and found the flight plan of the *Fafner*. Among the
listed on-board equipment, tantalizingly, the manifest
included the enigmatic item, "strong field modifier, prototype."

I learned the exact second of the ship's departure.
I found its nominal destination, though that could change
through subsequent course corrections or changes of
mind. I obtained a complete list of subsequent engine
firings, which even without the record sent back from

the *Fafner*'s inertial navigation system would allow us to pinpoint the ship's last known location. After all the engine firings, a certain stochastic element affected the *Fafner*'s movements depending on the vagaries of gravitational perturbation by small bodies and variations in solar wind. But natural body positions for anything substantial were in the data banks on an hour-by-hour basis, and the programs to compensate for their effects were routine.

The calculations took a while, even with McAndrew's talent for instant shortcuts. Once we had answers we borrowed the synthetic aperture distributed observation system for a few days and surveyed the sky sector where the *Fafner* should be found.

Result: nothing. Not a sign. No *Fafner*, not in the region we had defined as most probable or in one ten times as big in all directions. The ship had disappeared.

I checked the calculations, redoing everything the long way. The *Fafner* was not a big ship, nothing to compare with a cargo carrier or even a large passenger vessel, but it was thirty meters long and almost fifteen across. Anything that size would stand out prominently on the observations made by the big scope, especially when you used a time exposure to sort out moving objects within the Solar System from the fixed celestial background. Comparison with known natural bodies ought to do the rest.

I found nothing wrong with McAndrew's calculations. He checked my checking. That took two more days. Finally we were ready to admit defeat. By this time a dozen others at the Institute were taking an interest. McAndrew phrased the dilemma for all of us. "Objects just can't disappear. Here are the possibilities: The *Fafner* might have totally disintegrated. It might have hidden away inside another object. Or it might be deliberately covered with nonreflective material at the wavelengths used by the Institute scopes."

"Or stolen away by aliens," I added. I was *tired*.

McAndrew nodded as though that was a serious

possibility. "In any case," he said, "we've gone as far as we can just sitting and looking."

"The ship can't be far away from where we calculated," I said. I could see where the discussion was heading, and I knew that we faced a very tough job. "It's in the Inner System, and near the plane of the ecliptic. In the Asteroid Belt, almost certainly."

McAndrew nodded and looked gloomy. "Aye. Wouldn't you just know it'd be that way?"

The others muttered vague expressions of sympathy.

To see why, imagine that you are asked to look for something small. Would you rather search a large volume or a small one?

The answer to that question depends where you are and what you are seeking. The region of the Solar System that includes the Sun, planets, moons, asteroids, and the odd collection of misfit bodies forming the Edgeworth-Kuiper Belt is a substantial volume; it is shaped like a flat pillbox, about thirty billion kilometers across and maybe forty million deep. Say, a billion billion cubic kilometers of volume altogether. But that's infinitesimal compared with the space bounded by the inner edge of the Oort cloud. There, we are talking a spherical region with a radius of a twentieth of a light-year. The volume in cubic kilometers is a number with thirty-five zeroes, too many for me to be comfortable with. You can subtract the volume of the pillbox, and it makes no noticeable difference.

The odd thing, though, is that inside the pillbox it's much harder to find something. And if you had to pick one place where the search is more difficult than any other, the Inner Belt of the asteroids is where you'd least like to be.

The key word is *clutter*. There are far too many natural bodies in orbit. The Asteroid Belt contains everything from substantial bodies like Ceres, seven hundred and fifty kilometers across, all the way down to house-sized boulders, pebbles, and grains of sand. One good rule of thumb is that for every object of a given size, there will be ten times as many one-third that size.

The data bases at the Institute keep dynamic track of every body of any size, down to ten meters across. The *Fafner* was much bigger than that, so it ought to have been picked up in our search. Recognize that it hadn't been, and where does that leave you? You know there are countless millions of objects near where the missing ship ought to be, and you have no idea at all why your original search failed.

So we would fly out there and take a look for ourselves, and hope that our human brains could spot an anomaly able to fool the smartest computers in the Solar System.

How? I had no idea.

McAndrew did. "If it's been blown apart to its component atoms," he said, "we'll never find it. But if it's still in one piece, there's a way that can't fail."

We were preparing to leave, and we were not using a ship with McAndrew's balanced drive. Instead he had picked out an old touring pinnace with a one-gee acceleration limit. After my initial surprise I decided that I knew why (it would turn out later that I was wrong). McAndrew, it seemed to me, wanted time to think. He'd never admit it, but his pride was hurt. It was bad enough that somebody would come up with a basic idea that he had missed, in an area of theoretical physics where he had thought longer and harder than any person alive. That the somebody was his own father—the father who had run off and deserted him and his mother—was even worse.

As the *Driscoll* eased away from the institute, I compared travel times. Even the most minimal ship equipped with the balanced drive was capable of continuous forty-gee acceleration. With that performance, our destination would have been a mere seventeen hours, standing start to standing finish. On the other hand, at the leisurely half-gee best suited to the *Driscoll*'s engines, we faced a journey of close to a week.

All right for McAndrew, perhaps; he was sitting barefoot, staring vacantly at the cabin wall and cracking his finger and toe joints in a way that I always found infuriating. I knew from experience that he was likely to sit for days, eating his meals like a zombie and washing only at my insistence. Meanwhile, what was I supposed to do, here in a ship that flew itself?

I reviewed everything we had learned so far. Heinrich Grunewald's paranoia had not ended when he left Mary McAndrew. The *Fafner* required a crew of three when it flew in cislunar space. Upon leaving that controlled region, Heinrich as soon as possible had the other two men ferried back to Earth station. He continued alone. His last recorded engine burn placed him in stable orbit in the middle of the Asteroid Belt. Any new engine burn would have been detected. None had been recorded. Any explosion in that location powerful enough to destroy a ship would have been seen. No instruments, on Earth or elsewhere, had seen such evidence.

The ship must be there. The ship was not there. I sat and wondered. Where's Heinrich?

McAndrew emerged from his trance when we still had a full day of flight time ahead. "I've got it," he said. "Or at least, part of it."

"Well, isn't that nice." I should have known better. Sarcasm is wasted on the man. He smiled at me. I went on, "So you know how changing the strong force would allow somebody to do the things that your father claimed?"

He stopped smiling. "Och, I've always known *that*. It's obvious."

"Not to me it isn't. I don't suppose you'd consider explaining?"

"The strong force holds nuclei together. So suppose you could make it more powerful and act over a longer range, for an indefinitely long period. That would lead to stable compressed matter, and you'd be able to squeeze anything you like into a smaller space. If you used the strong force to overcome electromagnetic repulsion between protons, you'd also be on the road to easy proton-proton fusion at room temperature.

"Now suppose you work the other way round, and know how to *weaken* the strong force. Then nuclei will be less strongly bound, and a lot of naturally stable elements will become unstable. That gives you induced radioactivity."

"But that's everything." It seemed to me he had covered everything on Heinrich Grunewald's list. "Why do you say you only have part of it?"

"Because I slipped something in there at the beginning. I said, suppose you could modify the strong force *for an indefinitely long period*. That's the killer, Jeanie. I can see a way to make changes, but they'd be unstable. Worse than that, they'd be *unpredictable*. You'd never know when the effect would reverse itself and things return to the way they were. And when I try to stabilize the situation over time, I need to assume the existence of isolated quarks. I might find a way around that when I give it a bit more of a think, but I still won't know what went wrong. Something surely did. There must be a missing piece—some trivial point, some fact that I've overlooked . . ."

He was all set to drift off again. I said, loudly, "Mac, we'd be a lot closer to the something you're missing if we knew how to find the *Fafner*. In another twenty-four hours we'll be sitting out in the middle of the Asteroid Belt, wondering what to do next."

He stared at me with those pale, vague eyes. "Why, I already know what we'll do. Why do you think I wanted to take the *Driscoll*, instead of something with a balanced drive?"

"Because you wanted time to think."

"Maybe. And I got that. But we'd have a problem if we'd used the balanced drive. The compressed matter plate on any of those ships masses trillions of tons."

"That's never given us any difficulty before."

"Because we've never had this situation before. Think about it, Jeanie. If the *Fafner's* still in one piece, what's the one thing about itself it can't hide?"

"Thermal signature?"

"That's not a bad answer for a ship that's alive. Anything with people on board has to generate and give off heat. But the *Fafner's* more than likely dead, so there would be no thermal signal. A ship can be at the same temperature as its surroundings, or it can change its size and shape, or it can be coated with an absorbing layer so it's hard to see. The one thing it still has, no matter what it does, is *mass.*"

When he spoke that one, final word I could see the rest for myself. We knew from the *Fafner's* records the ship's mass at the time of final engine burn: three hundred and thirty tons. Even if Grunewald had jettisoned material into space, the present value would not be far from that. If we were anywhere close to the ship we could locate it using our mass detector. The instrument was highly sensitive and it could be programmed to correct for every nearby object in the right size range. The trillion-ton mass of a compressed matter plate was something else. On a ship with a balanced drive, the plate's effects would overwhelm the gravity field of everything in the neighborhood.

It's my one big complaint with McAndrew. He assumes you understand what he understands. Even when you feel sure you know what goes on inside his head, you don't. One of his colleagues told me that the difference between McAndrew and other people is that Mac knows how to think around corners. It's probably true, but it doesn't help much.

I wondered if he got that talent from his father. I had no idea what Heinrich Grunewald had been doing out here, or why he had disappeared thirty years ago from the face of the Solar System. I thought of Mary McAndrew's words, "he was a wicked, obstinate, reckless man." Cut out the wicked part, and you had McAndrew.

I can't think around corners, but I have excellent instincts for danger. And I was feeling uneasy, more nervous than the situation seemed to justify.

❖   ❖   ❖

We had arrived, exactly at the place where the *Fafner* was supposed to be. I cut the drive and used the visible wavelength sensors to scan through a full four-pi solid angle.

Did I see the ship? Of course not. You might say I already knew I wouldn't, because if it had been there the scopes of the Penrose Institute would have found it before we ever left.

I pointed that out to McAndrew.

"Which is why we had to come out here and take a look for ourselves." He seemed filled with secret glee, his normal reaction when facing a scientific mystery. "Jeanie, keep the drive off and the displays on, and let's have a go with the mass detector."

I took a last look at the screens. The optical sensors would find and highlight any unknown body that subtended more than a fiftieth of a second of arc. That meant I would see something as small as a tenth of a meter across, even if it were a hundred kilometers away.

The displays showed absolutely nothing. The *Driscoll* sat in the middle of a large volume of emptiness.

Convinced that we were wasting our time, I turned on the mass detector. Instantly, a loud buzz from the instrument made me start upright in my seat.

"There we are." McAndrew clapped his hands in delight. "What do we show for mass and range?"

"Eighteen thousand tons," I said. "So that's not the *Fafner*, it's far too massive. It's at eighteen kilometers." I took another look at the optical sensor outputs. "But Mac, there's nothing there."

"We'll see. Take us that way—slowly."

I did as he asked, but at one kilometer away from the invisible target I stopped the *Driscoll*. "No closer, Mac. That's as near as we're going."

"But there's no possible danger—"

"This ship has to take us home. If you want a closer look, we use suits."

"Jeanie—"

"On a ship you can only have one captain." When I feel a certain way I can be as obstinate as McAndrew.

He knows it, too. He scowled at me, but he didn't argue. He went over and began to put on a suit. I locked the *Driscoll* to hold a fixed one-kilometer distance from whatever was exciting the mass detector, and went across to do the same.

Keeping an eye on McAndrew? Sure. But I had my own curiosity to satisfy. Why were the optical sensors and the mass detector at odds with each other?

He went a meter or two in front of me, heading for the place where the mass detector insisted that we would find an invisible eighteen-thousand ton object. The suit displays homed us in the location. McAndrew went slower and slower. He was using the light in his suit to illuminate the space ahead of him.

Finally he paused, and said, "There you have it!"

"There you have *what*?" I, only a meter behind him, saw nothing at all.

"The body—the eighteen-thousand ton body—that Heinrich used to test his strong force modifier. If he compressed it down to three billion tons per cubic centimeter, the radius would be a fraction of a millimeter— just about right."

Finally, I saw a mote of reflected light. When I moved my head within the suit helmet, I realized that the object was tiny and just a few feet in front of us.

"That thing?" I said. "That's what the mass detector picked up?"

"Of course. What I expected, and what I hoped we'd find."

He reached out with his gloved left hand. Before I could stop him he gripped the tiny particle between his thumb and forefinger. "As you'd expect," he said. "It's tiny, but it should have all the inertia of the original body. Let's see."

I saw him pull, but all that did was move his position. "Doesn't budge," he said. And then, in a different tone,

"This is the damnedest thing. Jeanie, I can't let go. My finger and thumb won't come apart—and they *hurt*."

He was wearing a tough, insulated suit. Cold or heat could not get through it, nor could radiation. If the suit had somehow developed a hole at finger or thumb, air would be jetting out into space. I saw no tell-tale sign of chilled vapor.

McAndrew turned on his suit jets. It changed his body position only by the length of his own outstretched arm. He was stuck, locked in place by an invisible mote.

I heard his grunt of pain and effort. Suddenly I imagined his father, floating outside the *Fafner* and with no one to help him, reaching out to touch the mote of compressed matter and held as McAndrew was held.

I still had no idea what was going on, so my next actions were pure instinct. I said, "Grit your teeth, Mac, this is going to hurt worse than it hurts already," and I took a metal shearing tool from the belt of my suit. Before McAndrew could do anything about it I moved to his suit and severed the top joint of his thumb and first finger.

He cried out in pain as a foam of blood and air spurted from his suit glove. In less than a second the suit sensors reacted and tightened a seal on the fingers. I used the thrustors on my own suit to pull us away toward the *Driscoll*. As we backed up I saw the first joints of the finger and thumb, still firmly attached to each other. In my over-stimulated condition they seemed to be moving closer to each other and shrinking at the ends.

McAndrew's suit had decided that he would be better off with a shot of anesthetic. He was still conscious when I hauled us both through the air lock of the *Driscoll* and peeled off our suits. I put him on a bunk and anxiously examined his left hand.

"How is it, Jeanie?" he said. The painkillers left him rational and quite calm.

"Not too bad. The cuts are clean. But there's no way to regrow the joints before we're back home."

"I'll manage," he said. "My own fault. That's what you get when you don't think before you act."

"We'll be home in less than a week." I was already at the controls of the *Driscoll*. "I'll keep you as comfortable as I can until we get there."

"Hey, we can't leave." He had been lying down, but now he sat suddenly upright. "Not without what we found."

"We're certainly not leaving with it. That thing, whatever it is, is lethal."

"It isn't, unless you were as careless as I was. Look, I'll tell you what happened. Then see what you think."

I paused in setting up our flight home. I looked at the mass detector readings, and confirmed that we were still a full kilometer away from the particle of compressed matter.

"Five minutes to persuade me," I said.

"It won't take that long. But you'll have to take my word on the numbers."

"I'll give you that much." When it comes to calculations, McAndrew doesn't know how to make mistakes.

"All right." He lay down again on the bunk and stared up at nothing. "You take a natural body, floating around here in the Asteroid Belt. You go to it, and you place in position there a piece of equipment that locally increases the strong force. Then you turn on the equipment—remotely, from a safe distance. The increase in the strong force makes the body collapse, until it has a density of three billion tons per cubic centimeter. That's what he claimed he could do, so let's believe him. If the body you started out with massed eighteen thousand tons, the one you end up with will be minute. About a quarter of a millimeter across."

"I didn't have any numbers," I said, "but I finally guessed that something like that had to be going on. It's the only way we'd have a strong signal from the mass detector, and not see anything. But you couldn't escape when you took hold of it, and the pain you felt—"

"My own fault entirely. I didn't do the other half of the calculation. Gravity's the weakest force in the Universe, but it follows an inverse square law. Take a mass of eighteen thousand tons, and squeeze it down into a quarter millimeter sphere. What's the gravity at the surface?"

That sounded like a rhetorical question. I waited.

"The field at the surface of the sphere is thousands of gees." He held up his damaged hand. "And I was fool enough to grab hold. I couldn't get my fingers free. Not only that—the field pulled in anything close enough. The material of my glove, then the tips of my finger and thumb. I could feel the blood sucking out."

"But I didn't notice a thing," I protested.

"No more you would. The inverse square law got me, but it saved you. Ten centimeters away from the sphere, the pull is down to a hundredth of a gee—not enough to feel. But close up . . . good thing you were there to cut me away, or I don't know what I'd have done."

I did. I could see it with awful clarity. The same thing would have happened to McAndrew as had happened to Heinrich Grunewald. Held by the tiny ball of compressed matter, unable to move back to the *Fafner* because of the immense eighteen-thousand ton inertia. Except that at the time it had been not quite eighteen thousand tons. The ball, slowly and inexorably, would have consumed Heinrich, drawing his body little by little into itself. And then, over a much longer time frame, the *Fafner* must have suffered the same fate. The gentle force of gravity would have tugged it gradually toward the speck of condensed matter, closer and close until there was finally physical contact. From that moment the *Fafner* was doomed, just as McAndrew's father had been doomed. As McAndrew himself, without my intervention . . .

I realized that he was speaking again. "But now we know what happened," he was saying in an unnaturally cheerful voice, "there's no danger at all. We'll bring the compressed matter on board, contain it electromagnetically, and take it back with us to the Institute."

"Not on this ship you won't." The most brilliant mind in the System, but sometimes you wonder if he's capable of learning anything. Maybe I ought to be charitable and blame the anesthetic. He was starting to sound decidedly woozy. I went on, "Didn't you tell me, just an hour or two ago, that the compressed matter might be unstable—it could revert unexpectedly to its original condition? Suppose that happened on the way back. Do you want to share your living quarters with an eighteen thousand ton lump of rock?"

"Ah, but I think I see a way around that. If we build the right piece of equipment—"

"You mean *when you've built* the right piece of equipment. After that's done, and it's been thoroughly tested, and you know it works in every case and there's no danger of compressed matter instability, *then* if you like we'll come back out here and collect your finger and thumb."

I wasn't worried about his finger and thumb, but I didn't want to say what was really in my mind. *Then maybe we'll be able to give your father a decent burial.*

Ignoring McAndrew, I set the final coordinates for home and turned on the drive. The Mighty Mote we were leaving behind was not going to run away. Heinrich Grunewald, in his strangest of sarcophagi, would still be waiting if and when we came back.

When Mary McAndrew left the Penrose Institute for the first time I would have bet good money that she would never return. Scientists like Plimpton and Monty Siclaro were all right for diversion, an occasional snack as it were, but not for her regular diet.

I would have lost. Mary showed up, one year to the day after her first visit, for the formal ceremony in which an award was made, posthumously, to Heinrich Grunewald for his part in the development of the Grunewald-McAndrew formalism for the modified strong interaction.

McAndrew had insisted that the names be listed in that order. He said that his own contribution, allowing a generator to amplify the strong field externally so that the equipment itself would not be destroyed, was minor. All the major insights for the theory had been provided by the late Heinrich Grunewald.

Mary sat quietly through the ceremony, though I don't think it had most of her attention. She looked very serious and smiled only once, when McAndrew held up Heinrich Grunewald's medal and citation for the visiting media to see. Her dress also seemed odd for the occasion. She wore a long black dress, with a single pearl pinned at the left shoulder. She looked stunning, but she seemed indifferent to the ogling male and female eyes of the media representatives.

After the ceremony was over McAndrew to his disgust had to submit to questions and an interview— Institute Director Rumford was not willing to give up such a wonderful opportunity for favorable publicity. As McAndrew left, Mary came over to me.

She got right down to the point. "Do you think you could show me Heinrich's remains? I want to pay my respects, but Artie refuses. He doesn't seem to like the idea, even though it's his own father."

"I have to agree with him, I don't think it's wise."

"Why not?"

"Well . . ."

"Look, I heard that Heinrich had some sort of accident, and was squashed real bad. But I'm a grown woman, I won't turn hysterical on you or anything."

I wasn't so sure of that. On the other hand, it sounded unreasonable to refuse anyone's request to see the remains of a loved one when a team from the Institute had trailed all the way out to the Asteroid Belt to recover the compressed matter asteroid, and as an incidental had brought back the *Fafner* plus Heinrich Grunewald and a couple of bits of McAndrew's fingers.

"Come on," I said.

I led the way from the auditorium, out along a rarely-used corridor to an annex far removed from the main body of the Institute, and into a small chamber. The Mighty Mote sat in the middle of it, magnetically suspended to prevent it coming anywhere near other matter. A sphere of glass, three feet across, surrounded the exhibit to provide added security.

Mary advanced and stared in through the curved window.

"Where is he?" She turned to me in bewilderment. "You don't understand. I wanted to see Heinrich, no matter how bad he was mashed up in the accident. I don't see anything in there at all."

She had just sat through a series of explanations, especially simplified for the media, about the significance of the work done by Grunewald and McAndrew. The emphasis had been on the inexpensive creation of compressed matter and the successful recovery of the prototype experiment on strong force enhancement. Apparently Mary had understood not a word.

I intensified the light level and adjusted the angle of the beam, so that the speck of compressed matter appeared as a tiny bright-blue spark.

"There," I said, "is Heinrich Grunewald."

"That?" Mary stepped close to the window.

"That." I resisted the urge to add, *And most of what you see isn't even him. He's squeezed in there along with the Fafner and eighteen thousand tons of rock*.

"Oh dear." Mary pressed her nose to the glass. "That little fly-speck of stuff? Heinrich wouldn't be pleased at all, not with him always going on about size—though I told him, over and over, it's what you do with it that counts. Is there any way of bringing him back the way he used to be?"

"McAndrew's working on it. He has ideas, but it's too soon to say if they'll work. Why do you ask?"

"Well, I don't have that much to remember Heinrich by, and they don't look like they're doing anything for him up here. And it's terribly lonely in this little room. So I was wondering, I don't suppose I could take the whole thing down to Earth with me, could I, and look after him there?"

"I'm afraid that's impossible. What you're looking at is small, but it's enormously dense. That little sphere with Heinrich's remains weighs—" I caught myself in time. She'd wonder about eighteen thousand tons. I finished "—a lot more than you'd think. There would be no way to stop it sinking right down to the center of the planet."

"Oh dear. Then, no. I'm sure Heinrich would like it there even less than being up here." She turned away. "They should have left him out where he was, among the stars. He'd have preferred that. I'm going to say goodbye to Artie, and then I'm leaving."

I trailed along behind, waited while she had a private few minutes with McAndrew, and the three of us went along to the loading dock. She waved, and was gone.

Next day I was gone, too, on a routine delivery of a kernel assembly to Umbriel. I was away for a month. On the way back I dropped by the Institute, now free-orbiting beyond the Moon.

McAndrew was in his office. It was as crowded and cluttered as ever, with one important difference. Over in a clear corner sat a three-foot ball of glass. Within it sat the grain of compressed matter, and alongside that blue speck stood a small hologram of a smiling Mary McAndrew.

"Mac! I thought you told me the compressed matter was unstable. If it changes back to its original form—"

"It won't." The buds of his finger and thumb joints were already growing nicely. "I worked all that out when you left. It will stay like that as long as we want it to."

"And you moved it in here."

"Well, yes. My mother didn't seem to like him being off by himself. I thought the two of them ought to be together."

"Does she know about this?"

He looked surprised. "Why, no. Or if she does, I didn't tell her."

But I did. After McAndrew and I had agreed to meet for dinner and a long catch-up evening, I left him and placed a call to Mary McAndrew. I tracked her down in Cap d'Antibes, at one of Fazool's mansions.

She listened in silence while I told her about the glass sphere and the hologram in McAndrew's office. Then she said, "I still miss him, you know. Look after him, won't you."

She had mixed two different hims in one sentence, but I had no trouble sorting them out. "I'll do my best," I said. "But you know your son."

"I do indeed. Just like his father. Come and see me, Jeanie. Fazool won't mind. You and Artie both."

"I will."

"In fact, Fazool will probably make a pass at you."

"I can stand that."

"I hope Artie can. Goodbye, Jeanie. Look after him, and give him my love."

"I will. Goodbye, Mary."

We hung up. *Look after him.* I'd spent twenty years trying to look after McAndrew and it didn't seem to be getting any easier.

I went to find the man to tell him that I had spoken with his mother and we needed to plan another visit to her.

McAndrew thinks he understands what the strong force is in the universe, and I wouldn't dream of disagreeing with him. But Mary McAndrew and I, we know better.

APPENDIX:

Science & Science Fiction

Writers, readers and critics of science fiction often seem unable to produce a workable definition of the field, but one of the things they usually agree on is the existence of a particular branch that is usually termed "hard" science fiction. People who like this branch will tell you it is the only subdivision that justifies the word *science*, and that everything else is simple fantasy; and they will use words like "authentic," "scientifically accurate," "extrapolative," and "inventive" to describe it. People who don't like it say it is dull and bland, and use words like "characterless," "mechanical," "gadgetry," or "rockets and rayguns" to describe it. Some people can't stand hard SF, others will read nothing else.

Hard science fiction can be defined in several different ways. My favorite definition is an operational one: if you can take the science and scientific speculation away from a story, and not do it serious injury, then it was not hard SF to begin with. Here is another definition that I like rather less well: in a hard SF story, the scientific techniques of observation, analysis, logical theory, and experimental test must be applied, no matter where or when the story takes place. My problem with this definition is that it would classify many mystery and fantasy stories as hard science fiction.

Whatever the exact definition, there is usually little difficulty deciding whether a particular story is "hard" or "soft" science fiction. And although a writer never knows quite what he or she has written, and readers often pull things out of a story that were never consciously put in, I certainly think of the book you are holding as probably the hardest SF that I write. Each story revolves around some element of science, and without that element the story would collapse. If the stories reflect any common theme, it is my own interest in science, particularly astronomy and physics. Because of this, and because the science is what I have elsewhere termed "borderland science" (*Borderlands of Science: How to Think Like A Scientist and Write Science Fiction*; Baen Books, 1999), I feel a responsibility to the reader. It is one that derives from my own early experiences with science fiction.

I discovered the field for myself as a teenager (as did almost everyone else I knew—in school we were tormented with Wordsworth and Bunyan, while Clarke and Heinlein had to be private after-school pleasures). Knowing at the time a negligible amount of real science, I swallowed whole and then regurgitated to my friends everything presented as science in the SF magazines. That quickly built me a reputation as a person stuffed with facts and theories—many of them wrong and some of them decidedly weird. The writers didn't bother to distinguish the scientific theories that they borrowed, from the often peculiarly unscientific theories that they made up for the story. Neither did I.

I knew all about the canals on Mars, the dust pools on the Moon, and the swamps on Venus, about the Dean drive and dianetics and the Hieronymus machine. I believed that men and pigs were more closely related than men and monkeys; that atoms were miniature solar systems; that you could shoot men to the moon with a cannon (a belief that didn't survive my first course in dynamics); that the pineal gland was certainly a rudimentary third eye and probably the seat of parapsychological powers; that Rhine's experiments at Duke University had made telepathy an unquestioned part of modern science; that with a little ingenuity and a few electronic bits and pieces you could build in your backyard a spacecraft to take you to the moon; and that, no matter what alien races might have developed on other worlds and be scattered around the Galaxy, humans would prove to be the smartest, most resourceful, and most wonderful species to be found anywhere.

That last point may even be true. As Pogo remarked long ago, true or false, either way it's a mighty sobering thought.

What I needed was a crib sheet. We had them in school for the works of Shakespeare. They were amazingly authoritative, little summaries that outlined the plot, told us just who did what and why, and even informed us exactly what was in Shakespeare's head when he was writing the play. If they didn't say what he had for lunch that day, it was only because that subject never appeared on examination papers. Today's CliffsNotes are less authoritative, but only I suspect because the changing climate of political correctness encourages commentators to be as bland as possible.

I didn't know it at the time, but the crib sheets were what I was missing in science fiction. Given the equivalent type of information about SF, I would not have assured my friends (as I did) that the brains of industrial robots made use of positrons, that the work of Dirac and Blackett would lead us to a faster-than-light drive, or that the notebooks of Leonardo da Vinci gave all the details needed to construct a moon rocket.

As Mark Twain remarked, it's not what we don't know that causes the trouble, it's the things we know that ain't so. (This is an example of the problem. I was sure this was said by Mark Twain, but when I looked it up I found it was a Josh Billings line. Since then I have seen it as attributed to Artemus Ward.) What follows, then, is my crib sheet for this book. This Appendix sorts out the real science, based on and consistent with today's theories (but probably not tomorrow's), from the "science" that I made up for these stories. I have tried to provide a clear dividing line, at the threshold where fact stops and fiction takes over. But even the invented material is designed to be consistent with and derived from what is known today. It does not contradict current theories, although you will not find papers about it in the *Physical Review* or the *Astrophysical Journal*.

The reader may ask, which issues of these publications? That's a very fair question. After all, these stories were written over a twenty-year period. In that time, science has advanced, and it's natural to ask how much of what I wrote still has scientific acceptance.

I reread each story with that in mind, and so far as I know everything still fits with current knowledge. A few things have even gained in plausibility. For example, when I wrote "Rogueworld" we had no direct evidence of any extra-solar planets. Now reports come in every month or two of another world around some other star, based not on direct observation of the planet but on small observed perturbations in the apparent position of the star itself. The idea of vacuum energy extraction, first introduced to science fiction in "All the Colors of the Vacuum," has proceeded from wild science fiction idea to funded research. Black holes, which at the time I wrote "Killing Vector" were purely theoretical entities, form a standard part of modern cosmology. A big black hole, about 2.5 million times the mass of the Sun, is believed to lie at the center of our own galaxy. Radiating black holes, which in 1977 were another way-out idea, are now firmly accepted. The Oort cloud, described in "The Manna Hunt," is a standard part of today's physical model of the extended Solar System.

So has there been nothing new in science in the past twenty years? Not at all. Molecular biology has changed so fast and so much since the 1970s that the field seen from that earlier point of view is almost unrecognizable, and the biggest changes still lie in the future. Computers have become smaller, more powerful, and ubiquitous, beyond what anyone predicted twenty years ago. We also stand today on the verge of quantum computation, which takes advantage of the fact that at the quantum level a system can exist in several states simultaneously. The long-term potential of that development is staggering.

Finally, in the very week that I write this, a report has appeared of the first successful experiment in "quantum teleportation." Via a process known as "entanglement," which couples the quantum state of two widely separated systems, a Caltech team "teleported" a pattern of information from one location to another, independent of the speed of light. If there isn't a new hard SF story in that report, I don't know where you'll find one.

Kernels, black holes, and singularities.

Kernels feature most prominently in the first chronicle, but they are assumed and used in all the others, too. A kernel is actually a Ker-N-le, which is shorthand for Kerr-Newman black hole.

To explain Kerr-Newman black holes, it is best to follow McAndrew's technique, and go back a long way in time. We begin in 1915. In that year, Albert Einstein published the field equations of general relativity in their present form. He had been trying different possible formulations since about 1908, but he was not satisfied with any of them before the 1915 set. His final statement consisted of ten coupled, nonlinear, partial differential equations, relating the curvature of space-time to the presence of matter.

The equations are very elegant and can be written down in tensor form as a single short line of algebra. But written out in full they are horrendously long and complex—so much so that Einstein himself did not expect to see any exact solutions, and thus perhaps didn't look very hard. When Karl Schwarzschild, just the next year, produced an exact solution to the "one-body problem" (he found the gravitational field produced by an isolated mass particle), Einstein was reportedly quite surprised.

This "Schwarzschild solution" was for many years considered mathematically interesting, but of no real physical importance. People were much more interested in looking at approximate solutions of Einstein's field equations that could provide possible tests of the theory. Everyone wanted to compare Einstein's ideas on gravity with those introduced two hundred and fifty years earlier by Isaac Newton, to see where there might be detectable differences. The "strong field" case covered by the Schwarzschild solution seemed less relevant to the real world.

For the next twenty years, little was discovered to lead us toward kernels. Soon after Schwarzschild published his solution, Reissner and Nordstrom solved the general relativity equations for a spherical mass particle that also carried an electric charge. This included the Schwarzschild solution as a special case, but it was considered to have no physical significance and it too remained a mathematical curiosity.

The situation finally changed in 1939. In that year, Oppenheimer and Snyder were studying the collapse of a star under gravitational forces—a situation which certainly *did* have physical significance, since it is a common stellar occurrence.

Two remarks made in their summary are worth quoting directly: "Unless fission due to rotation, the radiation of mass, or the blowing off of mass by radiation, reduce the star's mass to the order of the sun, this contraction will continue indefinitely." In other words, not only can a star collapse, but if it is heavy enough there is no way that the collapse and contraction can be stopped. And "the radius of the star approaches asymptotically its gravitational radius; light from the surface of the star is progressively reddened, and can escape over a progressively narrower range of angles." This is the first modern picture of a black hole, a body with a gravitational field so strong that light cannot escape from it. (We have to say "modern picture" because before 1800 it had been noted as a curiosity that a sufficiently massive body could have an escape velocity from its surface that exceeded the speed of light; in a sense, the black hole was predicted more than two hundred years ago.)

Notice that the collapsing body does not have to contract indefinitely if it is the size of the Sun or smaller, so we do not have to worry that the Earth, say, or the Moon, will shrink indefinitely to become a black hole. Notice also that there is a reference to the "gravitational radius" of the black hole. This was something that came straight out of the Schwarzschild solution, the distance where the reddening of light became infinite, so that any light coming from inside that radius could never be seen by an outside observer. Since the gravitational radius for the Sun is only about three kilometers, if the Sun were squeezed down to this size conditions inside the collapsed body defy the imagination. The density of matter must be about twenty billion tons per cubic centimeter.

You might think that Oppenheimer and Snyder's paper, with its apparently bizarre conclusions, would have produced a sensation. In fact, it aroused little notice for a long time. It too was looked at as a mathematical oddity, a result that physicists needn't take too seriously.

What was going on here? The Schwarzschild solution had been left on the shelf for a generation, and now the Oppenheimer results were in their turn regarded with no more than mild interest.

One could argue that in the 1920s the attention of leading physicists was elsewhere, as they tried to drink from the fire-hose flood of theory and experiment that established quantum theory. But what about the 1940s and 1950s? Why didn't whole groups of physicists explore the consequences for general relativity and astrophysics of an indefinitely collapsing stellar mass?

Various explanations could be offered, but I favor one that can be stated in a single word: Einstein. He was a gigantic figure, stretching out over everything in physics for the first half of this century. Even now, he casts an enormous shadow over the whole field. Until his death in 1955, researchers in general relativity and gravitation felt a constant awareness of his presence, of his genius peering over their shoulder. If Einstein had not been able to penetrate the mystery, went the unspoken argument, what chance do the rest of us have? Not until after his death was there a resurgence of interest and spectacular progress in general relativity. And it was one of the leaders of that resurgence, John Wheeler, who in 1958 provided the inspired name for the Schwarzschild solution needed to capture everyone's fancy: the *black hole*.

We still have not reached the kernel. The black hole that Wheeler named was still the Schwarzschild black hole, the object that McAndrew spoke of with such derision. It had a mass, and possibly an electric charge, but that was all. The next development came in 1963, and it was a big surprise to everyone working in the field.

Roy Kerr, at that time associated with the University of Texas at Austin, had been exploring a particular set of Einstein's field equations that assumed an unusually simple form for the metric (the metric is the thing that defines distances in a curved space-time). The analysis was highly mathematical and seemed wholly abstract, until Kerr found that he could produce a form of exact solution to the equations. The solution included the Schwarzschild solution as a special case, but there was more; it provided in addition another quantity that Kerr was able to associate with *spin*.

In the *Physical Review Letters* of September, 1963, Kerr published a one-page paper with the not-too-catchy title, "Gravitational field of a spinning mass as an example of algebraically special metrics." In this paper he described the Kerr solution for a *spinning black hole*. I think it is fair to say that everyone, probably including Kerr himself, was astonished.

The Kerr black hole has a number of fascinating properties, but before we get to them let us take the one final step needed to reach the kernel. In 1965 Ezra Newman and colleagues at the University of Pittsburgh published a short note in the *Journal of Mathematical Physics*, pointing out that the Kerr solution could be generated from the Schwarzschild solution by a curious mathematical trick, in which a real coordinate was replaced by a complex one. They also realized that the same trick could be applied to the charged black hole, and thus they were able to provide a solution for a rotating, *charged* black hole: the Kerr-Newman black hole, that I call the *kernel*.

The kernel has all the nice features admired by McAndrew. Because it is charged, you can move it about using electric and magnetic fields. Because you can add and withdraw rotational energy, you can use it as a power source and a power reservoir. A Schwarzschild black hole lacks these desirable qualities. As McAndrew says, it just sits there.

One might think that this is just the beginning. There could be black holes that have mass, charge, spin, axial asymmetry, dipole moments, quadrupole moments, and many other properties. It turns out that this is not the case. *The only properties that a black hole can possess are mass, charge, spin and magnetic moment*—and the last one is uniquely fixed by the other three.

This strange result, often stated as the theorem "A black hole has no hair" (i.e. no detailed structure) was established to most people's satisfaction in a powerful series of papers in 1967-1972 by Werner Israel, Brandon Carter, and Stephen Hawking. A black hole is fixed uniquely by its mass, spin, and electric charge. Kernels are the end of the line, and they represent the most general kind of black hole that physics permits.

After 1965, more people were working on general relativity and gravitation, and other properties of the Kerr-Newman black holes rapidly followed. Some of them were very strange. For example, the Schwarzschild black hole has a characteristic surface associated with it, a sphere where the reddening of light becomes infinite, and from within which no information can ever be sent to the outside world. This surface has various names: the surface of infinite red shift, the trapping surface, the one-way membrane, and the event horizon. But the Kerr-Newman black holes turn out to have *two* characteristic surfaces associated with them, and the surface of infinite red shift is in this case distinct from the event horizon.

To visualize these surfaces, take a hamburger bun and hollow out the inside enough to let you put a round hamburger patty entirely within it. For a Kerr-Newman black hole, the outer surface of the bread (which is a sort of ellipsoid in shape) is the surface of infinite red shift, the "static limit" within which no particle can remain at rest, no matter how hard its rocket engines work. Inside the bun, the surface of the meat patty is a sphere, the "event horizon," from which no light or particle can ever escape. We can never find out anything about what goes on within the meat patty's surface, so its composition must be a complete mystery (you may have eaten hamburgers that left the same impression). For a rotating black hole, these bun and patty surfaces touch only at the north and south poles of the axis of rotation (the top and bottom centers of the bun). The really interesting region, however, is that between these two surfaces—the remaining bread, usually called the *ergosphere*. It has a property which allows the kernel to become a power kernel.

Roger Penrose (whom we will meet again in a later chronicle) pointed out in 1969 that it is possible for a particle to dive in towards a Kerr black hole, split in two when it is inside the ergosphere, and then have part of it ejected in such a way that it has more total energy than the whole particle that went in. If this is done, we have extracted energy from the black hole.

Where has that energy come from? Black holes may be mysterious, but we still do not expect that energy can be created from nothing.

Note that we said a *Kerr* black hole—not a Schwarzschild black hole. The energy we extract comes from the rotational energy of the spinning black hole, and if a hole is not spinning, no energy can possibly be extracted from it in this way. As McAndrew remarked, a Schwarzschild hole is dull, a dead object that cannot be used to provide power. A Kerr black hole, on the other hand, is one of the most efficient energy sources imaginable, better by far than most nuclear fission or fusion processes. (A Kerr-Newman black hole allows the same energy extraction process, but we have to be a little more careful, since only part of the ergosphere can be used.)

If a Kerr-Newman black hole starts out with only a little spin energy, the energy-extraction process can be worked in reverse, to provide more rotational energy— the process that McAndrew referred to as "spin-up" of the kernel. "Spin-down" is the opposite process, the one that extracts energy. A brief paper by Christodoulou in the *Physical Review Letters* of 1970 discussed the limits on this process, and pointed out that you could only spin-up a kernel to a certain limit, termed an "extreme" Kerr solution. Past that limit (which can never be achieved using the Penrose process) a solution can be written to the Einstein field equations. This was done by Tomimatsu and Sato, and presented in 1972 in another one-page paper in *Physical Review Letters*. It is a very odd solution indeed. It has no event horizon, which means that activities there are not shielded from the rest of the Universe as they are for the usual kernels. And it has what is referred to as a "naked singularity" associated with it, where cause and effect relationships no longer apply. This bizarre object was discussed by Gibbons and Russell-Clark, in 1973, in yet another paper in *Physical Review Letters*.

That seems to leave us in pretty good shape. Everything so far has been completely consistent with current physics. We have kernels that can be spun up and spun down by well-defined procedures—and if we allow that McAndrew could somehow take a kernel past the extreme form, we would indeed have something with a naked singularity. It seems improbable that such a physical situation could exist, but if it did, space-time there would be highly peculiar. The existence of certain space-time symmetry directions—called killing vectors—that we find for all usual Kerr-Newman black holes would not be guaranteed. Everything is fine.

Or is it?

Oppenheimer and Snyder pointed out that black holes are created when big masses, larger than the Sun, contract under gravitational collapse. The kernels that we want are much smaller than that. We need to be able to move them around the solar system, and the gravitational field of an object the mass of the Sun would tear the system apart. Unfortunately, there was no prescription in Oppenheimer's work, or elsewhere, to allow us to make small black holes.

Stephen Hawking finally came to the rescue. Apart from being created by collapsing stars, he said, black holes could also be created in the extreme conditions of pressure that existed during the Big Bang that started our Universe. Small black holes, weighing no more than a hundredth of a milligram, could have been born then. Over billions of years, these could interact with each other to produce more massive black holes, of any size you care to mention. We seem to have the mechanism that will produce the kernels of the size we need.

Unfortunately, what Hawking gave he soon took away. In perhaps the biggest surprise of all in black hole theory, he showed that *black holes are not black*.

General relativity and quantum theory were both developed in this century, but they have never been combined in a satisfactory way. Physicists have known this and been uneasy about it for a long time. In attempting to move towards what John Wheeler terms the "fiery marriage of general relativity with quantum theory," Hawking studied quantum mechanical effects in the vicinity of a black hole. He found that particles and radiation can (and must) be emitted from the hole. The smaller the hole, the faster the rate of radiation. He was able to relate the mass of the black hole to a *temperature*, and as one would expect a "hotter" black hole pours out radiation and particles much faster than a "cold" one. For a black hole the mass of the Sun, the associated temperature is lower than the background temperature of the Universe. Such a black hole receives more than it emits, so it will steadily increase in mass. However, for a small black hole, with the few billion tons of mass that we want in a kernel, the temperature is so high (ten billion degrees) that the black hole will radiate itself away in a gigantic and rapid burst of radiation and particles. Furthermore, a rapidly spinning kernel will preferentially radiate particles that decrease its spin, and a highly charged one will prefer to radiate charged particles that reduce its overall charge.

These results are so strange that in 1972 and 1973 Hawking spent a lot of time trying to find the mistake in his own analysis. Only when he had performed every check that he could think of was he finally forced to accept the conclusion: black holes aren't black after all; and the smallest black holes are the least black.

That gives us a problem when we want to use power kernels in a story. First, the argument that they are readily available, as leftovers from the birth of the Universe, has been destroyed. Second, a Kerr-Newman black hole is a dangerous object to be near. It gives off high energy radiation and particles.

This is the point where the science of Kerr-Newman black holes stops and the science fiction begins. I assume in these stories that there is some as-yet-unknown natural process which creates sizeable black holes on a continuing basis. They can't be created too close to Earth, or we would see them. However, there is plenty of room outside the known Solar System—perhaps in the region occupied by the long-period comets, from beyond the orbit of Pluto out to perhaps a light-year from the Sun.

Second, I assume that a kernel can be surrounded by

a shield (not of matter, but of electromagnetic fields) which is able to reflect all the emitted particles and radiation back into the black hole. Humans can thus work close to the kernels without being fried in a storm of radiation and high-energy particles.

Even surrounded by such a shield, a rotating black hole would still be noticed by a nearby observer. Its gravitational field would still be felt, and it would also produce a curious effect known as "inertial dragging."

We have pointed out that the inside of a black hole is completely shielded from the rest of the Universe, so that we can never know what is going on there. It is as though the inside of a black hole is a separate Universe, possibly with its own different physical laws. Inertial dragging adds to that idea. We are used to the notion that when we spin something around, we do it relative to a well-defined and fixed reference frame. Newton pointed out in his *Principia Mathematica* that a rotating bucket of water, from the shape of the water's surface, provides evidence of an "absolute" rotation relative to the stars. This is true here on Earth, or over in the Andromeda Galaxy, or out in the Virgo Cluster. It is not true, however, near a rotating black hole. The closer that we get to one, the less that our usual absolute reference frame applies. The kernel defines its own absolute frame, one that rotates with it. Closer than a certain distance to the kernel (the "static limit" mentioned earlier) everything *must* revolve—dragged along and forced to adopt the rotating reference frame defined by the spinning black hole.

The McAndrew balanced drive.

This device makes a first appearance in the second chronicle, and is assumed in all the subsequent stories.

Let us begin with well-established science. Again it starts at the beginning of the century, in the work of Einstein. In 1908, he wrote as follows:

"We . . . assume the complete physical equivalence of a gravitational field and of a corresponding acceleration of the reference system . . ."

And in 1913:

"An observer enclosed in an elevator has no way to decide whether the elevator is at rest in a static gravitational field or whether the elevator is located in gravitation-free space in an accelerated motion that is maintained by forces acting on the elevator (equivalence hypothesis)."

This equivalence hypothesis, or equivalence principle, is central to general relativity. If you could be accelerated in one direction at a thousand gees, and simultaneously pulled in the other direction by an intense gravitational force producing a thousand gees, you would feel *no force whatsoever*. It would be just the same as if you were in free fall.

As McAndrew said, once you realize that fact, the rest is mere mechanics. You take a large circular disk of condensed matter (more on that in a moment), sufficient to produce a gravitational acceleration of, say, 50 gees on a test object (such as a human being) sitting on the middle of the plate. You also provide a drive that can accelerate the plate away from the human at 50 gees. The net force on the person at the middle of the plate is then zero. If you increase the acceleration of the plate gradually, from zero to 50 gees, then to remain comfortable the person must also be moved in gradually, starting well away from disk and finishing in contact with it. The life capsule must thus move in and out along the axis of the disk, depending on the ship's acceleration: high acceleration, close to disk; low acceleration, far from disk.

There is one other variable of importance, and that is the *tidal forces* on the human passenger. These are caused by the changes in gravitational force with distance—it would be no good having a person's head feeling a force of one gee, if his feet felt a force of thirty gees. Let us therefore insist that the rate of change of acceleration be no more than one gee per meter when the acceleration caused by the disk is 50 gees.

The gravitational acceleration produced along the axis of a thin circular disk of matter of total mass M and radius R is a textbook problem of classical potential theory. Taking the radius of the disk to be 50 meters, the gravitational acceleration acting on a test object at the center of the disk to be 50 gees, and the tidal force there to be one gee per meter, we can solve for the total mass M, together with the gravitational and tidal forces acting on a body at different distances Z along the axis of the disk.

We find that if the distance of the passengers from the center of the plate is 246 meters, the plate produces gravitational acceleration on passengers of 1 gee, so if the drive is off there is a net force of 1 gee on them; at zero meters (on the plate itself) the plate produces a gravitational acceleration on passengers of 50 gees, so if the drive accelerates them at 50 gees, they feel as though they are in free fall. The tidal force is a maximum, at one gee per meter, when the passengers are closest to the disk.

This device will actually work as described, with no science fiction involved at all, if you can provide the plate of condensed matter and the necessary drive. Unfortunately, this turns out to be nontrivial. All the distances are reasonable, and so are the tidal forces. What is much less reasonable is the mass of the disk that we have used. It is a little more than 9 trillion tons; such a disk 100 meters across and one meter thick would have an average density of 1,170 tons per cubic centimeter.

This density is modest compared with that found in a neutron star, and tiny compared with what we find in a black hole. Thus we know that such densities do exist in the Universe. However, no materials available to us on Earth today even come close to such high values—they have densities that fall short by a factor of more than a million. And the massplate would not work as described, without the dense matter. We have a real problem.

It's science fiction time again: let us assume that in a couple of hundred years we will be able to compress matter to very high densities, and hold it there using powerful electromagnetic fields. If that is the case, the massplate needed for McAndrew's drive can be built. It's certainly massive, but that shouldn't be a limitation—the Solar System has plenty of spare matter available for construction materials. And although a 9 trillion ton mass may sound a lot, it's tiny by celestial standards, less than the mass of a modest asteroid.

With that one extrapolation of today's science it sounds as though we can have the McAndrew balanced drive. We can even suggest how that extrapolation might be performed, with plausible use of present physics.

Unfortunately, things are not as nice as they seem. There is a much bigger piece of science fiction that must be introduced before the McAndrew drive can exist as a useful device. We look at that next, and note that it is a central concern of the third chronicle.

Suppose that the drive mechanism is the most efficient one consistent with today's physics. This would be a photon drive, in which any fuel is completely converted to radiation and used to propel the ship. There is certainly nothing in present science that suggests such a drive is theoretically impossible, and some analysis of matter-antimatter reactions indicates that the photon drive could one day be built. Let us assume that we know how to construct it. Then, even with this "ultimate" drive, McAndrew's ship would have problems. It's not difficult to calculate that with a fifty gee drive, the conversion of matter to radiation needed to keep the drive going will quickly consume the ship's own mass. More than half the mass will be gone in a few days, and McAndrew's ship will disappear from under him.

Solution of this problem calls for a lot more fictional science than the simple task of producing stable condensed matter. We have to go back to present physics and look for loopholes. We need to find inconsistencies in the overall picture of the Universe provided by present day physics, and exploit these as necessary.

The best place to seek inconsistencies is where we already know we will find them—in the meeting of general relativity and quantum theory. If we calculate the energy associated with an absence of matter in quantum theory, the "vacuum state," we do not, as common sense would suggest, get zero.

Instead we get a large, positive value per unit volume. In classical thinking, one could argue that the zero point of energy is arbitrary, so that one can simply start measuring energies from the vacuum state value. But if we accept general relativity, this option is denied to us. Energy, of any form, produces space-time curvature. We are therefore not allowed to change the definition of the origin of the energy scale. Once this is accepted, the energy of the vacuum state cannot be talked out of existence. It is real, if elusive, and its presence provides the loophole that we need.

Again, we are at the point where the science fiction enters. If the vacuum state has an energy associated with it, I assume that this energy is capable of being tapped. Doesn't this then, according to relativity ($E = mc^2$), suggest that there is also mass associated with the vacuum, contrary to what we think of as vacuum? Yes, it does, and I'm sorry about that, but the paradox is not of my creation. It is implicit in the contradictions that arise as soon as you try to put general relativity and quantum theory together.

Richard Feynman, one of the founders of quantum electrodynamics, addressed the question of the vacuum energy, and computed an estimate for the equivalent mass per unit volume. The estimate came out to two billion tons per cubic centimeter. The energy in two billion tons of matter is more than enough to boil all Earth's oceans (powerful stuff, vacuum). Feynman, commenting on his vacuum energy estimate, remarks:

"Such a mass density would, at first sight at least, be

*expected to produce very large gravitational effects which
are not observed. It is possible that we are calculating
in a naive manner, and, if all of the consequences of the
general theory of relativity (such as the gravitational
effects produced by the large stresses implied here) were
included, the effects might cancel out; but nobody has
worked all this out yet. It is possible that some cutoff
procedure that not only yields a finite energy for the
vacuum state but also provides relativistic invariance may
be found. The implications of such a result are at present
completely unknown."*

With that degree of uncertainty at the highest levels
of present-day physics, I feel not at all uncomfortable in
exploiting the troublesome vacuum energy to service
McAndrew's drive.

The third chronicle introduces two other ideas that are
definitely science fiction today, even if they become science fact a few years from now. If there are ways to
isolate the human central nervous system and keep it alive
independently of the body, we certainly don't know much
about them. On the other hand, I see nothing that suggests this idea is impossible in principle—heart transplants
were not feasible forty years ago, and until this century
blood transfusions were rare and highly dangerous. A
century hence, today's medical impossibilities should be
routine.

The Sturm Invocation for vacuum survival is also
invented, but I believe that it, like the Izaak Walton introduced in the seventh chronicle, is a logical component
of any space-oriented future. Neither calls for technology beyond what we have today. The hypnotic control
implied in the Invocation, though advanced for most
practitioners, could already be achieved. And any competent engineering shop could build a Walton for you in
a few weeks—I am tempted to patent the idea, but fear
that it would be rejected as too obvious or inevitable a
development.

❖   ❖   ❖

Life in space and the Oort cloud.

Most chronicles take place at least partly in the Halo, or the Outer Solar System, which I define to extend from the distance of Pluto from the Sun, out to a little over a light-year. Within this radius, the Sun is still the primary gravitational influence, and controls the orbits of objects moving out there.

To give an idea of the size of the Halo, we note that Pluto lies at an average distance of about 6 billion kilometers from the Sun. This is about forty astronomical units, where the astronomical unit, usually abbreviated to AU, is defined as the mean distance of the Earth from the Sun. The AU provides a convenient yardstick for measurements within the Solar System. One light-year is about 63,000 AU (inches in a mile, is how I remember it). So the volume of space in the Halo is 4 billion times as large as the sphere enclosing the nine known planets.

By Solar System standards, the Halo is thus a huge region. But beyond Neptune and Pluto, we know little about it. There are a number of "trans-Neptunian objects," but no one knows how many. Some of them may be big enough to qualify as planets. The search for Pluto was inspired early this century by differences between theory and observation in the orbits of Uranus and Neptune. When Pluto was found, it soon became clear that it was not nearly heavy enough to produce the observed irregularities. The obvious explanation is yet another planet, farther out than the ones we know.

Calculations of the orbit and size of a tenth planet needed to reconcile observation and theory for Uranus and Neptune suggest a rather improbable object, out of the orbital plane that all the other planets move in and about seventy times the mass of the Earth. I don't believe this particular object exists.

On the other hand, observational equipment and techniques for faint objects are improving rapidly. The number of known trans-Neptunian objects increases almost every month.

The other thing we know for sure about the Halo is that it is populated by comets. The Halo is often called the Oort cloud, since the Dutch astronomer Oort suggested thirty years ago that the entire Solar System is enveloped by a cloud of cometary material, to a radius of perhaps a light-year. He regarded this region as a "cometary reservoir," containing perhaps a hundred billion comets. Close encounters between comets out in the Halo would occasionally disturb the orbit of one of them enough to divert it to the Inner System, where it would appear as a long-period comet when it came close enough to the Sun. Further interactions with Jupiter and the other planets would then sometimes convert the long-period comet to a short-period comet, such as Halley's or Encke's comet, which we observe repeatedly each time they swing by close to the Sun.

Most comets, however, continue their lonely orbits out in the cloud, never approaching the Inner System. They do not have to be small to be invisible to us. The amount of sunlight a body receives is inversely proportional to the square of its distance from the Sun; the apparent area it presents to our telescopes is also inversely proportional to the square of its distance from Earth. For bodies in the Halo, the reflected light that we receive from them thus varies as the inverse fourth power of their distance from the Sun. A planet with the size and composition of Uranus, but half a light-year away, would be seven trillion times as faint. And we should remember that Uranus itself is faint enough that it was not discovered until 1781, when high-quality telescopes were available. So far as present-day detection powers are concerned, there could be almost anything out there in the Halo.

One of the things that may be there is life. In a carefully argued but controversial theory developed over the past thirty years, Hoyle and Wickramasinghe have advanced the idea that space is the natural place for the creation of "pre-biotic" molecules in large quantities. Pre-biotic molecules are compounds such as carbohydrates, amino acids, and chlorophyll, which form the necessary building blocks for the development of life. Simpler organic molecules, such as methyl cyanide and ethanol, have already been observed in interstellar clouds.

Hoyle and Wickramasinghe go further. They state explicitly: *"We shall argue that primitive living organisms evolve in the mixture of organic molecules, ices and silicate smoke which make up a comet's head."*

The science fiction of the fourth chronicle consists of these two assumptions:

1. The complex organic molecules described by Hoyle and Wickramasinghe are located in a particular region of the Halo, a "life ring" that lies between 3,200 and 4,000 AU from the Sun;
2. The "primitive living organism" have evolved quite a bit further than Hoyle and Wickramasinghe expected, on at least one body of the Oort cloud.

Missing matter and the beginning of the Universe.

Today's so-called "standard model" of cosmology suggests that the Universe began in a "Big Bang" somewhere between ten and twenty billion years ago. Since we have been able to study the Universe in detail for less than four hundred years (the telescope was invented about 1608), any attempt to say something about the origin of the Universe implies considerable extrapolation into the past. There is a chance of success only because the basic physical laws of the Universe that govern events on both the smallest scale (atoms and subatomic particles) and the largest scale (stars, galaxies, and clusters of galaxies) appear not to have changed since its earliest days.

The primary evidence for a finite age for the whole Universe comes from observation of distant galaxies. When we observe the light that they emit, we find, as was suggested by Carl Wirtz in 1924 and confirmed by Edwin Hubble in 1929, that more distant galaxies appear *redder* than nearer ones.

To be more specific, in the fainter (and therefore presumably more distant) galaxies, every wavelength of light emitted has been shifted toward a longer wavelength. The question is, what could cause such a shift?

The most plausible mechanism, to a physicist, is called the *Doppler effect*. According to the Doppler effect, light from a receding object will be shifted to longer (redder) wavelengths; light from an approaching object will be shifted to shorter (bluer) wavelengths. Exactly the same thing works for sound, which is why a speeding police car's siren seems to drop in pitch as it passes by.

If we accept the Doppler effect as the cause of the reddened appearance of the galaxies, we are led (as was Hubble) to an immediate conclusion: the whole Universe must be *expanding*, at a close to constant rate, because the red shift of the galaxies corresponds to their brightness, and therefore to their distance.

Note that this does not mean that the Universe is expanding *into* some other space. There is no other space. It is the *whole Universe*—everything there is—that has grown over time to its present dimension.

And from this we can draw another immediate conclusion. If expansion proceeded in the past as it does today, there must have been a time when everything in the whole Universe was drawn together to a single point. It is logical to call the time that has elapsed since everything was in that infinitely dense singularity *the age of the Universe*. The Hubble galactic redshift allows us to calculate how long ago that happened.

Our estimate is bounded on the one hand by the constancy of the laws of physics (how far back can we go, before the Universe would be totally unrecognizable and far from the place where we believe today's physical laws are valid?); and on the other hand by our knowledge of the distance of the galaxies, as determined by other methods.

Curiously, it is the second problem that forms the major constraint. When we say that the Universe is between ten and twenty billion years old, that uncertainty of a factor of two betrays our ignorance of galactic distances.

It is remarkable that observation of the faint agglomerations of stars known as galaxies leads us, very directly and cleanly, to the conclusion that we live in a Universe of finite and determinable age. A century ago, no one could have offered even an approximate age for the Universe. For an upper bound, most nonreligious scientists would probably have said "forever." For a lower bound, all they had was the age of the Earth.

Asking one question, *How old is the Universe?* inevitably leads us to another: *What was the Universe like, ten or twenty billion years ago, when it was compressed into a very small volume?*

That question was tackled by a Belgian, Georges Lemaître. Early in the 1930s Lemaître went backwards mentally in time, to a period when the whole Universe was a "primeval atom." In this first and single atom, everything was squashed into a sphere only a few times as big as the Sun, with no space between atoms, or even between nuclei. As Lemaître saw it, this unit must then have exploded, fragmenting into the atoms and stars and galaxies and everything else in the Universe that we know today. He might justifiably have called it the *Big Bang*, but he didn't. That name seems to have been coined by Fred Hoyle, whom we met in the previous chronicle.

Lemaître did not ask the next question, namely, where did the primeval atom come from? Since he was an ordained Catholic priest, he probably felt that the answer to that was a given. Lemaître also did not worry too much about the composition of his primeval atom—what was it made of? It might be thought that the easiest assumption is that everything in the Universe was already there, much as it is now. But that cannot be true, because as we go back in time, the Universe had to be hotter as well as more dense. Before a certain point, atoms as we know them could not exist, because they would be torn apart by the intense radiation that permeated the whole Universe.

The person who did worry about the composition of the primeval atom was George Gamow. In the 1940s, he conjectured that the original stuff of the Universe was nothing more than densely packed neutrons. Certainly, it seemed reasonable to suppose that the Universe at its outset had no net charge, since it seems to have no net charge today. Also, a neutron left to itself has a fifty percent chance that it will, in about thirteen minutes, decay radioactively to form an electron and a proton. One electron and one proton form an atom of hydrogen; and even today, the Universe is predominantly atomic hydrogen. So neutrons could account for most, if not all, of today's Universe.

If the early Universe was very hot and very dense and all hydrogen, some of it ought to have fused and become helium, carbon, and other elements. The question, *How much of each?* was one that Gamow and his student, Ralph Alpher, set out to answer. They calculated that about a quarter of the matter in the primeval Universe should have turned to helium, a figure very consistent with the present composition of the oldest stars. They published their results on April 1, 1948. In one of physics' best-known jokes, Hans Bethe (pronounced *Bay-ter*, like the Greek letter Beta) allowed his name to be added to the paper, although he had nothing to do with its writing. The authors thus became Alpher, Bethe, and Gamow.

Apart from showing how to calculate the ratio of hydrogen to helium after the Big Bang, Gamow and his colleagues did one other thing whose full significance probably escaped them. In 1948 they produced an equation that allowed one to compute the present background temperature of the Universe from its age, assuming a Universe that expanded uniformly since its beginning in the Big Bang. The background radiation, corresponding to a temperature of 2.7 degrees above absolute zero, was discovered by Arno Penzias and Robert Wilson in 1964, and made the Big Bang theory fully respectable for the first time.

We now believe that hydrogen fused to form helium when the Universe was between three and four *minutes* old. What about even earlier times? Let us run the clock backwards, as far as we can towards the Big Bang.

How far back do we want to start the clock? Well, when the Universe was smaller in size, it was also hotter. In a hot enough environment, atoms as we know them cannot hold together. High-energy radiation rips them apart as fast as they form. A good time to begin our backward running of the clock might then be the period when atoms could form and persist as stable units. Although stars and galaxies would not yet exist, at least the Universe would be made up of familiar components, hydrogen and helium atoms that we would recognize.

Atoms can form, and hold together, somewhere between half a million and a million years after the Big Bang. Before that time, matter and radiation interacted continuously, and the Universe was almost opaque to radiation. After it, matter and radiation "decoupled," became near-independent, and went their separate ways. The temperature of the Universe when this happened was about 3,000 degrees. Ever since then, the expansion of the Universe has lengthened the wavelength of the background radiation, and thus lowered its temperature. The cosmic background radiation discovered by Penzias and Wilson is nothing more than the radiation at the time when it decoupled from matter, now grown old.

Continuing backwards, even before atoms could form, helium and hydrogen nuclei and free electrons could combine to form atoms; but they could not remain in combination, because radiation broke them apart. The content of the Universe was, in effect, controlled by radiation energetic enough to prevent the formation of atoms.

This situation held from about three minutes to one million years A.C. (After Creation).

If we go back to a period less than three minutes A.C., radiation was even more dominant. It prevented the build-up even of helium nuclei. As noted earlier, the fusion of hydrogen to helium requires hot temperatures, such as we find in the center of stars. But fusion cannot take place if it is *too* hot, as it was before three minutes after the Big Bang. Before helium could form, the Universe had to "cool" to about a billion degrees. All that existed before then were electrons (and their positively charged forms, positrons), neutrons, protons, neutrinos (a chargeless particle, until recently assumed to be massless but now thought to possess a tiny mass), and radiation.

Until three minutes A.C., it might seem as though radiation controlled events. But this is not the case. As we proceed farther backwards and the temperature of the primordial fireball continues to increase, we reach a point where the temperature is so high (above ten billion degrees) that large numbers of electron-positron pairs can be created from pure radiation. That happened from one second up to fourteen seconds A.C. After that, the number of electron-positron pairs decreased rapidly. Less were being generated than were annihilating themselves and returning to pure radiation. After the Universe cooled to ten billion degrees, neutrinos also decoupled from other forms of matter.

Still we have a long way to go, physically speaking, to the moment of creation. As we continue backwards, temperatures rise and rise. At a tenth of a second A.C., the temperature of the Universe is thirty billion degrees. The Universe is a soup of electrons, protons, neutrons, neutrinos, and radiation. As the kinetic energy of particle motion becomes greater and greater, effects caused by differences of particle mass are less important. At thirty billion degrees, an electron easily carries enough energy to convert a proton into the slightly heavier neutron. Thus in this period, free neutrons are constantly trying to decay to form protons and electrons; but energetic proton-electron collisions go on remaking neutrons.

We keep the clock running. Now the important time intervals become shorter and shorter. At one ten-thousandth of a second A.C., the temperature is one thousand billion degrees. The Universe is so small that the density of matter, everywhere, is as great as that in the nucleus of an atom today (about 100 million tons per cubic centimeter; a fair-sized asteroid, at this density, would squeeze down to fit in a match box). Modern theory says that the nucleus is best regarded not as protons and neutrons, but as quarks, elementary particles from which the neutrons and protons themselves are made. Thus at this early time, 0.0001 seconds A.C. the Universe was a sea of quarks, electrons, neutrinos, and energetic radiation. We move on, to the time, 10^{-36} seconds A.C., when the Universe went through a super-rapid "inflationary" phase, growing from the size of a proton to the size of a basketball in about 5×10^{-32} seconds. We are almost back as far as we can go. Finally we reach a time 10^{-43} seconds A.C, (called the *Plank time*), when according to a class of theories known as *supersymmetry* theories, the force of gravity decoupled from everything else, and remains decoupled to this day.

This may already sound like pure science fiction. It is not. It is today's science—though it certainly may be wrong. But at last we have reached the time when McAndrew's "hidden matter" was created. And today's Universe seems to require that something very like it exist.

The argument for hidden matter goes as follows: The Universe is expanding. Every cosmologist today agrees on that. Will it go on expanding forever, or will it one day slow to a halt, reverse direction, and fall back in on itself to end in a Big Crunch? Or is the Universe poised on the infinitely narrow dividing line between expansion and ultimate contraction, so that it will increase more and more slowly, and finally (but after infinite time) stop its growth?

The thing that decides which of these three possibilities will occur is the total amount of mass in the Universe, or rather, since we do not care what form mass takes and mass and energy are totally equivalent, the future of the Universe is decided by the total mass-energy content per unit volume.

If the mass-energy is too big, the Universe will end in the Big Crunch. If it is too small, the Universe will fly apart forever. And only in the Goldilocks situation, where the mass-energy is "just right," will the Universe ultimately reach a "flat" condition. The amount of matter needed to stop the expansion is not large, by terrestrial standards. It calls for only three hydrogen atoms per cubic meter.

Is there that much available?

If we estimate the mass and energy from visible material in stars and galaxies, we find a value nowhere near the "critical density" needed to make the Universe finally flat. If we say that the critical mass-energy density has to be equal to unity just to slow the expansion, we observe in visible matter only a value of about 0.01.

There is evidence, though, from the rotation of galaxies, that there is a lot more "dark matter" present there than we see as stars. It is not clear what this dark matter is—black holes, very dim stars, clouds of neutrinos—but when we are examining the future of the Universe, we don't care. All we worry about is the amount. And that amount, from galactic dynamics, could be at least ten times as much as the visible matter. Enough to bring the density to 0.1, or possible even 0.2. But no more than that.

One might say, all right, that's it. There is not enough matter in the Universe to stop the expansion, by a factor of about ten, so we have confirmed that we live in a forever-expanding Universe. Recent (1999) observations seem to confirm that result.

Unfortunately, that is not the answer that most cosmologists would really like to hear. The problem comes because the most acceptable cosmological models tell us that if the density is as much as 0.1 today, then in the past it must have been much closer to unity. For example, at one second A.C., the density would have had to be within one part in a million billion of unity, in order for it to be 0.1 today. It would be an amazing coincidence if, by accident, the actual density were so close to the critical density.

Most cosmologists therefore say that, today's observations notwithstanding, the density of the Universe is really exactly equal to the critical value. In this case, the Universe will expand forever, but more and more slowly.

The problem, of course, is then to account for the matter that we don't observe. Where could the "missing matter" be, that makes up the other nine-tenths of the universe?

There are several candidates. One suggestion is that the Universe is filled with energetic ("hot") neutrinos, each with a small but non-zero mass. However, there are problems with the Hot Neutrino theory. If they are the source of the mass that stops the expansion of the Universe, the galaxies, according to today's models, should not have developed as early as they did in the history of the Universe.

What about other candidates? Well, the class of theories already alluded to and known as supersymmetry theories require that as-yet undiscovered particles ought to exist.

There are *axions*, which are particles that help to preserve certain symmetries (charge, parity, and time-reversal) in elementary particle physics; and there are *photinos*, *gravitinos*, and others, based on theoretical supersymmetries between particles and radiation. These candidates are slow moving (and so considered "cold") but some of them have substantial mass. They too would have been around soon after the Big Bang. These slow-moving particles clump more easily together, so the formation of galaxies could take place earlier than with the hot neutrinos. We seem to have a better candidate for the missing matter—except that no one has yet observed the necessary particles. At least neutrinos are known to exist!

Supersymmetry, in a particular form known as *superstring theory*, offers another possible source of hidden mass. This one is easily the most speculative. Back at a time, 10^{-43} seconds A.C., when gravity decoupled from everything else, a second class of matter may have been created that is able to interact with normal matter and radiation, today, only through the gravitational force. We can never observe such matter, in the usual sense, because our observational methods, from ordinary telescopes to radio telescopes to gamma ray detectors, all rely on *electromagnetic* interaction with matter.

This "shadow matter" produced at the time of gravitational decoupling lacks any such interaction with the matter of the familiar Universe. We can determine its existence only by the gravitational effects it produces, which, of course, is exactly what we need to "close the Universe," and also exactly what we needed for the fifth chronicle.

One can thus argue that the fifth chronicle is all straight science; or, if you are more skeptical, that it and the theories on which it is based are both science fiction. I think that I prefer not to give an opinion.

Invariance and science.

In mathematics and physics, an invariant is something that does not change when certain changes of condition are made. For example, the "connectedness" or "connectivity" of an object remains the same, no matter how we deform its surface shape, provided only that no cutting or merging of surface parts is permitted. A grapefruit and a banana have the same connectedness—one of them can, with a little effort, be squashed to look like the other (at least in principle, though it does sound messy). A coffee cup with one handle and a donut have the same connectedness; but both have a different connectedness from that of a two-handled mug, or from a mug with no handle. You and I have the same connectedness—unless you happen to have had one or both of your ears pierced, or wear a ring through your nose.

The "knottedness" of a piece of rope is similarly unchanging, provided that we keep hold of the ends and don't break the string, There is an elaborate vocabulary of knots. A "knot of degree zero" is one that is equivalent to no knot at all, so that pulling the ends of the rope in such a case will give a straight piece of string—a knot trick known to every magician. But when Alexander the Great "solved" the problem of the Gordian Knot by cutting it in two with his sword, he was cheating.

Invariants may sound useless, or at best trivial. Why bother with them? Simply for this reason: they often allow us to make general statements, true in a wide variety of circumstances, where otherwise we would have to deal with lots of specific and different cases.

For example, the statement that a partial differential equation is of elliptic, parabolic, or hyperbolic type is based on a particular invariant, and it tells us a great deal about the possible solutions of such equations before we ever begin to try to solve them. And the statement that a real number is rational or irrational is invariant, independent of the number base that we are using, and it too says something profound about the nature of that number.

What about the invariants of physics, which interested McAndrew? Some invariants are so obvious, we may feel they hardly justify being mentioned. For example, we certainly expect the area or volume of a solid body to be the same, no matter what coordinate system we may use to define it.

Similarly, we expect physical laws to be "invariant under translation" (so they don't depend on the actual position of the measuring instrument) and "invariant under rotation" (it should not matter which direction our experimental system is pointing) and "invariant under time translation" (we ought to get the same results tomorrow as we did yesterday). Most scientists took such invariants for granted for hundreds of years, although each of these is actually making a profound statement about the physical nature of the Universe.

So, too, is the notion that physical laws should be "invariant under constant motion." But assuming this, and rigorously applying it, led Einstein straight to the theory of special relativity. The idea of invariance under accelerated motion took him in turn to the theory of general relativity.

Both these theories, and the invariants that go with them, are linked inevitably with the name of one man, Albert Einstein. Another great invariant, linear momentum, is coupled in my mind with the names of two men, Galileo Galilei and Isaac Newton. Although the first explicit statement of this invariant is given in Newton's First Law of Motion (*Every body will continue in its state of rest or of uniform motion in a straight line except in so far as it is compelled to change that state by impressed force.*), Galileo, fifty years earlier, was certainly familiar with the general principle.

Some of the other "great invariants" needed the efforts of many people before they were firmly defined and their significance was appreciated. The idea that mass was an invariant came about through the efforts of chemists, beginning with Dalton and Lavoisier, who weighed combustion products and found that the total was the same before and after. The equivalence of different forms of energy (heat, motion, potential energy, and electromagnetic energy), and the invariance of total energy of all forms, developed even later. It was a combined effort by Count Rumford, Joule, Maxwell, Lord Kelvin, Helmholtz and others. The merger of the two invariants became possible when Einstein showed the equivalence of mass and energy, after which it was only the combined mass-energy total that was conserved.

Finally, although the idea that angular momentum must be conserved seems to arise naturally in classical mechanics from the conservation of linear momentum, in quantum physics it is much more of an independent invariant because particles such as protons, neutrons, electrons, and neutrinos have an intrinsic, internal spin, whose existence is not so much seen as *deduced* in order to make angular momentum a conserved quantity.

This sounds rather like a circular argument, but it isn't, because intrinsic spin couples with orbital angular momentum, and quantum theory cannot make predictions that match experiments without both of them. And as McAndrew remarks, Wolfgang Pauli in 1931 introduced the idea of a new particle to physics, the neutrino, just in order to preserve the laws of conservation of energy and momentum.

There are other important invariants in the quantum world, However, some things which "common sense" would insist to be invariants may be no such thing. For example, it was widely believed that parity (which is symmetry upon reflection in a mirror) must be a conserved quantity, because the Universe should have no preference for left-handed sub-nuclear processes over right-handed ones. But in 1956, Tsung Dao Lee and Chen Ning Yang suggested this might not be the case, and their radical idea was confirmed experimentally by C.S. Wu's team in 1957. Today, only a combination of parity, charge, and time-reversal is regarded as a fully conserved quantity.

Given the overall importance of invariants and conservation principles to science, there is no doubt that McAndrew would have pursued any suggestion of a new basic invariant. But if invariants are real, where is the fiction in the sixth chronicle? I'm afraid there isn't any, because the nature of the new invariant is never defined.

Wait a moment, you may say. What about the Geotron?

That is not fiction science, either, at least so far as principles are concerned. Such an instrument was seriously proposed a few years ago by Robert Wilson, the former director of the Fermilab accelerator. His design called for a donut-shaped device thirty-two miles across, in which protons would be accelerated to very high energies and then strike a metal target, to produce a beam of neutrinos. The Geotron designers wanted to use the machine to probe the interior structure of the Earth, and in particular to prospect for oil, gas, and valuable deep-seated metal deposits.

So maybe there is no fiction at all in the sixth chronicle—just a little pessimism about how long it will take before someone builds a Geotron.

Rogue planets.

The Halo beyond the known Solar System offers so much scope for interesting celestial objects of every description that I assume we will find a few more there. In the second chronicle, I introduced collapsed objects, high-density bodies that are neither stars nor conventional planets. The dividing line between stars and planets is usually decided by whether or not the center of the object supports a nuclear fusion process and contains a high density core of "degenerate" matter. Present theories place that dividing line at about a hundredth of the Sun's mass— smaller than that, you have a planet; bigger than that you must have a star. I assume that there are in-between bodies out in the Halo, made largely of degenerate matter but only a little more massive than Jupiter.

I also assume that there is a "kernel ring" of Kerr-Newman black holes, about 300 to 400 AU from the Sun, and that this same region contains many of the collapsed objects. Such bodies would be completely undetectable using any techniques of present-day astronomy. This is science fiction, not science.

Are rogue planets also science fiction? This brings us to *Vandell's Fifth Problem*, and the seventh chronicle.

David Hilbert did indeed pose a set of mathematical problems in 1900, and they served as much more than a summary of things that were "hard to solve." They were concise and exact statements of questions, which, if answered, would have profound implications for many other problems in mathematics. The Hilbert problems are both deep and difficult, and have attracted the attention of almost every mathematician of the twentieth century. Several problems of the set, for example, ask whether certain numbers are "transcendental"—which means they can never occur as solutions to the usual equations of algebra (more precisely, they cannot be roots of finite algebraic equations with algebraic coefficients). These questions were not disposed of until 1930, when Kusmin and Siegel proved a more general result than the one that Hilbert had posed. In 1934 Gelfond provided another generalization.

At the moment there is no such "super-problem" set defined for astronomy and cosmology. If there were, the one I invented as Vandell's Fifth Problem would certainly be a worthy candidate, and might take generations to solve. (Hilbert's Fifth Problem, concerning a conjecture in topological group theory, was finally solved in 1952 by Gleason, Montgomery, and Zippin.) We cannot even imagine a technique, observational instrument or procedure that would have a chance of detecting a rogue planet. The existence, frequency of occurrence, and mode of escape of rogue planets raise many questions concerning the stability of multiple-body systems moving under their mutual gravitational attractions—questions that cannot be answered yet by astronomers and mathematicians.

In general relativity, the exact solution of the "one-body problem" as given by Schwarzschild has been known for more than 80 years. The relativistic "two-body problem," of two objects orbiting each other under mutual gravitational influence, has not yet been solved. In nonrelativistic or Newtonian mechanics, the two-body problem was disposed of three hundred years ago by Newton. But the nonrelativistic solution for more than two bodies has not been found to this day, despite three centuries of hard work.

A good deal of progress has been made for a rather simpler situation that is termed the "restricted three-body problem." In this, a small mass (such as a planet or small moon) moves under the influence of two much larger ones (stars or large planets). The large bodies define the gravitational field, and the small body moves in this field without contributing significantly to it. The restricted three-body problem applies to the case of a planet moving in the gravitational field of a binary pair of stars, or an asteroid moving in the combined fields of the Sun and Jupiter. It also offers a good approximation for the motion of a small body moving in the combined field of the Earth and Moon. Thus the problem is of practical interest, and the list of workers who have studied it in the past 200 years includes several of history's most famous mathematicians: Euler, Lagrange, Jacobi, Poincaré, and Birkhoff. (Lagrange in particular provided certain exact solutions that include the L-4 and L-5 points, famous today as proposed sites for large space colonies.)

The number of papers written on the subject is huge—Victor Szebehely, in a 1967 book on the topic, listed over 500 references, and restricted himself to only the major source works.

Thanks to the efforts of all these workers, a good deal is known about the possible solutions of the restricted three-body problem. One established fact is that the small object cannot be thrown away to infinity by the gravitational interactions of its two large companions. Like much of modern astronomy, this result is not established by looking at the orbits themselves. It is proved by general arguments based on a particular constant of the motion, termed the Jacobian integral.

Unfortunately, those arguments cannot be applied in the

general three-body problem, or in the N-body problem whenever N is bigger than two. It is presently *conjectured* by astronomers, but not generally proved, that ejection to infinity is possible whenever more than three bodies are involved. In such a situation, the lightest member of the system is most likely to be the one ejected. Thus, rogue planets can probably be produced when a stellar system has more than two stars in it. As it happens, this is rather common. Solitary stars, like the Sun, are in the minority. Once separated from its stellar parents, the chances that a rogue world will ever again be captured to form part of a star system are remote. To this point, the seventh chronicle's discussion of solitary planets fits known theory, although it is an admittedly incomplete theory.

So how many rogue planets are there? There could conceivably be as many as there are stars, strewn thick across the Galaxy but completely undetectable to our instruments. Half a dozen may lie closer to us than the nearest star. Or they may be an endangered species, vanishingly rare among the varied bodies that comprise the celestial zoo.

In the seventh chronicle I suggest that they are rather common—and that's acceptable to me as science fiction. Maybe they are, because certainly planets around other stars seem far more common than we used to think. Up to 1996, there was no evidence at all that even one planet existed around any star other than Sol. Now we know of a dozen or more. Every one is Jupiter's size or bigger, but that does not imply that most planets in the universe are massive. It merely shows that our detection methods can find only big planets. Possibly there are other, smaller planets in every system where a Jupiter-sized giant has been discovered.

If we cannot actually see a planet, how can we possibly know that it exists? There are two methods. First, it is not accurate to say that a planet orbits a star. The bodies orbit around their common center of mass. That means, if the orbit lies at right angles to the direction of the star as seen from Earth, the star's apparent position in the sky will show a variation over the period of the planetary year. That change will be tiny, but if the planet is large, the movement of the star might be small enough to measure.

The other (and to this date more successful) method of detection relies on the periodic shift in the wavelengths of light that we receive from a star and planet orbiting around their common center of gravity. When the star is approaching us because the planet is moving away from us, the light will be shifted toward the blue. When the star is moving away from us because the planet is approaching us, the star's light will be shifted toward the red. The tiny difference between these two cases allows us, from the wavelength changes in the star's light, to infer the existence of a planet in orbit around it.

Since both methods of detection depend for their success on the planet's mass being an appreciable fraction of the star's mass, it is no surprise that we are able to detect only the existence of massive planets, Jupiter-sized or bigger. And so far as rogue worlds are concerned, far from any stellar primary, our methods for the detection of extra-solar planets are no use at all.

The solar focus.

We go to general relativity again. According to that theory, the gravitational field of the Sun will bend light beams that pass by it (actually, Newtonian theory also turns out to predict a similar effect, a factor of two less in magnitude). Rays of light coming from a source at infinity and just missing the Sun will be bent the most, and they will converge at a distance from the Sun of 550 astronomical units, which is about 82.5 billion kilometers. To gain a feeling for that number, note that the average distance of the planet Pluto from the Sun is 5.9 billion kilometers; the *solar focus*, as the convergence point is known, is a fair distance out.

Those numbers apply for a spherical Sun. Since Sol rotates and so has a bulge at its equator, the Sun considered as a lens is slightly astigmatic.

If the source of light (or radio signal, which is simply another form of electromagnetic wave) is not at infinity, but closer, then the rays will still be converged in their passage by the Sun, but they will be drawn to a point at a different location. As McAndrew correctly points out in the eighth chronicle, a standard result in geometrical optics applies. If a lens converges a parallel beam of light at a distance F from the lens, then light starting at a distance S from the lens will be converged at a distance D beyond it, where $1/F = 1/S + 1/D$.

This much is straightforward. The more central element of this chronicle involves far more speculation. When, or if you prefer it, if, will it be possible to produce an artificial intelligence, an "AI," that rivals or surpasses human intelligence?

It depends which writers you believe as to how you answer that question. Some, such as Hans Moravec, have suggested that this will happen in fifty years or less. Others, while not accepting any specific date, still feel that it is sure to come to pass. Our brains are, in Marvin Minsky's words, "computers made of meat." It may be difficult and take a long time, but eventually we will have an AI able to think as well or better than we do.

However, not everyone accepts this. Roger Penrose, whom we have already mentioned in connection with energy extraction from kernels, has argued that an AI will never be achieved by the further development of computers as we know them today, because the human brain is "non-algorithmic."

In a difficult book that was a surprising best-seller, *The Emperor's New Mind* (1989), he claimed that some functions of the human brain will never be duplicated by computers developed along today's lines. The brain, he asserts, performs some functions for which no computer program can be written.

This idea has been received with skepticism and even outrage by many workers in the field of AI and computer science. So what does Penrose say that is so upsetting to so many? He argues that human thought employs physics and procedures drawn from the world of quantum theory. In Penrose's words, "Might a quantum world be *required* so that thinking, perceiving creatures, such as ourselves, can be constructed from its substance?"

His answer to his own question is, yes, a quantum world-view is required. In that world, a particle does not necessarily have a well-defined spin, speed, or position. Rather, it has a number of different possible positions or speeds or spins, and until we make an observation of it, all we can know are the probabilities associated with each possible spin, speed, and position. Only when an observation is made does the particle occupy a well-defined state, in which the measured variable is precisely known. This change, from undefined to well-defined status, is called the "collapse of the quantum mechanical wave function." It is a well-known, if not well-understood, element of standard quantum theory.

What Penrose suggests is that the human brain itself is a kind of quantum device. In particular, the same processes that collapse the quantum mechanical wave function in sub-atomic particles are at work in the brain. When humans are considering many different possibilities, Penrose argues that we are operating in a highly parallel, quantum mechanical mode. Our thinking resolves and "collapses to a thought" at some point when the wave function collapses, and at that time the many millions or billions of possibilities become a single definite idea.

This is certainly a peculiar notion. However, when quantum theory was introduced in the 1920s, most of its ideas seemed no less strange. Now they are accepted by almost all physicists. Who is to say that in another half-century, Penrose will not be equally accepted when he asserts, "there is an essential *non*-algorithmic ingredient to (conscious) thought processes" and "I believe that (conscious) minds are *not* algorithmic entities"?

Meanwhile, almost everyone in the AI community (who, it might be argued, are hardly disinterested parties) listens to what Penrose has to say, then dismisses it as just plain wrong. Part of the problem is Penrose's suggestion as to the mechanism employed within the brain, which seems bizarre indeed.

As he points out in a second book, *Shadows of the Mind* (Penrose, 1994), he is not the first to suggest that quantum effects are important to human thought. Herbert Fröhlich, in 1968, noted that there was a high-frequency microwave activity in the brain, produced, he said, by a biological quantum resonance. In 1992, John Eccles proposed a brain structure called the *presynaptic vesicular grid*, which is a kind of crystalline lattice in the brain's pyramidal cells, as a suitable site for quantum activity.

Penrose himself favors a different location and mechanism. He suggests, though not dogmatically, that the quantum world is evoked in elements of a neuron known as microtubules. A microtubule is a tiny tube, with an outer diameter of about twenty-five nanometers and an inner diameter of fourteen nanometers. The tube is made up of peanut-shaped objects called *tubulin dimers*. Each dimer has about ten thousand atoms in it. Penrose proposes that each dimer is a basic computational unit, operating using quantum effects. If he is right, the computing power of the brain is grossly underestimated if neurons are considered as the basic computing element. There are about ten million dimers per neuron, and because of their tiny size each one ought to operate about a million times as fast as a neuron can fire. Only with such a mechanism, Penrose argues, can the rather complex behavior of a single-celled animal such as a paramecium (which totally lacks a nervous system) be explained.

Penrose's critics point out that microtubules are also found elsewhere in the body, in everything from livers to lungs. Does this mean that your spleen, big toe, and kidneys are to be credited with intelligence?

My own feeling is that Penrose's ideas sounded a lot better before he suggested a mechanism. The microtubule idea feels weak and unpersuasive.

Fortunately I don't have to take sides. In the eighth chronicle, I was deliberately silent on how the AI came into existence. However, as a personal observation, I would be much surprised if in our future we do not have human-level AI's, through whatever method of development, before humans routinely travel to the satellites of Jupiter and Saturn; and I believe that the latter will surely happen in less than five hundred years.

Compressed matter.

We know that compressed matter exists. In a neutron star, matter has been squeezed together so hard that the individual protons and electrons that normally make up atoms have combined to form neutrons. A neutron star with the mass of the Sun can be as little as twenty kilometers across, and a simple calculation tells us that the average density of such a body is about 475 million tons per cubic centimeter. That is still not at the limit of how far matter can be compressed. If the Sun were to become a black hole, as mentioned earlier, its Schwarzschild radius would be about three kilometers and its mean density twenty billion tons per cubic centimeter. McAndrew's illustrious but unfortunate father developed an unspecified way of squeezing matter down to something between neutron star and black hole densities.

It is easy to calculate what it would be like if you were unwise enough to take hold of a speck of such compressed matter. And it might well be a speck. An eighteen thousand ton asteroid in normal conditions would be a substantial lump of rock about twenty meters across. Squeeze it to a density of three billion tons per cubic centimeter, and it becomes a tiny ball with radius 0.11 millimeters. Its surface gravity is almost ten thousand gees.

The gravitational force falls off rapidly with distance, so if you were a meter away from the mote of matter you would probably be unaware of its existence. It would pull you toward it with a mere ten-millionth of a gee. But take hold of it, and that's a different story. Ten thousand gees would suck any known material, no matter how strong, toward and into the ball. That process would continue, until either you sacrificed some skin and broke free, or you were eventually totally absorbed. In practice, I think that McAndrew's father would have realized what was happening and found a way to free himself. He would have plenty of time, because the absorption process into the compressed matter sphere would be slow. That, however, would not have made as interesting a story.

The way that McAndrew's father produced compressed matter remains pure science fiction. However, the "strong force" itself is an accepted part of modern physics, one of four basic known forces. The other three are gravity, the electromagnetic force, and the so-called "weak force" responsible for beta decay (emission of an electron or positron) in a nucleus. Although there is an adequate theory of the strong force, embodied in what is known as *quantum chromodynamics*, there is not the slightest hint in that theory of a method to make such a force either stronger or weaker than it is.

That's all right. Five hundred years ago, magnetism was a curious property of certain materials, and no one knew what it was or had any way of generating it artificially. That had to wait until another strange phenomenon, electricity, had been explored, and experimenters such as Ampère, Oersted, and Faraday proved a link between electricity and magnetism. After that could come Maxwell, providing a unified theory for the two ideas that led to such practical devices as radios, dynamos, and powerful electromagnets.

It is not unreasonable to model the future on the past.

A few hundred years from now, maybe we will be able to play our own games with all the known forces in the context of a unified theory, creating or modifying them as we choose. The weak force and the electromagnetic force have already been unified, work for which Glashow, Weinberg, and Salam were awarded the Nobel prize in physics in 1979.

I cannot resist a couple of personal reminiscences regarding the late Abdus Salam. He was my mathematics supervisor when I was a new undergraduate. His personal style of solving the problems that I and my supervision partner brought to him was unique. More often than not, he would look at the result to be derived and say, "Consider the following identity." He would then write down a mathematical result which was far from obvious and usually new to us. Applying the identity certainly gave the required answer, but it didn't help us much with our struggles.

Salam also had one endearing but disconcerting habit. He did not drink, but he must have been told that it was a tradition at Cambridge for tutors to serve sherry to their students on holiday occasions. He offered my partner and me sherry, an offer which we readily accepted. He then, unfamiliar with sherry as a drink, poured a large tumbler for each of us. We were too polite to refuse, or not to drink what we had been given, but we emerged from the supervision session much the worse for wear.

There is a throwaway comment in the ninth chronicle, that McAndrew was going off to hear a lecture entitled "Higher-dimensional complex manifolds and a new proof of the Riemann Conjecture." This is a joke intended for mathematicians. In the nineteenth century, the great German mathematician Bernhard Riemann conjectured, but did not prove, that all the zeroes of a function known as the zeta function lay in a certain region of the complex plane. Riemann could not prove the result, and since then no one has managed to do so. It remains the most important unproven conjecture in mathematics, far more central to the field than the long-unproved but finally disposed-of Fermat Last Theorem.

People will keep chipping away at the Riemann conjecture, precisely because it *is* unproven. Just as we will keep pushing for better observing instruments, more rapid and sophisticated interplanetary or interstellar probes, quantum computers, artificial intelligence, higher temperature superconductors, faster-than-light travel, treatment for all known diseases, and human life extension.

The future in which McAndrew lives is fiction, but I believe that the science and technology of the real future will be far more surprising. There will indeed be ships, built by humans and their intellectual companions, computers, headed for the stars. They will not be powered by Kerr-Newman black holes, nor employ the McAndrew balanced drive, nor will they tap the resonance modes of the vacuum zero-point energy. They will not be multi-generation arks, nor will they find life-bearing planetoids in the Oort cloud, or rogue planets in the interstellar void. What they will be, and what they will find, will be far stranger and more interesting than that. And they will make today's boldest science fiction conjectures appear timid, near-sighted, small-scale, and lacking in imagination.

Writing of this I wish, like Benjamin Franklin, that I could be pickled in a barrel for a couple of hundred years, to experience the surprising future that I'm sure lies ahead. If I can't do that and don't last that long, here is a message to my descendants two centuries from now: On my behalf, make the most of it.

DOOMSDAY CAME
ABOUT EVERY FIVE YEARS ...

Someone Out There really hated humans. Twenty years have passed since Shiva I swept aside Earth's crude defenses and rained down destruction. Now Shiva V has entered the Solar System, more powerful than any of its predecessors.

The Shiva cannot be destroyed by fleets of ships: we tried, and it was the fleets that were destroyed. There is only way way to defeat a Shiva: get inside and kill it. Once again, in the personae of five champions, four billion of us are about to do just that, using the ...

EARTHWEB
Marc Stiegler

"A high-voltage adventure story—and an intriguing look at what the worldwide web may become."   **—Vernor Vinge**

"A brilliant vision of our future networked intelligence."
                              —Max Moore, Ph.D, President of the Extropy
                              Institute and the *Extropy Newsletter*

                    ISBN 57809-X ◆ $6.99   □

DAVID WEBER

The Honor Harrington series: *(cont.)*

Flag in Exile

Hounded into retirement and disgrace by political enemies, Honor Harrington has retreated to planet Grayson, where powerful men plot to reverse the changes she has brought to their world. And for their plans to succeed, Honor Harrington must die!

Honor Among Enemies

Offered a chance to end her exile and again command a ship, Honor Harrington must use a crew drawn from the dregs of the service to stop pirates who are plundering commerce. Her enemies have chosen the mission carefully, thinking that either she will stop the raiders or they will kill her . . . and either way, her enemies will win. . . .

In Enemy Hands

After being ambushed, Honor finds herself aboard an enemy cruiser, bound for her scheduled execution. But one lesson Honor has never learned is how to give up!

Echoes of Honor

ìBrilliant! Brilliant! Brilliant!îô *Anne McCaffrey*

Ashes of Victory

Honor has escaped from the prison planet called Hell and returned to the Manticoran Alliance, to the heart of a furnace of new weapons, new strategies, new tactics, spies, diplomacy, and assassination.

continued (☞

EXPLORE OUR WEB SITE